Praise for Minerva Spencer & S.M. LaViolette's THE ACADEMY OF LOVE series:

"[A] pitch perfect Regency …. Readers will be hooked." (THE MUSIC OF LOVE)
★*Publishers Weekly STARRED REVIEW*

"An offbeat story that offers unexpected twists on a familiar setup." (A FIGURE OF LOVE)
"[A] consistently entertaining read." (A FIGURE OF LOVE)
Kirkus

Praise for Minerva Spencer's THE OUTCASTS:

"Minerva Spencer's writing is sophisticated and wickedly witty. Dangerous is a delight from start to finish with swashbuckling action, scorching love scenes, and a coolly arrogant hero to die for. Spencer is my new auto-buy!"
-*NYT Bestselling Author* Elizabeth Hoyt

"Fans of Amanda Quick's early historicals will find much to savor."
★*Booklist STARRED REVIEW*

"Sexy, witty, and fiercely entertaining."
★*Kirkus STARRED REVIEW*

D0873129

More books by S.M. LaViolette & Minerva Spencer:

THE ACADEMY OF LOVE SERIES

The Music of Love
A Figure of Love
A Portrait of Love*

THE OUTCASTS SERIES

Dangerous
Barbarous
Scandalous
Notorious*

THE MASQUERADERS
The Footman
The Postilion*
The Bastard*

THE SEDUCERS
Melissa and The Vicar
Joss and The Countess
Hugo and The Maiden*

VICTORIAN DECADENCE
His Harlot
His Valet
His Countess

ANTHOLOGIES:

BACHELORS OF BOND STREET
THE ARRANGEMENT
*upcoming books

JOSS
And The
COUNTESS

The Seducers Book 2

S.M. LAVIOLETTE

Crooked
Sixpence
CS
P
Press

CROOKED SIXPENCE BOOKS are published by

CROOKED SIXPENCE PRESS
2 State Road 230
El Prado, NM 87529

First printing June 2020

ISBN: 978-1-951662-40-0

10 9 8 7 6 5 4 3 2 1

Photo stock by Period Images
Printed in the United States of America.

Chapter One

Alicia, Countess of Selwood, pulled on her black kid gloves and turned to the naked man on the bed.

Lord Byerly was asleep, the fine Irish linen sheets he favored twisted around his slim body like the pale arms of a lover.

He was an attractive man but barely adequate when it came to bed sport.

He was also becoming a bore.

They'd been seeing one another for only a little over two months and already he'd become cloying, clingy, and apt to put his "mark" on her in public situations.

She picked up her reticule, opened the door, and closed it quietly behind her.

Thankfully Byerly kept his family's house open in London even though he was a bachelor. Alicia wouldn't have consented to this liaison if she'd had to meet him in some dreadful lodgings.

But although he stayed in the mansion, he didn't have the money to properly staff it, which was also good because it meant she had no need to dodge servants and their prying eyes.

The only servant in the foyer when she descended the stairs was hers.

Jocelyn Gormley looked up from something he held in his hands—it would be a book, which he was never without—but swiftly closed and slid into the pocket of his greatcoat. He got to his feet before she reached the bottom of the stairs and left to find a hackney without her having to ask.

Alicia went to the mirror that hung above a dusty console table and inspected her reflection.

Her pale, ash-blond hair was pulled back in a smooth chignon rather than the fussier styles favored by younger women. Her skin was translucent, and free of wrinkles—at least in the dim lighting of the foyer.

And her silver silk gown was as fresh-looking as it had been when she'd left her house four hours earlier.

She looked exactly like the Ice Countess, a name applied behind her back and one she found amusing.

Gormley reentered, his massive frame filling even the oversized doorway of Byerly House.

"The hack is here, my lady." His voice was the low, rough rasp of a man who rarely used it.

Alicia preceded him out the door and into the waiting carriage without speaking. The old, but clean, carriage dipped precariously on its worn springs when Gormley climbed in behind her.

He was a huge man with a history of prize fighting, which was partly why she had hired him. He was also taciturn and self-contained—two other reasons why she chose to employ him as the servant who accompanied her on her most private of errands.

Alicia had not spoken more than a dozen words with the man since employing him a little over two months earlier—right before she'd ended her affair with Sir Henry, the first lover she'd ever taken, and yet another mediocre selection.

Gormley was perfect for her needs. In addition to handling all the messages between herself and her paramour, he was also unflappable, polite, and unusually well-spoken for a man of his class. He also appeared utterly incurious about her and what she did on her late-night jaunts.

According to Alicia's maid—Maude—Gormley wasn't only closed-mouthed around her; he was universally discreet.

Maude, Alicia's spying eyes in the servants' hall, assured Alicia that she'd hardly heard the enormous man exchange two words with anyone, and that he never spoke about his mistress.

"I can't decide if he's dull-witted or extremely sharp," Maude admitted.

Maude herself fell into the second category.

Alicia hadn't told her maid that Gormley appeared to spend his time waiting for her occupied with a book—an activity which would indicate he was not a stupid man.

Not that all smart people read. Alicia considered herself fairly smart but she never read if she could help it.

She looked away from her silent servant and stared out the window at the passing streets, which were peopled by men returning home after a night of debauchery, or perhaps just setting out for one. Young bucks bent on sensual pleasure—just like Alicia, in other words.

2

She thought back to her evening with Byerly and snorted. Pleasure? Well, in theory.

The viscount—a good decade younger than her own thirty-nine years—was selfish and pedestrian between the sheets. Rather than satisfy her shameful urges—which, admittedly, she'd never confessed to either Byerly or any another human being—their trysts had left her increasingly frustrated.

Why had she ever believed that she could find what she needed? Especially when what she *needed* was considered a sinful perversion by God and man?

She straightened the seams on her already straight gloves, wishing she could straighten out her life just as easily.

Edward had died thirteen months ago and yet here she was, still mixing among people who despised her, but who couldn't entirely reject her because of her wealth.

Allie Benton, or what was left of her, chuckled somewhere in the dark confines of Alicia's mind. Oh, if only these arrogant aristocrats knew who she really was.

Society hadn't been any warmer toward her back in New York City—quite the reverse, in fact—but at least she hadn't felt so foreign there.

Some days—or nights, more often—she missed her country of birth. Other days, she enjoyed being a visitor here, no real need to settle in and learn the customs because she would one day move on.

But she couldn't leave yet—not until she could take Elizabeth with her, and that wasn't for another four years.

Alicia sighed. It was a vicious trap: she could not go to New York without Lizzy, and David would never let Alicia take her daughter out of Britain.

She sucked her lower lip into her mouth and chewed it, allowing herself something she did not often permit: a moment of despair.

But then she recalled she was not alone.

She turned to look at her servant.

Gormley appeared to be sleeping—or at least resting; he was certainly not paying any attention to her.

Even so, she closed the door on the hopelessness that always threatened to leak out if she was not vigilant.

Besides, it was self-deluding to yearn for New York. There was nothing for her there; nothing but a past she'd been in a hurry to leave behind after Horace died.

Something inside her twisted at the thought of her first husband.

Forty years her senior, the iron magnate had been in his sixties when they'd married. His body had been wrinkled, sagging, and covered with a pelt-like mass of gray hair—but that did not mean Alicia hadn't welcomed his hands on her. Indeed, she had labored and schemed for the day he would take her to his bed.

Alicia now knew how fortunate she'd been in her choice of matrimonial target. Horace had been one of the wealthiest men in New York and could have done whatever he'd wished with the seventeen-year-old niece of his washerwoman and nobody would have raised an eyebrow.

Instead of using and discarding her—as so many men would have done—he'd done the unthinkable and married her.

She smiled. *That* had certainly raised enough eyebrows.

Horace had been good to her, and she'd given him everything she had in return.

But really, how much had her body been worth?

After all, she now gave herself to a sneering aristocrat who offered almost nothing in return.

Alicia turned from her black thoughts to the silent man's profile.

It occurred to her, not for the first time, to wonder what he made of her activities. She was not so much to-the-manner-born that she did not know servants had minds, brains, and curiosity.

Out of all the applicants to her rather peculiar advertisement, Alicia had liked this huge, brutish-looking, and well-spoken man best.

Before coming to Alicia he'd been a groom to Viscount Easton for almost six years. Easton was a high stickler who'd sent along a glowing letter of recommendation for Gormley.

Not that Alicia had taken the viscount's word alone.

No, she'd hired her own man to investigate her new servant: Nathaniel Shelly, whom she'd used several times in the past for sensitive matters.

Mr. Shelly had followed Gormley for two weeks before Alicia had decided to hire him.

While she knew such caution might seem excessive, it wasn't. If David learned about her private life, he would make her suffer.

So, whoever she hired must, above all things, be discreet and trustworthy.

Shelly's report had been short:

"Jocelyn Gormley, twenty-eight, grew up in London. His elderly father owns a prosperous butcher shop, he has two married brothers with children—the eldest operates the butchers now and the other works as a clerk in a counting house. One younger sister who keeps house for the father. Gormley visits them every servant half-day."

"His mother?"

"She died when Gormley was fifteen. It seems she was a gentleman's daughter who'd fallen on hard times. Worked as a governess before marrying Gormley. Neighbors remember her as a "lady" who taught not only her own children to read and write, but also several in the neighborhood. Apparently all four of the Gormley children are exceptionally well-spoken."

Alicia had guessed Gormley had some schooling from the brief interview. He was a man of few words, and those were not spoken in the accent of the streets.

Instead, he sounded like that amorphous group of Britons who put effort into aping their betters but could never quite manage to replicate the diamond-hard, clipped accents of the aristocracy.

"Where did Gormley work before the Viscount's," she'd asked.

"Well, he had a rather interesting journey. After his mother died the schooling stopped so he went to work for his father. When his father became ill, his oldest brother took over the butchers and Gormley left."

"Is that when he went to Easton?"

"No. From what I can tell he pursued his fighting for four years— from eighteen to twenty-two. After that, his uncle—on his father's side—brought him on as a stable hand at the viscount's." Shelly cleared his throat. "Apparently he's quite sharp. Not that you'd know it to look at him."

Alicia had chuckled at that. "He *does* look like a prize fighter."

"He was still fighting those first few years he worked for the viscount. It seems Lord Easton enjoys wagering on a good mill and gave Gormley unusual freedom to pursue his pastime."

"Why is he leaving Lord Easton?"

"I spoke to a couple of the stable lads, who say Lord Easton's fifteen-year-old daughter has been loitering around Gormley lately and, well—"

Alicia took mercy on the blushing man. "I understand. She took a fancy to our Mr. Gormley."

"Aye, my lady. He could hardly tell his lordship, so he applied for this position."

His actions indicated wisdom, morals, fear, or perhaps all three.

"Does our paragon of virtue have a lady friend?"

"None that I saw, my lady. Viscount Easton gave Gormley his evenings free, but the man no longer fights and he only left his lodgings twice at night in the two weeks I followed him." Shelly had grimaced, an unprecedented display of agitation, before adding, "His destination both times was a very exclusive and rather unusual, er, brothel."

Alicia's pulse had sped up at that information. "Indeed?"

"It's so exclusive no amount of bribery could gain *me* access. Nor could I bribe or purchase reliable information as to what or with whom Gormley spent most of his evening, not departing until the early morning hours."

Alicia's interest had been caught by the introduction of such a prurient, taboo subject. "Continue."

"The brothel is operated by a Mrs. Melissa Griffin, a woman who is known to be exceptionally selective when it comes to her lovers. It is rumored she even declined the great Wellington. It seems unlikely that Gormley could afford such a place, so he was probably visiting somebody who works there—a maid or somebody on the kitchen staff."

"You mentioned the place was unusual—how?"

The poor man had looked like he'd wanted to melt into the floor. "Er, it caters to, er, well," he'd scratched his head, his face flaming. "Well, it caters to birching and the like."

Alicia's heart, which had already been beating fast, had raced at his information.

She had burned to ask more questions, but had let the matter rest, unwilling to expose her prurient fascination to a man who was essentially her employee.

Alicia had entertained herself more than once wondering what Mr. Gormley did at the exclusive brothel.

Just what would a sexual encounter with such a dour hulk of a man be like?

He was the farthest thing from attractive, his features rough-hewn, his nose bent and re-set at least a few times, his heavy-lidded eyes a non-descript muddy shade of green and brown. And his mouth an impassive slash with thin lips that never smiled.

But his body ….

Alicia allowed herself a quick look at his well-clothed form now: he was one of the biggest men she had ever seen.

Even in America, where the people tended to be larger, she couldn't recall seeing a man so huge. He should have looked laughable in the expensive, well-cut clothing she'd had made for him—like a gorilla dressed in a suit—but instead he looked powerful and menacing.

She remembered him closing his book earlier and shoving it into his pocket. He was a butcher's son/boxer/groom who liked to read. The man was something of a curiosity.

Joss surveyed his mistress from beneath heavy lids. She had an odd expression on her beautiful face. He'd seen the look more than once—usually when she came away from one of these trysts.

He felt his face shift into a slight, self-mocking smile. *Tryst.* Just listen to him, using a fancy word for knocking off a piece, for making the beast with two backs, for *fucking.*

He'd been around toffs for years, in one form of service or another—but never an American toff.

Since coming to work in her house he'd heard all the rumors about her—and there were wagonloads.

Joss wasn't sure which ones he believed. Not that it mattered what he believed. She was so far beyond his reach that she might as well be one of those exotic, tropical islands in the Caribbean he'd read about.

Still, that didn't mean he couldn't think about her. She might own his time, but his thoughts still belonged to him.

Well, that was a bloody lie.

The truth was that all Joss's thoughts had belonged to the countess since the first moment he'd laid eyes on her.

Seeing her for the first-time reminded Joss of when his brother Gordon had accidentally struck him in the head with an entire side of hog.

But there'd been no Gordon in the Countess of Selwood's study to slap Joss's slack-jawed face back to awareness, so he'd gaped at her like a yokel.

Joss knew he wasn't alone in his stunned reaction to her. But to still be in awe of her months later and—he had to be honest—to be *obsessed* with her? No, his fellow servants appeared smarter than that.

Only a romantic fool like Joss was stupid enough to wander down *that* fork in the road. Yes, romantic foolery—yet another crime he could lay at his mother's door.

But he didn't want to think of his mother.

Instead, he took the opportunity to drink her in.

Never had he seen a woman so physically perfect—and Joss knew plenty of beautiful women.

She was tall enough to come up to his shoulder and had a waist so tiny a man's hands twitched to span it. Her hips and breasts would make an hourglass envious. Skin like cream, red, full lips that promised dark, sinful things, and hair an impossibly pale, silky blond, like the rich silk of some of the gowns she wore—garments that shrieked wealth, status, and unattainability.

But it was her eyes—fringed in sooty, rather than blond lashes—that were the real shock. They were a pale sapphire blue unlike anything he'd ever seen: crystalline, perfect, and as remote as the moon.

Not that Joss often looked directly into them. No, it wasn't the place of a groom-cum-footman-cum-whatever-the-hell-he-was to meet the eyes of his mistress.

But in his dreams and fantasies those eyes had looked at *him* times beyond counting as he slid into her body.

They'd been hooded and heavy as he'd taken her from behind, taunting him over her shoulder. And they'd gazed down at him in queenly hauteur as she straddled him—posting him the way she rode her fine hacks.

Yes, he'd done things to her in his imagination that would get him jailed, hanged, or transported if anyone could see the contents of his head.

A man couldn't look at a woman like her without primal, lustful thoughts; even a man like Joss: a mere servant who was expected to never even look, not to mention *think* about touching.

Just catching a glimpse of her on the way from the house to her carriage was like the taste of something expensive and elusive—a brief holiday from the mundane, drab realities of life.

But it was a holiday that never lasted more than a few minutes. Right on its heels was the gut-churning despair of knowing a man like him could never possess her. Except in his dreams.

Each and every male in her London establishment had fantasies of their glorious employer just like Joss did. Well, perhaps not the *very* same.

The general consensus among the male servants was that Lady Selwood was as cold, untouchable, and icy as the name the nobs gave her: The Ice Countess.

But Joss knew better.

Only Joss among her servants knew what she was really doing when she was supposed to be attending routs or balls or whatever rubbish rich folk spent their time doing.

There was no denying her façade was cool, but beneath it was something else entirely.

And Joss's body responded instinctively to what lay buried under all that ice.

He knew, without her telling him, what she craved and he knew he could give her exactly what she needed.

Was that an arrogant assumption? Probably, but it was still true. And Joss had bloody well earned the right make such a claim.

Unfortunately, if his body's response to her was bad, his mind entertained even more dangerous impulses: he'd begun to obsess about what lay behind her beautiful face.

Why would he care about what sort of person she was?

Because he was an idiot.

The closest he'd ever come to knowing her would be looking.

In his months with her he'd seen her with two different men. Oh, not *seen* her, of course, but waited for her to sate her desires and for those lily-white-handed nobs to sate theirs using her body.

The knowledge that she spent her evenings with men who looked like they knew as much about pleasuring a woman as they did about digging a ditch or butchering a hog rankled. But what rankled even more was the knowledge there wasn't a damned thing he could do to stop her.

Joss knew he wasn't the smartest of men, but even a fool would realize the work he'd done for Melissa had given him thoughts and ideas that weren't suited to a man of his station.

It was natural, he supposed, to begin to think of aristocrats as people—at least the women—when you'd seen them naked, been inside them, and learned they were just a collection of wants and needs like anyone else.

He knew that money couldn't buy happiness—but it could buy pleasure.

And it had certainly bought Joss often enough in the past.

He shoved away the depressing thought.

As was usual when he was in her company, he'd worked himself up. His cock was as hard as cast iron and his stomach churned with all the desire he was forced to swallow while he waited and imagined.

The gnawing want and envy was wearing on him.

He would be glad to leave her tonight, although such partings usually left him feeling restless and not a little despairing.

Tonight he would go to his snug room in the mews and he'd beat the living fuck out of his bag, until his knuckles bled, until he was too bloody fagged to do anything but pass out. Sometimes that afforded him a certain . . . release.

"What were you reading earlier, Gormley?"

Joss startled; she'd rarely spoken to him directly in the months he'd worked for her—and never anything personal. And now she'd fixed her disconcerting silver-blue gaze on him and expected an answer.

"What book do you have in your pocket?" she repeated.

Joss fished the book from his coat and handed it to her. He watched her face as she flipped it open, staring at it for so long he thought she might have fallen asleep.

"Shakespeare?" She said the word with an inflection of amazement, as if she'd just discovered one of her carriage horses could read. When she looked up at him her eyebrows were arched.

Her surprise was like salt on a raw wound and Joss felt his mouth twist into a smile that held no humor. "I like to look at the pictures, my lady."

She glanced down at the book in her hands, quickly flicking through the pages and, of course, found no pictures.

Even in the dim light Joss could see the slight flush that spread over her magnificent cheekbones. He sighed. Here it came, the sacking he'd expected since the first week he'd begun to work for her, when he'd realized he wanted her and that his blazing yearning was making him even surlier than usual.

But she surprised him.

"I didn't mean to imply I doubted your ability to read Shakespeare." She closed the book and handed it back to him. "I've never read Shakespeare, myself. Is Antony and Cleopatra your favorite?"

"It's one of them."

"Why do you like it?"

Mercifully, the carriage came to a shuddering halt and Joss was spared from having to answer.

He flipped down the steps and stood to the side of the door, his breath like steam from a kettle in the frigid night air.

She gave him her hand, always gloved, always two barriers between his skin and hers, and he released her almost before he'd touched her, mounting the eight steps to the house and unlocking the door for her with the key she'd given him.

No servants waited up for her.

"Goodnight, Gormley." She spoke the words without pausing or looking at him, picking up the candlestick that waited for her on the console table and heading for the marble stairs that led to her chambers.

"Goodnight, my lady." He murmured the words quietly, too soft for her to hear over the muted clicking of her heeled slippers on the hard stone steps. Only when she'd disappeared did he close and lock the door.

He walked down the narrow alley that led to the mews which serviced this block of houses.

The servant quarters above Lady Selwood's carriage house were more private than those in the house. Joss had occupied the same type of quarters at Viscount Easton's and made sure it was part of his employment contract to have a bedchamber and the small room next to it for his personal use.

Joss took the stairs to his room two at a time, stopping abruptly when he found the door to his quarters ajar. When he pushed it open, he saw the unmistakably naked body of a woman lying across his double bed.

Chapter Two

Joss's double bed was his most expensive possession—and the only item of furniture in the small quarters that he owned.

A man his size couldn't sleep on a regular bed—at least not the size to be found in a servant's quarters.

He stopped in the middle of the room and removed his hat, tossing it onto the nearby table with a dull *thunk*.

The body on the bed jerked upright, allowing him to see the face, not that he'd been in any doubt.

"I thought you'd never get back. I was just about to leave." Annie Philips was a parlor maid, and, as such, she was a good-looking girl. She came from the country, so she wasn't like the pale, slight girls one often found in London. Instead, she was what his father would call a proper armful, or a *strapping wench*.

Joss let his eyes drift over her body, taking his time unbuttoning the expensive coat Lady Selwood had provided for him, the cut of the garment distinguishing him from her other servants.

The countess dressed Joss in gentleman's clothing rather than the usual garments that branded a man a servant: velvet breeches and clownishly laced coats. Indeed, Joss's coat was no different than that of any toff, a rich black wool that was unadorned by foppery.

His cock, which had just begun to deflate with some distance from his mistress, was once again alert, aware, and interested. How could it not be with such a vista before him?

Annie had curly brown hair, long, long, legs, and breasts that would fill both his hands twice: and Joss had very big hands.

She'd stripped down to her stockings, which must have been her best pair, her garters covered in needlework flowers, like a garden bordering her dark brown bush.

Joss hung up his coat, never taking his eyes from her body, and then leisurely removed his cravat and waistcoat before dropping into the room's only chair, his knees spread to offer some relief for his cramped organ.

"How'd you get in?"

She had to sit upright to see him over the end of the bed. She brought her knees up to her chest, shielding her breasts from his gaze but inadvertently exposing another, even more private, part of her body in the process. Joss's eyes dropped to the small pink peak that thrust from the tangle of brown curls. It took a hellish amount of effort to force his eyes back up.

She bit her lower lip between even, white teeth, lowering her lids to display a thick sweep of dark lashes. Her coquettish look made him wonder just how inadvertent her pose really was.

"I borrowed Mr. Feehan's keys. But I put them back," she rushed to add.

Joss was impressed. After all, who didn't like being wanted enough by a pretty girl that she would steal and risk immediate discharge just to be with you?

"Help me off with my boots," he said, not bothering to make it a polite request. If she wanted him, she'd better know right now exactly what it was she was wanting.

When it came to fucking—at least if Joss wasn't being paid for it—he liked things his way.

If she found that unacceptable, it was best they both knew it before things went any further.

She scrambled from the bed without hesitation and he raised one foot, amused and aroused when she turned her generous bottom toward him. Joss enjoyed the show, throbbing so hard by the time she'd straddled him twice he was in actual pain.

When she'd finished the second boot, he jerked his chin toward the cupboard in the corner of the room. "Put them inside and then come back here."

Joss brooded on what he was about to do while she followed his orders; her eagerness to please arousing him far more than was normal or healthy. But he'd long given up wondering why he enjoyed submission in his lovers.

He knew it was unwise to fuck where one ate, but he'd been dodging Annie's attentions for months.

It had been a long time since he'd had a woman. Working for Lady Selwood and knowing what it was she did when he accompanied her on these nights had left him raw and wanting. He'd been behaving like a monk, as if he were saving himself. For her?

Joss snorted at the stupid thought.

As for Annie? Well, he was tired of rejecting what the girl offered him day after relentless day: mindless pleasure and release.

She came to stand before him and he gave her another chance.

"Have you considered what you're doing, Annie?"

She raised her chin. "I'm not a maiden."

He supposed that was an answer, of sorts.

"And I'm not looking for a wife."

She flinched at his words and her cheeks darkened; Joss thought she might leave.

"And *I'm* not lookin' for a husband, Mr. High-and-Mighty. Just because *Herself* dresses you like a nob and you've always got your nose in a book doesn't make you better. Just because *you* think you're such a fine catch doesn't mean the rest of us do."

Joss was amused by her fire. But just because her words were brave didn't make them more convincing. Still, he'd fought her for weeks, how much was a man supposed to take?

He spread his thighs wider and she swallowed, the musculature of her throat fascinating to watch in the dim light of the tallow candle.

Hers was not the kind of body Joss was accustomed to seeing naked. Instead of soft and of middle years, Annie's body was young and firm thanks to hard work.

"Kneel," he said, pointing to the floor between his wide-spread feet.

A dark flush spread over her neck and chest, her muscles tensing and flexing as she slowly knelt between his legs.

As ever, his cock hardened and lengthened in response to such immediate obedience. "Undress me."

Her hands shook as they reached for the fastenings of his trousers.

Joss's coats, trousers, and shirts had been made especially for him, the only such garments he'd ever owned. He knew why he wore them because Lady Selwood had told him.

"Your position in my household is singular and you will be seen with me in a variety of social situations, so you shall dress accordingly. I shan't need you all the time, but when I do, you will be attired like a gentleman. When I have no need of you, you may present yourself to my stable master, Mr. Carling. He has been informed of your skills and has also been informed he will have to accommodate your unique position. In other words, my needs will supersede his."

Carling, a big, bluff, good-natured bloke, had smirked at Joss the first time he'd reported to the stables.

"Aye, I know who you are. Lady Selwood's groom-cum-secretary-cum-whatever." But he'd laughed when he'd spoken. "Lady Selwood is an American," he'd said, as if that explained her strange behavior. "And they do things different over there."

The other servants had not been nearly as sanguine, but they'd eventually adjusted to seeing Joss dressed like a gentleman—not that they'd grown to like it.

Annie reached the last button and Joss lifted his hips. She pulled the fabric down, handling the garment with reverence and folding the trousers without being instructed before setting them aside and turning back.

His white linen drawers were monstrously tented, a wet spot making the thin fabric transparent.

"That's for you," he lied, but only partly.

While it was true he'd been hard for hours, on and off, imagining what his mistress was doing with her effete, aristocratic fop, his body had become eager for the woman kneeling before him since the moment he'd seen her naked on his bed.

He was a man, after all.

She pulled the tape and freed him.

Joss grunted and gave himself up to her care, letting his head fall back, and closing his eyes. Her hand was work-roughened, but the friction was not unpleasant. And the way she gripped and stroked him told Joss she'd done this more than a few times in the past.

Good; he had no interest in innocents.

Her hot mouth lowered over him and her tongue swirled his head while she sucked him hard enough to be painful, but a good pain.

Pictures formed behind his closed lids: another woman kneeling between his thighs; another woman worshipping him with her mouth; another woman ready to be filled by him.

Joss *ached* at the thought of spending into the mouth of his fantasy woman and he reached out to fist her glossy, smooth hair.

But it was thick, tight curls his hand encountered.

Frustration and lust mingled inside him as the carefully constructed image in his mind's eye wavered and began to dissipate. *No, not yet. Don't go yet.*

But it was too late, his brain chose reality rather than fantasy: it was the girl he felt, not the woman.

He opened his eyes and loosened his grip on her hair, freeing her. But she didn't pull away. Instead, she took him deeper with no pressure from his hands, no thrusting from his hips.

Her willingness to please him shot Joss full of guilt and the last vestiges of his fantasy lover disappeared like a thin taper of smoke from a cigar. The girl's curly brown head—bobbing up and down so eagerly— might not be the one he imagined every night and a good part of each day, but she was here, she was real, and she wanted him.

Joss relaxed and enjoyed her enthusiastic, if clumsy, efforts for a few moments before sliding his fingers beneath her jaws and gently lifting her head. When she looked up, it was with glassy and questioning eyes.

"D-didn't you like it?"

His thumb went of its own volition to her slick, swollen lips. Her mouth opened to take him, but he merely stroked the soft, wet skin. "I liked it."

Her lips curved and her cheeks tinged with pink at his meager praise. He stood and lifted her to her feet before pulling his shirt over his head and tossing it onto the chair.

"Get on the bed."

While she obeyed, he opened the drawer in the only nightstand. Inside he had a small leather envelope. He extracted the flattened not-quite translucent rectangle and put it in the washbasin, pouring water over it to turn it supple and soft. He turned to find her watching, her eyes wider than ever.

Joss lifted the sheath. "You have not seen one of these?"

She shook her head.

Joss put the softened tube against his swollen head, wincing as the cool, wet sheep's intestine touched his hot skin. He began to pull the snug sheath up his shaft.

"It will protect us both—from disease, from pregnancy."

Her creamy skin flushed brick red. "I've got no diseases."

"Nor do I."

"Then . . ."

Joss tied the sheath tight. "I don't want to put a child inside you."

Annie's face took on an odd expression and Joss wondered if it wasn't that of a person thwarted. But then she smiled, her eyes dropping to his erection as she reached for him.

He brushed aside her hands and took her by the hips, pulling her generous bottom to the edge of the bed and pressing her thighs wide with his knees.

"Lay back," he ordered. He dropped into a crouch, parted her lips with his thumbs, and sucked her tight bud into his mouth. She was hot, sweet, and as responsive as hell and it took only moments to bring her to orgasm.

She came fast and hard, her young body taut and slick with sweat as she thrashed beneath him, grinding herself against him and using him to bring on a second climax.

He waited until her body went still before he positioned himself at her opening and entered her in one long, smooth glide.

She cried out and bucked against him when he rammed his length home.

Joss kept her filled with his cock as he lifted her hips off the bed, his hands beneath her smooth thighs and his knees bent for balance and strength as he began to pump.

She lay stretched out before him like a banquet and he gazed down the length of her ripe, curvy body, his eyes lingering on her breasts, which were full, hard tipped, and bounced with each savage thrust. He regretted neglecting them, but his balls could no longer be denied.

He reached down to where their bodies were joined, thumbing her while he watched the mesmerizing sight of her body stretching to accommodate his. He made her come quickly—and then again.

She shook her head from side to side as her contractions faded. "Please, Joss," she begged as his thumb began to caress her again. "I …can't…. Not again."

He smiled, both at her begging and at her contractions, which drove him toward the edge of self-control, until all he cared about was his own pleasure and the oblivion it would bring.

Joss gripped her legs so hard his fingers ached and he fucked into her with brutal stabbing thrusts, until his body stiffened and he held himself deep within her convulsing heat.

He came until it hurt, until he was drained of everything: everything except futility and frustration. Everything except the knowledge of who he was and why he would never, ever have what he wanted.

Chapter Three

Joss wondered if Lady Selwood began talking to him merely to torment him.

Surely she could have no interest in his reading habits, his family, or his life in general.

Or perhaps it was because she was bored?

Whatever the reason, over the coming days she did not miss an opportunity to grill him.

"Tell me about your family, Gormley," she asked when he was escorting her home from some gaming party where she'd gone to meet Byerly, but then—surprisingly—left early and without the annoying young lord.

His family?

"I expect the courtesy of an answer," she said when he failed to respond.

Joss had to look down to hide his smile. For some reason, he enjoyed it when she became starchy with him.

He cleared his throat and looked up, meeting her questioning gaze. "I have two brothers and a sister who lives with my father."

"Your mother?"

"She is dead." Joss ignored the hornet's sting to his conscience.

"Ah." For a moment he thought she might be finished. But no. "Your brothers are older or younger?"

"Older, both of them—my lady," he added, when he realized his confusion had caused him to momentarily forget himself.

"And your sister?"

"She is the baby of the family, my lady."

"And are you close to your family?"

Joss squinted through the dim light. "Close, my lady?"

Her smile grew and it made him more than a little anxious. He wondered if she'd been imbibing spirits and sniffed the air as subtly as possible. He smelled nothing but the elusive scent of her undoubtedly expensive perfume.

"Yes, close." She said "Do you see them often? Do you enjoy their company? Will you miss them if I decide to move my household elsewhere? Have you ever been away from them? That sort of thing—close, in the emotional sense, Gormley."

Joss turned his hat in circles. "I see them every week. I enjoy seeing them, but once a week is usually plenty, my lady." He stopped and she nodded encouragingly. "I've been away before, when I was a lad. I recall missing them, but not, er, over much."

"Do you have a favorite sibling?"

Joss cocked his head.

"Is that a rude question?" She absently tugged at the fingers of one glove, turning to look out the window as the carriage passed a streetlamp. "I don't have brothers or sisters," she said, turning back to him. "So I've always been curious about those who do."

She was *curious* about her servant's brothers and sisters? To say her behavior was odd was an understatement. Lord Easton, for whom he'd worked for almost eight years—and also a man who'd attended every one of Joss's fights—had never asked him anything more personal than the current odds.

She cleared her throat, delicately, but Joss got the hint.

"Ah, a favorite," he said, wondering just how honest he wished to be with this woman, whose glorious, expectant eyes were focused only on him. He realized, to his disgust, he would do a lot to keep her looking at him that way. "I suppose my sister is my favorite."

"What is her name?"

"Annabelle, my lady."

"That's very pretty—and unusual."

He knew what she meant, unusual for a girl of Joss's class. Well, his mother had been unusual.

He glanced out the window, relieved to see familiar landmarks: they would be home soon and this exquisitely uncomfortable yet dangerously addictive interlude would be over.

"How old is she?"

"She is three-and-twenty, my lady."

"Are you a protective older brother? Do you vet and scrutinize all her swains, making quick work of any who are unsuitable?"

A laugh burst out of him before he could stop it.

She looked at him as though he'd sprouted a second head.

"I beg your pardon, my lady," he said, his face again composed. "When she was little I kept the other children who lived on our street from teasing her. And now? Well, I suppose I am protective of her, but all three of us—my other brothers included—look out for her."

Her expression was almost wistful. "She must like that—it must make her feel very . . . safe."

Joss had no earthly idea how to answer that. Luckily it seemed she didn't require an answer.

"I will be bringing my daughter to stay with me before Christmas."

Joss blinked. She had a *daughter?* This was the first Joss had heard of it.

"She has been raised in the country and this will be her first visit to London." She gazed out the window and Joss saw they had turned onto their street. He desperately wished, suddenly, that the journey was not almost at an end. Something about her was so very *sad.*

But the carriage rolled to a smooth stop and Joss helped her out. The only thing she said before disappearing up the stairs was the usual, "Good night, Gormley."

She resumed her questions two nights later, when he'd escorted her to Lord Byerly's; except this time the interrogation topic had been—of all things—how one went about becoming a groom.

But the return journey from Lord Byerly's—which had taken place a scant quarter of an hour after her *arrival*—had taken place in stony silence.

The interior of the carriage had crackled like the sky before a storm; it had been the first time Joss had seen his mistress discomposed.

Whatever had happened up in Byerly's chambers, it hadn't ended well. Joss had wanted to cheer at her speedy departure from the effete nobleman's ramshackle and neglected lair. He'd kept his elation to himself.

Lady Selwood's jaw had been tight and her beautiful face had worn twin slashes of color when she'd descended the staircase. Byerly had stood at the top of the stairs, clad only in a silk robe that had been open, affording Joss a vision that would require a chisel and mallet to eradicate from his brain.

"Bloody hell, Alicia! I said I was sorry. What else do you want from me?"

Lady Selwood ignored the nobleman's pleading.

She'd tapped the toe of one foot the entire ride home and Joss had been astounded how such a small, delicate slipper could create such a menacing sound.

Joss thought about her name—one delicious new piece of information to come out of the aborted evening—while she stewed:

Alicia. It gave him the shivers just thinking it. He hadn't spoken it aloud; not even when he was alone.

He was a pitiful fool.

She hadn't used him for three nights after that.

But tonight, he was accompanying her in her own carriage rather than a hack. Their destination was Lord Delmore's rambling mansion on the other side of the river, far beyond the fashionable part of town. Joss had been once before, but Byerly had been there that night to escort Lady Selwood so Joss had stayed with the carriage. Tonight Joss would be her guardian.

"Do you gamble, Gormley?"

The question came from the darkness of the coach. As usual, she'd not wanted the inside lanterns lighted and the streetlights had become scarce as they left the City.

"Do you mean cards, my lady?" Joss still didn't find it easy to talk to her—to ask *her* questions—but he had come to realize she enjoyed these brief tết-à-têts. And so did he.

"Cards, horses, anything."

"I occasionally wager on a mill."

"Ah. But not cards?"

"No, my lady, I like better odds than a game of cards can offer."

She chuckled in a way that gave him goosebumps. "There speaks a man who does not understand the game."

Joss shrugged, and then remembered to whom he was speaking. "I am sure you are correct, my lady."

"Take the game of vingt-et-un, for example. Do you know it?"

"Yes, my lady." But he'd only ever played it with his family, and for pennies.

There was gambling at The White House, but that was on the male side of the business, and Joss would not have been welcome at those tables, even if he'd wished to play.

"While there is still an element of chance involved, sticking to a consistent system will yield results that might surprise you."

"Of course, my lady."

"I believe you are patronizing me, Gormley."

Joss coughed to cover a laugh. "I would never do that, my lady."

She laughed, not bothering to hide it. "You are a clever man, Gormley, but not clever enough to deceive me."

Joss was gob-smacked. She thought him clever?

"Tell me, what book do you have in your pocket tonight?"

"What makes you think I have a book in my pocket, my lady?" Joss felt foolishly proud when his rather cheeky retort elicited another laugh.

"Oh come, you must think me terribly unobservant if you believe I have not noticed you *always* have your nose in a book while you wait for me."

Joss *had* thought her unobservant, at least when it came to him.

"It is Henry Neele's *Odes and Other Poems.*"

"Ah, you are partial to poetry."

The carriage, as well-sprung as it was, jolted violently as it passed over a particularly poor segment of road. Lady Selwood was thrown to one side and began to slide forward. Joss saw a flash of wide-open eyes and blindly reached forward. As it happened, one hand ended up on her shoulder, the other on her very generous bosom. He righted her quickly and yanked back his hand, as if burned.

"I beg your pardon, my lady." Joss wondered if his face glowed red in the near darkness.

She gave a breathy laugh. "Thanks to your quick thinking and even quicker reflexes I am not on my knees, Gormley."

The picture her words evoked was like a roundhouse to the jaw and Joss was grateful he was seated. He tucked away the erotic image for later, when he was alone and could take it out and examine it more fully.

———❤———

Alicia didn't want to consider her reasons for driving all the way out to Delmore's house, which was really more of a high-stakes gaming hell than merely the earl's house.

The earl had been an associate of Alicia's last husband. She'd never liked him, but she had to admit he knew how to assemble some of the most skilled and outrageous gamblers in Britain.

She'd made the mistake of introducing Byerly to the exclusive group some weeks earlier, when she arranged to meet him here and then had been forced to watch him lose repeatedly. The man was a horrid card player and also addicted to the pursuit.

She hadn't made the mistake of inviting him again. The only reason to ask him along the first time was because showing up unescorted was problematic.

But now she had Gormley and he was enough to deter anyone from bothering her; not that being bothered was much of a concern. Delmore's was a fairly respectable house—as such things went.

Alicia told herself she'd only brought Gormley as a deterrent, but that was a bald lie. She found the massive, reserved man interesting. Indeed, she found him *too* interesting.

Her body, in particular, appeared to find him *most* interesting. She shivered at the memory of his powerful hands on her side—and breast.

He'd moved like lightning and lifted her onto the seat with an ease that had sent heat arrowing to her sex. It had been—

"I understand you'll be staying in town all winter, Lady Selwood."

Alicia looked up from her lustful musing to find the Honorable Ronald Skipton looking at her. She wanted to ask him how he knew about her private business, but guessed the source was most likely Byerly.

She nodded at the dealer who gave her another card. It was a four, which brought her to twenty.

"I'll stick," she said, before turning to Skipton and saying, "Yes."

He looked nonplussed at her brief and very uncommunicative answer and then opened his mouth.

The Duke of Beckingdon, a man famous for his hatred of small-talk at the card table—one of the main reasons Alicia enjoyed playing with him, the other being he was a fine card player—cleared his throat and glared at the younger man. Skipton shrank back into his chair and the play continued in silence.

Alicia could not see Gormley as he stood behind her, beside the door where he could keep an eye on her but not assist her playing—although nobody had dared suggest such a thing.

She felt a brief pang of remorse—no doubt he would rather be sitting somewhere with his big, bent nose tucked in a book.

The play continued deep for the next hour.

Skipton threw in his cards and shook his head as a new banker came to their table. "That's it for me, too rich for my blood."

Beckingdon merely grunted and turned to Alicia, his obvious dismissal of the younger man causing Skipton's face to burn a fiery red.

The duke smiled at her, a rare, and rather ghastly sight with his yellow, snaggled teeth. "I read about your triumph in the last paper from New York, Lady Selwood. Congratulations."

Alicia smiled. "Thank you, Your Grace." She could guess what was on the wily old bird's mind.

"What triumph is that, Becky?" Lord Grimsby asked, his hands trembling with a palsy Alicia had heard was from syphilis.

"Lady Selwood had enough foresight to purchase land from Albany, New York to some lake in the back of beyond. Coincidentally, the same route as the new canal that is to be built." The duke didn't take his eyes from her.

Grimsby barked a laugh, signaling the hovering waiter for yet another brandy. "Lord, a canal? What the devil for? Selling goods to savages?"

The other two members of the table, men Alicia had never played with before, chuckled. But the duke did not.

"It is some three hundred and sixty miles in length, is it not?"

Alicia smiled. "Three hundred and sixty-three miles."

The duke's eyes kindled and Alicia knew it was not for her smile. The man needed money, just like every other aristocrat in Britain. "I should love to hear more about this engineering feat, Lady Selwood."

"You must come to dinner sometime, Your Grace."

"Her Grace and I will be staying in the city over Christmas."

Alicia almost laughed at his blatant invitation. She could just imagine the reaction of his high-stickler wife when she learned she would be dining with Lady Selwood.

"I am having a dinner party Christmas Day; you would honor me with your presence."

"Here then, what's this?"

Alicia sighed at the sound of the slurred, familiar voice that came from behind her. The duke looked over her shoulder, his habitual frown back in place. He grunted and turned back to the table.

Alicia looked up to find Byerly beside her, and none-too-steady. He stared at her through bleary eyes and then nudged the man who'd taken Skipton's seat.

"Move over, Kingston, I wish to sit next to Lady Selwood. It's been ages since we've last chatted."

"Byerly," the duke barked.

All heads turned to the duke.

Beckingdon had upgraded from a frown to a scowl. "This is a *card* table, for playing *cards*. If you wish to *chat* I suggest you pay morning calls. No doubt my wife would be thrilled to oblige your chatter."

The others laughed outright and even Alicia bit back a smile.

Charles flushed and looked uncertainly from Alicia, to the banker, who was studiously avoiding the viscount's eyes. Alicia could guess what that meant: Charles had already outlived his welcome—and his credit—at Lord Delmore's tables.

Charles stared at her, as if expecting her to offer to frank him.

"Well, are you in or out, Byerly?" Beckingdon demanded testily.

Byerly crossed his arms. "I believe I shall just watch for a while."

"Fine, see that you do so with your mouth closed."

Alicia continued to win, as did the duke, which helped to ease his frown. Charles, on the other hand, became more and more restless and when the table broke for supper he hovered, waiting for her. But Alicia had had enough.

"I'm finished for the evening," she told the duke, who appeared to be waiting to take her in to supper, also. How awkward.

The older man shot Charles a filthy look and then nodded, taking her hand and bowing over it. "You are a superlative player, my lady and I enjoyed it. I shall see you at Christmas."

"Thank you, Your Grace."

Alicia and Charles watched him walk away and then Alicia gathered up her winnings. Charles eyed her money with embarrassing desperation.

"Here, Charles," she picked up his hand and placed the roll of flimsies into the middle of his palm, closing his fingers around it. She collected her reticule and nodded to Gormley, who stood by the doorway, watching and waiting. She took a few steps toward him but Charles's hand stopped her.

He opened his mouth, closed it, and then puckered his lips and leaned toward her, as if to kiss her.

She recoiled. "Never in public."

"I just wanted to thank you." He looked as petulant as he sounded and Alicia knew he'd had far too much to drink to talk reasonably. She realized Gormley had crossed the room, his massive body taut and coiled, his eyes locked on Charles. She gave a slight shake of her head and he hesitated and frowned but stepped aside.

"Good night, Charles."

She expected him to come after her and did not relax the set of her shoulders until she was again inside the carriage.

As they rumbled down Delmore's poorly maintained driveway Alicia asked herself why she had come.

She ignored the answer her brain provided, but her willful eyes sought out her servant, catching glimpses of Gormley's harsh features as shafts of moonlight flickered through the window.

—❤—

At first Joss thought they might make the journey home in peace and quiet.

He'd seen she was distracted, if not exactly upset, by the appearance of her current lover.

Byerly had looked rough and ragged and he'd taken the money she'd offered like a man grasping at a lifeline. Joss rarely wagered, but he would place all the money he had on the odds of Byerly leaving Delmore's house without a penny of Lady Selwood's money left in his pocket.

Her voice interrupted his internal wagering.

"Was that your first journey to a gaming hell, Gormley?"

"No, my lady. Although I've never been to one in an aristocrat's house."

"Oh, where did you go?"

He hesitated.

"A brothel, perhaps?"

Joss blinked. Now, why would she have said that?

"I daresay there are not many differences between one hell and another," she continued, apparently deciding to leave the subject of brothels alone. "But what did you think?"

"The stakes were considerably higher, my lady."

"Oh, is that so?" She sounded genuinely surprised.

"Yes, my lady." At any given time there had been at least a thousand pounds on that table. She'd played as if they were pennies. He estimated she had won at least two thousand in the course of the evening. And then she had given it all to that louse.

"You disapprove of me giving my winnings to Lord Byerly." Her chuckle was velvety and mysterious in the near blackness of the carriage. "I could see it in your face. You are, in general, a difficult man to read, Gormley. But you were as open as ... a book when I put the money in his hand. Tell me, what were you thinking at that moment? I would like to know."

Joss snorted softly.

"You don't believe me?"

"I don't think you would like what I was thinking, my lady." He wanted to take the words back, but of course he couldn't.

She leaned forward, until her face was only inches away. "You were angry—you are *still* angry."

"Very well, my lady. You are correct, I am angry."

She sat back, and he was again facing the darkness. "Why is that?"

Joss rolled his eyes.

"I saw that, Gormley."

He gaped. "It's *dark* in here, how—"

"I have the eyes of a cat." He heard the smile in her voice. "But you were saying?"

26

Fine, she wanted his opinion, she could have it. "There must have been almost two thousand pounds in that roll."

He heard the rustle of silk and knew she'd shrugged. "Closer to three. What of it?"

Could she really not understand? "That is a fortune and he will lose it. All of it—and most likely tonight."

A sigh came out of the darkness. "Yes, I believe you are right. It is quite sad."

"Sad?" he demanded before he could stop himself.

"What would you call it?"

"I would call it foolish to the point of criminal."

They both knew he did not mean Byerly's gambling, but her giving him the money. Joss knew he should shut his mouth, but the box had been opened and the contents could not be shoved back inside.

"That is more than a well-paid servant will make in a decade, my lady."

The carriage was heavy with silence and Joss thought he had finally stepped over the line.

He expected to be scolded—at the very least—but, instead, she sighed. "You are correct of course. There were many other better uses for the money." Her eyes glinted in the darkness. "Tell me, how would *you* spend three thousand pounds, Mr. Gormley?"

Joss looked away, unnerved now that he knew her vision was so keen. She could see him, but he could not see her. He did not like it. "I don't know, my lady."

She chuckled. "That was a lie. But you do not owe me such confidences. I will make you a promise, Gormley." She paused. "Don't you wish to know what it is?" she asked.

He couldn't help smiling, even though he was still more than a little angry and frustrated.

She spoke before he could answer, "The next time I gamble I'll give *you* my winnings. But only if you confide in me how you will spend it."

"But what if you lose, my lady?"

She laughed. "I shouldn't worry about that if I were you, Mr. Gormley."

"Are you really that lucky, my lady?"

"No, I'm really that good."

This time Joss kept his opinion to himself, not that it seemed to matter.

"I can hear your skepticism."

It was his turn to chuckle. "Are you a mind-reader, my lady"

"I know men." Her tone was no longer humorous. In fact, she sounded sad. Sad and tired and resigned.

Chapter Four

Alicia looked at the long, pleading message penned on the heavy white paper and felt her eyes blur with the effort of reading it. Not that she needed to read it in order to discern the contents: it was the fifth missive he'd sent in as many days.

Charles was behaving recklessly—foolishly—and she should end it. I She dropped the letter in disgust.

You wouldn't have these problems if you could just keep your knees together. It was her auntie's voice, which seemed to have carved out a niche in her head and moved in permanently, even though her Aunt Giddy had been dead for more than two decades.

Her aunt had said the same thing dozens of times when she'd been alive, when Alicia had first understood how men looked at her. And that she liked their looks and the power it gave her.

She'd been fifteen, but as tall and physically developed as she was now. More than once her aunt had threatened to tie her to a chair in the tiny room they called home.

"A decent man won't want a soiled dove, Allie."

Alicia had laughed. "I'm hardly a dove, Aunt Giddy."

"Oh, you're so clever, aren't you? Smarter than the three wise men all wrapped into one? Well let me tell you, miss, I know a sight more about men and what they want than *you* do. And the only thing most of 'em are interested in is to scratch their itches with that thing you've got tucked between your legs. And once they've scratched it?" She'd shrugged, leaving the conclusion up to Alicia's younger self's active imagination.

Alicia remembered wanting to ask her aunt about *her* itches and why it didn't matter what Alicia needed scratching. Also, why could the itch only be scratched once? And why was getting it scratched so very bad?

Of course she'd asked none of those things.

Her aunt's words had worried her enough to convince Alicia to keep her knees together—and she had continued to do so until the day she married. *No decent man will want you if you are soiled.* And if no decent man wanted her, well what would she have then?

She looked up at the sound of knocking on her boudoir door.

"Come."

Maude, stood in the doorway, pinched faced and disapproving. "You wanted Gormley?"

"Drat." Alicia had forgotten she'd rung for the man. "Have him wait in my study. I'll have a message for him to deliver in a moment."

Her maid *hmmphed* and closed the door with a pointed *click*. Sometimes Alicia thought her life would be more pleasant if she discharged the sour-faced, judgmental older woman, but of course she never would.

Something about Maude reminded her of her Aunt Giddy. She often couldn't decide if that was a good thing, or a bad thing. Yet, here was Maude, still with her after almost twenty years.

Alicia stopped dithering and avoiding the task at hand and pulled out a fresh sheet of paper, picked up her quill, and began the laborious process of drafting a message.

—❤—

Joss had been in this study dozens of times over the past months, but only rarely had he caught a glimpse into her inner sanctum. He didn't know much about this side of rich, titled women, but Lady Selwood's sitting room was unlike anything that he would have imagined.

If he'd been led in here without knowing the owner he would have said it was a man's room.

The floor was an unusual milk-white wood that had been buffed to a glossy shine. Scattered on top were thick, plush rugs in hundreds of shades of rich brown; Joss hadn't realized there were so many different types of brown.

The furniture was heavy; no gilt, no spindly carved legs, no frilled skirts, no piles of cushions. Nothing but dark wood upholstered in rich blond leather the color of her hair. It was a man's room, or at least a room Joss would have enjoyed lounging in, if he did things like lounge.

The door across from him opened and Lady Selwood stepped inside. She was swathed head to toe in a dressing gown of heavy cream-colored silk, a shade remarkably similar to her skin.

The complete lack of color should have washed her out and made her insignificant. But instead it made her look stark, compelling, and achingly untouchable—all of which she was.

She held out her hand. "Here is a message for Lord Byerly."

Joss closed the distance between them in three strides and took the letter. "Very good, my lady. I will go directly." He turned to leave.

"Gormley?"

Joss stopped and pivoted on one heel. "Yes, my lady?"

Her full, bloodred lips twisted slightly. "His lordship will probably want you to wait while he composes a reply," she hesitated, a flicker of indecision crossing her usually impassive face. Joss darted a look at her eyes and found they'd gone vague.

"Do you wish me to wait for a response, my lady?"

She inhaled deeply, teasing his eyes to look lower, which he prudently avoided. She nodded. "You will wait if he requests it."

"Is there anything else, my lady?"

Her pale eyes sharpened and focused on his. Like a moth held by a flame he could not look away.

"Yes. Before you leave tell Cook I shall be eating at home tonight." She turned without waiting for a response, the door closing soundlessly behind her.

The room felt as if it had dimmed.

"You bloody fool, Gormley," he muttered under his breath.

Joss took the back stairs to the first floor, deciding he would walk the distance to Lord Byerly's house rather than take a hackney.

In the kitchen he found a scattering of servants gathered around the battered wooden table where Cook held court when she was not laboring over the massive stove—which was most of the time since the mistress of the house was rarely at home for dinner. And when she was, she ate "barely enough to keep a bird alive" as Cook phrased it.

"Off on a mission for Herself, are ye?" Cook always behaved more freely when Feehan was not in attendance.

Joss nodded, looking from Cook to Annie, who sat sipping her tea, her cap on the table beside her, her brown curls mussed in a way that reminded him of that night. The way she was staring at him told him that she was thinking the same thing.

She'd come back to his quarters again, two nights after their tussle, and he'd sent her away. The last thing he wanted was her thinking they were a couple. Judging by the yearning looks she was cutting him; he was already too late.

"Her Ladyship will dine in tonight," he said.

Cook's heavy face lightened. "Ah, good, time to earn my keep. It's been two weeks since her last dinner. I sometimes wonder why she keeps me at all," she muttered.

"I've got a message to deliver. I'm going to walk rather than take a hack, if anyone should ask," he told the room at large.

Cook heaved herself to her feet. "Aye, 'tis a beautiful day for a walk, Gormley." She cast a glance around at the others. "Best be gettin' on with youse. Annie, you know 'is Nibs wanted them curtains done. Hiram, that marble won't polish itself." She gestured to her three lounging kitchen helpers and clapped her meaty hands. "Up and ready, lazybones, we've got a dinner to prepare."

Joss left them to it, taking his overcoat from the hook by the door.

A hand on his sleeve stopped him and he was not surprised to find Annie smiling provocatively up at him.

"I've my half day tomorrow," she said, her hands deftly tucking and pinning on the mobcap that covered her crowning glory.

Joss knew she had a half day because they *all* had a half day.

"I'm going to see my family," he said, buttoning his coat. He could see she was struggling to say something. He sighed and picked up his hat from the table before taking her arm and leading her away from the bustling entrance to the kitchen.

"Annie, that was one time. I never said it would be more."

She pressed closer, her breast soft and warm on his arm. "But you never said it wouldn't, either."

Joss couldn't help smiling at her persistence, a mistake, because she took his rare smile for encouragement. She caught his sleeve. "A few of us are meeting up before coming back here. You know, just a friendly pint or two."

Joss knew. He'd been avoiding servant socializing since he'd been hired. It had taken a few weeks, but finally the men had stopped asking him. He knew they thought he was high in the instep because he didn't gossip about his mistress, wouldn't meet at a pub, wouldn't talk about his past.

"Please?"

He looked down and wanted to curse at the pleading expression in her eyes. It was the same look women always got. Well, the same look unmarried women always got, at least: that marrying look.

"Just an hour? What could an hour hurt?"

Joss worked his jaw from left to right, willing his lips to form the word *no.*

"Fine," he said, gently tugging away his sleeve. "An hour."

She grinned as if he'd just promised her the crown jewels with the moon and stars to go with them.

"Now, I've got to go—and so do you or you'll get a proper raking."

She giggled but moved away.

Joss shook his head and headed for the door. It wasn't that Annie wasn't a nice girl, it was that he had a rule. One woman, one night. Never twice. He couldn't risk becoming entangled with a woman who would resent the care his sister would require—that was a promise he'd made to himself years ago, when their mother had left them.

So he'd lived by his "one night" rule for years, ever since leaving Melissa's and taking a proper job.

The rule had worked well for him at Lord Easton's London house, a position he enjoyed greatly—until Lord Easton's daughter had begun casting languishing looks in Joss's direction.

He snorted; he'd escaped from adolescent infatuation and tears by the skin of his teeth and now he'd jeopardized his new position with his own foolishness. Not that Annie was seventeen or a viscount's daughter. She was in her early twenties for all that she was behaving like a schoolroom chit.

Joss pushed the aggravation from his mind and enjoyed the weather, which was sunny and unexpectedly warm for this time of year.

He tossed a penny to a street sweeper and turned left on North Audley Street.

He'd not thought to still be in London at Christmas, but it turned out Lady Selwood would not go to the country this year.

That meant Joss would be able to spend some part of the holidays with his family.

Of course Michael and Gordon had families of their own, but Belle was tied to home by both their father and her condition. Thinking of his sister's unmarried state brought Annie back to mind.

Joss had never understood what it was that women saw in him. He was not a handsome man, he knew that. His only attractive sibling was Michael, who'd inherited their mother's green eyes and slight build.

Gordon, Joss, and—God help her, Annabelle—all took after their father. Tall, strapping builds with big features and muddy colored eyes.

At least Joss had inherited his mother's thick brown hair. Both Gordon and Annabelle had wispy dusty-colored locks which, in Gordon's case, had given way to a naked pate at the age of thirty. Thankfully the same had not happened to his poor sister, who had enough to contend with without losing her hair.

Joss realized his mind had drifted around to Belle and forced it back to the errand at hand.

He loathed Viscount Byerly and would have done so even had the man not been bedding Lady Selwood. Byerly represented everything Joss hated about the aristocracy. He was effete, useless, ornamental, and he had everything Joss did not: money, power, respect, and Alicia Selwood in his bed. Although he doubted Byerly would have her for much longer.

Joss's mouth curled into a tight smile at the thought.

Byerly's house was on Berkeley Square, a great block of a place that was directly across from Selwood House. Joss knew the current earl lived there when he was in town—which apparently was not right now—and he also knew from listening to servant gossip that Lady Selwood did not get along with her stepson, who was apparently something of a high stickler.

Joss doubted Lord Selwood would take kindly to the knowledge that his father's widow was fucking the man who lived across the square from him.

When he reached Byerly House he went round back rather than to the front entrance, where he usually went if he had a message for somebody in a grand house. But Byerly's house was so poorly staffed there was rarely anyone near the front door.

He knocked, waited, and then knocked again. A maid answered just as he was about to try the front door.

Her mouth tipped into a wicked smile as she assessed him. She appeared to be his age, her cap and gown grubby, her neck unwashed.

Joss handed her the message. "From Lady Selwood. I've been instructed to wait if there is a response."

Her smile grew and exposed a row of teeth with several blackened. "Sure ducks." She opened the door wider. "We're just havin' a cuppa."

Joss followed her swaying form into the kitchen. The difference between the kitchen he'd just left and this one was extreme. Slatternly looking servants of both genders surrounded the servants' table, which was cluttered with dirty crockery and spills and stains. Joss abhorred dirt and filth; in fact, he had something of a mania for cleanliness. This kitchen made his skin crawl.

"'Ave a seat, 'ansome." The maid leered up at him and handed the message to a footman wearing the dingiest livery Joss had ever seen.

Joss glanced down at the chair in question, crumbs and other unidentifiable bits of food sticking to the hard wood seat.

"Thank you, I'll stand."

She raised her eyebrows. "Ohh, crikey! *I'll stand, thank you.*"

The others chuckled at her mockery and even Joss had to smile at the apt imitation.

She slumped into her seat and gestured to the steaming pot.

"I just had tea," he lied.

She smirked, knowing his words for a lie, but not challenging him. "'Imself is in quite a taking," an older woman said, the words an obvious gambit.

"Is he?" Joss glanced around the dank, dimly lighted kitchen, grateful he didn't have to eat any food that came out of it.

The maid poured herself some inky black liquid. "Aye, 'ee 'ad 'is 'opes up for yer lady, dint 'e? As did we all." The others grumbled at her words and Joss could only assume wages were in arrears. He could sympathize, although he'd never been in such a situation himself. Both Lord Easton and Lady Selwood paid their servants well and on time.

The door opened and the scruffy footman slouched back into the room. "He wants you."

Joss's eyebrows shot up.

The footman gave him an annoyed, impatient nod. "Aye, you. Now."

Joss followed him down the ill-lighted servant corridor and up to the second floor. The master's hallway was no cleaner or better illuminated than that of his servants.

The footman opened a door and jerked his thumb toward it.

Joss stepped inside a very dim room, a study, he guessed.

"You may go, Thomas."

The door closed behind him and Joss saw Viscount Byerly's form lurking in the darkness at the far end of the room.

"Come here," Byerly ordered.

Joss navigated the darkened room with care, the floor and table surfaces as cluttered as those below in the kitchen, before coming to a stop in front of the man's heaped desk.

Byerly looked rather worse for wear. He was, Joss had to grudgingly acknowledge, a handsome man, although the lifestyle he led was taking its toll. Lines radiated from his limpid blue eyes and deep grooves of dissipation ran from his fine, aquiline nose to his thin aristocratic lips. His skin was as pale as Lady Selwood's, but splotched and pasty. His hair—golden blond curls that no man should have—appeared dry and brittle even in the poor light. He wore no cravat and his shirt was limp and sweat-stained, his waistcoat shapeless and grimy from too much wear.

"You are the servant who usually accompanies Lady Selwood here." The lord's tone was sharp and the words were not really a question.

"Yes, my lord."

Byerly's eyes flickered over him, as if searching for some sign of what he might be thinking. But Joss had been trained by the best to hide his true thoughts and Byerly's sharp eyes found nothing.

"Does she go to other houses—to see other men?" His voice broke on the last word. Joss should have been expecting this; should have devised a response. He hesitated, and Byerly rushed on. "I know you cannot be disloyal to your mistress, but—" he gestured helplessly with one long, pale elegant hand, the motion churning the air as if the words he sought might be floating somewhere just beyond his grasp.

Joss stared straight ahead. "I am sorry, my lord."

Byerly's jaw moved side to side, his left eye twitching. He gave an abrupt nod. "You are a good and loyal servant. I shall commend Lady Selwood on your discretion." He motioned toward the door. "Go wait in the hall. I shall have something for you shortly."

Joss waited out in the hall for over an hour until Byerly summoned him.

One of the candles had guttered out, leaving the room even darker. Joss could smell alcohol mixed with despair. He could almost feel sorry for Byerly, whose blond hair was tufted and clumped in greasy wads, as if he'd been tugging on it nonstop this past hour.

For all the time he'd taken, he held out a single folded sheet, not bothering to seal it. No doubt he assumed Joss could not read, or at least not well enough to matter.

Joss took the missive, bowed, and turned to leave.

"Stop."

The word caught him with his hand on the door and he turned.

"You will not tell her of my condition." Again, it was not a question.

Joss could have told the man that she would never ask such a question and he would never volunteer, but he didn't.

"I do whatever Lady Selwood tells me to do, my lord."

The other man snorted, his sneering lips twisting unpleasantly. "I'll just bet you do. Now get the hell out."

Chapter Five

Joss wished, for the hundredth time, he had not agreed to meet Annie at the Crown and Shield. He fisted his hands in his coat—not the black wool he worked in, but his far less elegant brown rough weave, which he'd been so proud of when he'd bought all those years ago—and hunched his shoulders against the blast of cold; it seemed winter was officially here.

He'd enjoyed his afternoon at his father's house. Belle had been cheerful and excited about the coming holiday, her homely face creased with a smile when he showed up on the doorstep.

"Oh, Joss!" She'd thrown her arms around him, hugging him close. "I'm so glad you are here." She drew back and looked up at him, her eyes—a drab brownish green like his—sparkling and pretty. "You look good."

"And you, too," he said, not needing to lie. She *did* look good, her fine hair skillfully dressed to soften, rather than hide, some of the worst scars on her jaws and forehead.

"I brought these for Father." He handed her the package of sugar plums he'd bought. Their father, who'd become more and more childlike, seemed to brighten up for sweets.

"He will be so happy! Although I shall have to take care he does not eat them all at once." She took his hat. "We were beginning to worry you might not come."

"I'm sorry I'm late, Belle. My hackney got held up behind an accident and I just decided to walk." He shrugged out of his coat and handed her the scarf she'd knitted him for Christmas last year. It was a beautiful black and gray checked thing that he greatly treasured. Belle knew better than anyone how much he liked fine things.

"I'm just glad you're here," she'd said, casting a furtive glance toward the kitchen.

Joss grimaced. Their brother Michael's wife, Susan, could be a chore. Especially toward Belle, whose position as mistress of the house she would take once their father died. "Is she—"

Belle shook her head. "Nothing I cannot manage," she said, smiling.

Joss knew there were no doubt countless petty slights his sister endured without complaint, but he could see she did not wish to discuss it. "I've got to leave a bit early," he warned, following her toward the sound of his family's voices.

She grinned up at him. "Oh? Someone special."

"No, just a drink with the mates."

"That's not like you, Joss."

"I know, that's why I'm making an effort; they're thinking I'm top-lofty."

"Then they'd be right, wouldn't they?"

"Cheeky wench," he muttered.

She chuckled and he opened the door to his family's warm, cozy kitchen.

"Joss!" Michael, his most demonstrative sibling, came to embrace him. "You're looking as ugly as ever," he said.

"Aye, and you as pretty."

After that, Joss had been swept into the fold of his loud, boisterous family. He kept busy dandling nieces and nephews, listening to the mild marital squabbles, mostly good natured, between his brothers and their wives, and answering his father's polite questions about who he was and why he was there. The hours had passed quickly and all too soon it was time to leave.

Now, as he approached the glowing, fogged window of the Crown, he wished he had the bollocks to just head home. If he went back to his room now, he'd be able to relax and enjoy some peace before changing back into his work clothes. His half-day was over at ten o'clock. Most weeks Her Ladyship did not need him on Sunday night, but he was to be prepared in case she summoned him.

He hesitated and had just taken a step back from the heavy oak door when a voice came from behind him.

"Gormley, ye bastard!"

Joss started and turned to find Mr. Carling approaching.

His lips curved into a smile. He liked the bluff, older man, who was his superior in the hierarchy of Lady Selwood's household, but never made a point of it.

"Good evening, Mr. Carling."

"Come to rub shoulders with the likes of us mortals? Or to rub other things with the likes of Annie?"

Joss's face heated just like a boy at the other man's good-natured ribbing. He sighed, shook his head, and opened the door to the pub, the

Carling's laughter booming around him as they entered the heat and noise.

━━◖♥◗━━

"It's been an age since I saw you, Alicia. Tell me, you secretive wretch, why are you staying in the city over Christmas?"

Alicia looked away from her reflection at the sound of Lady Constance de Veaux's question. They were in her dressing room, where Alicia was running late thanks to yet another *urgent* message from Byerly.

"I'm staying because Selwood sent me a letter last month saying he was bringing Lizzy to town for the first time."

Connie's rather plain face lit up at the news. "How wonderful! When? You must be thrilled to pieces to see her."

"I am. I'd thought we'd be forced to interact only by letter until next summer. Selwood has not said yet *when* they will arrive." Just another way to bait and torment her.

"I'm thrilled for you, but why is he bringing her here in winter of all times?"

"Selwood has come early for some session-related business and the countess is spending the holidays with her family. There was water damage to The Willows from that dreadful storm last month and Selwood decided the workmen need Lizzy out. You know I've not had many opportunities to see her since the earl moved into the house."

Connie did not need to have the matter spelled out. She knew that Lizzy lived at the country seat of the Earls of Selwood and Alicia could hardly visit the house unless she received an invitation. And of course her stepson, the current earl, delighted in depriving her of one.

"And he will let you see Elizabeth on Christmas?"

Alicia screwed the pearl-drop earring into her left lobe and sat back. Yes, these would do quite nicely. She liked the bold look of the onyx and pearl together and the way they complemented her gown, a cream and black confection Madam Silvi had fought tooth-and-nail, until she'd finally seen the unusual design made up to Alicia's specifications. The earrings were inexpensive but she liked them because she had chosen them for herself. Buying her own jewelry might seem unimportant, but it was one of the things she enjoyed about being her own woman. No longer did she have to tolerate a man branding her with his choices.

Alicia realized Connie was waiting for an answer. "Selwood has promised to let me bring her here at Christmas and keep her until The Willows is again fit for habitation."

Connie's eyes widened. "Goodness, that's hardly like him, is it?"

"No, it isn't." Alicia didn't say what she was thinking: that she'd believe her stepson would let her keep Lizzy when it actually happened.

"Whatever have you done to make him so obliging?"

Alicia clasped on her bracelet and stood. "There, I am finally ready. I'm sorry for being so dreadfully late."

Connie's eyes flickered over her and she shook her head, forgetting that Alicia had not answered her question. "Lord, I should hate you."

Alicia laughed.

"Oh, you can laugh, you don't have to stand beside somebody who looks like you and watch men's faces," Connie said, pulling on her gloves.

"And *you* don't have to endure the constant snubs of their wives."

Lady Constance chortled. "Yes, well there is that."

Tonight the two of them were going to a dinner party at the Earl of Broughton's house.

"I do wish you'd reconsider and join us at the theater after dinner," Connie said after they'd settled themselves into Alicia's luxurious coach.

Alicia smiled across at her friend. "Alas, darling, I'm not as youthful as you. I need my beauty sleep if I'm not to look a fright."

"Oh what bosh! You couldn't look a fright if you tried. I know we are all younger than you, Alicia, but we are hardly children. Cynthia and Elinor will be there." She hesitated, and then added, "Piers will be there, too, and I know you enjoy his company."

Piers was the young Duke of Sunderland. Alicia *did* enjoy his company; indeed, she'd considered accepting his bold advances when she'd decided to take a lover. But she had seen the occasional, yearning look Connie cast at the gorgeous aristocrat. Her friend probably didn't even recognize her own attraction, but Alicia certainly did.

The two young people were delightful and would make a charming couple. If Alicia stayed away from Piers then perhaps he might recognize the treasure that was right in front of him and see that his childhood friend was the woman he *really* wanted.

And so Alicia said, "Maybe next time, Connie."

"You always say that."

"Tell me," Alicia said, not-so-subtly changing the subject, "Do you believe the rumor that Lady Broughton is having an affair with that handsome blond footman?"

It was the perfect distraction and the subject of Alicia and her evening did not come up again.

❤

40

Joss grimaced. The night had been the mistake he'd known it would be.

Annie had rubbed up on him like a bitch in heat from the moment he'd entered the pub. When he made it plain he wasn't interested she'd become sulky and spiteful. And then she'd turned her attention toward the new footman, William, a boy a few years younger than Annie and star-struck by her sudden interest.

When she'd understood that Joss was relieved rather than jealous, she'd become argumentative. He knew it was likely the alcohol talking as the girl had consumed at least two pints in his company and had been there before him.

As the evening wore on, Joss felt guiltier and guiltier about bedding her. She might be only a year or so younger than Joss, but she was decades younger in experience. He wished she had some male relative to keep her from throwing herself away—or, even worse—getting herself pregnant and discharged.

But that was hardly his business.

When Carling threw back the last of his third pint and said something about her ladyship coming home earlier tonight, Joss leapt at the excuse to leave.

The cold air felt good after the stifling, hot, sweaty pub.

"You'd best stay away from that one," Carling said as they both hunkered low and walked fast.

Joss just snorted.

"If she ain't got a bun in the oven yet, she soon will have."

"How do you know that?" he asked, wondering if Carling had been the one to put it there—or was considering it. He'd thought the older man happily married, but people were a constant source of surprise.

The stable master shrugged his bull-like shoulders. "I know it because I've seen it before. Girl comes from the country, loses her bearings, spreads her thighs, and then," he snapped his fingers, the sound a loud crack in the frigid air. "She finds herself without a job and on the street. Happens all the time."

Joss wasn't naïve, he knew it happened all the time. After all, something similar had happened to his own mother.

They arrived back just as Lady Selwood's town carriage rolled to a stop in front of the house. Joss hesitated, wondering if he should see to her, but Carling squeezed his shoulder.

"Not dressed like that, my lad."

Joss blinked. Ah, right; his clothing. He turned, regretfully leaving sher in the hands of the servants who'd accompanied her carriage.

Once in his quarters, Joss stripped out of his street clothes, broke the ice on the basin of water and hurriedly washed his face, frowning at the heavy smell of smoke in his hair, wishing he had enough water to wash it and then cursing himself for a fool. Even if the countess used him tonight, she'd hardly be sniffing his hair.

As he changed his clothing Joss thought about the odd, conflicting emotions that stirred in his belly. Part of him always wanted her to use his services—no matter what the errand. The other part knew what he would be doing if she summoned him: taking her to her lover. And, truth be told, that was beginning to rankle.

He snorted at his reflection as he buttoned his waistcoat. That was a lie. It had rankled almost from the start. It was now gnawing at him, like a rat that could never get enough to eat. His imagination, always active, envisioned the things she did with Byerly.

The thoughts always started out the same way: her with another man. The two of them were unclothed and writhing, on a bed, the floor, a chair, it didn't matter; Joss had envisioned her naked on every surface imaginable.

Somewhere in the process of his imaginings the man in his mind's eye turned into Joss.

"You idiot," he said to the fool in the mirror, turning away from the glass and shrugging into his coat.

Once he was dressed, he tidied his already neat room.

Joss's mother had left when he was fifteen, but the one thing she'd instilled in him was a mania for cleanliness. Well, that and an embarrassing penchant for poetry.

His mother had been the daughter of a bank clerk and raised to be a lady. Her expectations had been destroyed by her father's sudden death, after which she'd had to take a position as a governess—a position that had left her pregnant by the master.

The last part of the story Joss had only learned after she left—when their Nana—his father's mother—had taken charge of the household.

His mother had always told her children a different version.

"Your father was such a gentle man." She'd always made sure to sound out the words, as if to make sure they understood she wasn't calling big Clive Gormley a *gentleman.*

"I'd grown up with a cook and two maids and even a footman before Papa died." Her chin had quivered whenever she spoke of their grandfather, whose death had left his wife and daughter penniless.

And so pretty Laura Smithers had taken a governess job—a godsend, she and her mother had believed, as the gentleman who offered her the position had been a friend of her father's.

Laura had also, on occasion, gone to market for her mother on her half-day. That was when Clive Gormley first saw her.

Joss imagined that his father had never before beheld such a lovely, dainty, well-mannered thing as his mother. Clive had been a good deal older than her: a quiet, shy middle-aged giant who'd taken over the family business early, after his own father had died. He'd supported his spinster sister and his mother for years, and they kept house for him.

Laura had liked to whisper to her children how *jealous* her mother and sister-in-law had been, and continued to be, after she married their father and took her place as mistress of his house.

"They could not understand why my hands were so smooth and white, why my clothes were so fine," she'd confided, her small hands work-roughened by the time she told Joss this story.

Looking back on his mother's behavior from the vantage point of over a decade Joss realized that she'd hardly been more than a girl when she'd become pregnant by the master of the house. Once that happened, her life as a teacher was over.

Had it not been for Joss's father—a man kind enough to take a pregnant woman to wife—she would have ended up without a roof over her head.

But she'd never counted those blessings. Instead, she'd remained dissatisfied with her new station in life until the day she'd left them. Left *him*.

Joss would never forget the morning he'd gone down to breakfast to find Nana Gormley rather than his mother.

Nana—raised on hard work—had been called back to duty thanks to her daughter-in-law's desertion.

Joss's father, who'd already been quiet, hardly spoke at all after his wife left.

Although nobody ever told him outright, Joss somehow learned that his mother had run off with the man who came twice a year to sharpen and repair blades for his father.

Joss frowned at the old, yet still painful memories. Why was he thinking about his mother now?

Probably because he was cleaning his quarters as obsessively as she'd taught him to do.

Joss shoved his mother into the back of his mind and set about changing his bed linens, even though he annoyed Lady Selwood's washerwoman by changing the bedding twice as often as any other servant.

The last thing he did was sweep the wooden, rug-less floor, and then put away the broom and dustpan he'd purchased with his own money.

Joss checked his watch, a well-made but not ostentatious piece which his father had given him on his sixteenth birthday: it was half-past eleven. If she did not call for him by midnight, she usually would not.

He looked at the three new books he'd taken from the circulating library he belonged to: *Waverley, The Rights of Man*, and *Heart of the Midlothian Bride*. He took *Waverley* and settled into his chair.

He'd read for perhaps ten minutes when there was a knock.

Joss wasn't surprised to find the countess's personal maid on the other side of the door.

"Good evening, Miss Finch."

The sour old bird glared up at him, as if it were *his* fault that their mistress had sent for him to take her on one of her wicked jaunts.

"She'll be ready in a half hour." She turned on her heel and stomped off before he could answer.

Joss smiled at her retreating back. She was abrupt and rude, but she had an honesty about her that he liked.

He put on his overcoat and drew on his black gloves. They were made from a leather that was slightly thicker than kid and they fit his hands like a second skin.

He completed his outfit with a black woolen scarf and high-crowned hat before snuffing his candles and closing the door.

He located one of the hacks that now hovered about the area after realizing there was often well-paid work to be found at odd hours of the night.

It was too cold for the man to wait his horses until Lady Selwood deigned to come down—which Joss knew from experience would not be in the promised half-hour—so he told the driver to circle the area, and that he would be paid for his time starting immediately.

Joss then went into the black and white marble entry hall and waited.

Lady Selwood arrived only a scant fifteen minutes after the time she'd said.

"The hackney will be only a moment, my lady."

She nodded absently and went to look in the foyer mirror. Joss stepped outside and raised a lantern to summon the hack from the far end of the street.

"To Lord Byerly's," she murmured to Joss as he handed her into the carriage.

He gave the driver the destination and within moments they were on their way.

Joss was gazing out the window when she spoke.

"Tell me what it is like to be a prizefighter?"

By now, her questions shouldn't have surprised him, but this one did.

She gave a low, throaty chuckle that shrieked of tangled bedding and flushed, naked flesh.

"Your expression is quite telling, Gormley."

They passed a streetlamp and he saw she was looking at him, her expression one he'd not seen before, almost puckish.

"Humor me, Gormley. Tell me what it was like. Did you enjoy it?"

That was easy to answer. "No, my lady."

"Then why did you do it?"

"Because it pays well." Her eyebrows shot up at his sarcastic tone. "Ah, begging your pardon, my lady."

"You needn't beg my pardon when I ask a foolish question. What do you think about while you are engaged in fighting?"

As usual, Joss burned to ask her why she was asking about such things. He did not.

"I don't think so much as watch, I let my body's knowledge and skill guide my actions." Joss wished he could take back the foolish—pompous—words, but they were already out in the world.

Her eyes widened. "Why, you sound poetical, Gormley."

He sounded like a tosser, is what he sounded like. Joss hoped that had been the last question.

His hopes were not to be granted.

"You used to work in your father's butcher shop?"

"Yes, my lady."

"But then you went to work for your uncle—as a groom?"

"I started as a hand around the stable." Just where was this going?

"Was that your aspiration?"

"I beg your pardon?"

"Aspiration? It means—"

Joss smiled. "I know what it means, your ladyship."

"So?"

He sighed. "No, it wasn't."

"Was it being a butcher?"

"No, I always knew the shop would go to my eldest brother." He hesitated and then thought, *what the hell?* "I'd once thought to become a teacher."

There was a long pause, but at least no laughter. "How interesting. And why didn't you?"

Thankfully the carriage rolled to a halt; Joss sighed and reached for the door.

"We shall continue this conversation some other time, Gormley."

Joss heard the amusement in her tone.

He escorted her to the door, which was unlocked, as it always was. Joss was lifting her cloak from her shoulders when a voice spoke from the top of the stairs.

"Oh, so you've deigned to come, have you?"

Byerly stood a few steps down from the second floor landing, a glass glinting in one hand, wearing a gaudy red banyan and nothing else.

Lady Selwood removed her hat, her movements unhurried, and handed it to Joss before answering.

"Shall we discuss this upstairs, Charles?"

The nobleman, intoxicated based on the way he was swaying, gave a nasty laugh and turned on his heel.

Joss stood motionless, her hat in one hand, her cloak in the other. The hairs on the back of his neck were prickling, as they'd done from the moment Byerly spoke.

Lady Selwood smoothed her already perfect hair in the gilt-framed mirror and their eyes met in the glass. "I will not be long. Have another carriage waiting in half an hour."

He watched her mount the stairs. Her gown had an hourglass panel of white in the front but was black in the back. The thin silk slid over her curvaceous body like dark water and Joss had to swallow to rid his mouth of excess moisture. He set aside her possessions and immediately went to find a hackney driver.

When he returned, he went to the foot of the stairs, his body tense and aware, just as it had been since arriving. He'd stood for perhaps five minutes and was considering going back to his chair when he heard the unmistakable sound of a woman crying out.

Chapter Six

Alicia had known it was foolish to meet Charles one last time even before he'd drunkenly shouted from the top of the stairs.

She'd known it when she received his last angry, pleading message, she'd known it after sending a message agreeing to see him, and she'd known it when she'd sent Maude to fetch Gormley.

She'd *told* herself that she needed to see Byerly in person in order to put an end to things.

But that was a barefaced lie.

The pitiful, pathetic, undeniable truth was that she'd agreed to see Byerly again just so she could spend time with her enigmatic servant.

Yes, that was the truth, it really was. Admitting it made her want to bang her head on something hard, as if that might shake the mad desire from her thick skull.

Alicia should have guessed she was lost when she'd enjoyed talking to Gormley on the carriage ride to and from Delemor's far more than she'd liked her evening of cards.

Honestly, she didn't know what it was about the quiet, rather brutish-looking man that she found so appealing.

But her growing fascination for him had become worrisome.

Unfortunately, her worry could not compete with her curiosity—which had become overwhelming.

If there was one thing Alicia was good at—her only skill, really—it was single-mindedly pursuing and then acquiring the things she wanted.

It was a skill she'd not always employed wisely, and she tried to convince herself to consider *exactly* what she wanted this time.

After all, the last time she'd thought she wanted something, she'd ended up married to the Earl of Selwood.

That sobering thought should have dimmed her growing obsession.

But it hadn't.

Alicia *needed* to know more about her inscrutable servant. One way to do so, without exposing her humiliating curiosity, was to read what he did.

So, she'd decided to read one of his favorites: *Antony and Cleopatra.*

Alicia had a library stuffed with books that she had paid her steward to choose; it was a room she'd always avoided like the plague.

She knew it was likely that she had Shakespeare among those thousands of books. But when she imagined herself searching the shelves, painstakingly sounding out and reading every title, frustration and anger boiled inside her.

So, Alicia ignored her library and went—for the first time in her life—to a bookseller's.

The entire time she'd mentally mocked and berated herself: she was going to purchase a book just because one of her *servants* was reading it.

She'd been captivated. And not only by a servant, but by a man who was ten years younger than her.

Closer to eleven, her Aunt Giddy had helpfully pointed out.

Alicia had taken her volume of Shakespeare home and spent the next few nights reading it rather than accepting Byerly's increasingly desperate invitations.

Her behavior had stunned Maude.

"You? Reading? A book," she added, just in case Alicia might be too stupid to know what she meant. "You went to a bookseller's? And you *bought* a book of Shakespeare's plays?"

"Why do you find that so amusing?"

"Not amusing—*strange*. Like coming home and finding your cat trying to play the piano."

Alicia had tried to ignore her after that, but Maude had made sly comments about her new pastime until Alicia had finally snapped at the viper-tongued woman.

"I've had more than enough of your disrespectful attitude, *Miss Finch*. Perhaps you'd like passage on the next ship back to New York?"

Maude had merely laughed. "I should take you up on your invitation, *my lady*. And then where would you be?"

"I would be reading, rather than arguing with you. Now, leave me be and go laugh somewhere else."

Maude had smirked, but she'd left her alone after that. Which was just as well because the first twenty pages were incomprehensible.

Alicia had become angrier and angrier, until she'd finally thrown the book across the room. After getting out of bed and picking it up, she'd tried another play—something called *Troilus and Cressida*—thinking it might be easier.

But no, it was also obscure, at least to a sapskull like her.

When her head had pounded so severely that she'd believed she would cast up her accounts, she'd put the book aside.

And then forced herself to pick it up again the next day, reading only until her eyes began to ache, and then put it aside.

She'd done this several times every day. It had been miserable.

It had taken a great deal of work, but even her wretched reading ability and the archaic language could not obscure the emotions that pulsed from the pages: love, hate, pain, pleasure, and an agonizing jealousy so steeped in frustration and rejection that death was preferable.

She'd wanted desperately to ask Gormley questions about the play but had stopped only at the last moment from exposing her ignorance to a mere servant.

As she mounted the stairs that led to Charles's room, she cursed her own cowardice, promising herself that she'd be braver on the journey home.

Alicia opened the door to Charles's chambers, experiencing a near-crushing urge to turn and run down to the big man in the entry hall.

But her feet wouldn't obey.

Some stubborn part of her—maybe all that was left of Allie Benton—refused to let this nagging wreck of a man cow her. He was not her husband—not her lord and master who could do whatever he wanted with her person.

Once inside the room, she glanced around. Clothing was strewn all over, trays filled with dirty crockery covered every surface, and the smell of his unclean body was nauseating.

"Have you discharged your man," she asked, making no effort to hide her revulsion.

"He left, Alicia, as did the rest of them."

She squinted through the gloom at him. Only three candles burned and those were smoky tallow candles one usually found in servants' quarters.

"What do you mean, *they left?*"

He gave an ugly laugh, replenishing his glass and offering her nothing, not that she wished for a drink.

He waved the cut crystal so wildly that liquid sprayed over the top, the droplets catching the dim light and scattering into the darkness like black diamonds.

"Left as in buggered off. All of them, every blasted one." He took a gulp and giggled in a way that sent chills down her spine. "We are alone but for that brute of yours."

Alicia had known he was strapped for money, but not so badly that he could not pay his servants.

She stripped off her gloves but then could find no clean place to put them.

"Tell me what happened," she said, although she had no desire to know.

"What *happened*? I'm ruined, that is what *happened*."

Alicia bristled at his accusatory tone. "Dare I say this has something to do with cards, Charles? Perhaps you might have dangled my name—and your connection with me—to establish more credit?"

He looked like a boy caught filching pastries.

Furious, Alicia strode toward him. "Imagine my *chagrin* when I learned you were using our connection to frank your current lifestyle."

"Who told you?" he asked, raising his glass with a shaking hand.

"Does it matter?"

He flinched at her tone, but then laughed. "No, I suppose not." He cut her a look that held all the contempt she'd always suspected he felt for her. "I offered you the honor of my name—a name that goes back to the Conqueror, and you rejected me. *You*. A nobody from nowhere, a woman who bought her way in to our midst. God only knows what you did to acquire your wealth, although I suspect you did it on your back."

His words lacked the ability to hurt. When people meant nothing, they lacked the power to cause pain.

"Don't fool yourself, Charles. What you offered me was the honor of your debts."

"You led me—"

"I led you to nothing more than your bed. A journey whose destination has been singularly unrewarding, I might add."

Alicia had foolishly believed he was too foxed to move as fast as he did. The painful sting of his slap took her by surprise.

"You *bitch*!" he roared, winding up for a second blow, this time with his fist.

She spun around, but he flung himself onto her back before she could take more than a few steps, his body slamming her to the floor.

Agonizing, blinding white spangles filled her head. But that was nothing compared to the sudden failure of her lungs.

Alicia opened her mouth and gasped like a fish, but no air would come. His weight crushed her and she writhed and thrashed to free herself. But he clung like a burr, his hands sliding around her neck.

I'm going to die! Her mind shrieked as she struggled for breath.

50

Suddenly, the weight of Charles's body disappeared.

Something large and dark flickered across the room.

Charles's voice rang out, "Unhand me you brute! Do you know who I am?" A dull thump followed his question and then a whimper.

Alicia felt a strange *pop* in her chest and noisily sucked in air until it felt like her lungs would explode.

Dark eyes hovered above her as warm, strong hands slid beneath her thighs and back, cradling her against a wall of warm wool.

"Are you hurt, my lady?"

"Wha-what?"

"Are you hurt?" he repeated calmly.

"N-no, I'm not hurt. What about—"

"Take that, you fucking ape!"

"*Ufff!*" Gormley grunted and staggered forward but didn't drop her. Instead, he lowered her gently into the nearest chair.

Something glittered on the shoulder of his coat when he turned but before she could identify it his arm drew back and she heard a sickening crunch and the unmistakable sound of a body hitting the floor followed by glass breaking.

And then Gormley was there again and powerful arms slid beneath her knees and around her shoulders.

He strode through the open doorway, carrying her toward the stairs in smooth, long strides.

Alicia had no memory of ever being carried and held like this, not even when she was a child. It was beyond comforting.

They were in the foyer before she knew it.

"Can you stand, my lady?"

His voice was a low, impossibly deep rumble against her temple and she raised her head to see his face. Only his eyes showed any emotion, and they were creased with concern.

"Y-yes, of course."

He lowered her to her feet but continued to hold her upper arm, picking up her cloak with his free hand and draping it over her shoulders. "Are you steady?" he asked.

"Yes, I am fine. Go. Get a hackney."

"It is already waiting."

She almost wept: of course it was. She put on her hat with shaking hands and realized she had no gloves; they must have fallen when Charles struck her. She stared at her naked, trembling fingers.

"Here." He thrust gloves into her hands—his, by the look of it—and his lips twisted into a grimace. "There's a bite in the air."

She pulled on the huge gloves without speaking.

Outside a carriage waited at the curb.

"It's about bloody time, mate!" the driver snapped.

Gormley said nothing, but she felt his big body tense under her hand. He helped her into the carriage and then began to follow, but the driver's voice stopped him.

"'Ere then! You're dripping. You'll get—" Whatever else he was going to say was cut off by a grunt and then, "Alright, alright. Bleedin' 'ell! Lemme go!"

Gormley hopped into the carriage and the cab tipped precariously on its springs.

"Are you cold, my lady?"

Alicia was shaking. Badly. She pulled her heavy cloak tighter. "No, I'm not cold." Her voice was odd, hoarse, and did not sound normal.

He reached out and she flinched back.

"I just want to have a look, my lady," he said, his eyes on the right side of her face—the side Charles had struck. She remained still and he lifted her chin, tilting her so that he could see her face. He frowned at whatever his saw, his mouth tight, his expression beyond menacing.

"Is it bad?"

His eyes flickered to hers and he dropped his hand. "Bad enough." He shifted in his seat and she saw him wince.

"Are you hurt?"

"It's nothing."

"Then why are you wincing?"

"It's nothing," he repeated in a tone no good servant would use.

Alicia overlooked it, more interested in whatever it was he was trying to hide.

"Gormley, you will answer me," she said using her best Countess Voice.

He pressed his lips together and for a moment she thought he would disobey her, but he grudgingly met her eyes. "I was foolish to turn my back on him. He hit me with a bottle."

Alicia forgot her own aches. "My God, are you cut?"

He chewed the inside of his cheek, clearly annoyed.

"Are you *cut*, Gormley?" This time she didn't bother to keep the anger and fear from her voice.

"Aye, he cut me."

Alicia rose on shaky legs.

"Here then, my lady, what—"

"Hush," she ordered, turning awkwardly in the confined space—which was made even smaller with a man his size in it—and dropping gracelessly beside him on the seat, another awkward task since the entire bench was full of him. "Turn and let me look."

He glared down at her.

"*Turn.*"

He made a low, animal growl, but he turned.

"Good God!"

The thick wool of his coat and the two layers of cloth beneath had been sliced and the fabric sagged, heavy with blood.

A wave of nausea rose inside her and she had to swallow to force it back down.

"This will need stitching."

"I'll take care of it, my lady," the stubborn man said, beginning to shift away from her.

"One more word, Gormley, and I shall discharge you. One. Word."

His muscles tightened beneath her hand and anger rolled off him in waves. But her threat had its intended effect and he remained quiet for the remainder of the drive.

She let him help her from the hackney but stopped him when he would have picked her up and carried her to the door.

"I shall walk. Pay the driver."

His eyes met and held hers for one dangerously long moment but he gritted his jaws and complied. Again, it was not the look of a servant, but then he'd seen her tonight in a way most servants would never see their employers. The line between them had shifted.

Once inside the foyer she turned to him. "You will accompany me to my chambers." His lips parted. She lifted her hand. "One word, Gormley."

His mouth snapped shut and she preceded him up the stairs.

Even injured he managed to get in front of her and open the door to her sitting room, but when it came to entering her bedchamber he hesitated just long enough that Alicia opened the door.

Maude was sitting beside the fire but sprang to her feet. "What—"

"Mr. Gormley is injured, fetch hot water, clean cloths, and a needle and   thread."

Chapter Seven

An agonizing pain lanced his shoulder, like somebody had struck him across the back with a fiery sword or a whip made of nettles.

Joss wished he'd not been so hasty to refuse the liquor or laudanum.

But then *she* squeezed his hand and made him glad he'd refrained.

"Would you care for a drink now, Mr. Gormley?"

"No, thank you, my lady," he forced between gritted teeth. No, indeed. Why would he want to dull his senses when he was lying stripped to the waist in *her* bed, with *her* holding his hand, and *her* lush bottom pressed against his side?

Of course her harpy of a maid was on the other side, jabbing him with a needle and doing so with entirely too much relish.

Still, it was worth the agony to touch her; to smell her and lay on the bed where she slept. The sheets were unbearably soft against his skin— but he'd lain in good sheets before. No, it was the scent—her scent. He couldn't recall smelling anything so enticing in his entire life. He didn't have the olfactory experience to define it—peaches? Lavender? Or something like lemons, but not quite. Whatever it was he wanted to inhale her into every pore of his body. He wanted to take her in his mouth and consume her.

Another lash of fire on his shoulder made him bite his lip hard enough to draw blood.

And then a cool, soft hand brushed his damp hair off his brow and he almost howled, but for entirely different reasons. *Great. Bloody. Hell.*

"Gormley?" Her breath feathered his temple and he squeezed his eyes shut so his lustful thoughts and filthy desires could not leak out. "Are you conscious?" she asked softly the words tickling his ear, her breath sweet and warm, making his rock-hard cock pulse even worse than it had when she helped her maid cut off his clothing.

Joss swallowed, almost delirious from the delicious mix of pain and pleasure. "I'm awake, my lady," he said, the last word breaking as he endured another jab of the needle.

"Maude!" Lady Selwood's tone was chastising. "Must you be so savage?"

Joss silently echoed her words, not that it mattered much, the pain in his shoulder was nothing to the painful pleasure of her touch.

Such a poet, some snide part of him observed.

"You can stitch him yourself if you're so concerned," the old crone snapped.

And that was another thing; the way her maid spoke to her. Joss had never heard anyone speak to the Countess of Selwood with such a lack of respect. But rather than be angered, Lady Selwood appeared not to notice.

Her hand stroked his forehead again and Joss had to concentrate on not spending in his trousers, crying out in ecstasy, or drooling on the fine white silk of her comforter. Already he'd bloodied more than a little of her bedding.

Another harsh jab in his shoulder made him tense, but he was past feeling pain.

"I'm surprised this hasn't happened sooner," the older woman said, her words jarring Joss out of his blissful stupor.

"Oh, hush. Why should you expect any such thing?" Lady Selwood demanded, thankfully not stopping her stroking of his brow. Joss considered purring.

"Because you drive them half-mad, making them dance on a string, wanting you, wanting your—"

"Maude." The hand giving him pleasure froze, her fingers tense, the soft voice turning hard and cold.

Joss heard an answering snort on the other side; the woman halted her scolding but was obviously not cowed.

"Are you almost finished?"

Please, God. Never, ever finish. Joss begged silently, wishing the cut went down his back, beneath his trousers, down his—

"Aye." Miss Finch gave a sharp tug and then a snip. "There, that's the best I can do."

"That looks very nice, Maude."

Again the other woman snorted, and then touched him with a cool cloth.

Joss sucked in his breath and bit his lip. Hard. But his brain screamed, *FIRE!FIRE!FIRE!*

"Did that sting, Gormley?" The hand returned to his brow, her tone solicitous, like a nurse with a patient.

Joss could do little more than grunt, his eyes tearing, his shoulder a raging inferno, and his cock throbbing.

"That stinging sensation is from brandy, which Maude believes will cleanse your wound."

"We'd best get him up and out of here, my lady."

The hand stroking his forehead stopped.

No, no, no, no, no—

Lady Selwood sighed softly beside him and Joss began to move before she had to ask him. Her hands slid from his person and he ignored the ludicrous feeling of abandonment that swept over him.

"Here, let me help you," she said, her slender, cool fingers landing on his upper arm, as if she could somehow lift him.

"I can stand, my lady." The words were harsher than he'd intended, but he needed to get away from her. Now.

He did feel rather woozy when he stood, gripping the post at the end of her bed for balance and blinking until his vision cleared. And then wishing it hadn't.

"Oh, my lady, your gown—" Joss could only stare in horror.

She glanced down at the front of her dress, which was now streaked red and wrinkled. She looked up at him and shook her head.

"This is hardly your fault, Gormley. Besides," a slight shudder wracked her elegant frame. "It would have been far worse if you had not come for me."

Joss's face heated and he looked away, grateful his shirt was still tucked into his trousers, hanging down in bloody tatters, but at least they were covering the disgraceful erection he could not seem to suppress.

"My coat—" he began.

"Right here." The maid stood behind him, holding the coat up for him to put on. Joss slid his arms into the sleeves and then shrugged into the coat before recalling his injury. His vision blackened from pain and when it cleared, he found his mistress standing in front of him, her smooth brow furrowed with concern.

"Do you require assistance to get to your—"

"I'll be better on my own, my lady." Joss gave her a quick bow and turned. The maid already held open the door.

"You must stay in bed tomorrow, Gormley. That is an order." Her voice floated behind him, but Joss didn't stop or turn. He heard the click of a latch when he was half-way down the hall and sighed with relief, slowing his pace and buttoning his overcoat all the way. It was a short journey to the mews, but it would be a cold one.

When Joss opened the door to the stairs that led to his quarters he collided with a body.

"Oof!" He staggered back and reached out to take hold of the door jam, his vision again going black with pain.

"Are you ill, Mr. Gormley?"

Joss grimaced at the sound of Annie's voice. Wasn't this just perfect?

"Are you foxed?" she asked, her eyes wide with fascination.

Joss seized the convenient idea and let his features go slack. He grinned. "Annie!"

"You *are* foxed!"

He chuckled. "Nah I'm not." He slewed to one side and came up on the step above her.

"Do you want me to help you to your quarters?" The hopefulness in her voice made him curse his stupidity for at least the hundredth time.

He gave an exaggerated shake of his head, unwilling to turn around and expose the torn coat. "Nah, goin' to bed. G'night, Annie." He stood grinning, his swaying posture not entirely feigned. He was bloody tired and sore and needed sleep. He was also as stiff as a plank, but this time he would have the sense to take care of his condition himself.

Annie's lips turned down in a mulish expression that told Joss she'd not be giving up on him any time soon.

Alicia had thought she was so tired she'd fall asleep immediately.

But even after the delay of Maude fussing around with her bedding, taking a much-needed soak in her big copper tub, and drinking one of Maude's disgusting potions, she still could not sleep.

Instead, she ran through the events of the evening. Over and over she replayed her argument with Charles, as if she might see where she'd gone wrong, how she'd managed to misinterpret him, underestimate him, and lose control of the situation.

She cursed herself for being too unaware to have noticed Gormley's arrival, but she saw, in her mind's eye, the fluid motion of his torso as he delivered the felling blow to Byerly.

Every time she relived that moment her body tightened with some emotion she couldn't identify, something so . . . primitive. . . that it left her skintight and prickly

And then there was the way he'd carried her, expending as much effort as if he were carrying a child.

Best of all was the memory of him in her bedroom—in her bed, exactly where she was lying right now.

Maude had stripped the bed to its ticking so Alicia knew the smell that was teasing her nostrils—the masculine scent of sweat, the metallic tang of blood, and the underlying odor of soap—could not really exist. But her memory of his body, yes, that existed, and in blinding clarity.

He'd been even bigger than she'd imagined—something she'd been doing far too often lately.

He was brawnier, rawer; slab upon slab of hard muscle, the striations beneath his smooth white skin as taut as wire. He was massive.

When he'd given her his gloves, she'd felt like a child trying on her mother's shoes.

As upset as she'd been at that moment, slipping her hands inside the warm leather—curved by use and shaped to his body—had been uncomfortably intimate yet deliciously sensual.

Alicia reached beneath her mattress, where she'd tucked the gloves earlier—when Maude was busy clearing away the mess.

She frowned as her hand sought blindly for the soft leather, finding nothing.

Had she only imagined hiding them—what if—

But, no—there they were.

Alicia heaved a sigh and brought them to her face, her motions hesitant, as if she were doing something shameful.

She inhaled deeply, closing her eyes to focus all her attention on drawing his essence into her lungs. But all she smelled was leather.

She lowered the gloves, letting them slide over her cheek, her chin, her neck, before lowering them over her chest and down to her stomach, which was quivering with anticipation, as if she were lowering not just his gloves, but his hands.

Alicia opened her eyes and expelled the breath that was burning her lungs, her entire being now focused on the items on her belly.

After a long moment's hesitation, she fumbled in the darkness, under the covers, and then slid her hands into them, smiling at how huge they were.

She ran her hands up her arms, shivering foolishly at the sensation, which surely was no different than it usually was.

And yet ...

"Alicia you fool," she whispered.

Images resolved themselves in the velvety blackness above her head: Gormley, his torso naked. His arms, bigger around than her waist, or so it seemed.

His own waist: narrow, taut, and corded, flaring out to shoulders that could have modeled for Atlas.

He was pale, not like the men Alicia usually saw naked, aristocrats who took the time to bask in the sunshine at their country homes, playing like carefree otters in the rivers and lakes on their lands.

A nightmarish image of David—her son-in-law—flickered through her brain, his body sleek and browned after a month spent at The Willows.

Her throat convulsed and her eyes flew open.

No! she screamed, thankfully inside her head.

"No," she whispered fiercely.

There was no place for her stepson in this fantasy—or anywhere else in her life.

Alicia had worked hard to root and scrape and pull every memory of David from her brain. It had not been easy, his handsome face— loathsome to her—had clung like a stubborn weed between cobbles. But she'd done it. Or at least she'd believed she had.

She closed her eyes and tried to recapture the other image. Him. Gormley, his powerful arms shielding her, protecting her, hurting those who would hurt her.

Her lips curved; yes, his body, pale, strong, and laid out exactly where she was right now.

Alicia realized she'd been flexing her hips, her thighs, her private muscles as she imagined him. She was wet, tight, *needing.* This sensation was not unique.

No, this was the nagging, driving, relentless urge that had given her the strength to stamp out her nightmarish memories of her marriage to the earl and take control of her life—her body.

This persistent, aching need was why she'd decided to take a man like Byerly as her lover, not that he'd ever done anything about assuaging the desire between her thighs—something *she*'d needed to see to after their trysts.

Still, Byerly was hardly unique in his inability to bring her to climax. Alicia had never experienced sexual satisfaction with another.

She'd been too young with Horace, and too scared of doing something wrong. And later, when she might have enjoyed his kind attentions and gentle lovemaking, he'd been too ill to give them.

And her second husband—the earl?

Alicia shivered. No.

It was likely there was something wrong with her. Why else did she have these unnatural urges? Urges that only she could satisfy.

She'd never met another woman who was driven by such lusts, at least none who would admit to it.

As ever, her body's demands filled her with irritation, anger, and finally resignation. The feeling would not go away—not unless she addressed the problem.

So, she sighed and pulled up the expensive lawn of her nightgown, the fabric whispering over her skin like ghostly fingers. Her body vibrated with expectation as the material drifted up her thighs, over her mound, and finally her belly.

She spread her knees and reached down, only to realize she still wore the oversized gloves—*his* gloves. Her hesitation was momentary, pushed aside by her anger. Was it more wanton to pleasure herself with his glove on her hand? Wasn't her soul condemned to hell merely for thinking about what she was about to do?

Alicia snorted; as if her soul hadn't been condemned to hell decades ago.

She let her knees fall open and skimmed the glove over her mound, shuddering at the anonymous feeling of cool leather grazing her hot skin. Her breathing became ragged and she spread wider, stroking herself harder.

If she was going to hell, she might as well enjoy the journey.

.

Chapter Eight

It was barely after dawn when a rap on his door startled Joss awake.

Miss Finch stormed into his room without waiting for permission, bearing a tray of food.

Joss didn't own a nightshirt so he pulled his bedding higher, scooting up against the smooth pine headboard, and sitting upright.

"This wasn't my idea; her ladyship sent me," she announced flatly.

Joss hardly needed her to tell him that.

Instead of bringing the tray to the bed she set it on his small table and fixed her hostile gaze on him.

"I need to check your wound before you eat." She marched to the head of the bed and Joss leaned forward.

Unlike last night, her fingers were light and gentle as they skimmed his injury. "Not too much swelling, no weeping, not too hot or red." She dropped her hands to his pillow and shoved it up behind him. "Sit back."

Joss did so.

She gave a rude snort. "A man of few words, aren't you?" She didn't wait for an answer. "Where's your coat?"

He gestured to his clothes cupboard. He'd tried to rid the fine wool of some of the blood, but the small bowl of wash water had become as red as a slaughterhouse floor.

She eyed it. "Tried to clean it, did you. Well, I'll be able to mend it so you'll hardly notice." She looked up from the torn bloody garment. "The shirt, on the other hand, won't be good for anything but patches, but I'll see what I can do with the waistcoat." She shook her head and Joss knew she was thinking back to her mistress, who'd insisted on cutting off his garments, impatient to get him stitched.

It was an unusual toff who would think a servant's skin more important than bespoke clothing.

Maude put aside the coat and brought the tray.

He let her set it on his lap, not bothering to conceal his morning erection. It wasn't his job to hide himself if a woman came uninvited into his room. Not that she appeared to notice or care.

"Thank you," he said.

She ignored him. "Her ladyship says to remind you that you are to rest." She rolled her eyes. "Just do as she ordered. Somebody will bring you a midday meal and your tea and I'll bring your dinner and check your back again. Do you need anything else?"

"I'm not to leave my room?"

"You're not to leave your *bed* for two days," she amended. "Unless it is necessary, of course. Do you need anything else," she repeated.

"Aye, a pitcher of wash water."

Her eyes flickered slightly, whether in surprise at his tone or his request, he could not have said. She made a *hrumphing* sound and left without answering.

Joss looked down at his tray. Fresh scones, whipped butter, strawberry jam—his favorite—two slabs of ham, a small crock of coddle eggs, toast, and a steaming pot of tea with cream. He grinned; it was a far nicer breakfast than he'd be eating in the servants' quarters. Perhaps staying in bed wouldn't be so hard, after all.

Alicia dithered about what to do for five whole days.

She dreaded facing Gormley again after the dreams she'd been having about him. Not to mention the things she'd been *doing* while dreaming about him.

The dreams didn't just come at night, but also assaulted her throughout the day. Insidious, dangerous, erotic dreams that refused to go away.

She could not forget the image of his naked torso stretched across her bed.

Nor could she forget the way he'd rescued her, taking charge of the chaotic situation quickly, calmly, and masterfully.

Alicia was accustomed to rescuing herself—or going un-rescued, as had been the case with her last husband and his rotten son.

The feeling of putting oneself into another's hands was . . . well, she didn't know quite what it was, exactly, but she burned to find out more about her intriguing servant.

A debate raged inside her head for five days.

On one side was that part of her that recoiled from the mere *idea* of conducting an affair with a servant.

On the other—and far more vocal—side, was the deep physical attraction she felt for this strong, self-contained, and quietly intelligent man.

While it was perfectly acceptable for male aristocrats to chase their chambermaids around their bedchambers, people would sit up and take notice if an upstart American countess bedded her groom.

Alicia had worked her entire adult life to distance herself from her hardscrabble beginnings; she simply could not allow her feelings—her physical *needs*—to jeopardize everything she'd struggled so hard to achieve.

Or so she told herself.

But as hard as she tried to control her thoughts, her mind kept returning over and over, like an annoying homing pigeon, to the memory of how gentle and safe his arms had felt when they'd held her. How could somebody so powerful be so gentle?

Quit lyin' to yourself, Allie—it ain't thoughts of his gentleness that make your quim wet and hot, her aunt taunted with a raucous laugh.

Alicia knew it wasn't *really* her Aunt Giddy's voice speaking in her head—not that her aunt would have hesitated to chastise her for her earthy wants if she were still alive. Aunt Giddy had firmly believed that all women's problems originated between their thighs.

Keep your purse shut tight, young Allie, nothin' good can come of you openin' it up for some man.

You'd think Alicia would have taken that advice to heart by now, but her mental debate about Gormley was still raging five days after the Byerly incident.

And then, quite suddenly, the lustful half of her mind—more like three-quarters, if she were honest—came up with an argument that tipped the scales in lust's favor.

The weather had been cold—dreadfully cold—and Alicia still had Gormley's gloves.

She had no idea whether a servant would have two sets of gloves. What if he didn't? Was he suffering because of her thoughtlessness?

Summoning him to her rooms seemed rather callous given the fact that she had *stolen* the gloves and hidden them.

And she could hardly send Maude to return them without having to tolerate a raft of impertinent questions.

Besides, shouldn't she thank him for what he'd done?

Send the gloves along with a note, Aunt Giddy barked.

Alicia ignored the suggestion.

It was only proper—and *decent*—that she thank him in person.

Her heart thudded with anticipation.

Yes, she should thank him. And she could do it that very evening.

She'd planned to use her own carriage and John Coachman to take her to the wretched masquerade ball her friend Connie had talked her into attending.

Instead, she would have Gormley attend her, even though it wasn't his normal duty to escort her to *ton* functions.

Connie had sent over several costumes for Alicia to choose from and one was Cleopatra.

It had taken Alicia hours upon hours to finish reading that blasted play. She'd cried her eyes out when she reached the end, greatly admiring the willful, clever, and much-maligned ancient queen.

The costume lacked originality—there were likely to be a dozen Cleopatras at the ball—but it would be amusing to see Gormley's reaction.

Oh, Allie.

She refused to allow her aunt to spoil things.

Besides, the more she thought about it, the more sense it made to have Gormley fetch a hackney to take her.

The last thing she needed was for her carriage to be spotted outside Lord Pinkney's house during a masquerade.

Alicia shivered; not wanting to think about how her son-in-law would respond to such information.

She shoved David from her mind, turning to more pleasant thoughts.

She would use Gormley—just the two of them. That would be far better, she told herself. Far better.

———❤———

Joss had just removed his cravat when there was a knock on his door.

Now who the devil could that be?

Not her ladyship because he'd been told he wouldn't be needed tonight as the countess was going to a ball with friends.

Joss gritted his teeth and said a silent prayer: *Please, don't let this be Annie.*

But when he opened the door, he found Miss Finch outside, her sharp gaze flickering to his open shirt and unbuttoned waistcoat.

"She changed her mind, so you'll be escorting her. Fetch a hackney."

Joss nodded, but she'd already turned and left.

He splashed some water on his face before taking a fresh neckcloth from his cupboard.

As he tied it, Joss studied his face in the mirror. He looked . . . hostile. And he was feeling hostile, too.

If she wanted the anonymity of a hackney rather than her carriage it meant she would be going to meet some lover rather than going to a ball.

He scowled at his reflection. Surely she would not be going to meet Byerly?

No, that was impossible.

Even if it wasn't Byerly, Joss wasn't sure he could stomach waiting for her while she gave herself to yet another man who didn't deserve her.

Unlike you, of course.

No, Joss didn't ever expect her to even notice him—or so he told himself—but he sure as hell didn't want to wait while she engaged in bedsport with somebody else.

That's why she hired you, fool.

Dammit, he knew that. But that didn't mean he had to like it.

Take yourself in hand, Joss.

Yes, he'd better.

He fixed a blank look on his face—his servant expression—and went to secure a hackney.

Once he'd done that, he went to the entry hall, prepared to wait. But she was already there.

Joss's jaw dropped and an embarrassing noise came out of his mouth. She was swathed head-to-toe in a cloak of lustrous dark fur and her eyes were lined with kohl.

And she wore a serpent-shaped crown on her smooth blond hair.

She cut him her customary, cool look. "Good evening, Gormley."

"Er, my lady."

She moved toward the door and he made haste to open it. Her heavy cloak glistened black as sin in the low light, the red eyes of the serpent winking.

He helped her inside the hack and waited until she was comfortably settled.

"Where shall I tell him to take you, my lady?"

"Lord Pinkney's house on Grosvenor Square."

Joss's head jerked up at the unknown address. She wasn't looking at him, but down at her hands.

She wore black lambskin opera gloves, covering her bare arms up past the elbow. The butter soft leather would be nowhere as soft as her skin. He knew that, now, after touching her that night . . . in her bed.

She cleared her throat and Joss realized he'd been staring and turned to give the waiting driver the address.

When he moved to shut the door and take his place on the rumble seat, she said, "In here, Gormley."

So, he climbed into the carriage and shut the door.

They rode in silence for a few moments.

"I am going to a masquerade ball."

That made Joss smile. "I gathered as much, my lady."

"Can you guess who I am?"

"Cleopatra?"

"I suppose that was rather an easy question for a man who reads Shakespeare. Tell me, Gormley, which of the Bard's descriptions fits me best? *Lustful gipsy*? *Wrangling queen*?" She hesitated. "*Whore?*"

Joss's breathing hitched at hearing the vulgar word on her tongue. "I was thinking an enchantress who has made Antony *'the noble ruin of her magic.'*"

She laughed. "Bravo, Gormley, bravo." She was still chuckling when she extended one hand toward him.

Joss looked down. "My gloves." He'd believed they'd been lost that night. "Thank you, my lady."

"You must have been cold. I'm sorry I did not think to return them sooner."

He smiled at her concern and pulled them on. "I hardly noticed, my lady."

When he looked up, he saw she was staring at her hands, adjusting the seams on her already straight gloves. Her fingers were long, delicate, and unspeakably sensual encased in tight leather.

And then there was her gown.

Her fur cloak had fallen open, exposing a white sleeveless affair that was cinched tight with a gold girdle at her waist.

She wore no undergarments and the hard, dark circles of her nipples thrust against the silk.

Joss wrenched his eyes away and looked up at her beautiful face.

And stared.

Her lips were parted, her nostrils flared, and her chest rose and fell in shallow jerks beneath the whisper-thin silk.

And the expression in her darkened eyes …

Joss shook himself. *No, he had to be wrong.*

But he knew he wasn't. After all, it was a look he knew all too well, although he'd not seen it in a few years.

He wanted to laugh. And then jump out of the moving hackney.

Christ. It was happening again.

—◦♥◦—

What are you doing? What are you doing?

It seemed the voice in her head had run out of any other words. Over and over the same thought went round, a chant, almost.

Indeed, what was she doing?

She looked up from her hands to find his eyes on her. He was looking at her. Not over her shoulder, not at her feet. But *at* her.

His face was as harsh and unreadable as ever, but something had changed behind the rock wall he presented to the world.

Alicia focused on not fidgeting with her hands—something she never did—and breathing evenly: a thing she was finding it difficult to do.

He turned away to stare out the window, giving her his harsh profile.

Alicia saw his lips twitch—ever so slightly.

Her eyes narrowed. Had he noticed something? Did he think—

Did he notice you are like a bitch in heat for him and does he find your behavior amusing? her Aunt Giddy suggested with a chuckle.

The corner of his mouth pulled up higher, his expression no longer in question.

Alicia sucked in a harsh breath; why, the arrogant *bastard!* How dare he think—

—that you want him?

A sudden, horrid, thought assaulted her—something that Shelly had said when he'd given his report about Gormley—that he'd been driven to leave his last post when the viscount's adolescent daughter had become enamored of him.

Alicia bit her lip to keep from groaning; she was no better than a schoolroom chit. He'd seen the desire on her face.

Oh God. How utterly mortifying.

Let that be a lesson to you, her aunt said, smugly.

Alicia ground her teeth, glaring at the man across from her, as if her infatuation were *his* fault.

She had to try and convince him that he'd not seen what he thought he'd seen. She could redirect his suspicions with a few subtle questions and comments.

"I know that you patronize a place called the White House." Alicia wanted to kick herself.

So much for subtlety, Allie.

He turned toward her slowly, his thin lips curved in an amused—and oddly resigned—smile. He studied her in silence, entirely justified in not answering such an invasive question.

Alicia should have clamped her jaws shut, but her mouth had other plans. "You don't look surprised that I know."

"Actually, it does surprise me, my lady."

It was the same low, harsh voice as ever, but now there was a lack of restraint. Oh, he hadn't raised his voice, but his inflection was no longer the subservient tone of a mere groom.

And whose fault was that?

Fine! she snapped at her aunt, *It's my fault. Does that make you happy?*

But her aunt had gone, leaving her to decide what to do next.

Why stop now? She'd already made a fool of herself.

"Tell me, Gormley, do you go there often?"

Something flickered in his dark eyes but Alicia could not identify it. Whatever it was, it made her face heat. Which only annoyed her more.

"When I ask you a question, I expect you to answer me," she said more sharply than she'd intended.

Rather than appear chastened by her obnoxious command, he wore that same smirk "Perhaps once or twice a month."

Jealousy flared in her stomach.

Her body's ridiculous reaction infuriated her.

It also stiffened her spine. "Tell me, what kind of place is it."

One of his eyebrows—they were the only elegant feature on his rough-hewn face—cocked. "You already know what kind of place it is."

"Yes, but I understand the White House is singular when it comes to . . ." She floundered like an idiot. "Well, places like that."

"Surely you could ask such questions of one of your lovers?" There was not-so-subtle mockery in his voice.

And Alicia didn't like it; it was past time he remembered who she was.

"I could ask whoever I choose. I choose to ask *you*. And when I ask one of my *servants* a question, I expect a timely answer."

He leaned forward so suddenly she flinched back. "People *fuck* when they go there, m*y lady*."

She gaped, more stunned by his quiet ferocity than his foul language.

Beneath her shock was another emotion: powerful, intoxicating arousal.

The words tumbled out of her. "Tell me about your activities there? I understand the place offers—" she gulped, unsure of what word to use, which phrase would be least embarrassing. "Er, well, deviant practices." Her voice was breathy and the question was more of a plea, but she didn't care. "Is that what you do?" Her voice was soft she hoped he hadn't heard the question.

But he had.

"Why?" He looked sullen and mulish.

Stop, Allie! You're behaving like an infatuated fool!

"Why?" she repeated dumbly. Her addled brain spun, looking for a quick, clever response but all that came was the same tired line: "Because I employ you and when I ask a question, I expect you to—"

"Fine.   I   quit."

Chapter Nine

Gormley rapped on the roof. "Turn back," he ordered when the vent opened.

"What do you think you are doing?" Alicia demanded, her voice breathy and weak.

"I'd get out right here, but I don't want to leave you unattended." He stared out the window.

His words were the cool, impassive words of a proper servant but they cut her more than a yell.

She had misjudged him, seriously misjudged him.

Not only that, but he'd saved her and she had responded to his noble actions by ordering him to disclose the most personal details of his life as if he didn't have a right to his privacy. As if she owned him.

And all because she was *obsessed* with him.

She rapped on the roof and the vent opened. "Take us for a drive."

The driver coughed. "Ah, beggin' yer pardon, ma'am, but where to?"

"It doesn't matter. Just keep driving."

There was a pause, but the vent closed.

Gormley cocked one eyebrow.

"I'm sorry."

His expression alone was worth the apology. The shocked disbelief was comical, bringing his stone face to life. He stared at her for a long, uncomfortable before nodding abruptly.

Relief flooded her; why did she care so much for a servant's forgiveness?

Because you're not entirely cast away yet, Allie Benton. Aunt Giddy was back.

The low rumble of his voice pulled her from her misery.

"How did you find out about the White House?"

The last thing Alicia wanted to tell him was that she'd hired a man to follow him.

"I shouldn't have—I was just—" She closed her eyes and dropped her head back, too ashamed to finish. After all, what could she say? "*I was hoping to use the information to pressure you into being my lover?*" or "*I have been entertaining wanton thoughts about you day and night and scheming as to how I can force you to act them out with me?*" Or—

"Yes, you were just . . ." he prodded.

His tone was gentle, patient, and slightly amused.

She opened her eyes and found him leaning toward her, his forearms resting on his thighs, an action which brought his face close to hers in the cramped confines of the carriage.

Alicia could see herself doing it, but she had no control over her body.

She closed the distance between them and kissed those thin, stern lips.

—❤—

If there was one thing Joss knew about wealthy women and sex, it was how to read their expressions. After all, it had been his bread and butter for almost four years.

He could have avoided her mouth without making it obvious; he could have salvaged her pride and his job.

Instead, he crushed her lips while sliding his arms around her soft, slender body and lifting her onto his lap.

She gave a soft grunt of surprise, her lips clinging to his.

Joss thrust into her like a green boy, no finesse, only hunger and want. She moaned and her fingers slid from his chest to his neck, cool soft leather on his hot skin. Her hands were delicate but strong as they pulled his head lower, her tongue shoving his aside to plunder him.

God. She tasted like—like—

Heaven.

He parted the folds of her heavy cloak and unfastened the gold clasp at her throat. The luxurious fur fell away to expose a gown as insubstantial as his self-control.

Joss slid his fingers down her body, throbbing at the sight of his big hand caressing her generous curves.

He'd had countless women—slim, fat, tall, short, young, old, pretty, not so pretty—but none of them had ever felt like her. Not a one.

He stroked her with the heel of his hand, pressing firmly over her mound, her stomach, the unforgiving bone between her soft breasts, all the way to her throat.

A golden collar hugged her long, elegant neck; a fortune in jewels that wasn't worth even a fraction of the woman who wore them.

Joss lowered his hand over the cool metal, feeling the fragile cords and sinews of her neck tighten at his touch. "You look well in a collar, my lady."

Her lips parted and her chest expanded with a deep breath, the pulse above her collarbone pounding, her eyes wide and lush lips parted.

Joss insinuated a finger between metal and skin and gave a soft tug, offering her one last chance to take a different fork in the road

"Do you want me to tell the driver to turn around and take you to your party? Or do you want—" His hand tightened around her delicate throat, fingers flexing. "Or do you want *this*?"

She spoke without hesitating: "This."

Joss was relieved that she'd made the decision for them.

He lowered his mouth over hers and she thrust into him, their tongues tangling, their hands stroking, events moving much too quickly. He wanted to savor this; he wanted this to *last and last and last*. Because he doubted she would ever succumb to a momentary hunger again.

He pulled away from her sweet mouth, the raw yearning in her eyes sending a brutal ache to his groin.

Joss yearned to kiss and caress and love her, but that wasn't what she wanted.

She wanted a brute—a beast who would dominate her, *taking* what he wanted.

It was a bedroom game that he had once loved to play—and would still welcome with a woman who loved him—until he'd discovered that sex without love was, ultimately, unfulfilling.

His body was desperate to take what she offered—no matter that it would wreck him.

Maybe you're wrong, Joss. Maybe you aren't the world expert on female sexual behavior that you fancy yourself to be. Why don't you give her a chance before you decide what she wants?

He grimaced at the smug voice, but forced his mouth into a cruel sneer. "Tell me what you want," he ordered, stroking her throat in the way that caused her eyelids to flutter. "I want to hear you to beg for it."

Her entire body shuddered beneath his hand and her lips parted as her chest rose and fell in shallow jerks.

No, not wrong, after all.

Joss didn't care; if it was master and slave games she wanted, he could give her all she wanted and more.

"Tell me," he ordered, his grip tightening on her delicate throat. "Beg for it. Or do I need to put you on your knees right here in this dirty hackney? Yes—I like the sound of that." He began to lift her.

Her lips moved, and he hesitated. "What's that?"

Her expression was a mixture of lust and mortification. "I don't . . . I can't . . ." she made a frustrated sound—but her legs moved apart.

He snorted rudely. "Want my hand on your cunny—*inside* your cunt? Say *please* Mr. Gormley, I want you to make me come. *Say it!*" he snapped.

She jolted at his sharp command, her pale skin flushed with passion. "P-Please, Mr. Gormley, make me c-come."

It was Joss's turn to shudder and his hand shook badly as he caressed over her thighs, past her bent knees, to the hem of her gown.

It was winter, and a cold one at that, but she wore only a single, fine petticoat beneath the liquid silk. His groan was audible even over the clatter of the carriage wheels as the coach traversed what sounded to be ragged cobbles.

"You dressed like this—exposing your body—for me, didn't you?" he snarled. "I'm going to use you *hard*, my lady—harder even than the whores I use at The White House. Is that what you want? To be my *whore?*"

She whimpered, "Yes. *Yes*," she whispered, her thighs parting. "Your ... *whore*."

Christ!

Joss's lifted his hand—stunned it wasn't shaking with the force of his lust—pulling off his glove with his teeth, finger by finger.

Her eyes were black as she watched his deliberate actions.

When his hand was bare, Joss held up his thick middle finger. "I'm going to fuck you until you scream."

Her jaw dropped and Joss claimed her mouth in a kiss that was for him—not that of a rude and crude brute, but a slow, sensual exploration, unhurried, just like his fingers as they slid up past her garters to the naked flesh of her thigh.

Joss squeezed his eyes shut at the exquisite heat of her, the realness of damp, quivering skin.

For one jarring second he felt like he was in the middle of one of his dreams. Any minute now he would wake up alone, his cock hard, weeping, and wanting—

The carriage jolted and the driver yelled something rude, snapping him back to the here and now.

Joss slid his naked hand to the apex of her thighs and traced the seam of her lower lips, worshipping her with his gentle caress.

She pushed her sex against his palm. "*Please*."

Once again, Joss put aside his foolish desire and gave her what she wanted.

—❤—

Alicia turned her head into the arm cradling her, biting his bicep to muffle her groan; biting him hard enough to make him hiss.

"You like that," he rasped, his big, thick finger roughly circling her swollen core. "This is what you've been needing." His thumb rubbed her in a way that made every muscle in her body clench with utter joy. "Say you need it."

"Yes." She forced the word through her gritted teeth, breathing like a horse that had been ridden to a lather. "I *need* it."

He gave an ugly, demeaning chuckle that both thrilled and shamed her. "I know you do. Such a tiny little thing," he whispered, doing something unspeakably delicious that made her buck and bite his arm yet again to keep from screaming. "Poor countess," he mockingly crooned. "You want to come, don't you—a wanton harlot, spreading your thighs wide for your servant."

He might be your servant, but at this moment you are his slave and you both know it.

She risked a glance up at him and saw one brow was cocked, his nostrils slightly flared, as if he knew exactly what was going through her head.

Her obedient servant had transformed into something diabolical. "Do you like it fast and light," he demonstrated, his thumb dexterous beyond belief as he swirled, barely touching. "Or slow and hard."

She made a low, growling sound that caused her face to heat.

He chuckled with smug satisfaction; the slightly rough pad of his thumb magical.

Alicia bit down hard on her lower lip and tried not to humiliate herself. It was pointless; she groaned and squirmed like a wanton.

Her tenuous hold snapped and she shuddered, coming apart under his expert fingers.

"Good girl," he praised as her inner muscles convulsed, the pleasure almost unbearable. "Such a responsive cunny you've got."

Without warning, he shoved his thick finger into her slick, swollen entrance, the action forcing a low, mortifying whimper from deep in her chest.

He pumped her with deep, almost violent thrusts.

"Look at me," he ordered.

It was all she could do to lift her heavy lids.

"Do you want more?" he asked, not stopping his thrusting.

There was more? If there was, she couldn't recall it at the moment. When had a man touched her so patiently, skillfully, intently?

His face went slack. "You're just as lovely on the inside," he murmured so softly she almost didn't hear it.

But then his face twisted into a feral grin. "What you need is a proper fucking with a big, fat prick, but this will have to do. For now."

His words sent a shock through her and his powerful arm began to work her, pumping her relentlessly until he stroked some part of her body she didn't even know existed, and causing her entire body to spasm.

She thrashed but he held her immobile with one arm while he stroked her to a climax that threatened to turn her inside out .

"Yes, that's right," he praised, his arm pumping with increasingly savage thrusts, quickly driving her toward madness.

It was too much sensation—too much pleasure.

"I can't," she whispered, even as her hips rose to meet his hand. "I can't…it's too much, please, . . ."

His mouth flexed into a cruel smile. "Come for me, my lady."

His raw, vulgar words catapulted her over the edge, into a climax that rolled through her and hung on and on and on, as intense and relentless as the man who'd summoned it.

Alicia opened her eyes some moments later to find him watching her, his lids heavy, his expression slack, almost as if he'd had his release.

But he hadn't.

She knew he hadn't because she could still feel his long, hard shaft pressing against her hip.

She'd never been with a man who gave pleasure without taking it. She'd never been with a man who'd known exactly what she needed and wanted—no matter how base and humiliating.

And she'd *never, ever* behaved the way she had these past few minutes.

Memories of her spread thighs, thrusting hips, begging, crying out, and shameless writhing flooded her and Alicia struggled to sit up—as if she could escape her shocking behavior.

When she reached down to cover herself, she saw he'd already straightened her gown and fastened the clasp of her cloak, wrapping her up against the cold.

The realization was like a slap: He'd tended and cared for her while she'd basked in pleasure, utterly unaware.

Without warning, he lifted her up and lowered her gently onto her seat.

His coat was still buttoned, his hat still on, his face that of an impassive servant.

The demon whose fingers had been inside her—the vulgar, crass, cruel magician who'd said and done those things to her? He was gone.

She could only drop her eyes in shame. They landed on his hands, one of them bare and clutching his glove with white-knuckled fingers.

He'd given without taking anything for himself.

Why?

Because she employed him?

How else was a servant supposed to respond when his mistress demanded such things? Aunt Giddy demanded.

Self-loathing flooded her belly and Alicia tore her eyes away from him and looked out the window, but there was nothing to see—nothing but her own mortified reflection.

Across from her he gave a barely audible sigh and knocked on the roof.

"Take us back home," he ordered coolly when the vent opened.

They rode back in silence.

Chapter Ten

Alicia only managed to stay away from Gormley four days this time.

She'd thought—*prayed*—that she could just ignore that evening, but each day the memory took up more space in her mind—and in her dreams.

She needed to speak to him and clarify what had happened. She needed to promise him it would not happen again.

Or . . .

Alicia buried her face in her hands. Or what? Just what was it that she wanted from him? To make it happen again?

Before she could stop herself, she rang for Maude.

"Fetch me the plainest hat and cloak I own," she said when her maid appeared a few moments later.

Maude squinted. "It's past midnight, my lady."

"I didn't summon you to ask the time, Maude. I asked you to fetch me the plainest hat and cloak I own."

"You're going out, my lady?"

Alicia gritted her teeth. "Yes."

"Shall I call for the carriage?"

"Did I ask for the carriage? Just the clothes, Maude." Why were these things never as simple as they seemed in her imagination?

"Do you want me to have Gormley go fetch a hack?"

"No. All I want is the cloak and hat."

"But—"

"Maude."

The older woman rolled her eyes. "Fine. I suppose you want that rig you used when you were seeing Sir Henry and—"

"Yes, yes, that will be fine."

Lord! As if Alicia wanted to be reminded of the useless lover she'd chosen first—the one before Byerly.

Maude went to find the garments, moving at a speed that would have shamed even a tortoise.

She returned with pursed lips and a plain gray servant's cloak. They locked eyes and Maude's narrowed, her expression judging and assessing. Alicia snatched the cloak from her.

"Are you sure you wouldn't like me to summon somebody for you, my lady?"

"No, Maude, I do *not* want you to summon anyone. What I would like is for you to give me the hat I requested."

"If you do this, you know you'll have to discharge him."

The words only stung because she'd been thinking the very same thing herself. "Nonsense," Alicia said, tying the cloak at her neck. "Besides, I am merely going to thank him for—well, something. It's none of your affair."

Maude's expression loudly proclaimed what she thought of that.

Alicia heaved a sigh. "Very well. Let's say—just for the sake of argument—that you are correct and I am going to visit him. I've never had any trouble—" she broke off as an image of Byerly's rage-distorted face floated to the surface of her memory like a bloated corpse. "Fine," she amended. "I u*sually* have no trouble afterward. I didn't with Sir Henry—did I?" She sounded desperate even to her own ears.

Maude tied the plain black ribbon on the straw bonnet and fixed the veil. "It might not bother you, my lady. But what about him?"

Alicia opened her mouth, but then closed it. Why bother lying to Maude, or herself. The truth was, she wanted him: consequences be damned.

❤

Joss was reading when the knock came. He glanced at his watch: it was just past midnight. He put a marker in his book and set it aside, drumming his fingers on the arm of his chair.

Annie had sneaked into his room again this week.

This time he'd told her—in no uncertain terms—that this had to stop. Her eyes had watered and she'd fled, leaving him feeling like a beast for crushing her spirit.

He doubted it was Miss Finch as Lady Selwood was staying in tonight. Besides, the countess had been avoiding him after the episode in the hackney. Even so, he'd dressed for her summons every night, just like some lovelorn, neglected swain. And when she failed to call for him, he went to his bed and fisted himself raw to the memory of her spread across his lap.

There was another knock, sharper this time.

It had to be Annie.

He went to the door and yanked it open, his mouth already open to deliver a scolding.

"Gormley." The woman across from him was shrouded in a rough, gray cloak, the type of thing a servant girl would wear. She wore a broad straw hat with a veil, again, a rude garment that was cheap and ill-made. But he would know her anywhere, and he certainly knew that cool, commanding, and exotically accented voice.

"Lady Selwood."

She flinched at the name and glanced to both sides, as if somebody might have overheard. "May I come in?"

Joss looked down at his clothing—his shirt and trousers—grimaced, and looked up at her. He opened his mouth, but she waved a hand.

"What you are wearing is adequate."

Joss opened the door wider and stepped to the side.

She entered and Joss closed the door, trying to arrange his features into something other than stupefaction before turning. But she wasn't even looking at him. Instead, she was glancing around at his small room as if she'd not seen it before.

"I've not seen these quarters before," she said, echoing his thoughts. "I purchased the house without looking at it," she explained, her eyes flickered away from his and stopping on the small table beside his chair. "You were reading?"

"Yes."

Her lips twitched into a smile. "More Shakespeare?"

"Not this evening, my lady."

She crossed the small room and picked up the book. "You are reading *Common Sense.*"

Joss clasped his hands behind his back and relaxed his weight on his heels. "Yes, my lady."

"He was a countryman of mine."

"I am aware of that."

She replaced the book on the table and turned, her gaze skittering around the room. She was as nervous as a cat, her beautiful full lips turned down at the corners as if she were unhappy to find herself here.

Joss realized she was still standing.

"Would you like to sit, my lady."

She exhaled a long, shaky breath. "Yes."

"May I take your cloak?"

"Oh, yes." She divested herself of the cloak and then removed the bonnet, turning it in her hands. She wore a plain gown of white muslin that made her look younger and almost girlish—as did her somewhat dazed expression.

Joss stood across from her, hands behind his back, and waited silently like the good servant he was for what he knew was coming.

When she looked up at him, her eyes were unusually dark. "I never thanked you for that night at L-lord Byerly's house."

She had, but he was hardly going to correct her.

She was so bloody gorgeous it hurt to look at her.

He should have been overjoyed that she was here—his cock had certainly perked up and taken notice—but his joy was tempered by regret.

Joss didn't fool himself; she didn't want him. She wanted a service he could offer.

He realized she was still staring up at him, waiting for an answer.

"Protecting you is what you pay me for, my lady."

"And is that the only reason you did it?"

Joss blinked at the heat in her tone. "Of course not, my lady."

She seemed to deflate at his words. "No, of course not. I know that. I beg your pardon." She looked so young, lost, and forlorn.

Joss knew he was lost when his strongest impulse was to take her in his arms and comfort her.

But it wasn't comfort that she'd come for.

So he once again pushed aside his foolish desires and prepared to give her what she wanted.

Alicia didn't understand why things had become so awkward. In her mind, she'd simply approached him and said what she wanted.

Reality was proving to be something infinitely more complicated.

She'd consumed two glasses of brandy before making her way to the carriage house. At the time, she'd felt confident and fearless. Somehow all that changed the moment she began to mount the stairs—to enter his domain. And now—now that she sat in the chair in this tiny, sparse impeccably clean and tidy room—a room that smelled intoxicatingly of *him*—she'd never felt so mortified in her entire life.

What had she been thinking?

He was standing across from her, his hands behind his back, feet spread, eyes downcast. It was the posture of an obedient servant waiting for his mistress to speak. His lids were so low she could hardly see his eyes. Not that it mattered since he never gave anything away.

The silence grew, along with her embarrassment. Her brain encouraged her, strongly, to head for the door. To run.

All the while she dithered, he watched.

"What is in there?" she blurted, pointing to a door.

His expression didn't change, but she could tell her question amused him; as if he knew of the struggle inside her and *that* amused him, too.

"I believe it was meant to be a lumber room or perhaps a small bedroom. But I use it for practice."

"Practice?"

"Pugilism, my lady."

"Ah." She paused. "How does one practice pugilism, exactly? I know men do it all the time at Jacksons."

"That would be sparring, my lady." His lips curled in a manner that shrieked derision. "Or pretending to spar with men like John Jackson, who knows how to butter his bread."

"What do you keep in there?"

"There are two bags and a pallet." He raised his eyebrows. "Would you like to see?" Before she could answer, he picked up the candle from beside the chair and crossed the room in a few long strides, his body brushing hers in the close confines of the room. He did not apologize for touching her.

He opened the door, put the candle in the wall sconce, and stood aside.

The small room was scrupulously clean and tidy, just like the rest of the small quarters.

The "bags" he mentioned were made from canvas. On the floor was a thin leather pallet. It was just as he'd described.

"What do you do in here?"

"Exercises."

She frowned at the unfamiliar word. "Exercises?"

He nodded, crossing his arms and leaning against the door frame, not the posture of a well-behaved servant. "Just like drills or practicing for the piano or grammar."

Alicia tried not to show how his knowledge of such things surprised her. Why should it? She already knew the man was better educated than she was. Not that that was saying much.

"It is a way to keep physically fit," he added.

She turned toward him at that, her eyes roaming his body, as if to test the veracity of his words. Yes, he was physically fit. She swallowed and looked up.

81

"Do you know why I went to Lord Byerly's house?"

He looked so startled that she couldn't help smiling.

"I, er, beg your pardon, my lady. Do I know *why* you went to his house?"

Alicia was beginning to gain a sense of him, and this was one of his favorite techniques, repeating her words while he stalled for time. For some reason, this small sign of weakness made her feel more confident.

"Yes, why do you think I went to him?"

A slight flush stained his cheeks. "He's your lover." His voice was deeper and harsher than usual and she saw something flare in his eyes.

"He *was* my lover." She kept her eyes on his, taking one step closer. He inhaled, the intake of air causing his already huge chest to expand even more. "Do you find me attractive, Gormley?"

His features hardened, his eyes becoming darker, but cold. "What is it that I can do for you, my lady?"

His words were like a slap, making her see herself in his eyes.

It was a revolting phrase, but it was the only one that fit: she was behaving like a bitch in heat. Again.

Alice shook her head at the unattractive image and spun on her heel, desperate to get away.

He caught her wrist and she gasped, glaring down to where his huge hand encircled her arm, his skin warm and rough. "What do you think you are doing?"

He turned her easily, leading her back to the chair.

"Sit."

A bonfire roared low in her belly at the soft command. They locked eyes, his glinting with amusement—and—by God, *authority*. How she wanted to reject him, but her body was already obeying.

He nodded slightly when she'd complied, as if he'd never expected any other response.

He dropped to his haunches, the action so sudden she flinched.

"Shhh," he murmured, resting his big hands lightly on her knees, the unsolicited touch sending more heat surging through her.

She had to look down at him now, an odd shift in perception that left her feeling off balance. His hair was a bit long and flopped over his forehead, the wavy brown locks exhibiting interesting glints of red gold in the light of the tallow candle. He made soft circles on her knees with his thumbs, the action pulling her eyes back to his.

"You come here tonight to continue what we began the other night in your carriage, didn't you?" He asked the question in the same quiet, respectful tone he used to ask if she wanted him to fetch a hackney.

Why did he not look subjugated in such a position? What kind of man could lower himself to a woman's feet and look so . . . strong, so powerful?

"Answer me," he said.

Every muscle in her body was taut with expectation and it was all she could do to manage an infinitesimal nod.

"Lift your skirt."

She started at the raw order.

"If you want to stay, you will do as I tell you."

A bolt of lightning could not have produced more of an effect in her body. *If she wanted to stay?* Why the arrogant, conceited, obnox—

But her hands had begun lifting the hem of her gown, stopping when the hem of the dress reached her knees.

"Higher," he ordered.

The muslin moved jerkily, slowly.

His eyes dropped to her exposed garters and his hands slid around her knees. When he tried to spread her thighs, she clamped them tight.

He raised his eyes to her face, his expression harsh and pitiless. The only sign of his desire for her were his swollen pupils.

"My lady."

Alicia swallowed and forced her body to relax.

He pulled her toward him, not stopping until her bottom reached the edge of the chair, and then he spread her legs wide, until her hips ached.

Her body grew hot with a bizarre mixture of embarrassment and lust.

He stared at her forever, his thin, hard lips curving into a smile as he took in her stocking-clad legs all the way up past her garters, his gaze halting at the bottom edge of her chemise, an insubstantial wisp of muslin that did nothing to conceal the dark triangle beneath.

"Lovely," he murmured, leaning forward, hot breath skimming the tops of her stockings.

He lowered his hot mouth over her silk-clad thigh and bit her, sucking her flesh into his mouth and flexing his jaws, marking her.

He growled and the sound vibrated up her leg, into her sex, into her core.

He pulled away and stared at the red oval of flesh, smiling.

"I want to look at you. Lift your chemise."

His arrogant, abrupt command sent a shock through her body but, again, her hands were in motion before her brain gave the order and they both dropped their eyes to watch as she exposed herself to him.

"Ah," he sighed, his gaze riveted to her spread sex and his hands moving toward her.

"But—"

He glanced up. "But?"

She gestured to the table, which held the two candles he used to read. "The light." She reached to snuff it.

"No, leave it."

Her head turned sharply at his harsh tone.

"I want to look at you, to watch your face and see your expression when I make you orgasm."

They both heard the gulping sound she made and he smiled slightly.

"And I want you to see me. I want you to watch me lick, suck, and finger you."

The room seemed to sway around her.

"Breathe, my lady."

Alicia exhaled noisily before filling her lungs again.

"Do you like it when I use raw language, my lady? Does it make you throb here," he dragged a finger over her swollen lips.

Alicia could only stare: Who *was* this man? He looked like her servant—he even sounded a bit like him. But, otherwise—

"Answer me."

She blinked rapidly, as if to clear the steam from her eyes. "Yes." It was so soft she was amazed he could hear it.

His eyes dropped to her chest. "Pull your bodice down beneath your breasts."

She squeezed her eyes shut as her core clenched or pulsed or convulsed or did something that made every muscle in her body thrum.

"Open your eyes."

Her eyes flew open at the sharp command.

His gaze was hungry and intense. "I said to pull your bodice beneath your breasts. The next time you fail to obey me, you can leave."

Her jaw dropped, but her shaking hands moved to her bodice, which was already so low it took very little to lift her breasts over. The stretched muslin held them high, their tips hard, rose-colored pebbles that tightened even more when exposed to the chill air—and his piercing gaze.

His hooded eyes glittered in the candlelight. "You are very lovely." The hungry look and subtle praise fed a yearning in her, a desire to please him, to have him say more.

"Your nipples are hard. Tell me, do they hurt—do they ache?"

She shuddered at the word *nipples*. "They ache."

He rewarded her with another half-smile. "Touch them—pinch them. Hard."

She froze like an animal in the glare of a lantern.

He cocked his head. "Did you not hear me or understand my words?"

"I uh-understood."

"Then do as I say."

His order caused a—now predictable—ache in her sex. Her cool, trembling fingers slid over her hard tips and she gasped.

His nostrils flared. "Again, harder."

Her body bucked at the painful pleasure that arrowed from her breasts to her belly and pelvis.

His lips shifted into a satisfied smile and his eyebrows rose.

She pinched herself again, not needing to be told, shuddering, her eyelids impossibly heavy.

His thumbs stroked a feather-light touch over her damp, plump lips, and then parted them, opening her to his probing gaze.

"My God you're beautiful. I want to taste you."

She made a mortifying squeak.

His lips curved, his eyes still on her sex. "Is that a yes?"

Alicia nodded, as if in a trance.

He leaned close and laved from her entrance to her core.

She sucked her lower lip into her mouth and bit down to stifle a cry, but a strangled grunt escaped her.

He looked up at the sound, sitting back on his haunches, absently stroking her slick, still spread lips with his thumbs.

Alicia's head was so hot she was surprised she didn't lose consciousness.

"Don't you like my mouth on you?"

God—she loved it! But still …

"Yes, but—" if she admitted to being embarrassed, would he stop? Because that was the last thing she wanted.

He cocked his head. "Have you never had a man make love to you with his mouth, my lady?" Whatever expression he saw on her speechless face made him frown. His eyes flickered from her face to her sex, which his thumbs were continuing to tease.

"But—"

He glanced up. "Yes?"

"It is so . . . *dirty*."

To her surprise, he laughed—a quick, startling illumination of his harsh features. But his amusement fled as quickly as it had appeared.

This time, when he lowered his mouth, he kept his eyes locked on hers while he bathed her in exquisite, wet, heat.

He groaned as he sucked her into his mouth, his eyelids fluttering.

Alicia's head dropped against the back of the chair with a soft *thud*. *Good. Lord.*

He stroked that most sensitive part of her with his lips and tongue, moaning as he worked—as if he *enjoyed* what he was doing.

Just like the other evening, he drove her toward her climax far too quickly.

As she shuddered, her flesh painfully sensitive, he released her swollen bud and moved to her entrance, spearing her with his tongue.

He kept her open, his suggestive, rhythmic penetration leaving her in no doubt as to what he wanted.

Alicia forced her heavy lids up; she needed to see him. She needed to watch as he feasted—yes, there was no other word for it—on her body.

He'd dropped to his knees at some point, his broad shoulders shoving her knees wide as his dark head bobbed between her thighs.

The heat in his eyes made her gasp.

When he pulled away, his chest was heaving, his lips, chin, and even his nose glistening.

He licked her wetness from his lips. "You taste delicious, my lady." He slid one of his big fingers into her, his eyes watching his hand, his expression wondrous. "So soft and wet." He withdrew and pushed back in, his arm trembling, as if he were restraining himself.

The sound of their labored breathing was deafening in the silent room. He began to pump her as he'd done in the carriage, and then he lowered his mouth over her throbbing peak and commenced to drive her wild.

Alicia felt like she was racing toward the edge of a cliff in a vehicle she had not a chance of stopping. She thrust her hands into his thick hair, as if to cling to him.

Her passion built quickly—too quickly, she didn't want it to end, but every muscle in her body grew tighter and tighter—until she exploded.

—❤—

Joss hurt with wanting her.

She looked like a haughty queen as she stared down at him, her jewel-blue eyes dark with passion, full lips slack, cheeks and chest and breasts flushed. Yes, a queen, and not one made of ice.

Her eyelids were heavy and he wasn't surprised when they drifted shut and her breathing became more measured.

Joss shoved a hand through his hair and winced—she'd just about pulled it out by the roots. But the pain only made him harder, reminding him of how she'd come apart.

He also realized just how easily and quickly he'd slipped back into performing for a woman who cared about as much for him as she had for Byerly.

She came to you, not some toff. The greedy, wanting part of him pointed out. *She all but begged you. Now take her to bed and possess her. Bury yourself in her so deeply you—*

Joss shrugged away the goading voice and stood. He stooped to lift her from the chair, her body warm, soft, and yielding.

She blinked up at him, confused and sleepy. "Where—"

"Shh," he said, taking her to his bed, grateful he'd changed his sheets today. He lay her down and pulled the bedding over her, folding her into an envelope of blankets.

"You've no fire." The words were slurred and dreamy.

"I will soon." Joss went to the dormant fireplace and lit the fire that had been laid for ages. It would take a long time for the fire to catch and warm the room. In the meantime, he would warm her with his body.

His blood thundered to his cock at the thought of wrapping himself around her.

But when he returned to the bed it was to find her sleeping soundly.

She looked like a princess from a children's story: skin white as snow, lips like cherries, and long, thick lashes fanning her cheeks. Her pale, lustrous hair had come loose from its moorings and tendrils lay spread across the pillow—*his* pillow.

Well.

Joss tucked the blankets in around her and went back to his chair. A chair that was already becoming precious to him as he could now imagine her sitting in it, thighs spread, her eyes dark and her mouth open and panting as she came. For him.

Joss lowered himself into his chair, picked up his book, and tried to read.

Chapter Eleven

Naturally Maude was awake and waiting for Alicia when she entered her rooms just before dawn.

"I told you not to wait up." Alicia took off the hat and tossed it onto the bed along with her cloak. Maude immediately picked up both items and marched into her dressing room without answering.

Alicia wanted to scream. She did not need another conscience berating her in addition to the one she already had.

She'd woken in near darkness, confused about where she was. A dim light had guttered and she realized she was in his room, asleep in *his* bed.

He was in his chair, an open book resting face down on his chest. He still wore his trousers and shirt, but had draped a robe over himself, no doubt to keep warm.

His head rested against the back of the chair and his lips were parted, his breathing deep and even. She'd taken the rare opportunity to study him unobserved. He looked younger in sleep, but his slack features were every bit as harsh and craggy. No, he was not a handsome man. Yet she had never met a man who drew her eyes so powerfully.

Like a thief in the night, she'd quietly gathered her things, terrified he would wake and they would be faced with an awkward scene.

Just the mere thought of seeing him again made her stomach clench.

Back in her own bed, it had taken hours to fall asleep and she'd not woken up until almost two o'clock.

She took her very late breakfast in bed and was just enjoying her second cup of chocolate when Maude entered.

Alicia cut her a glance and then returned her attention to the *Gazette*. "So."

She looked up at the word to find her maid with fisted hands planted on her hips.

Alicia sighed and lowered her cup. "How fortunate that you are speaking to me again." She didn't bother to keep the sarcasm from her voice. Maude had undressed her in silence and left without a word. And when Alicia had rung for her breakfast, it had been another maid who'd answered—the pretty, fresh-looking country girl named Annie.

"Why are you doing this?" Maude didn't bother to explain what she meant.

Her maid's censorious expression was like a hot poker, prodding her into recklessness. "I will answer your question, Maude. Not that I'm sure why you think you are in any position to demand explanations from me. I will see *him* whenever I wish." This was news to Alicia, who hadn't come to conclusions of any kind on the matter. Still, she did tend to react impulsively when baited or challenged.

"And what happens when you tire of him?"

Alicia had a difficult time imaging that would ever happen but she hardly wished to share that with Maude.

Instead she shrugged and picked up her cup. "Why should anything happen. We will go back to our usual roles."

Maude snorted. "Are you really so without any idea as to how other people—*normal* people—are put together?"

Alicia lowered her cup with a noisy clatter. "You are insolent, but you do amuse me so please go on. Tell me what it is you mean—but you had better explain it slowly, as I'm so deficient."

"What if he grows to care for you? What if he thinks this—this *whatever* you are doing—means something? What if he cannot simply curtail his emotions so easily or—" She paused and then added with emphasis, "What if he becomes angry and violent—like Viscount Byerly?"

Alicia thought of the calm, impassive man who'd given her such tender pleasure, who'd carried her from Byerly's house as if she were made of spun glass. "I don't believe that is his nature."

"What if you are *wrong?*" Maude hissed through gritted teeth.

Alicia shoved aside the tray and the blankets, not caring when crockery and cutlery clattered. "What if I am? So what if it's a servant? Does it matter who gets angry and behaves childishly—a viscount? A groom? A boatswain in His Majesty's Royal Navy? A gaucho from the South American Pampas?"

Alicia could see her logic had momentarily paralyzed the other woman. She marched toward her and didn't stop until their bodies were almost touching. Maude was a good five inches shorter than Alicia and had to tilt her head to an uncomfortable angle to meet her gaze.

"I am mistress here. I will make any decisions I please and I refuse to answer to anyone for them—even *you.* I will," she hesitated, and then narrowed her eyes, "I will *fuck,*" Maude was unshaken by the vulgar word, "anyone I please, as often as I please, wherever I please. If you don't like it, you know what to do."

Maude's jaw moved side to side as if she were chewing over possible retorts, and then swallowing them.

"Do you understand?" Alicia asked. She did not wish to humiliate the older woman, whom she loved, but she also did not wish to argue every time she decided to see the man.

The man? Her aunt Giddy's voice demanded. *You're so ashamed you can't even say his name.*

Joss. His name is Joss, and I will see him whenever and as often as I please.

Aunt Giddy did not respond.

"Very well, my lady." Maude's stiff words brought Alicia back to herself. "I have spoken my last word on the matter."

"Good," Alicia said, sounding far more certain than she felt. "I would like to take a bath."

—❤—

Alicia had behaved. She'd wanted to go to him every night—or to summon him to her—but she had exercised restraint. She knew she was doing so to impress Maude—to show *one* servant that she had *not* become obsessed with another.

Meanwhile, she spent her time obsessing about her groom. Obsessing about what he thought about *her*. Did he see her as just a lonely older—because she *was* older than him, by over a decade!—woman who was merely using him for sexual gratification?

Was that all she wanted from him?

She tried to convince herself that bed sport *was* all she wanted, but she couldn't lie convincingly enough to fool herself. She was. . . smitten by him.

God, the thought of being smitten at her age made her want to scream; but there it was. Perhaps it was only his air of mystery that had, er, smited her? Maybe if she got to know him she would lose interest in him?

Still, what if her interest *didn't* wane? What if she became even more obsessed? It had never happened to her before, but there was always a first time in life, wasn't there?

When she'd been young, she'd not been looking for love. When she'd married Edward, she'd first been mesmerized by his status—and then she'd spent the years with him merely struggling to stay alive.

And since Edward's death? Well, she'd just wanted something to make her *feel* alive. And now that she was feeling alive, she wasn't sure she liked it.

So, for the last four days she'd stayed away from him, a coward to her own emotions.

But today she had a legitimate excuse for summoning him. She needed him—wanted to have him with her when she picked up Elizabeth.

She told herself the reason she wanted him at hand was because she planned to use him for Elizabeth's needs while her stepdaughter stayed with her. The way he'd carried her that night—like a feather—had made Alicia think of him when it came to engaging a strong servant for Elizabeth.

But that wasn't the only reason—and not even the most compelling one. The truth was Alicia wanted him to accompany her to Selwood House and be nearby when she spoke to David.

She'd been more badly shaken by that night at Byerly House than she'd expected. She wasn't sure why it had affected her so profoundly. After all, she'd endured far worse than Viscount Byerly: she had endured and survived her last husband. And his vile son.

She might not *need* Gormley nearby when she went to see David, but she wanted him there.

So, when the carriage was brought around later that afternoon it was Gormley who waited to hand her inside.

Alicia didn't know what she'd been expecting, but she couldn't help feeling a certain sense of anticlimax when he simply lowered the steps and offered his hand, his eyes downcast like any good servant's.

"My lady?"

Alicia realized she was staring at him. She ignored his quizzical look, her throat unable to produce any words even if her mind could have formulated them. She looked away and her gaze landed on his hand. On his gloves.

Gloves which had touched the most intimate part of her.

Gloves? What about those lips? That mouth? His tongue? Those fingers?

Her face, already hot from anticipating this first meeting, was now scalded.

He waited patiently until she was settled and then raised the steps. When he would have closed the door she stopped him.

"You will ride inside, Gormley, I wish to inform you of your new duties." Alicia made sure to speak loudly so that the other servants might hear. Not that she cared what they thought, but, no doubt, it made the man's life easier.

Alicia forced her body to relax against the luxurious leather as he folded his powerful body onto the seat across from her, her heart pounding as fast as a terrified rodent's.

"How is your shoulder?" She could see her question startled him.

And why wouldn't it? When was the last time you showed any concern for him or his needs?

Alicia grimaced at the too-accurate thought.

"It is almost healed, my lady."

"I somehow doubt that, but Finch says you have been working in the stables, so I assume it is not paining you too much."

"No, my lady."

"If you feel any twinges, I want you to tell Mr. Carling not to work you so hard."

He hesitated only a fraction of a second, but it made her consider what she'd just said: about working him hard.

Her face heated so quickly she felt dizzy. She lowered her eyes from his face and concentrated on even, deep breathing. Of course that just meant she was looking at his body. His huge, muscular body that had knelt between her thighs and—

"I am bringing you along today to carry my daughter," she blurted, her loud voice causing him to startle. "Lady Elizabeth is my stepdaughter, but I consider her my own." She paused, and then continued. "She is chair bound. She can walk a little, and it is possible she might, one day, become stronger, but for now she is—" Alicia hesitated, wondering how much one should tell a servant. She glanced at him.

He was attentive, but expressionless. He'd seen her lover beating her; he'd had his mouth on the most private part of her body, and he'd made her beg and writhe. What else could she possibly do or say to surprise him?

"She has spent all her life at the family house in the country. This is her first visit to London. I'm afraid Lord Selwood, her brother and my stepson, believes her too fragile for town pursuits. I do not. But he is her guardian and I have no say in the matter." That was hardly anything he needed to know. "As a result of her condition she is accustomed to spending almost all of her time at home—which means a good deal of time with servants. In particular she enjoyed her governess." Her lips twisted with fury.

"Unfortunately, Lord Selwood dismissed her governess several months back and I'm afraid Lady Elizabeth is at loose ends. Add to that the fact work is being done on Lord Selwood's country house, so," she stopped babbling and waited.

But he did not speak, because he was a servant. And servants did not volunteer opinions. Not even a servant who'd given his mistress the most exquisite pleasure she'd ever experienced.

Good God! Can you not complete a simple thought without digressing?

"What I am *trying* to say is that you will be needed often as I will be taking her out and about as much as possible. Do you understand?"

"Yes, my lady."

"Good." She looked away from him, embarrassed by the way she was behaving, as if both of them were not perfectly aware of what had happened.

He was hardly in a position to demand answers from her—or anything, really. It would be up to her to fix matters between them.

But not now. Not when she would have to see David in mere minutes.

The journey to Selwood House was both too quick and too slow, leaving her enough time with her chaotic thoughts to become even less composed, but not enough time to get either mind or body under control. And the presence of the silent man across from her did little to help.

She stared at Byerly House, which was across the square from Selwood House. The windows were dark and the steps were not cleared of the recent snow. Soon Charles's neighbors would notice the signs of neglect if they had not already. Alicia shivered. She'd been foolish to play her games so near David—even though he'd not been in town. If he ever discovered her behavior it would make a handy weapon to use against her. Not that he needed a reason to torment Alicia, an activity which seemed to give him inexplicable pleasure.

The carriage stopped. It was time.

You are doing this for Elizabeth, she reminded herself.

⸺❤⸺

Joss was still kicking himself about falling asleep that night.

Why hadn't he heard her leave?

He knew none of that mattered. What mattered is that she had *not* wanted to wake him and speak to him. And obviously she had not wanted to see him since that night, either. She had essentially banished him from her presence. Again.

And once again he'd waited in hourly expectation of being discharged—the toffs didn't like evidence of their weaknesses right under their noses, and that's what Joss was, a servant who'd seen his mistress at something less than her most proper.

Not only had he witnessed the affair with Byerly, he'd made her climax in his mouth.

Just thinking the raw words made him stiffen—not exactly something new. He'd been hard and wanting for days and should have blisters on his palms to show for all his nocturnal activity. Instead, all he had to show for it was yet another erection.

No doubt that was all he'd *ever* get from her—an erection he would have to deal with himself. Well, he'd guessed as much when she came to him that night. It wasn't as if he shouldn't have known. Women like her wanted what he had to offer—oh, they wanted that so very desperately and would pay dearly for it—but they did not want *him*. Why would they? He was a big, ugly, butcher's son; a brute of a man with the unfortunate habit of reading too much and getting ideas above his station. A whore.

Or at least an ex-whore.

God. It made him so tired. He should have stayed working for Melissa. Sleeping in a luxurious bed, eating rich food, fucking wealthy, eager women and being very well compensated for it. What kind of fool would leave that set-up?

A special kind, that was for certain.

So, here he was, a fool who was yanking his cock raw and wishing for somebody who didn't even believe he was human.

Knowing all that didn't keep him from getting boneless with relief when Hiram, the footman she'd been using lately instead of Joss, came into the stables and told him to be ready to escort her ladyship somewhere that afternoon.

The boy's lips had been petulant, like those of a displaced lover. Joss had wanted to grab the young cockerel's neck and squeeze him for his audacity. But then he'd realized he felt the exact same way. They were a right pair of idiotic bookends to think they had some claim on a woman who was as accessible as the moon.

Joss's mind churned in a way that left him nervy and angry. He was caged in here, barely a foot away from her and it was all he could do not to gawk at her. He tried to think of something else, to look somewhere else, but it was pointless.

So, he stared at her from beneath lowered lashes like some hole-and-corner pervert; unable to get enough of this woman who tied him in knots.

She was as gloriously beautiful as ever, her skin as pale as marble, her glossy blond hair pulled back to showcase her long elegant neck and exquisite features, her body clothed in the finest garments that money could buy.

But it was clear that all was not tranquil in her wealthy world.

She'd given him an abrupt little speech about her daughter and then turned to stare out the window. But Joss didn't think she saw anything. He thought she was looking at something inside her head, something she didn't like at all. He suspected that whatever was bothering her waited inside Selwood House.

Joss had never been to Selwood House before and had not seen the current earl.

They passed Byerly's house—which had an air of neglect—but Lady Selwood did not seem to notice.

The carriage slowed and she fussed with her reticule. He helped her down and escorted her up the front steps. A liveried servant opened the door before he could knock.

When he turned to go, her voice stopped him.

"I want you to wait inside, Mr. Gormley."

A man wearing the conservative black suit of a butler and cloaked in an overweening sense of superiority descended the stairs as they entered the foyer.

"Good afternoon, my lady. His Lordship is waiting for you in the library." His gaze flickered to Joss and the hovering footman.

Lady Selwood began stripping off her gloves. "Good afternoon, Beamish. This is Gormley. He is here to assist with Lady Elizabeth."

"Very good, my lady." He turned to the footman. "Thomas, show Mr. Gormley to the kitchen and—"

"No."

All three men turned at her sharp command and Joss saw an expression of uncertainty on her beautiful features.

She pulled off her second glove and slapped them both into one hand, the gesture a decisive counterpoint to her hesitation. "I shall not be long and I want Gormley close at hand when I am ready to leave. He can wait for me in the Yellow Saloon."

"Of course, my lady. If you'll follow me." The butler led them up the stairs.

Joss had to hand it to Beamish, he had a face made for buttling and an unflappable demeanor that spoke of years of experience. Seating servants in sitting rooms was not normal behavior—even for American countesses.

Joss had no idea what was going on here, but, whatever it was, she was   afraid.

Chapter Twelve

Alicia hated this house.

No matter how much she struggled to control her emotions, the reins always slipped when she stepped through the door and memories of the horror she'd endured during her marriage flooded her.

Today she'd exposed her agitation to Gormley.

Beamish was unflappable, but even he had been surprised by her unconventional request. She couldn't help it; she needed Gormley nearby.

Needed him. And when was the last time she'd needed someone? Or at least when was the last time she'd shown her need so very plainly?

She would have thought she'd learned her lesson long ago, when she'd been a child of six.

Her Aunt Giddy had made Alicia a doll out of an old sock. She'd sewed tiny clothing and stitched on a face and Alicia had loved that doll more than life itself. She'd named her Lily, and had confided in her, cared for her, and protected her from the other children in their rooming house, who'd mocked her cruelly for her attachment to a stuffed sock.

She hadn't cared. When Lily had been with her, she had felt so loved, so complete—even when her stomach had been gnawingly empty.

One day a girl from the rooming house—a nasty, rickety thing two or three years older than Alicia—had stolen Lily and left her gutted and torn on the front stoop.

Oh, how she'd cried.

Giddy had repaired the doll but Alicia's special confidant, her best and only friend, was gone: Lily was nothing more than a sock.

So, Alicia had learned it was better not to show how much you loved something—it just drew attention, and bad attention at that. She'd been so very good about hiding her love for years.

But then she'd met her stepdaughter and made a dreadful mistake: she'd loved Lizzy from the first. And the earl had seized on her affection and used it to squeeze more money out of her and make her life hell.

But had she learned from that?

No. Here she was showing her need for Gormley. Would he end up discarded and gutted?

Beamish opened the door to the library, pulling her away from unpleasant thoughts and shoving her into an unpleasant situation.

David looked up from his great desk, coming to his feet, a welcoming smile on his face.

"Alicia! How glad I am to see you." He came toward her, bent to kiss her cheek and it was all she could do not to flinch away at what was, undeniably, the quick flick of his tongue against her skin.

He smiled down at her, his probing, knowing eyes drinking in her discomfort. "Beamish, send up tea."

"That's not necessary, David, I—"

"Please, Alicia, it is Christmas—or near enough. Can't you spare a moment for your poor, lonely stepson?" He pushed out his lower lip, an expression of mocking self-pity on his handsome face. "Soon you will take Elizabeth and I will be all alone in this huge drafty pile for Christmas and weeks and weeks afterward."

Alicia knew his words were his subtle way of reminding her that the only reason she was allowed to have Elizabeth for so long was because it was his will—which he could change at any moment.

She smiled tightly at Beamish, who was waiting. "Yes, thank you, tea would be nice."

David gestured to the settee and chairs in front of the blazing fire, ushering her toward them, his hand hovering just over her shoulders, making her twitch, but never quite touching her.

She sat in the middle of the settee, just in case he got any notions. But he took the seat across from her, crossing one elegantly pantaloon-sheathed leg over the other, smiling at her with a face that appeared completely devoid of guile.

But Alicia knew better.

She wondered how many people knew what lurked behind that handsome face of his.

Not his wife, she suspected. The current Lady Selwood was a dull-eyed and phlegmatic woman who seemed consumed with her duties as countess—specifically her duty to produce an heir—and was either too incurious or too unimaginative to wonder what her handsome husband did with his time.

He swept her with warm hazel eyes, the caressing look making her throat tighten. "I'd ask how you've been keeping yourself, Alicia but I can see you are well. Very well, indeed."

"Thank you, David. You are looking well, also." And he was, but that was nothing new. Her dead husband's son was a very handsome man. Tall and imposing like his father, he was the consummate aristocrat, his bone structure the distillation of hundreds of years of careful breeding and selection. His bones long and elegant, his features fine but not effeminate. Most people would consider him an excessively attractive man. Most people.

"How are Rebecca and Amelia?"

His full lips curved into a smile at her question, as if it pleased him. But Alicia knew better than anyone how furious his wife's inability to carry a son made him.

Three live births and four miscarriages and all he had to show for it was one daughter.

Like his father, David burned for a son like an opium addict burned for his pipe. Without a son the earldom would descend to his cousin Cedric, a happy-go-lucky young man Alicia had met only once and liked very much.

Both David and her dead husband, Edward, had hated Cedric virulently. It was the need for money and a loathing for Cedric which had driven Edward Selwood to marry Alicia, but those had not been the only reasons.

If she'd been wiser, she might have looked more closely into the death of his two prior wives; but she had learned about their unpleasant ends too late to save herself.

"Rebecca is *enceinte* again," he smiled proudly, and Alicia had to clench her teeth to hold the bile at bay. "Amelia is budding into a beautiful young lady but she is still her father's little darling at fourteen and has promised to stay with me until I am old and gray." His smile made Alicia shiver. "Yes, they are doing well, thank you for asking, Alicia." He said her name the way all Englishmen did: Ah-lee-cee-yah. For some reason it always made her cringe. "They will spend the holidays with her parents at Kingsford and all Rebecca's siblings will be there. It will be a joyous event."

"You must regret that your duty is keeping you in town." She knew that was the last thing he felt about being away from his wife: regret.

His smile deepened at her subtle dig. "I am, indeed. But I'm afraid my mistress is a demanding one." Wicked glints lit his brown, beautifully lashed eyes at his words, which were not exactly proper when spoken with such relish. Especially given what Alicia knew of him and his flesh-

and-blood mistresses. He chuckled. "My mistress being a position on His Grace of Beckingdon's council, of course."

"Of course," she echoed.

The door opened and a maid appeared bearing a tray.

David gestured to the low table between them. "Will you serve, Alicia?"

"It would be my pleasure," she murmured, glad to have something to occupy her hands, which seemed determined to fiddle and twitch, as they always did in his company.

He turned to the pretty young maid, who was smoothing her skirts with hands that trembled worse than Alicia's.

"You may go, Molly." The girl darted from the room in a manner that spoke volumes, David's amused eyes following her. "One of the girls Rebecca brought with her from The Willows. Very shy, quiet, and diligent." He grinned. "Nothing quite like a country lass when it comes to working hard to please her master, is there? But skittish, I'm afraid."

Loathing and fury welled up inside her but she lowered her eyes to the tray, anger making her hands as steady as boulders.

"I take mine black, Alicia."

"I recall that." She did not look up.

He chuckled. "Of course you do. You have always been so sedulous when it comes to taking care of my needs and desires, haven't you? A perfect step-mama."

A flurry of violent, painful, and humiliating memories rampaged through her mind and the urge to flee almost overwhelmed her. Wisely, she ignored it.

"Speaking of remembering," she said. "Have you found a new governess for Lizzy?"

"Why no, my dear, but then I haven't been looking."

Alicia's head whipped up. "But it has been months now. I thought perhaps . . . "

David's expression did not alter, but she felt the shift in him, all the same. He became more . . . alert, his warm brown gaze arrested, his concentration that of a rapt child who didn't want to miss a moment of suffering after tearing the legs off some insect.

"Yes, what did you think?" he prodded.

"She is alone at The Willows for much of the time, David. She needs a companion."

"Not if she does not live in the country."

Her heart leapt "You mean she will stay in London?" She hated the hope she heard, knowing he would latch onto it, exploit it.

He did.

"Oh, no, no, no. That would be far too arduous for a girl with her condition." He glanced at the pot, which was still suspended, and raised his eyebrows, forcing Alicia to turn her eyes to her task, swallowing her scream and her urge to fling the boiling water at his head and use the pot to crush his skull and—

"I am beginning to believe she needs constant care, Alicia. The care of professionals."

She put the lid on the teapot with a clatter and stared at him. "Please tell me you are not going to put her in one of those *places*."

The expression on his face sickened her: it was arousal, pure sexual arousal. Just like it had always been when it came to taunting her, tormenting her.

He gave her an injured, pouting look. "I have not made my decision yet. I'm looking for only the best. She is my sister." He set the hook a bit deeper. "You know my father entrusted her to my care rather than—" he stopped and gave her an apologetic smile, as if he'd just stopped himself in time. "Well, rather than anyone else's."

Her care. He meant Alicia's care. Edward had deliberately left his daughter in his sadistic son's care so that he might have some leverage to use over Alicia, a way to control her—to control her money. And, oh how clever that had been. Even in the grave he was directing her life, determining her future, and bleeding her dry.

"I can give her better care than she would receive anywhere, David. I could pay for the best care that—"

He raised one hand in a halting gesture and chuckled tolerantly. "Please, you are becoming excitable, my dear." This time his smile let slip a hint of the cruelty that defined him. "A bit of your American passion coming out, I daresay." He shrugged. "We shall have to spend some time together—work closely with one another—on a solution for my sister. I look forward to that." His eyes gleamed and his slick, red lips curved into a smile. "But right now, I am parched."

It was all she could do not to fling herself across the table and scratch out his eyes. But that had worked out very badly for her the only time she'd tried it and she'd not seen Elizabeth for more than six months. He'd kept her at a painful distance, but not her money, of course.

David began talking about some of their mutual acquaintances while she resumed the feminine ritual and struggled to regain control of herself.

Alicia had been twenty-nine when she married the Earl of Selwood, who'd been in his mid-sixties. David, his son and heir, had been thirty-four.

At first Alicia hadn't believed the younger man had been bothered by his father's marriage. Indeed, David had acted openly welcoming. His wife had never been warm, but neither had she been disrespectful.

Although the earl had needed money, he'd not been utterly below the hatches like so many of his class. Even so, he'd needed to sell all but two of his estates, his seat—the Willows, which he could not sell—and a smaller property brought to the marriage by the earl's first wife.

The marriage settlement had made all the difference between a careful existence and a luxurious one. Thanks to Horace, her first husband, Alicia was one of the wealthiest women in

Horace's most trusted men of business, a pair of bachelor brothers whom she'd brought to England to hammer out the marriage contract, had taught their English counterparts a thing or two about American ingenuity. They'd made sure that Alicia remained a woman of means—living largely on the interest from her investments—while the vast majority of her wealth was put in settlements for any future children.

The Earl of Selwood would get enough of her money to make marriage to an American mongrel tolerable, but the bulk of her fortune would remain tied in a series of clever knots, forever beyond his reach.

The rapacious brothers had done an admirable job securing her wealth, but her person would still be the legal chattel of her new husband.

Alicia, idiot that she was, hadn't believe that taking Edward as her lord and master was anything to fear. After all, he was the consummate bloodless, emotionless aristocrat. Or so she'd believed.

"—and they say Byerly will remain there for the foreseeable future. Have you heard anything about it, Alicia?"

The sound of her name jarred her from her trancelike state. She saw she'd poured a cup of tea without realizing it and looked up.

"I beg your pardon?"

He waved an admonishing finger at her. "You were gathering wool! But I will repeat it, because it is a delicious piece of gossip. Byerly has fled the country."

The cup and saucer rattled in her hand.

"Ah," he said, leaning forward to take the cup and saucer, his long cool fingers brushing against hers. But not inadvertently. Never that.

"Oh, has he?" she said carefully, pouring her own cup with more care than was expended in the crowning of a king.

"Yes, it seems he is utterly below the hatches. He's gone to Paris, of course, like so many others who've lost their shirts in the current environment."

Alicia gestured to the biscuit tray.

"I'd better not." He laid one hand on his flat abdomen, stroking it with a sensual gesture, the inappropriate motion designed with only one intention in mind: to draw her gaze to his lower body. But Alicia never let her eyes dip below his. "I've been putting on my winter layer of fat, I'm afraid." He lifted his cup, his mouth a moue of self-reproach. "Lord knows how I'll find a way to work it all off in the city." He sighed. "Oh how I miss the vigorous exercise I am able to take while down at The Willows. You must recall those times? We did enjoy ourselves, didn't we?" His teeth flashed. "I do miss those long, hard rides we enjoyed so often—until we were both lathered and sore."

Acid surged up her throat, almost choking her. Her cup clattered as she set it down on the tray and she stood.

David was on his feet and beside her in an instant.

"Is everything all right, Alicia?" He gazed down at her with concern puckering his forehead. But his eyes glinted with barely suppressed glee. She'd forgotten how tall he was, almost as tall as Gormley, but nowhere as big or broad.

"I just remembered I invited Lady Constance to come over before dinner, to help Elizabeth settle in." She swallowed, giving him a cool smile—or at least the best she could muster. "I'm having a dinner party to celebrate her arrival."

He grinned, fully aware of her lie. "How charming—I haven't seen darling Connie in ages. Perhaps I might make the time to come over and—" he hesitated and her heart stuttered. His nostrils flared ever so slightly, the only overt sign of the amusement he was deriving from torturing her. "But, no—I'm afraid I cannot make it today. Perhaps later in the week, if I should have a moment to come up for air?"

"Of course, that would be delightful." It would never come about. That, at least, she could see to.

He caught her hand before she could snatch up her gloves and reticule. His skin was soft but the power in his long elegant fingers was latent. He raised her hand all the way to his mouth, lowering his lips to her skin, his eyes holding hers as his lips parted and the slick point of his tongued dragged slowly across the sensitive skin.

Alicia couldn't help the shudder that wracked her body and his lips curved into a boyish—almost innocent—smile. But his eyes promised something else. Dark things. For her.

—❤—

Joss was staring out the sitting room window, absently watching the activity on the street below when he heard the door open. It was Lady Selwood, and her face was even paler than usual, her blue eyes huge, her pupils pinpricks. He strode toward her, his hands out, without thinking, only stopping when a man appeared beside her.

The stranger—Lord Selwood, obviously—smiled and glanced from Joss to Lady Selwood. He chuckled for some reason. "Ah," he said, laying a hand on Lady Selwood's shoulder, not appearing to notice how she flinched at the touch. "I can guess why you brought this strapping lad with you."

Joss kept his face expressionless at the word *lad*, disappointed in himself that he would even allow such a thing to rankle. But that's what came of entertaining thoughts above one's self.

The earl turned a wide, jovial smile on him. "I gather you will serve as my sister's trusty steed? Her valiant mount." He grinned from Joss to the woman beside him, his amusement bearing an odd, uncomfortable edge.

Joss hesitated, unable to read his employer's face. "Yes, my lord."

Lord Selwood rocked back on his heels as if elated by his answer. "Excellent. Well, I shall say my goodbyes now, Alicia. Lizzy and I already had our parting last night, before her bedtime." He bent down to kiss her cheek. Joss noticed how her body went wooden and wondered if the other man noticed it, too. But if he did, he didn't appear to care.

He turned to Joss and gave him a brief nod. "Have a care with my sister, er—"

"Gormley, sir."

The tall lord nodded, his handsome face wreathed with good humor. "Ah, yes, well, be careful with my sister, she is very precious to me." He cut one last look at Lady Selwood and was gone.

Joss risked a quick look at his mistress's face, but she had already turned to go.

Outside, standing in the hall, was the butler.

The three of them went up one more flight of steps and to a door at the very end of the hall.

Beamish opened the door without knocking and Lady Selwood went inside, Beamish behind her. Joss hovered outside in the hall, listening to sounds of female excitement, laughter, and raised voices.

He was wondering what he was supposed to do when Beamish's head popped around the door jam.

"Inside, man, inside," he hissed.

Joss entered the room and saw Lady Selwood crouched low in front of somebody in a chair—a young girl, by the look of it.

The girl saw him first, and then Lady Selwood turned. Joss stopped as though somebody had hit him in the head with a plank. He had always thought his mistress the most beautiful woman he'd ever seen, but he had never before seen her smile, at least not like this, an open, joyous grin, her pale blue eyes sparkling her white skin flushed with pleasure, her red lips curled into a smile. Some part of his brain noticed her teeth, which he realized he'd never seen bared so openly. One of her canines was chipped and shorter than its partner.

A charming imperfection.

"Gormley, this is Lady Elizabeth, my daughter."

Joss saw the girl was staring at him and dropped a hasty bow.

"Hello Mr. Gormley. Mama says you are to have the arduous task of carrying me about during my visit?" Brown eyes sparkled up at him and Joss realized the girl bore a striking resemblance to the man he'd just met. Like the earl she was tall and fine-boned. But she had an unhealthy puffiness around her face that spoke of a sedentary lifestyle, or perhaps illness.

"It will be my pleasure, Lady Elizabeth."

The girl had a delightful, infectious laugh that made his lips twitch. "Oh, you did not mention how gallant he was, Mama."

"He is, isn't he? Perhaps that is because Mr. Gormley is a fan of reading plays and poetry and always keeps a volume in his pocket." Lady Selwood gave him an amused arch look—as if daring him to deny it or expecting him to look ashamed.

Lady Elizabeth clapped her hands. "But that is delightful! I adore plays *and* poetry but Mama will have none of it." She smiled shyly. "Tell me, what have you been reading today?"

"I'm afraid I didn't bring anything with me, my lady."

"Well, it was very wicked of Mama to share that information, for now I shall be ringing for you to haul me up and down the stairs all day, just to discuss books."

Both women laughed at whatever they saw on his face—which had already heated at all the unexpected attention.

"We are embarrassing him," the girl said, her tone one of exaggerated confidence.

Lady Selwood stood. "Yes, we are. And it is also time to go." She turned to Beamish. "Her trunks have been loaded?"

"Yes, my lady, as well as Her Ladyship's spare chair."

Lady Selwood turned to Joss. "Lady Elizabeth's condition makes it difficult for her to walk but she can still feel pain. Do be careful."

The girl shook her head. "Don't let her frighten you Mr. Gormley, I'm not a piece of fine china." She pushed the wheels of her chair and rolled toward him, smiling her sunny smile. "I am ready, sir."

Joss felt humbled by her good humor in the face of her condition. He slid an arm beneath her knees and another between her back and the chair and lifted her.

She looked up at him, sliding an arm around his neck to steady herself, obviously accustomed to being carried this way. "I am terribly sorry, I know I am not a feather. Am I too heavy for you?"

"You are not heavy," he said. She was no lightweight like Lady Selwood, but certainly nothing Joss couldn't manage.

"You are too kind." She had a smile that made him want to smile.

By the time he'd gone down two flights of stairs and out to the street he was perspiring a little and the freezing wind felt good.

The footman had the door to the carriage open.

It was a bit of a trick to get her through the narrow door and into the carriage without jostling her, but when he'd finished, she gave him another smile and the carriage seemed to warm. "Thank you."

"It was my pleasure, my lady." Joss realized after he said it that he wasn't lying.

He handed in Lady Selwood.

"You will ride on the box, Gormley," she said, coolly.

Ah, dismissed.

"Yes, my lady." Joss closed the door, her words putting him firmly back in his place.

Chapter Thirteen

Joss immediately learned that Lady Elizabeth was serious about discussing books..

He brought her down to dinner her first night but the youngest footman, Hiram, transported her to her quarters afterward. The girl was not as heavy as she liked to believe and any of the male servants could have carried her the short distances she required. But, it seemed she had decided it would be Lady Selwood's prose-and-poetry-reading groom she would call on most often.

When she rang for him the following day, he was helping Carling with one of the new carriage horses and, as a result, was covered in hair and sweat.

"Hurry up and go change, Gormley," the older man had said, "I'll get Byron to finish this. Go on," he'd urged when Joss hesitated.

Even changing quickly and washing only his hands and face, it still took him half an hour to answer her summons.

When he arrived at her chambers it was to find not the girl, but Lady Selwood waiting for him. Judging by the expression on her face, she was not pleased by the delay.

"When Lady Elizabeth summons you, you will come immediately." She didn't raise her voice, but her accent seemed to subtly change, to become more . . . foreign.

Joss bowed his head. "Of course, my lady. I apologize."

He could hear something tapping and realized it was her foot. "What took you so long?"

"I was in the stables helping Mr. Carling with the horses. I had to, er, change out of my leathers."

The tapping stopped. "Oh, I see," she said, her tone both embarrassed and grudging. "Well, for the duration of my daughter's stay you are to place yourself at her service. That means you are to dress accordingly and present yourself to Mr. Feehan every morning—I doubt Lady Elizabeth will want you before ten o'clock, but be ready, all the same." She hesitated, her jaw working slightly and the telltale flush that colored her cheekbones told him she was not entirely comfortable. And why would that be, he wondered? Did she not like chiding him—disciplining him—after what he'd done to her body?

The thought almost made him smile. He was so pathetic that even being scolded by her was enough to make him harden.

She met his gaze, her cheeks almost fiery. "In fact, I would have you tell Mr. Carling he should not count on your services for the foreseeable future. Is that understood, Gormley?"

"Yes, my lady."

She stared up at him as if waiting for something.

Joss stared back.

She cleared her throat. "Very well, then. She is in the library, where Hiram has carried her. Go to her and see if she has need of you." She turned on her heel, not waiting for his response.

Joss could not resist watching her receding figure. Her anger seemed excessive to the occasion and sometimes he felt there were emotional currents at work that he couldn't see.

Joss snorted. She was a woman, there were *always* emotional currents.

"Well, didn't you get a right bollocking."

Joss turned at the sound of Annie's voice.

She was dressed in her maid's uniform and wearing a smirk. "I guess being Her Ladyship's pet means you get the lash more often than the rest of us lowly mortals."

Joss ignored her digs. "Which room is the library?"

She stepped closer and took his hand.

Joss pulled away and glanced around. "What the devil are you about, Annie? Trying to get us both sacked?"

"I was only going to take you to the library," she said, all wide-eyed innocence.

She hardly needed to take his hand to do that, but Joss forbore pointing that out. "Will you show me or do I need to find somebody else?"

She huffed but started walking. "You're no fun, do you know that Mister Jocelyn Gormley."

"I know."

She made a disgusted clucking sound. "I don't know why I bother with you."

"I wish you wouldn't."

She spun around and slapped his face—hard—the motion so fast it was a blur. Joss was momentarily ashamed by how poor his reflexes were now that he no longer boxed.

"You're a bastard!" she hissed. "Always thinkin' you're so much finer than the rest of us just because you wear those fancy clothes and do whatever you like."

Joss wondered if he had a handprint on his face. "I'm sorry, Annie, I shouldn't have said what I did. I *know* I'm a servant." Did he ever. "I also know this is my job—my livelihood, and *yours*. We'd best not be seen chattering or holding hands," his lips twitched, "or slapping each other."

She narrowed her eyes, turned with a flounce, and resumed her journey.

The library was on the second floor and seemed to take up one side of the long hall.

"You wait here," Annie said. She knocked, opened the door, and stepped inside, dropping a curtsy. "Gormley to see you, my lady."

"Oh, good. Tell him to come in—thank you Annie."

Annie motioned Joss inside, rubbing her body against his on her way out.

Lady Elizabeth sat in a chair beside the fireplace and was smiling at him. "Good afternoon, Mr. Gormley."

"Good afternoon, my lady."

She made a beckoning motion with one hand. "Come, sit down beside me and help me with my list."

Joss took the chair she indicated.

"Here," she handed him a piece of parchment.

It was a list of titles, some novels, some books of verse. Joss looked up. "I don't understand, my lady. How can I help?"

"You could give me some of your own suggestions."

Joss stared.

"Oh." She sat back in her chair, her smile dimming a little. "You think me odd." He opened his mouth to deny it but she shook her head. "No, it's quite all right: I *am* odd. I'm afraid being in the country by myself most of the time has made me that way." Her mouth pulled into a lopsided smile. "The only people I see every day are servants." Her round cheeks tinted pink, making her look younger. "They are my only friends. I spend time in the kitchen with Cook, Mr. Higgins takes me to the stables—or at least he used to, before my special gig went in for repairs, and—" She stopped abruptly, her expression momentarily stricken before she shook her head.

"In any case, most of them have known me since I was born, so they tolerate my foibles—if they even notice them." She bit her lip, her brown eyes imploring. "Ever since Miss Tate left—my governess—I've had nobody to discuss books with."

Joss couldn't stop himself from asking, "Does Lady Selwood not like discussing books?"

Lady Elizabeth's sandy eyebrows descended. "You know, she is not a great reader." Her gaze flickered to Joss. "I know there are many people who do not enjoy reading, but . . ."

"But you are not one of them," Joss finished for her.

"No." She grinned. "And neither are you, I think."

This conversation—sitting in this room, surrounded by books—was beyond anything Joss had ever experienced as a servant.

Well, except for those two nights with the mistress of the house, of course.

So, it was now part of his job to discuss books with the sister of an earl? What if he said the wrong thing—disagreed with her? Or mentioned something. . . inappropriate?

"You needn't, you know."

"I beg your pardon, my lady?"

"I said you needn't do this—stay with me. I can tell Mama I changed my mind."

Lord, her quiet acceptance of his possible rejection in her eyes gutted him; he couldn't recall ever seeing anyone who was quite so lonely.

"I would like to stay," he said. "It's just—"

"I know, it is odd and you are uncomfortable."

Joss nodded, relieved not to have to explain.

"If you don't mind me asking, where did you get your love of poetry?"

"From my mother." Joss hesitated, and then added "She was a governess before marrying my father. She had a great love of books—they were her prize possessions." They'd certainly been more prized than any of her children, whom she'd left behind, while taking her books.

"She died?"

Joss raised his brows.

"You said *she had*, so I assumed she died."

She certainly had for Joss and his family. He nodded. "Yes, when I was fifteen."

They were silent for a moment, and Joss wondered if she was thinking of her own mother, the first Lady Selwood, who, unlike his, really *had* died.

"That is a list Miss Tate drew up before she left. Have you read many of the books?"

Joss studied the piece of paper she'd handed him, which held perhaps twenty books. He looked up to find her waiting, her expression expectant. "I've read all but these three at the bottom." He gave her back the list.

"Ah," she said, tilting her head and squinting suspiciously. "You don't care for women novelists?"

Joss smiled at her mock arch tone. "My circulating library has a long waiting list for the more popular books."

The door opened and Lady Selwood entered. Joss sprang to his feet and she motioned him back down. "No, sit, sit. I shouldn't like to disturb your book society."

"Have you read any of these, Mama?"

Lady Selwood hesitated before taking the outstretched sheet. While she looked, her stepdaughter continued. "I am a very fast reader—are you, Mr. Gormley?"

"I am adequate, my lady." In fact, Joss *was* rather fast. Reading subscription books was a quick business as one didn't get the book for very long.

"Do you have a preference? Or would you perhaps prefer some verse? Mama said you were reading Shakespeare—"

Lady Selwood looked up from the sheet she'd been studying. "I don't think that would be appropriate, Lizzy."

Both Joss and Lady Elizabeth blinked at her rather sharp tone.

"Oh. Well, do you have a preference, Mr. Gormley?"

"No, my lady," he said, his gaze still on his employer. What was she finding that was so fascinating on that list?

"Would you like to read *Persuasion* first?" Lady Elizabeth asked him.

"*Persuasion* would be fine, my lady."

Lady Elizabeth glanced at her stepmother, who was still looking at the list. "*Persuasion* is for young ladies, Mama. It is quite proper." The countess finally lowered the sheet of paper. "Have you read it?" the younger woman asked.

"No, darling, I haven't. But that sounds fine."

"Excellent! *Persuasion* it is. Would you like to join us, Mama?"

"I'm afraid I'm going to be rather frantic with all these plans for our holiday pleasure."

He could see the girl was disappointed, but he could also tell she was accustomed to putting the best face on things.

"I just came down to remind you that we are to have dinner a bit earlier tonight. Remember, we are going to the theater."

"How could I forget." She turned to grin at Joss. "You are going, too, Mr. Gormley. It's a production of *The Tempest*, have you read it?"

"Yes, my lady, I have." Joss glanced at Lady Selwood.

"Lady Elizabeth will require assistance as her chair is not practical at the theater. You will remain in the box to wait on her. Please be ready with the carriage immediately after dinner. Now," she said, dismissing him and turning back to her stepdaughter, her icy expression melting. "You can probably discuss novels for an hour, but then Gormley should return you to your chambers if you're to be ready on time."

"Of course, Mama."

She kissed her daughter's cheek and left without another glance at Joss.

When he looked at the younger woman, she smiled and handed him another sheet. "Now, for the fun part. This is a list of what I have *already* read this year. Which of these have you read recently—so that we might discuss it?"

Joss had to admit he was more excited than he should be. He'd seen plays—many times—but he had never watched from anywhere other than the pit when he'd gone to the Drury.

Although he could have easily afforded tickets when he worked for Melissa he'd been saving his money, not splurging on extravagances.

Lady Selwood had arranged for them to use a side entrance to the theater so they were able to avoid the chaos out front. They'd also come a bit early so Joss encountered very few patrons as he carried Lady Elizabeth to the luxurious box that apparently belonged to Lady Selwood.

Once Lady Elizabeth was comfortably installed, Lady Selwood turned to him. "You may sit here," she gestured to the seat right behind her daughter. He must have looked surprised, having expected to stand at the back of the box, because she said, "I want you to be near if Lady Elizabeth has need of you."

"Of course, my lady." But when he cut a glance at the girl, he saw she was grinning at him. So, he had her to thank for the seat.

They were the first to arrive, but others soon swelled the box.

It was apparent that Lady Elizabeth and Joss were the only ones who were more interested in the play than what was going on around them.

But even with the nonstop chattering, flirting, and conspiring Joss was able to hear most of what happened on the stage.

It was a quality production and worthy of the theater: the experience was transporting.

All too soon it was intermission.

Joss stood and went to the back corner while the guests left the box. Soon there was nobody left except Lady Selwood, Lady Elizabeth, and three younger friends of her ladyship's whom Joss did not know.

He saw Lady Selwood lean down and say something to her daughter, but the girl shook her head. Lady Selwood looked at Joss and gave a very slight shake of her head. So, he was not needed to carry her.

The group of five were chatting and laughing when a tall form entered the box.

Joss knew from Lady Selwood's expression who the newcomer was before he saw him.

Lord Selwood greeted the younger guests first, saving his stepmother and sister until last.

"What a pleasure, Alicia. And you, too, Lizzy. Tell me, are you enjoying yourself?"

The girl turned to answer her brother and her expression shocked Joss: Gone was the smiling, gregarious, pretty young woman. In her place was a wooden, pale, and awkward person he scarcely recognized.

Whatever she said was too quiet for him to hear. Her gaze, however, flickered to Joss and her lips trembled into a smile, almost as if she were glad to see him. Her brother immediately turned, following her line of sight.

"What's this?" His teeth were a flash of white. "Ah, I see you've brought your beast of burden with you, Lizzy."

"His name is Mr. Gormley, David." The girl's voice was uncharacteristically sharp and an awkward silence filled the box. Joss was distantly aware of the others shuffling uncomfortably, but he could not take his eyes from Lord Selwood, who was still smiling, but not in a pleasant way.

"Yes, of course. *Mr.* Gormley."

Joss's hackles were well and fully raised.

Lady Selwood stepped forward, putting her person between the earl and Joss. "I'm pleased to see you've found some time for entertainment, David."

Joss could see the other man knew what she was doing and that it amused him.

"I always make time for pleasure, Alicia."

The conversation slid back into well-worn ruts and the next ten minutes ground by. The only one enjoying the exchange was Selwood.

"Well, my dears," he finally said, "I'd best take my leave." The tall lord kissed his sister and Lady Selwood, once again appearing not to recognize their body language. Only Joss saw his face before he turned, and it was almost unrecognizable. Gone was the gregarious, friendly brother and son-in-law. In his place was a man who was about to stick the knife in—and enjoy it.

"Oh, by the way, Alicia. It seems I'll be free for dinner on Christmas Day, after all. I do hope you still have a place for me?"

Lady Selwood would have resembled a marble statue if not for the red that stained her high cheekbones. She smiled and Joss could see it cost her. "We would love to have you."

Selwood turned, raising his brows and grinning at Joss, as if the two of them were co-conspirators.

When the door closed behind the earl, Joss realized he felt dirty—dirtier than he'd ever felt after a day of work at the butchers.

Chapter Fourteen

Alicia closed the door to Lizzy's room and leaned against it, releasing the sigh she'd been holding all evening—or at least since David had intruded on their pleasant night.

He'd come to let her know he was watching her, an activity he'd always enjoyed because he knew it unnerved her.

But his reaction to Mr. Gormley—to Joss—had been more than a little worrisome. It had been like a meeting of two predators inimical to each other.

Alicia snorted at her melodramatic thought, crossing through her sitting room into the bedchamber beyond. Maude had helped her out of her evening clothes into her nightgown after she and Lizzy had arrived home.

"Don't worry about my hair, Maude, Lizzy will brush it for me. You may go to bed."

Alicia and Lizzy had spent an hour gossiping and brushing each other's hair. And now? Now she was alone. And wide awake.

She was in her cloak and hat in a trice and on her way out the door when she paused. She would need to say something to him this time—not like the last time when she'd merely blustered into his rooms and thrown herself at him.

Alicia acted before she could talk herself out of it; she would think of something to say when she got there.

Her eyes alighted on a decanter of ludicrously expensive cognac. She snatched up two glasses from the mirrored tray, putting one in each cloak pocket, and then held the bottle to her chest. She was halfway to his rooms before she accepted what she was doing: running headlong into disaster. Again.

But she couldn't help it. She kept remembering his expression tonight when he'd looked at David. There had been no worry or humility in his eyes. The way he'd looked at the powerful, wealthy lord had been fearless. It had been. . . arousing. He'd resembled a gladiator or some mythical knight, prepared to fight to protect what was his.

She was breathless when she reached the top of the stairs. Before she could knock, the door swung open, making her yelp.

It was him. *Joss.* Again, he wore only his trousers and shirt. He looked at her without speaking, his expression the stone wall it always was. And then he stepped back and let her inside.

Joss was surprised to see her. He'd begun to wonder if his memories of those two nights were dreams or hallucinations.

He closed the door and waited for her to speak.

She brought her hands from beneath her cloak. "I come bearing gifts."

Joss glanced from the crystal decanter to her face. She wasn't smiling, but hope was shining in her eyes. Hope and something he was far more familiar with: lust.

He took the bottle and went to the battered wooden table.

"Here." She took two cut crystal glasses from the pockets of her cloak.

Joss poured them both a drink while she plucked off her hat and cloak and laid them over the wooden-backed chair and then turned to him.

She was wearing a dressing gown—the white silk one he'd seen her wear that day she sent the message for Byerly—and her hair was caught up in a loose knot, as if she'd hastily put it up.

He handed her a glass.

She raised it to her face and inhaled. "Cognac." She cut him a glance from beneath her thick, unusually dark lashes. "Cognac is a—"

"I know where cognac is from and what it is." He lifted his glass, inhaled, and then took a drink, savoring it on his tongue, letting it roll slowly over the part of his palate best suited to appreciating such a delicacy.

She took a drink and studied him, her gaze no longer open, hopeful, and lustful, but shuttered. Joss felt a small, mean surge of triumph at having squashed her so quickly. After all, she'd squashed *him* utterly flat days ago and rolled over him again and again each day she'd ignored him.

"I am sorry."

He raised his eyebrows. Well, this should be interesting.

She gave him a wry smile. "I can see you're not in a conciliatory mood."

Joss gestured to the chair in the other room. "Would you like a seat?"

"Yes." She looked at the rickety wooden backed chair. "Please bring that chair. I want to sit and talk. Not to you, but *with you.*"

116

He picked up the chair, placing it across from her in his tiny sitting area before lowering himself onto it.

She chewed her lip, took a substantial drink from her glass, and began. "You must be wondering what would happen if you refused me."

It was not a question, so he didn't answer.

"I want you to know your position here is not dependent on what happens here tonight." She gave him a direct look and he realized she wanted some verbal confirmation.

"Thank you, my lady."

"Why do I feel like you don't believe me?"

"I couldn't say, my lady."

She frowned and put down her glass with a thump. "After what we did—*you* did—the last time, you should call me Alicia."

Joss took a drink before he answered, wanting to rein in the fury he felt. "Is that an order, my lady?"

She recoiled. "No, of course it isn't. I apologize if it sounded that way." She stared hard at him. "Do you want me to leave? To forget all of this and go on as if nothing has happened?"

That made him smile. "You mean the way you have been doing?"

She opened her mouth, and then shut it.

Joss nodded, even though she'd said nothing. "Yes, perhaps you see the way things are. One of us makes the decisions and the other complies. I am the one who complies, *my lady*."

"So, you are angry."

"I am." He was beyond angry. He was furious. And hurt. Stupidly, foolishly, deeply hurt.

"I've behaved. . . high-handedly."

He laughed.

Her cheeks darkened. "I'm sorry."

"Sorry for what? Banishing me to the stables?"

"I didn't—" Joss cocked his head and she stopped, her shoulders slumping with defeat. "Fine. I did banish you."

"You've done it twice."

She sighed and then nodded. "Yes, twice."

"Why?"

She hesitated, and then said, "Because I was embarrassed."

He felt as though he'd been punched in the face, but he controlled his expression, lifted his glass and sipped, savoring the cognac the way it deserved.

"I apologize for embarrassing you."

"What? No! Of course I'm not embarrassed about you."

"Oh, so you'd like to make our—" Joss searched for the correct word, but couldn't find one. "Our *whatever it is* generally known."

She glared at him. "You're being purposely obtuse."

He sipped his drink.

"I meant I was embarrassed about what happened, of course."

"And what *did* happen?"

Color invaded her pale cheeks and her chin dropped. "You want me to tell you what embarrassed me?"

Joss actually wanted to know what the hell she wanted from him.

But now that she'd brought it up, he decided that hearing her describe what he'd done—in detail—would be more amusing than arguing with her. He nodded slowly.

Her mouth twitched at the corners, until she could not hold back a smile. "I think you just want to hear me say wicked things."

Joss kept nodding and she laughed.

The sound was so unexpected, so delicious, that he wanted to savor it more thoroughly than the liquor in his glass.

She set aside her drink and stood, her hands going to the belt of her dressing gown. "I don't think I would be very good at saying wicked things." Her fingers loosened the sash and then parted the robe.

Joss, who'd been erect since opening the door, sat up straight.

She gave an elegant shrug and the silk slid to the ground, puddling around her feet like rich crème.

Her nightgown had been spun by angels—or perhaps the Devil Himself. It was gossamer thin, twin rows of lace running from her shoulders down to the hem, falling just so across the hardened tips of her breasts.

He realized she'd stilled and looked up at her face.

"I'm probably not even very good at *doing* wicked things. But perhaps . . ." She chewed her lip.

"Perhaps?" Joss prodded, his voice like the rasp of a dull saw.

"Perhaps you might tell me how to . . . please you."

A shudder rocked his body and his shaft throbbed painfully hard.

"I've been selfish," she said, her voice breathy. "Taking from you without giving."

Joss could have told her that was a bloody lie; kneeling for her the last time had been one of the best experiences of his life.

No, it hadn't been the lack of an orgasm that had left him angry and empty, but the knowledge that sexual gratification was all she'd ever want from him.

"I want to give you the same pleasure."

It was all he could do to calm his breathing enough to speak.

"Take off your nightgown."

It was her turn to shudder, her face flushing at his tone of command, just as she had the last time.

Her shaky hands moved to the high neck of her gown and began the long, sensual process of undoing the tiny buttons. Her hands weren't the only ones shaking and he put down his glass, focusing all his attention on the fantasy unfolding in front of him.

Joss leaned back in his chair, spreading his thighs to give himself a little relief. Her eyes dropped to his trouser front and her hands faltered.

Joss curled his fingers around his straining erection and stroked himself over the cloth.

A choked noise broke out of her and her hands stilled. He stopped his stroking and she looked up. He raised his brows and looked at her gown, which was not yet unbuttoned.

She resumed her journey; Joss resumed his stroking.

"Remove it," he said when her hand reached the last button.

She hesitated and again he raised his brows. "You know my rules—or have you forgotten?"

She swallowed, visibly aroused by his curt words. "I haven't forgotten."

"So?"

"I—"

"Yes?"

"I'm older than you."

Joss's hand froze. "I beg your pardon?"

"I am not a young woman."

It was the last thing he expected or imagined her saying. This woman—the physical embodiment of poetry, symphonies, masterpieces—was concerned about her age?

Joss gave a laugh of disbelief. "You are the most beautiful woman I've seen in my entire life. Ever."

Her face colored furiously, as though she'd never heard that before. Aristocratic men really were fucking idiots.

"Remove your gown and let me look at you."

She lifted the garment off with shaking hands, and then let it flutter to the floor.

"My God."

She ducked her head at his words.

"Look at me," he ordered.

Her chest was rising and falling fast, telling him of the effort it took to stand before him naked. When she met his eyes, he saw that hers had gone dark.

"You're magnificent," he said in a raspy voice, rubbing his cock painfully hard with the heel of his hand. "You want to give me pleasure?"

"Yes."

The catch in her voice made him throb. He stood. "Come here and unbutton my trousers."

She stepped forward without hesitation.

Joss had done this hundreds of times—perhaps even thousands. Never, except for the first few times when he'd been sixteen, had he been in danger of spending in his drawers.

But when her shaky hands began to unbutton him, his control began to unravel. How many times had he envisioned, fantasized, dreamed about this? And now, it was happening. And it was happening too damned fast.

His loosened trousers slid to the ground and he stepped out of them and looked from the tented fabric of his drawers to her face. She was staring with parted lips that made his cock twitch.

"Touch me."

Her eyes flickered up to his and then back down, her palm flat as she lowered it over the damp circle.

He sucked in a breath and pulled the tape, pushing the fabric away and bringing himself into view.

She made a low gurgling sound deep in her throat and his balls clenched so tight it was a miracle he didn't explode.

He held himself in a loose grip, slowly stroking his aching shaft while she watched.

Her lips parted in a way that said she knew what he wanted, and— miraculously—her flared pupils said she wanted it, too.

"I want to hear you to say it."

She looked dazed. "Say it?"

"I want to hear you say, *I want to pleasure you with my mouth, Gormley.*"

Her jaw dropped and Joss didn't think she would do it. But then . . .

"I wa—" she had to clear her throat. "I want to p-pleasure you with my mouth ... *Joss*."

"Ah, God," he groaned, shuddering. "I love hearing you say my name. Say it again."

"Joss."

"Have you done this before?" It wasn't a fair question, but the imp that drove him would not be cheated of such an opportunity to ask her questions.

Her lids lifted and she looked at him, searing him with her black gaze. "Yes."

He paused on a downward stroke, holding himself taut and proud and rigid, the thick vein that pulsed beneath the sensitive skin throbbing so hard it was making him almost light-headed. A bead of moisture formed at the small slit.

"Get down on your knees and taste me."

A shudder wracked her frame but she sank to her knees, holding his hips to steady herself and stretching out her tongue before her knees had even hit the floor.

Her eagerness caused him to utter something unspeakably vulgar as the pink tip of her tongue flicked the glistening slit.

His hips jerked and he hissed through clenched jaws. "Again."

Her next stroke was longer, harder, the pointed tip probing the sensitive opening. His hips shook.

"Take me in your mouth."

One of her hands slipped over his before he'd even finished his sentence, her fingers cool, smooth, and delicate, but strong. Unspeakable softness enveloped the sensitive crown and Joss watched in greedy wonder as his mistress took him deeper, her plump lips stretched thin to accommodate his girth.

The volume of moisture in her mouth increased as she worked him and he felt the softly ridged palate on his glans as she attempted to take him deeper.

He was lost.

—◦♥◦—

Alicia wrapped her hand around the thick base of him and took him as deeply as she could—which was still not enough for her.

She saw his eyelids flutter and close, his head drop back.

Yes, she'd done this before—too many times—but never had she *wanted* to do it. To bring him the pleasure he'd brought her.

Her body's response to kneeling and taking him in her mouth mortified her. Wetness rolled down the insides of her thighs as she sucked him, sounds that should have embarrassed her—that *had* embarrassed her in the past—filling the room.

His hips gently pulsing, his big, scarred hands lightly tracing her jaw, her temple, her tightly stretched lips.

He opened his eyes and lifted his head, as if it weighed a thousand pounds, his gaze riveted to where her lips held him captive.

"God, I love watching you take me." He pushed slowly in, deeper, until she began to fear she couldn't breathe. But before she could become frantic—as she had in the past—he pulled out and she clung to him, not wanting to let go. But he removed himself entirely, took her hand, and helped her to her feet.

When he kissed her, his tongue was rough and questing. "I can taste myself on you," he murmured in her ear when he pulled away. "I don't know what was more satisfying, the feel of your hot mouth around me, or watching my cock slide in and out of those plump lips."

She gaped up at him.

He chuckled at her shocked expression. "Go lie on the bed," he said, giving her a gentle push.

Alicia hated for him to see her broad, fleshy backside, so she backed toward the bed and watched him. His erect penis jutted out, pushing against the fine cotton of his shirt, which he grasped and drew over his head.

Good lord.

She dropped onto the bed and stared. She'd seen his naked torso before, of course, but the circumstances had hardly been conducive to enjoying the sight.

His body was *magnificent*, and not just his erect organ.

In addition to her husbands, she'd been with three other men, all from the higher social orders.

She'd picked them based on a combination of looks and other elements like availability and unmarried state. Byerly was very handsome, indeed. But his elegant, aristocratic body could not rival this man's. She couldn't pull her eyes away from that most male part of him. It wasn't as if she hadn't seen the male organ before. She had seen it too often. . . especially David's—

No.

Alicia clenched her jaws tight enough to hurt.

No. She would not allow memories of David to poison this.

Instead, she feasted on the body before her, like a ruminant turned loose in a lush, green pasture. She wished desperately that there were more than just the two smoky tallow candles.

He was a masterpiece. Muscles upon muscles—braided, roped, ridged, slabbed, every part of him defined and chiseled and *hard*.

She swallowed and looked up. He met her gaze with an impassive stare that rocked her more than the sight of his body. Did *nothing* discountenance this man? How could he stand before her, every part of him exposed, and still appear so confident and unashamed?

He came toward her and she instinctively inched back.

He stopped, a flicker of uncertainty crossing his harsh features. "Would you like to leave, my lady?"

"No," she hastened to assure him. "I want to stay—more than ever. But I want you to call me by my name. Say it—Alicia."

His mouth twisted into an oddly shy smile. "All-ee-sha."

She grinned like an idiot. "Yes, like that. That is the way people say it back home. Say it again."

He shook his head. "You first, say mine."

They laughed like a pair of nervous children.

"Joss."

"Alicia."

They spoke at the same time and couldn't seem to stop laughing. She held out a hand, "Come, it is cold."

To her surprise, he came to her. But instead of getting into the bed he lifted the covers. "Get beneath and I'll start a fire."

"Don't go."

He looked up, surprised.

So was Alicia. Her face heated at her bold behavior, but she made herself speak her mind. "I want you, right now. Come and keep me warm."

A flush spread up his neck and turned him brick red. He could stand naked, do all manner of things kneeling before her, but a simple invitation to bed made him blush. She held up the covers for him and the entire bed shifted so that she rolled toward him, laughing. Well, actually, she *giggled*.

He chuckled as well, scooting close to her as the weight of his body compressed the mattress. The bed was absolutely filled with hot male body. With Joss.

His arm slid beneath her and he rolled her on top of him with the ease of a man lifting up a doll. He pulled her tight, their bodies meeting

123

from shoulders to hips, the hard length of him pressed into her belly and telling her he might be laughing, but he was still aroused. For her.

He stroked up and down the sides of her body, the gentle friction raising the temperature beneath the blankets. She leaned up on her elbows to look at him. The light in the room was dimmer by the bed, more romantic for a woman her age.

The intimacy of being only an inch from his face should have been uncomfortable—it always had been in the past—but his eyes looked into hers openly and honestly.

"Joss."

His lips twitched into that same shy smile, making her realize just how rarely she'd seen it.

"Yes … All-ee-sha?"

She closed her eyes and laughed, opening them when she felt his hands in her hair.

"I want to see it down."

"Yes, please."

His big fingers were gentle and deft.

"It's so soft, like spun silk. I knew it would feel this way."

"You-you've thought about my hair?"

He nodded, his expression unsmiling as his fingers removed pins.

"What else have you thought about, Joss?" Her voice was hoarse, unrecognizable.

"I'll show you," he promised.

The heavy coil slid down her neck and over her shoulders.

He reached out blindly and dropped the pins in the direction of the nightstand, but some hit the floor, *pinging* off the hard wood.

"Whoops," he whispered, thrusting his fingers into the rope of hair and closing his eyes, a beatific smile on his face.

Alicia leaned down and kissed his parted lips, stroking into him, tasting cognac and Joss.

His hand moved between their bodies, to the source of her pleasure. His fingers worked magic while his hips gently pulsed, rubbing his thick shaft against her as he effortlessly drove her toward a shattering climax.

Big warm hands stroked her back and shoulders afterward, bringing her gently back to awareness.

He whispered in her ear. "I want to be inside you."

"Yes." She nodded jerkily.

He lifted and moved her to the side before sliding out of bed.

"Where are you going?"

He opened the drawer, pulled out a slim leather envelope and removed a sheath.

Alicia stared in wonder. A man who voluntarily sheathed his organ?

He wet the tube in the basin on his dresser before returning to the bed. When he touched it to his shaft, he winced.

"Cold?" she asked, although she knew the answer.

He nodded.

She reached out and took him in both hands. "Let me."

His eyes widened, but his hands fell away.

She smoothed the thin membrane over him in slow, upward strokes.

His big body shuddered and his eyelids drooped, his hips pushing toward her. "You make me want to purr."

She smiled, needing to tug firmly to make the snug tube fit his length and girth.

Once it was tied, he looked down at her. "Lie back."

She did, and he knelt between her thighs, his hand going to her sex, his nimble clever fingers working their magic. Just how did he know such things?

Their eyes locked as he drank in her pleasure. "I need you . . . Alicia."

She opened wide for him.

He entered her in a slow, endless glide.

Alicia bit her lip to keep from crying out; he was thick and long, the largest man she'd ever had inside her.

"Is that good?" he asked as he pulled almost all the way out, hesitating an agonizing moment before thrusting back in.

"Yes." The word was more of a groan.

"You like this?" he hissed in her ear. "Me filling you, stretching you, *fucking* you?"

Her entire body contracted at his filthy words.

"You don't like it," he said, pulling out. "You *love* it." He thrust into her so hard her head bumped the headboard.

Alicia didn't care.

"You're so bloody tight." He grunted and thrust deep. "I can't get far enough inside."

She tilted her pelvis and took him deeper, wrapping her legs around his taut buttocks.

He made a sound that was half laugh, half groan, doubling his thrusts, deepening them, pounding into her until both their bodies were shaking.

"I'm sorry," he grated, his hips snapping faster and harder, his body slick even in the coolness of the room. "I can't hold back much longer, love—"

A flurry of savage thrusts were followed by a guttural yell and then he froze, all except the hard pulsing part that was buried deep within her.

He shuddered violently and then his body went limp.

Alicia felt as though a wagon had collapsed on top of her. A hot, sweaty, glorious wagon. She should have felt trapped, but instead she felt sheltered.

Unfortunately, it was over all too soon.

He shook his head like a big dog waking from a deep slumber and pushed up on one elbow, his hand going to where they were joined, holding the sheath when he pulled out.

He stared at her, intent and unsmiling, swooping down to give her a hard kiss. "That was selfish; you did not come with me, but I could not wait."

Alicia   laughed   weakly.   Oh,   this   man.

Chapter Fifteen

Joss was half expecting—dreading—that she would be gone when he came out of the small box room where he kept the necessary.

But she was still there, in his bed, real—no mirage. He crouched down and lit the fire, vowing to himself that from now on he would burn one every evening just in case she came to him.

He had wet a cloth in the basin of icy water and held it in front of the fire as the initial flames grudgingly flickered to life. When he stood, it was to find her watching him, her head propped up on her hand.

He gestured to the cloth. "I've warmed it, but it's not hot."

She cocked her head, her expression uncomprehending, and Joss mentally cursed, bloody toffs.

"Lift the covers," he ordered, and then hesitated. What was he doing, still speaking to her that way?

But she lifted the covers without hesitating. He lowered himself onto the mattress carefully, so as not to jostle her. "Spread your legs for me," he said, loving the flush that crept up her long elegant neck as she complied.

He cleaned her, reveling in the intimacy of this simple action; thrilling at the way her eyes consumed him. He threw the used cloth into the basin and then slid in beside her and pulled the blankets to their chins. They lay like boards, staring at the ceiling.

"I'm so sorry you were injured helping me that night."

"It was nothing."

"Yes, it was." She hesitated. "It was irresponsible and foolish of me; I should have guessed how he would be."

Joss turned to her. "You should have guessed he would *strike* you? Attack you?"

"He was drunk, and angry, and hurt."

"Not all men strike women when they are drunk, angry, or hurt. It's not a natural or acceptable reaction."

She smiled and he noticed, for the first time, the lines around her stunning blue eyes. Eyes he'd always thought looked like hard blue diamonds. But right now, they held all the possibilities of an endless summer sky.

"You are a conundrum, Joss."

God, his name on her lips made his cock as hard as iron. "How so?"

"You're a big—huge," she amended with a smile, "powerful man and yet you're so very gentle."

He never gave much thought to his size, other than how it led others to misjudge him. A big dumb oaf, that was what he was accustomed to seeing in other people's eyes.

He reached up and skimmed the curve of her jaw with one finger, knowing he would kick himself later for not touching her more. Her eyelids fluttered, the dark brown thickets brushing her skin.

The words slipped out before he could stop them: "How could anyone ever be anything but gentle with you?"

Her lids squeezed shut and he was horrified when tears leaked out.

He propped himself onto his elbow. "Good God, my lady. I'm—I'm sorry."

But the tears kept coming faster.

She shook her head back and forth, chuckling, a watery embarrassed sound. "No," she said, her eyes opening, tears still falling. "It is I who should apologize." She grabbed his hand and lifted it to her cheek. "That felt lovely; please don't stop."

Joss could only stare.

Alicia felt like a bloody fool. But his kindness had undone her, had unlaced her control like stays that had been too tight for too long. And now she could not lace herself up again.

How could she ever have believed that she shared a background with this man? His poor background had somehow made him kind, gentle, and good while hers had made her manipulative, greedy, and suspicious.

"Have you ever thought of going to America?"

He looked as surprised as she felt at the question, his eyebrows lowering, forehead furrowed. "No, I've not considered it," he hesitated. "Which is not to say I *would not* consider it."

She saw the question in his eyes and cursed her impulsive question.

"Are you thinking of returning?" he asked.

Right now she was. She was thinking of grabbing Lizzy and this man and running as fast and far as she could. With her money their lives would be luxurious wherever they went. But such an action would make her a criminal—and she knew David would come after Lizzy. She couldn't do that to her daughter, the only person she loved.

So she said, "Not now, maybe someday."

"Do you miss it? America?"

"Sometimes I do."

His hand gently stroked her throat, her shoulders, and then settled on one breast. "Tell me something about it," he said, his big thumb caressing her nipple and making it tight and hard.

Oh, the things she could tell him.

"It's difficult to convey the sheer overwhelmingness of it. It is the opposite of Britain, in which every square inch has been struggled over, marked, owned, and known for generations.

"In America the frontier is immense and unknown. At least by Europeans. England is like—" Alicia struggled to describe the sense of weight, expectation, and restraint she felt in this country. "England is like a very old painting, darkened by age, heavy with years. America is an unfinished sketch."

He pulled her closer. "You're a poet." He was smiling at her and it made her smile in return.

"What happened to your tooth?" he asked, and then flushed. "I'm sorry, I shouldn't—"

She took his beard-roughened jaw in her hand. "We are lovers, Joss. Lovers should ask each other things." Not that she would answer *all* his questions. "Besides, it's nothing deep and dark," not like so many of her other secrets. "I was playing with other children—they were all older than me and tried to leave me behind. But I followed them. They'd built themselves a fort, the way children do, and it was in a rickety old building. I was climbing the rotting stairs when one broke." She shrugged. "I was lucky to do no more than chip a tooth."

"You grew up in the city?"

"Yes, in New York City." Flashes of two New Yorks flickered through her mind: the grim streets of her youth and the gilded mansions of her married life. Two different worlds entirely.

"You said you had no siblings. Did you have other family?"

"My Aunt Giddy raised me." She hesitated, sorely tempted to tell him the truth—to let him *know* her: Allie Benton. But then she looked into his eyes—eyes unshadowed by disgust—and knew she couldn't.

"My parents died during a typhus outbreak when I was a baby." That was the story she'd always told because it was unbearable to admit the truth: her mother had been a whore and she'd not known who her father was.

"Giddy?" His big warm hand slid up and down her side in a way that was beginning to heat the rest of her.

She leaned into his touch. "Yes, her name was Edith—she went by Edie, which I somehow changed to *Giddy*."

"Is your aunt still in New York?"

"No, she died. A long time ago."

He nodded, his lips pursed, as if he regretted asking the question. She rolled closer to him, until their bodies were pressed tight, hot hardness thrusting against her belly.

She slid her hand between them. "I'm tired of talking, Joss."

—❤—

The few days before Christmas passed quickly.

Joss had to admit this was the best job he'd ever had. Who wouldn't like getting paid to dress in fine clothing, sit in a wonderful library, and discuss literature with an intelligent and enthusiastic woman?

As planned, they read *Persuasion* once Lady Elizabeth provided them both with copies—which he assumed she must have bought. How nice must it be to afford to buy all the books you needed or wanted, and even duplicates to spare?

They read to a certain point during the days—or evenings in Joss's case—before Alicia came to him—and would discuss it the following day. By the end of the week, they'd finished it.

They were in a heated debate about Mrs. Russell's role in Anne Elliot's life when the door to the library opened.

It was Lady Selwood—he forced himself to think of her by that name, except when they were in bed. There was a maid with her—Joss grimaced, Annie, of course—bearing a tea tray.

"I thought I'd better bring some tea to put out the flames," Lady Selwood said, smiling at her daughter.

Lady Elizabeth laughed. "Oh no, were we being dreadfully loud? That would've been me, I've been abusing Mr. Gormley dreadfully, I'm afraid."

Lady Selwood's gaze rested on him for a long moment, a smile in her eyes. Annie looked from the countess to Joss in a way that was far too curious.

"That will be all, Annie."

Annie dropped a curtsey and shot Joss a venomous look before leaving.

"Will you pour, darling?" Lady Selwood was speaking to her daughter, but her eyes were on Joss, and the look in them was speculative. He returned her stare with one of his own, and she flushed and turned away.

Seeing her fully clothed and wearing a guarded expression just made thinking of her naked with his cock in her mouth even more arousing. He began to harden.

It was time to go.

He closed his copy of *Persuasion* and stood.

"Where are you going, Gormley?"

He froze, looking from the countess to the younger woman. "I thought you wished to take your tea, my lady?"

"I do. But I have also come to join your book club. At least for today."

Lady Elizabeth was even more stunned than Joss and didn't notice his reaction.

Lady Selwood's daughter was one of the topics they had not discussed over the past seven nights together, so the subject of book meetings had never been raised and he had no clue she'd been planning to attend.

Lady Elizabeth clapped her hands. "I'm so pleased."

Lady Selwood flushed and gestured for Joss to resume his seat. "I didn't want to promise anything just in case I wasn't able to finish the book. Have you been discussing it all week?"

"Yes, but we can talk about anything you like." She turned to Joss. "How do you take your tea, Mr. Gormley?"

"Black with three sugars," Lady Selwood answered, and then froze.

But Lady Elizabeth didn't notice the slip. Instead, she turned to Joss and laughed. "Oh, I see I've found your weakness, you have a sweet tooth. We can go on with our discussion while I do this." She turned to her stepmother. "Mr. Gormley insists that Mrs. Russell was no true friend to Anne. But I differ. What do you think, Mama?"

Instead of answering, Lady Selwood turned her pale, penetrating gaze on Joss.

"Oh, and why is that, Gormley?" she asked, her cool stare as distant as ever—even though Joss knew he would make her eyes spit blue fire tonight in his bed.

"Mrs. Russell does not put her friend's concerns and needs first, although she claims to," he said.

"But she *knows* Anne's circumstances and understands that she would have been unhappy married to an impoverished sailor," Lady Elizabeth answered before Lady Selwood could speak.

"That is true, but those were not Anne's only choices: marriage or no marriage," Joss pointed out.

Lady Selwood laughed. "Pray, what *are* her myriad other options? I don't think you understand a woman's choices, Gormley."

The words stung, as he believed she'd meant them to do.

He bowed his head but was far from *feeling* bowed.

"You are correct, my lady: I do not understand many things when it comes to gently born females." He cut a quick glance at Lady Elizabeth and smiled. "Or women in general."

The younger woman laughed, having teased him about his relationship with his sister earlier in the week.

Joss turned back to Lady Selwood, who was watching him with the intensity of a hawk.

"But I do know it would have cost Anne nothing—yet given her and Captain Wentworth the time both of them needed—if she'd been allowed to commit to a long engagement. The only reason to cut him entirely was Lady Russell's belief that an association with such a man would naturally lower Anne's standing in society." Joss took a sip of tea.

Lady Elizabeth clapped her hands. "Bravo, Mr. Gormley!" She looked pointedly at her stepmother, who, Joss saw, was nodding slowly, her expression as guarded as the crown jewels.

"Yes, Bravo. Tell me," she said, turning to her stepdaughter. "What did you think of Mr. Elliot, Lizzy?"

Joss slowly released the air he'd been holding, feeling like he'd just gone a round against a brutal opponent.

❤

That night, as they laid hot, slick, and sated beside one another, staring at the ceiling, Alicia brought up the afternoon.

"I enjoyed joining your book discussion today." She turned toward him. "Did you?" she asked.

His eyes were dark, the pupils and irises very close in color in the low light of the room.

"It was a spirited discussion," he said, his guarded answer dodging her question.

"You think I was too harsh—that I have a cold heart to condemn Anne and Captain Wentworth to years of loneliness."

They both knew what she really meant.

"I think it is a novel, my lady."

She flinched at his use of her title—but really, wasn't that what she wanted? To make sure he understood that she, like Lady Russell, had a healthy respect for position and convention—no matter how she might flaunt it during these nights together.

"You are condemning me for my lack of romance." She said, trying to lighten the heavy mood. It did not work. Instead of joining in with her playfulness, he turned to stare at the ceiling, giving her his harsh profile.

"I think you were right in what you said, my lady—that I don't really know what it is like for women of your class."

Chapter Sixteen

Lady Selwood had given all but a handful of servants the entire day off at Christmas, not just half of it. Apparently it was her custom to give those who stayed to work Christmas Day all of New Year's Day. Once again, it was a generous custom he'd never heard of in any other household.

He'd not seen her since the night she'd come to discuss books with him and Lady Elizabeth. So, three nights without her.

Joss told himself it was because she was busy with her daughter. That was true, but he also felt her pulling away, as if she were preparing herself for a more permanent separation.

Why that should come as any surprise to him, he didn't know.

While she'd not paid him nightly, as the women had at the White House had done, she'd come to him for the exact same reason as all his other customers: the illusion of submitting to a cruel, brutish servant.

Joss was an idiot, but then, he'd known that all along.

Carling had consulted Joss on which day he preferred off. Joss thought of his family, all crowded around at Christmas, the noise, the fratching, the constant eating, the non-stop cooking, and—coward that he was—decided to take New Year's. He would visit then and it would be far quieter, just Belle and Da, as his brothers had their wives' families to visit.

He could also see Melissa after having dinner with his family and he could spend the evening with her. It had been a while since he'd seen her and he missed her. All in all, he was looking forward to some time away.

But first there was the holiday entertaining to be endured.

The diminished staff meant Joss was pressed into a variety of duties in addition to waiting on Lady Elizabeth.

There would be only Cook—who apparently never took *any* days off—Annie, whom Joss suspected of angling to work the day to be near him, two kitchen maids, a stable lad and the groom who was just below Joss, a young lad named Byron. That meant one of them would be pressed into footman duty and Lady Selwood indicated it should be Joss. Or at least Maude indicated that on behalf of her mistress.

Once again, Maude had delivered her mistress's message to his quarters.

"How may I help you, Miss Finch." He liked to call her that even though everyone else called her Finch. She was a little thing, but scrappy and somehow dignified. She was also a good two decades older than him and deserved some respect.

She just sneered at his greeting. "You'll add yet another title to your duties tomorrow. Her Ladyship will have an evening of entertainment and she will require you to act as footman," she said, even though Joss had already heard as much. "She has hired some extra help for the kitchen and dining room, so you won't be run off your feet."

"Aye, ma'am." He would handle all the carriages, mainly because he wasn't sure Byron was up to the job, but it wasn't his place to make those decisions. He probably could have asked Lady Selwood that in bed—had she come to him lately—but they'd steadfastly avoided topics of daily life. Particularly those which centered on him being her servant.

"Take off your coats."

Joss blinked. "Excuse me?"

She scowled. "Don't worry, I've got no designs on your virtue, lad. I want to see your shoulder."

"My shoulder is fine." He rolled it, as if to demonstrate, and winced.

She gave a rude laugh. "I can see that. Don't be a nervous Nellie."

Joss sighed and began unbuttoning his coat. Her eyes flickered to his hands as they worked and then away, sweeping his small room.

"Somebody taught you to be clean and tidy."

"Aye, my ma." She'd forbidden her children to call her *ma*. It had always been *mother*.

Her gaze landed on the tiny fireplace, which was cold and dark. "You've got no fire."

Tonight was the first night he'd not lighted it; a sign that he'd given up on seeing the countess.

"Can't slip anything past your sharp eyes."

To his surprise, she laughed. A quick, rusty bark, as if she'd not laughed in a long time.

Joss laid his coat and waistcoat over the chair and began to unbutton his shirt.

"You needn't strip all the way, I've already been thrilled," she muttered. "Just pull it off your shoulder enough for me to see. And sit down."

He did so and waited as she tugged down the white muslin. She gave a few noncommittal grunts. "Raise your arm."

He did.

"How does that feel? Does the skin pull?"

"No, but the muscle is still a bit sore."

"And it will be. But I don't think the scar will limit your motion any. You can get dressed." She stepped away from his chair and headed for the door.

"Thank you," he called after her. "I know it's due to your clever needle that I'm in such fine fettle. Thank you also for mending my coat." He'd found it in his quarters the day after his bedrest. It had been almost impossible to find the tear.

She snorted and kept walking, slamming the door behind her.

Joss smiled; he thought she might actually like him.

Alicia screwed in her diamond and sapphire earbobs, absently staring at her reflection in the mirror.

She both loved and hated having Lizzy with her.

She loved it because Lizzy was the only daughter she would ever have.

But she hated it because she knew their time together would have to end—just like her time with Joss.

Joss. The name caused a confusing flood of emotions to roll through her body.

Christmas had curtailed her adventures with her far-too-interesting servant, which was just as well: Alicia needed to impose some order on the situation with Joss because it had begun to get out of hand. At least for her.

They'd spent some part of every night together for over a week and she'd begun to look forward to seeing him far too much.

It wasn't only the physical satisfaction he gave her; she found him clever, dry witted, and interesting. He was more well-read and thoughtful than anyone she could think of—male or female.

He was also kind and considerate and appreciative, making her feel like a young, hopeful woman.

Yes, Joss was truly a treasure.

He'll make some fortunate, <u>nubile</u> young woman an excellent wife, Aunt Giddy said, her tone unnecessarily malicious.

She knew that. She also knew that what she had with Joss could not last for long. It was like a rare plant that only bloomed for a short, glorious period.

He was eleven—yes, she admitted it—years younger than her and would one day want a wife and children. Two things she could never give him.

Alicia forced herself to face the pain that realization caused in her chest. Yes, it was best to distance herself now. The longer she let herself have him, the harder it would be to end things.

She fastened on her matching diamond and sapphire bracelet and examined her appearance in the mirror: she was adequate.

The dress she was wearing was a new one: a silver silk sheath with a black net overdress scattered with pearls, the array becoming more dense as it approached the hem.

Tonight, for some reason, her characteristic neutral shades left her oddly depressed. Perhaps it was the bruised skin beneath her eyes, which would not dissipate no matter how many of Maude's remedies she employed.

"The only thing for that is sleep, my lady," her dour maid had said several days ago, staring pointedly at Alicia's nightstand, where a copy of *Persuasion* lay. Only Alicia and Maude knew how long each page took to read, and how her eyes had burned and head had ached.

But Alicia had done it—joined their group, even if just that one time.

She'd told herself she was reading the blasted book to discuss it with Lizzy—to make her happy. But that was a shameful lie.

Alicia closed her eyes and then opened them again when images of her servant immediately appeared.

The situation had become ridiculous. She would wait until after New Year and then she would—

The door behind her burst open.

"I *adore* it, Mama!"

Alicia turned to find Lizzy in the doorway between their rooms, Maude standing behind her chair, grinning.

"Oh, Lizzy!" Alicia lifted a hand to her mouth: Lizzy looked just like a young woman.

Well, she *was* a young woman—not a girl—as much as her brother tried to treat her like on.

Maude had clipped Lizzy's hair shorter, a fashion that was not for everyone, but which framed her sweetly rounded face to perfection.

Lizzy ran her hands down the shell pink skirt of her dress. "I love it," she said again, flushing. "This is my favorite color."

"It is?" Alicia gave her a look of mock surprise and Lizzy laughed. "I would never have guessed. Although it *is* the color of your room here, and at The Willows, and at Selwood House."

Lizzy laughed and Alicia grinned and waved her over. "Come, I have something for you. I didn't put it in your shoe because I wanted Christmas to last all day." She opened the drawer in her dressing table and took out a wooden box with an inlaid rose on the top.

"Pretty," Lizzy breathed, stroking the design with long, sensitive fingers. She glanced up. "What is it?"

"You must open it to find out."

"Maybe I will keep it this way, to draw out the suspense, savor it. Keep it for a day when the sky is gray. A day when I am not with you."

Something hard and cold twisted in Alicia's gut.

Lizzy must have seen it because her cheerful smile was back in a flash. "But I won't." She grinned impishly and lifted the lid. Her gasp told Alicia all she needed to know.

"It's . . . it's . . ." Lizzy shook her head.

Alicia laughed and nodded at Maude, who said, "Here, my lady, let me fasten it around your neck."

The necklace was probably too old for Lizzy, even though she was almost seventeen.

It wouldn't have been an appropriate gift if Lizzy were to have a Season, but what harm could a pretty bauble do when she would only wear it around family and close friends?

Indeed, tonight was probably the most exposure Lizzy would ever have to society. It was a shame there would be so few young people.

It was also a shame that David had insisted on attending dinner.

Alicia shoved away the disturbing thought. She would not allow it to interfere with her enjoyment of the evening.

"There," Maude said.

Alicia smiled. "It's perfect. Come look."

Maude wheeled Lizzy to the mirror and Alicia stood behind her. The necklace was a mix of pink pearls and topaz. It was an unconventional pairing and the hunched old man who'd taken the commission had looked skeptical when she'd described what she wanted.

But he'd come around to her side when he delivered the necklace.

"If you do not think me impertinent, Lady Selwood, you have an artist's eye." His own eyes had gleamed with respect.

Alicia knew she had an artistic flare when it came to clothing and jewelry. That wasn't much to be proud of when you had mountains of money to indulge your fancies.

She was elated that the necklace looked just as she'd hoped, the golden-brown stones brought a richness to the pink dress, making it appear a more subtle rose shade, and the creamy pink pearls added a touch of elegance.

"It's so beautiful," Lizzy marveled, her eyes on the necklace. Alicia's eyes were on Lizzy, a girl who was her daughter for all that they shared no blood.

"Yes," she said. "You are." She blinked away the gathering moisture in her eyes and became brisk. "Now, let's get you downstairs and comfortable."

Maude left to go find Joss—*Gormley,* she mentally corrected. It would hardly do to blurt out *Joss* in the middle of some conversation.

"You look lovely, as always, Mama."

"Thank you, darling."

"That is a beautiful dress." Lizzy sounded hesitant.

"Why do I think you're holding something back?"

Lizzy's short honey blond curls bounced. "I just wish you'd wear color more."

More? Alicia *never* wore color; it was all part of her Ice Queen façade.

Lizzy glanced up at her. "I haven't hurt your feelings, have I?"

Alicia chuckled. "Why would that hurt my feelings?"

"Good," Lizzy grinned, the sunshine coming back. "You would look beautiful wearing a grain sack."

The door opened and Maude entered, followed by Gormley.

Alicia had not seen him for several days. She'd hoped that some distance might have dimmed her yearning for him, but, if anything, her desire for him burned even hotter after evenings of self-imposed denial.

She yearned to bypass dinner and run up to his room—to his arms— *right* this moment.

That was not good; not good at all.

"Merry Christmas, Mr. Gormley," Lizzy said.

"Thank you, my lady." A slight smile curved his lips, transforming his harsh features into—well, they were still harsh, there no romanticizing him, not that Alicia wanted to, of course—but his smile made him fiercely attractive.

He was doubly appealing now that she knew he possessed an intriguing brain, a subtle sense of humor, and sexual prowess of mythical proportions.

"Are you ready to go downstairs, my lady?"

"I think the better question is are *you* ready?"

Alicia shook her head at her stepdaughter, who had recently become obsessed by how plump she'd become. "Really, Lizzy." She turned to Gormley, unable to meet his eyes when she gave him orders—yet another bad development. "She is ready. Please convey her to the Red Salon and return for her chair."

He scooped up Lizzy without any visible effort, his biceps bulging against his well-tailored coat.

Alicia sighed and followed them down the stairs. When would she stop behaving like such a smitten fool?

Joss was grateful the hired servants would take care of table service. He'd never done such duty before and had no desire to start now.

Even greeting people as they came in and taking their garments with the appropriate, servility didn't come naturally to him. Fortunately, he was never long with any guest or group of guests before Lady Selwood came to the foyer, welcoming people personally.

It was worth waiting on a bunch of arrogant toffs just to watch his secret lover.

She managed to be gracious and reserved while still appearing warm. Joss barely recognized her as the hot, uninhibited lover who knelt before him and then shared precious bits of her past while lying in his bed.

Watching her interact among her own kind made him realize why they called her the Ice Queen: she was serene, beautiful, and untouchable.

Seeing her in her element also drove home just how far apart they were socially—the barrier between them forever insurmountable.

Every day Joss reminded himself to be grateful for the little time he'd had.

When she gained a bit of confidence and learned to demand what she wanted in the bedroom—and discovered that there were men of her own station who could give it to her—she'd be on her way. He'd only had even this much time with her because Byerly had behaved like a fucking fool.

Joss needed to remember his place.

He thought back to Annie, who'd been shooting him angry, yearning looks all evening. Perhaps he should reconsider the girl. She was of his class, although not as well educated.

Thanks to his mother, Joss and his siblings all spoke proper English and not the London cant, a fact that had gotten him and his brothers into endless fights as youngsters, when other children on their street accused them of being toffy-nosed.

But proper speech and large vocabulary aside, Joss was nothing more than a shopkeeper's son. And his ma, his only connection to the genteel, had run off and left him; left her five-year-old daughter, who'd barely survived a sickness that left her scarred for life.

Sometimes Joss wondered if he'd bought into his mother's foolishness more than he'd realized. After all, who was he to fantasize about bedding the rarified creature who owned this house but look down his nose at a young girl offering him the best and only thing she had: herself?

A blast of arctic air hit him and Joss realized he'd been wool-gathering. He looked up to find Byron opening the door for three people and cutting Joss a glare. Joss nodded and opened the door wider.

"Good—" Joss's lungs froze, and not with cold.

"Yes, yes," the first man muttered, not noticing Joss's truncated greeting or even bothering to glance Joss's way as he pushed into the foyer, still talking to the woman beside him.

The same woman Joss was staring at.

And she was staring at Joss, too.

"—and so Selwood and I have a late session with Kettering, Ellen," the man's tone was abrupt and hectoring. "I'm relying on you to see that I shan't be roped into any foolishness like Speculation or chicken-stakes whist."

Joss started at the name *Selwood* and he realized the third person in the party was Alicia's son-in-law. And he was looking from Joss to the woman, his eyes sharper than freshly stropped razors.

The first man—who looked vaguely familiar to Joss—paused in the act of shrugging out of his overcoat and frowned at the woman. "Ellen?" His eyes slid to what she was staring at: Joss.

Joss immediately bowed. "Your coat, sir?"

When he didn't answer, Joss risked a glance up. The man's attention was still on the woman. As was Selwood's.

She—Ellen—had come about, but was paler than a glass of milk, her eyes now swiveling around the room and looking anywhere *but* Joss.

141

"I say. You're not ill are you, Ellen?"

Ellen, who Joss knew as Mrs. Ellen Fletcher, gave the man—her husband?—a sickly smile. "No, no, Beckingdon, I merely took a chill."

Beckingdon? The name gave Joss pause. Where had he heard that name before?

Beckingdon glared at Joss, his bushy white eyebrows low over eyes that reminded Joss of a falcon, although he'd never seen a falcon this close up, of course. "It's no surprise you've taken chill given how long we had to languish out there."

Selwood chuckled and handed Joss his coat. "Gormley, isn't it? My, my, but you do serve a variety of functions in Her Ladyship's household." The words dripped innuendo and Joss's face heated.

"Eh?" Beckingdon grunted, not waiting for a response before thrusting his coat and hat at Joss. His piercing gaze flickered over Joss's shoulder and a fatuous, smile transformed his cold, aquiline features.

"Lady Selwood, you see who I've come with—your very own stepson." He went to take Alicia's hand, fawning over it.

Ellen took the opportunity to stare at Joss, who gawked right back.

Selwood stared at both of them and rocked back on his heels, his expression almost gleeful.

Alicia's eyes flickered over all the faces, hovering on Selwood, who was gazing at Joss.

It was a bloody French farce.

"Welcome, Your Grace," Lady Selwood gave a low curtsy, turned to Ellen, and dropped another. "And Your Grace, what an honor you both do me. Good evening, David. Won't you all come in?"

Your Grace? Christ! That's where he'd heard the name—at the gambling hell! The man was a bloody duke!

"Thank you, my dear." Selwood took Alicia's hand and when he bowed over it, his tongue flicked over her skin.

Joss thought his eyes would roll out of his head. *What. The. Bleeding. Fuck?*

His body clenched, preparing to launch itself on Selwood and pound him to a pulp—right after Alicia slapped his smirking face.

But the Ice Queen gave no sign that anything was untoward.

Selwood grinned at Joss. And then the bastard winked.

Rage as hot and thick as lava oozed through him and he took a step toward the other man, envisioning violent, painful things.

"It's horrid out, is it not?" Alicia's voice, unnaturally loud, jolted Joss from his fury. She gave him a quick, speaking look before turning to the others. "Perhaps you'd enjoy something to warm you before dinner?"

"Yes, yes, deuced unpleasant." Beckingdon rubbed his hands together. "A nice glass of that exquisite cognac you had last time—if you've still got any."

And then he remembered what the Earl of Selwood's behavior had forced from his mind: this man was a duke and Ellen was the Duchess of Bloody Beckingdon.

Lady Selwood turned to her. "Your Grace? Is aught amiss?" she asked the older woman.

"I'm just a bit chilled, my lady."

Joss recognized her voice, although it was stiffer and more formal than it had been when he'd last heard it—when it had been rough from throating his cock and she'd begged him to do far from genteel things to her body.

"Thank you for having us on Christmas, Lady Selwood," the duchess said, not sounding very thankful.

Joss didn't know if that was because of his presence or because she didn't like Alicia. He was sure lots of women wouldn't like her—she made every female in her orbit pale in comparison.

Lady Selwood bestowed a gracious smile on the older woman. "David will lead you in, he knows the way. I shall join you in a moment."

"Yes, please follow me," Selwood said, his eyes glinting "We'll let Alicia have a word with her servant."

"Yes, my lady?"

She glanced behind her to make sure they'd gone and then asked, "Did something happen?" Her voice was almost a whisper.

"I was lax doing my duty and the duke and duchess were made to wait for longer than they should have in the cold."

"Oh, I see." Her forehead immediately smoothed.

Joss wondered what she'd *thought* had happened.

"There are only a few more guests. You can go down to the kitchen afterward. Where it is warm." A slight flush spread across her cheeks and she turned and strode from the room before he could answer.

Joss waited until she'd gone and then slumped against the front door, his thoughts roiling.

Good God—Ellen was a duchess?

And then he recalled Selwood and what he'd done when he'd greeted Alicia and all thoughts of Ellen fled.

Just what the devil was going on between the countess and her stepson?

Chapter Seventeen

Alicia had not planned to go to him that night, but being around David made her anxious, as if she'd gotten something filthy on her skin and couldn't wash it away.

So, she'd taken a very late bath, ignored Maude's judging expression, and made her way to the mews.

It was the first time she'd encountered anyone while going to him. It was the girl, Annie, one of her maids. She'd stopped and stared at Alicia for a moment—the longest moment of her life—but obviously could not see past the veil. When Alicia passed the girl, it wasn't recognition she saw in her face, but fury.

What was she doing out here? Alicia knew there were other quarters but could not recall who lived in them.

Joss's door was closed and no light came from beneath it. She hovered; her hand poised above the wood. She'd just lowered it when the door opened and his face appeared in the gap.

He smiled and she thought she saw relief as he opened it enough to let her slip inside. He'd dressed for bed—which meant his robe, with nothing beneath it.

"I didn't think you would come," he said, taking her hat and reaching for her cloak.

His jaw sagged when she removed it.

Alicia bit back a smile. Well, it appeared the money she'd spent on her new negligee had not been squandered.

"My God," he breathed, blindly extending the cloak toward the table and dropping it onto the floor, unable to take his eyes from her.

The gown was sheer lace—a deep green that somehow made her eyes appear almost violet in the low lighting.

"Turn," he ordered, the gruff command setting off the usual pulsing sensation between her thighs.

She held out her arms and turned, the lace skirt swirling around her naked legs. She came to a stop when she faced him again.

He was shaking his head, as if confronted with something that defied belief. "Color—it's the first time I've seen you in color."

She smiled, so warm inside—so utterly happy and safe and satisfied at this moment that she hardly even recognized herself.

"I bought it for you, Joss. Merry Christmas."

His smile grew slowly, taking over his face like the most spectacular sunrise conquering dawn. He laughed and scooped her up before she knew what he was doing, taking her toward the bed, where he laid her out.

She propped herself up on her elbows and watched as he pulled the sash and shrugged out of his robe, leaving it on the floor—quite a statement of desire for a man she knew was almost pathologically neat and tidy.

And also immensely hard.

He took the hem of her gown and lifted it.

"What are you doing?" she asked, her voice breathy, her blood pounding in her ears.

He grinned. "Unwrapping my present."

Tonight she wanted to talk rather than sleep after they'd sated themselves. Joss banked the fire, which he'd lighted earlier because it was so damned cold, and slid back into bed.

He lifted her on top of his body, the only place she could be comfortable with him taking up most of the bed.

"You need a bigger bed," she said.

He raised an eyebrow, his hands stroking her sides. "You don't like your part of it?" he asked, flexing his hips beneath her.

Her lips curved at his suggestive tone and gesture and she wiggled her hips, fully aware of what she was doing to him.

"I *love* my part of the bed." She kissed his shoulder, apparently unaware of what she'd just said. And certainly unaware of the way he could have taken it.

Of course he did not.

Instead, she looked over her shoulder and then back at him. "Your feet hang off the bottom."

He nodded.

"They must get cold."

He nodded.

She smiled. "Have you gone mute?"

He nodded.

She laughed and lowered her smiling lips over his, brushing them back and forth lightly, her tongue peeking out and flicking.

Joss groaned. "You're making me hard again."

Her body stiffened at his words. Oh how she liked it when he was coarse. And of course he did what she liked.

"Tell me something about yourself, Joss."

"What would you like to know?" he asked cautiously.

"Anything."

"There is not much to tell—at least not that you do not already know."

"Won't you tell me something you've never shared with another?"

The look she gave him made him reckless.

"My mother is not dead." Her lips parted and he hurried on before he lost his nerve. "That is just what my family tells everyone. The truth is that she left when I was fifteen." Saying the words out loud made his chest tighten, made breathing difficult. "She left my father, my sister—me."

"Oh, Joss." She leaned down and kissed him. "I'm sorry. I didn't mean to—"

"You didn't make me say anything I didn't want to." He smoothed her hair off her brow, momentarily distracted by several long strands of white among the blond. "Before she left us she managed to fill my head with rubbish—dreams of going to school and becoming a teacher. She did the same to my brother Gordon, who suffered the humiliation of being a charity boy to earn a place as an overworked and undercompensated bank clerk." His mouth flexed into a frown. "All my life she led me to believe she'd done my father some manner of favor by stooping to marry him. In truth it was my shy, quiet father who rescued her. She'd been a governess in the home of the same banker who'd employed her father. When she became pregnant, he turned her off. She told my father that her employer had forced himself on her."

"I'm so sorry," she murmured.

"It turned out that wasn't true. Gordon learned, much later, that the child was actually a footman's—a man who worked in the same house and refused to marry her."

Joss shrugged. "So, that was our oldest brother's father: not the master of the house, but his servant." Joss didn't tell her how furious he'd been when he'd learned the truth. Not because his mother had slept with a servant rather than the master, but because she had *lied* to them. All those years pretending she was somehow better than the situation she'd ended up in and the people she ended up living *with*. As if even her own children were beneath her.

He met her concerned gaze. "When I was fifteen and Belle only five, I woke up to find that she'd run off with the man who sharpened my father's knives." He snorted. "What kind of woman leaves a child who is little more than a baby?"

Alicia laid her head down on his shoulder and he slid both arms around her, burying his nose in her hair.

"Everything changed then. I went to work in the shop. Gordon was already in school and even with the scholarship my father couldn't afford to pay for two of us. And of course, Michael had married and the shop now needed to support two families." He shrugged. "It was a hard life and I never blamed her for wanting something easier—I just blamed her for making us all ashamed of who we were."

"What made you decide to be a groom?" she asked, breaking the silence.

"Da's younger brother had been in service to Lord Easton since he was a boy and he offered me a position as stable hand. I'd always liked horses and I've got a strong back. It was a good fit."

"I've not seen you ride," she murmured, tracing the scar on his chin with a soft finger. "I imagine you are an excellent horseman."

His harsh face flushed slightly. "I haven't ridden since leaving Lord Easton's. He had a big stable and I exercised his hacks most days."

"Do you miss it?"

"I still get to groom and care for them." He cut her a smile. "Besides, I'd look rather silly hacking your mounts."

She grinned, clearly amused by the thought of him on one of her dainty mares. She kissed him and sat up, naked and majestic as she straddled his body. "You might not be able to ride, but I can." Her hand settled on his erection and gave it a squeeze.

Joss laughed, unable to recall a Christmas when he had been happier.

Alicia was trapped by something invisible but utterly unshakeable. She knew there was something bad coming, she needed to run, but all her effort produced not even the smallest twitch.

"There you are, I've been looking all over for you, darling."

She tried to open her mouth, to scream, but only the tiniest whimper escaped, and that was suffocated by the sound of David's sickening, evil laughter.

His hands slid around her, more powerful than metal bands. "Why aren't you fighting me?" He murmured in her ear, his horrible fingers stroking her. "You know how much I like it when you fight me, don't you? Alicia? You know how much you love the things we do together, the things I do—"

Alicia screamed.

"Alicia? *Alicia*! *My lady*!"

Strong arms cradled her and a big hand caressed her back. "Shhhh, sweetheart. Shhhh, you're having a nightmare. You're here, with me. It's Joss."

Alicia stopped struggled and opened her eyes to a pitch-black room.

"Joss!" She pulled her arms out from where they were trapped between their bodies and wrapped them around his huge torso, squeezing until she couldn't breathe.

His body shook as a soft chuckle escaped. "It's al lright. It was just a dream." All the while his hand stroked her.

She closed her eyes. No, it was not a dream, it was a nightmare.

"What were you dreaming about?" He hesitated. "Or don't you wish to speak of it?"

She squeezed him tighter, gutted yet again by his sweetness. "I don't remember," she lied. "I was just running, trying to get away from— something, but I couldn't move."

She felt him nod. "Aye, I've had those. You're paralyzed."

"Yes, yes," she whispered, his stroking calming her, but also arousing her. She kissed his chest, his shoulder, her sex thumping wildly when he groaned with pleasure.

He liked his nipples sucked and nipped. She knew that now. She knew all manner of things about his magnificent body, and he knew even more about hers. She found the small pucker of flesh in the darkness and sucked it into her mouth.

"Ahhh, God. You know what that does to me." She smiled against him and he squeezed her tight. "You're a witch." He pushed a hand between them and she lifted her thigh so he could reach her core. "*Fuck.* You're drenched for me."

Her stomach, womb, and sex clenched at his vulgar declaration. He shook his head, his finger circling, his cock stiff against her thigh. "You're perfection," he muttered into her hair. "I want you again."

She bit his nipple. Hard.

He jolted and moved faster than should have been possible for a man his size, flipping her, until she was facedown, his knees bracketing her thighs.

He stroked his hardness between her cheeks and up her spine, his breathing heavy. "Have you ever seen a stallion mount a mare?" he asked, his hot breath on her ear one moment and his hot, wet mouth on her shoulder the next, his teeth sinking into the fleshy part of her shoulder.

She cried out as he bit her, his erection thrusting against the thin skin of her back.

"Have you?" he rasped, thrusting again, the slickness on her skin telling her how ready he was.

"Yes, Joss. Please."

"You want it hard? Rough? *Deep?*"

"*Please* . . . I—" she faltered and he froze.

"You *what?*" The words were low and menacing and pregnant with dark promise. He slid one huge hand beneath her throat and lifted her, arching her back until he held her in a position that left the front of her body exposed. "Tell me."

"I've imagined you taking me like this."

He released her in a flash. His knees shoved hers wide and he took her hips with both hands and jerked her up.

"Shoulders and head down on the bed," he ordered, "but this," he shoved a finger deep into her sex, the sudden penetration making her moan. "*This* I want up here, wet and tight for me." She clenched around him and he grunted. "So eager," he whispered, a second finger joining the first.

He worked her in deep, languid thrusts with one hand while his other stroked her crease, moving back and back until—

"I want to take you here." He ceased his thrusting and thumbed her back entrance.

Every muscle in Alicia's body tightened at the shocking words and sensation.

Joss laughed and pulled away, giving her buttocks a sharp slap. "Perhaps next time I'll take you that way, Alicia. But for now—"

He positioned himself at her entrance and slid into her with a brutal thrust that made them both gasp with pleasure.

—❤—

God how Joss wished the light was blazing so he could see every part of her in this deliciously submissive position.

He shook with desire, but made himself slow down, the gradual possession of her beyond intoxicating, inch by inch.

"Joss." She shuddered and pushed back against him and he almost came apart. Instead, he dropped over her, his belly on the gentle curve of her spine, his chest on her back and shoulders, holding himself inside her.

"How do I feel," he asked, because he wanted to know and also because he knew she loved hearing him talk, hearing him describe the things he would do to her, the things he wanted her to do to him.

"I'm so full of you—I don't feel like I could take any more. But I would, I would do anything for you," she added in a whisper.

Joss growled and began to move, stroking slowly—seating himself with each thrust, feeling her squeeze and caress every inch of him.

Which is when he realized that he'd come into her unsheathed. He froze.

She wiggled beneath him. "Joss?"

"I am not wearing a sheath."

She hesitated and then said, "I have no diseases."

He kissed her shoulder. "Neither do I."

She pressed her hips up against him and flexed her internal muscles, making him gasp. "I want you."

He hissed in a loud breath. "But. . ."

"I cannot have children."

She must have felt the hesitation in him at this disclosure—the most personal they had yet to share.

"I want to feel you spend inside me."

Her words erased all rational thought. Joss drove himself home, again and again, his hand finding the center of her pleasure and working a climax from her slick, tight body as he came, dissolving into pure sensation.

When he woke from his daze a few minutes later he was lying on top of her, his cock still buried inside her. He groaned and began to lift himself off.

"No, don't go."

"But I'm crushing you."

"I like it. Stay on me. In me."

He lowered himself onto her, keeping the bulk of his weight on his elbows.

"I want to tell you something."

"Yes?" he asked cautiously.

"I'm thirty-nine."

Which made her eleven or so years older than him. Joss smiled. So, that was why she was so concerned about her age. He stroked her hair and kissed her neck but had no idea what he should say. She was bloody gorgeous—perfect, in fact. What did he care how old she was?

"I—I just thought you should know. I am almost forty and I cannot have children." She hesitated. "I didn't mind so much with Selwood, but I loved my first husband—Horace—and I so wanted to give Horace a child." She shrugged. "I have no family left, except Elizabeth."

Joss traced a pattern on her shoulder, wondering why she had confided such things to him.

As if he'd spoken out loud, she said, "Only Maude knows this about me. I know it is unconventional, but I'm very close to her. We've been together a long, long time." She sighed. "As sad as it might be, Maude is my closest friend."

"I like her. She is a doughty one, but with a kind heart."

"Yes, you've summed her up perfectly."

"Why did you come to England?"

An odd expression flickered across her face, which he could only see in profile. "I came to England to be punished."

Joss cocked his head.

She shook her head. "No, it's your turn."

"My turn?"

"Yes, tell me something about you?"

"I've already told you all there is to know," he lied.

"Tell me more about your family."

Joss frowned. "My family?"

"Don't use those tricks with me?"

He grinned. "Tricks?"

Alicia shifted beneath him and he rolled off her onto his back, pulling his tumescent cock from her body with regret.

She muttered something beneath her breath and then straddled him, leaning low and capturing the nipple she'd been tormenting earlier. She sucked hard.

Joss gave a helpless laugh. "Ah! All right, all right! I'm sorry."

She looked up; her expression triumphant. "You admit that you use tricks with me?"

He hesitated and she leaned forward, mouth open.

"Yes!" he gasped, pressing himself back into the mattress, as if he could escape. "Yes, I was being evasive."

She grazed the skin below his nipple with her teeth, the harsh friction making him throb. He wanted her. Again.

"I'm sorry I kept you away from your family today."

"You needn't be, I was happy to take off New Year's instead."

"How will you celebrate an entire free day to yourself?"

"With my family."

"They will all gather?"

"No, for New Year's it will just be Belle, me, and my Da, although he might not even notice."

Her smile drained away. "I'm sorry—I didn't know about your father—is he very ill?"

"He's not well. He fell down about a year ago and when he woke up, he was mostly paralyzed. He can move and talk a little now, but he's not really quite there."

"Then I'm doubly sorry you missed being with your family today. I should have given you both days off."

Joss picked up one of her hands and kissed her fingertips, one by one, and then swiftly rolled her over, the action making her laugh.

"It doesn't matter about Christmas, my lady. I'd rather spend New Year's Eve with just Belle," he hesitated. "She is ... well, she has rather a lonely life."

She stared up at him as he rested on his elbows. "Because she nurses your father?"

"That, but also because she had the smallpox when she was five."

Alicia winced. "She was not vaccinated?"

"We all were. It seems there were a significant number of people who developed the disease regardless. It was less severe, but it left her scarred."

"Oh, Joss. Is it—is she—well, is the scarring very bad?"

"To me it does not seem to diminish her beauty, but many young men cannot seem to look beyond a few pockmarks. It is unfortunate that Belle and I both look like my father." He smiled. "A huge frame, big nose, and harsh features are bad enough on a man. But on a woman?"

"You poor, poor man." She made a theatrical moue of pity and placed both hands flat against his chest, exerting pressure.

Joss grinned. "Are you trying to push me over? *Again?*"

"Humor me."

He chuckled and rolled onto his back, their activities causing the bed frame to creak alarmingly.

She climbed on top of him, her knees bracketing his hips, her hot slickness on his erection. He reached out to take her hips and lift her but she shook her head. "Give me your hands."

Joss complied and she raised up on her knees, having to squirm and wiggle in a very enticing way to line him up with the entrance to her body. And then she sat down on him, hard.

Joss moaned.

She leaned forward, still holding his hands, and dropped a devastating piece of feminine artillery, "I will miss you terribly when you are away on New Year's Eve, Joss."

And what about all the nights after? He wanted to ask.

But,   of   course,   he   did   not.

Chapter Eighteen

"*Alicia:*

I want to speak to you on a matter of some importance. You will come to Selwood House for dinner tomorrow night. Do not bring either Lizzy and her savage looking body servant with you.

I will brook no excuses.
David"

Alicia's blood boiled as she re-read the brief missive.

She'd just come back from the mews—only to find this letter waiting on the salver in her sitting room. Which meant David had sent it sometime during the night. Had anyone knocked on her door to deliver it? Had David's man waited for a return message?

The temptation to run back and seek comfort in the small room over the stable was powerful, and that impulse frightened her.

Alicia closed her eyes; since when had she started to expect Joss to rescue her?

"My lady?"

She opened her eyes to find Maude staring at her, her serious gray eyes flickering from her face to the letter. "What is it?"

Alicia handed her the letter and began to pace.

"What do you think he wants?" Maude asked.

"God only knows."

"At least he hasn't told you to bring Miss Lizzy back."

That's exactly what Alicia had been thinking.

"What will you do?"

Alicia gave a choked laugh. "What *can* I do?"

❤

Joss was disappointed he did not see her again before his day off. But she'd been spending a good deal of time with her daughter, and he could not begrudge her that.

He headed over to his Da's bright and early on New Year's Eve. It was cold and clear and he walked, rather than waste money on a hackney.

The last weeks had been like a dream. A wet, hot, wonderful dream.

Joss realized he was grinning like an idiot because his teeth were cold. He cupped his hands around his mouth, breathing hot gouts of steam; the puffs of breath were white, fluffy clouds in the frigid morning air.

He needed to stop re-living their time together or he would walk directly under the wheels of a mail coach.

Instead, he thought back to Christmas dinner and the duchess and what—if anything—he should tell Melissa when he saw her later that night.

Joss had tried not to think about the duchess, which should have been easy. After all, he'd not seen her for years, it wasn't as if his memories were fresh.

Even so, she took up a certain amount of space in his thoughts.

She had aged well in the almost seven years since he'd last seen her. She must have been in her late fifties when he'd known her.

Her striking dark hair with its streak of silver was the same, although with more silver strands among the black, and the lines were deeper around her eyes and mouth—of course that could have been because of the shock of the moment—but she was still a very attractive woman.

Joss had always found older women more sexually arousing. His first lover, if you could call her that, since they'd only had sexual congress once—well, perhaps one and a half times was more accurate—had been Mrs. Lyons, the baker's widow.

Joss had been sixteen and she must have been somewhere around forty. He'd been helping out around the bakery, doing heavy lifting for her since her husband had been dead a few months and she had six daughters and no sons to help her. His father had felt bad for the woman and had offered up Joss's back.

Joss hadn't minded, she was kind to him in her brusque way and did her best to stuff him with pastries and bread. She'd also done a fine job of getting into his breeches.

He'd been carrying sacks of flour, the day a hot breezeless one that made a person forget London ever saw a snowflake.

The shop was closed and she'd come into the storeroom. He could still remember it. She'd not said a word, just pushed him back on a pile of flour sacks, yanked open his breeches, pulled out his rod, and lifted her dress. He'd been hard the way a young boy was hard: constantly, quickly, for no reason, for any reason.

He'd also been quick. Embarrassingly so.

Mrs. Lyons had been kind; she'd not mocked him or laughed at him. Instead, she'd taken his hand and brought it under her skirt, grinding against it until she shuddered and cried out.

By that point, Joss had been hard again and very interested in what she had beneath her skirt. She'd been of a forgiving nature and had used him again. Joss had redeemed himself that second time.

He shook his head; he'd not thought of her in years. One of her daughters ran the bakery with her husband now. Mrs. Lyons had gone to live with some relative out in the country.

Joss shoved his hands deeper into his pockets as he strode through early morning London. He'd walked today because he needed the cold and exercise to clear his muddled head. It was bloody freezing and he already wished he'd worn his gloves, but they were for work, and he made it a habit to only use work garments for work.

He shivered and rubbed his hands together. His mind, yet again, drifting back to Christmas dinner. That whole evening had been one long experiment in confusion.

Joss's duties that night had been few once all the guests sat down to dinner. After the meal was over, most of them stayed to play games or do whatever it was the Duke of Beckingdon had warned his wife he *didn't* want to do. As a result, the duke was the first to leave.

Lady Selwood had come with him to the door, the two speaking in low, intimate voices.

Joss had forced himself to ignore the rumbles of jealousy that had thrummed through his body as he'd wondered if the distinguished-looking older man had ever fucked his employer.

Instead of beating an answer out of the man— as he'd wanted—Joss had been ready with the duke's coat, hat, and carriage before anyone needed to ask for them.

His Grace had seemed loath to go once he had the beautiful countess alone. Alone but for Joss, who counted no more than a hat rack or boot scraper.

Beckingdon had laughed, flattered, flirted, and generally made an arse of himself while Joss ground his teeth and held his garments at the ready.

Finally, the duke was hatted, gloved, and cloaked. He took Lady Selwood's hand, promised to have Ellen invite her out to some nob house party at whatever godawful pile of bricks he called his country home, and kissed her hand. Repeatedly.

By the time he left, it was all Joss could do not to kick him down the steps.

Joss had been in the foyer for most of that night. Part of him wondered what the duchess was thinking. Part of him wondered if she would seek him out. Part of him wondered if he should leave now and start running, without stopping to pack.

Just what would a duke do if he learned his wife had fucked a groom?

He was a bloody duke; he could do whatever he wanted to an insignificant speck like Joss and nobody would lift a finger to stop him.

As it turned out, the duchess left several hours later with a small group of people, not looking at him even once when he helped her into her cloak.

Afterward, Joss had gone up to his freezing cold room and said a long, heartfelt prayer of thanks that the duchess had decided to spare him, to ignore him.

Perhaps she'd even told herself she'd been mistaken. He could imagine her thoughts as the evening progressed and even imagine her conclusion: how likely was that *other* man—a *whore*—and Lady Selwood's servant likely to be one and the same? No, it was an impossibility.

Joss sighed, the warm air he expelled as thick as a summer cloud in the cold morning air.

He'd been lucky this time. But what about the future? What if the next woman who recognized him was not so circumspect?

Christ. What if the next time the woman was some close acquaintance of Alicia's? Did women talk about such things? He knew they must or Melissa's clientele would not continue to grow the way it did.

He tried to imagine Alicia's response to the information that she was bedding a whore and shuddered: he should have told her, but he was a bloody coward.

Maybe Mel would have some idea as to what he should do. Not that his options were myriad. He could hardly call on a duchess and ask her to keep their past bed sport a secret.

His mind wandered back to the last evening he'd spent with Alicia, his cock stirring just thinking about it.

They'd seemed to cross some boundary—becoming not just bedmates, but lovers. They'd talked for hours. And their lovemaking had been more passionate and less inhibited than ever.

She had not wanted to go back to sheaths after that first time and he couldn't deny her, even though he knew it was foolish, no matter that she claimed to be barren.

Of course, thinking about how she'd felt around his naked cock made him instantly hard.

You're such a pitiful, romantic idiot. It was Mel's voice in his head. She'd told him the same thing more than once before.

Joss grimaced; Lord, Mel would carve him up into small pieces if he told her any of this. He laughed weakly at the thought; what a bloody mess.

—❤—

"Ring for another bath."

Maude went to summon a fresh bath and returned with a fresh towel. Alicia stepped from the tub, her skin red and raw. It didn't seem to matter how much she scrubbed; she could not feel clean.

Maude had not spoken a word since Alicia returned from David's house hours earlier. She had rung for baths and handed her fresh towels to dry herself between each of the three baths she had already had.

It was after two in the morning. Alicia knew she was being an arrogant aristocrat and running her servants ragged, servants who needed sleep, but she could not help it. She wanted to scrub the skin from her body. She would like to burn it off, along with the entire horrifying evening.

David had made her wait all the way through dinner, baiting her, teasing and toying with her, like a cat with a mouse that was barely moving.

It was not until after, when they were in his study, that he'd divulged the true reason for the evening.

"Good God, Alicia! How could you be so insensible to have hired a man who was a whore in an honest-to-God whorehouse—for *women* of all disgusting things." He'd appeared genuinely revolted "And probably men, too."

Even now, hours later, the words rang in her ears.

"Not only did you hire him, but as a servant for my young *sister*?" His face had been a mask of outrage. "You paid a man who sold himself for money to *touch* my sister."

Alicia had been just as horrified as David, albeit for different reasons.

Joss had *worked* at The White House? And he still went there—for what? To do what?

Alicia had struggled to absorb the shock, but David hadn't been finished.

His eyes had glinted with anticipation as he'd delivered the killing stroke. "It is bad enough he was even *near* Elizabeth. But then there are the *other* services you have used him for."

"What are you talking about?" she'd demanded weakly.

"Let us not pretend we don't both know what has been going on in that seedy little love nest in your mews."

The blood had drained from her head so fast she'd become dizzy. "How," she whispered.

He ignored her question. "You will discharge him. Do you understand me? If you do not get rid of him *immediately* I will find some reason to have him thrown into the deepest cell in Newgate. You know I have the authority—nobody would even question me." Anger, lust, brutality, and a dozen other unsavory emotions flickered across his face.

"H-how do you know this?" she asked again.

He smirked. "Never you mind about that, darling." He was on the big leather settee, his arm draped lazily along the back, his expression beginning to soften now that he'd obliterated all her defenses.

Beamish had knocked on the library door. "Do you require anything further, my lord?"

David had flicked a look at her. "Would you care for tea, my dear?"

"No," she croaked.

"You may take yourself off to bed, Beamish. Lady Selwood and I are family, we do not stand on ceremony and will not need anyone."

Alicia had ignored the butler's glance, which, coming from Beamish, was the equivalent of a full-blown gawk.

She knew the servants had suspected *something* went on between her and David. But it had never occurred to her that they might put such an incorrect interpretation on it: namely, that she *liked* or *encouraged* his attentions.

Beamish had left and David looked at her heated face, grinning.

"I believe Beamish might be a randy old goat beneath that rather stiff façade. What do you think, Alicia?"

"If I discharge him you will let her stay?" She'd despised the pleading, groveling note in her voice.

His mouth curled up at the corners. "It would be a good way to *begin* convincing me that I have not made a dreadful mistake trusting you." He placed his foot on the floor and shifted his hips, making sure she could see the arousal that strained against his skin-tight pantaloons. "Of course, there are more immediate—and pleasurable—things you could do to reassure me."

Bile had flooded her mouth, threatening to choke her.

Afterward, she wished it had; she wished that she'd choked to death and died in his bloody library. She wished she'd done *anything* other than what she ended up doing.

"My lady. *My lady.*"

Alicia looked up from the nightmare in her mind to find Maude staring.

"You must stop. Look," she took the towel Alicia was using and showed it to her. There was blood. Alicia looked down at her arm. Yes, she had taken off the skin. Tiny pinpricks of blood grew as she stared.

"Please. No more baths. Let me see to your poor face."

Ah, her face. Alicia had forgotten about that. It had been a long time since she'd needed Maude's extensive skills with cosmetics.

Maude's gentle fingers skimmed over the swelling on her cheekbone and Alicia winced.

"I'm sorry, my lady."

Alicia wasn't. She wanted the pain. She *deserved* everything David had done to her tonight and more. She deserved to be punished for what she'd done.

But, most of all, she deserved to be punished for what she was about to do.

❤

Everything changed after New Year's Day.

One day, Joss was in heaven, the next, somewhere worse than hell. One day he was her lover; the next day he didn't even exist for her.

Not only were the days miserable, but the hours seemed to pass with unnatural slowness, as if to give him the opportunity to enjoy his misery to the fullest.

Whether it was due to the bitter cold or her daughter's presence, her ladyship had hardly gone out the past week, staying in and choosing to have friends over. The daily book discussions had continued, but without Joss.

Whenever she required somebody to take messages or accompany her and her daughter, she'd used one of the footmen, making it patently clear she had no use for Joss.

And her nighttime visits had ceased as abruptly as they'd begun.

He didn't just miss *her*, he missed Lady Elizabeth. He missed the girl more than he'd thought. Those discussions had been mentally stimulating and invigorating and he'd looked forward to them.

He understood that things had to end, but why was Alicia behaving this way?

Ha! Alicia. It was back to Lady Selwood for him. And probably not even that for long, either.

Whatever was afoot, Joss expected to get the sack any moment. Getting sacked would have been far better than a slow and painful death by a thousand cuts.

A death that began when he presented himself to Feehan the day after New Year's Eve, dressed to carry Lady Elizabeth and discuss their current book.

He'd found Feehan supervising two maids—one of whom was Annie, who'd made no secret of the fact that she was miffed he was sitting in the library and taking tea with the daughter of the house.

"Just like one of the family, you are," she'd mocked one evening in the servants' hall. "Surprised you aren't sittin' upstairs with *them* for dinner." Her words had earned a few muffled snickers up and down the table.

"What's that, you say?" Feehan demanded from the head of the table, too far away to hear her.

"I said I do love mushy peas, Mr. Feehan." Her cheeky smile earned even more laughter.

Every day just brought more of the same abuse.

"Ah, Gormley," Feehan had said the morning after his day away. "You will report to Mr. Carling for the foreseeable future."

Annie snorted, not bothering to hide it.

Feehan frowned at her. "I do hope you have not taken ill, Annie," Feehan said before turning back to Joss and frowning.

"Er, what was that, Gormley?"

"Shall I report to Carling for the remainder of the day, sir?"

"Miss Finch indicated you would not be needed the rest of this week. She will fetch you if that changes."

He'd felt rejected, but he'd believed she would explain everything when she came to him that night. But she didn't come to him.

Not that night, or the next, or the night after that.

So, it seemed Joss was to be relegated to the stables.

He reminded himself—often—that his official job title was that of groom. But the reminder did no good and he felt like a man who'd been cast from paradise.

The first few days he was so bloody wound up it was a miracle he hadn't accidentally been kicked half to death by her ladyship's frisky new hack—an enormous gelding that had been delivered two days after the New Year.

"Lord almighty, Gormley!" Carling had yelled when he found Joss standing only inches behind the skittish animal, staring blindly into space.

Joss had apologized profusely, deeply ashamed at his behavior.

"Alright, alright—that's enough," Carling had said, half-scowling, half-laughing. "Just keep yer mind off whoever she is while you're here with me." He'd gestured to the huge dappled gray horse. "You'd better take this brute out and exercise him. He's too much for wee Byron to handle and I've got my hands full." He'd scratched his curly gray head, his wrinkled face creased. "Lord knows what the devil she bought *him* for." He'd shaken his head and muttered. "Americans!"

That was the first time Joss had really looked at the big gray and understood who the horse was for.

The realization had flooded him with hope as he'd recalled the pillow talk they'd had before his life had turned to shite. She'd bought a horse for him to hack, just because he'd said he missed it?

That knowledge had kept him hoping for those first days. He'd ridden the magnificent horse every morning in the park, foolishly believing that she would join him.

By the time Sunday came around, there'd been no sign or word from her.

He'd been so distracted that he'd only stayed a few hours with his family on his half-day, cutting his visit short so he could go and see Mel—something that always cheered him up.

But not his time.

In fact, he'd left The White House far more agitated than when he'd arrived.

Melissa had looked worn to a nub, nothing like her usual, vibrant self.

The change in the beautiful young madam's appearance from the last time they'd seen each other—a mere week earlier—had been shocking.

She'd seen Joss's worried expression and had given him a jaunty smile. Or she'd tried to.

"It's just this cold weather wearing on me. Don't you remember how it was with me when I was a nipper—how much I hated winter?"

Yes, he remembered. Melissa Griffin—who'd had a different name back then—had lived only a few buildings down from Joss's father's shop.

She'd been so pretty with her dark auburn hair and green eyes that Joss had been sweet on her, teasing her mercilessly even though she'd been a few years older than him.

Everyone knew her mother struggled to support them both by taking in washing. But, with the self-absorption of youth, Joss hadn't realized things were rough—that Melissa had become thinner and played less often—until one day he'd come home from the day school where their mother insisted on sending them, and discovered that Mel was gone.

Not long afterward his own Ma ran off, and he'd faced more pressing problems than the disappearance of a neighbor girl.

It wasn't until years later that he learned what happened to her.

Joss had been working at his father's shop when Mel came to see him. He'd been up front rather than in back—which is where he usually spent his days—while his Da recuperated from a foot butcher who'd cut off his bunions with less finesse than his father used to trim a roast.

Joss hadn't recognized Melissa at first, mistaking her for a rich toff with her glossy, well-fed appearance and expensive clothes.

From that day forward she'd enticed, seduced, and ensorcelled him, not that he'd offered up any resistance. On the contrary, he fell for her like a bird shot from the sky.

She'd told him upfront that she worked in a brothel.

Joss—the romantic, idealistic, and deeply infatuated fool that he'd been—developed grand visions of marrying her and taking her away from the ugliness of her past.

He'd behaved like a mooncalf, believing he was courting her when, all along, it had been Melissa courting him.

"You want me to work in a whorehouse for *women*?" He must have repeated that six times the day she brought up the subject.

After she'd finally convinced him that she wasn't jesting, Joss had become stuck in a second rut.

"I'm too bloody ugly, Melissa!"

"You've got something, Joss. And Mrs. Hensleigh agrees."

Venetia Hensleigh was the owner of The White House, but was planning her retirement from the business.

"You're not handsome, that's for sure. It's something about you." Mel had grinned. "I think it's the fact that you like women—*really* like them, want to see them happy, to give them pleasure." She'd given him a smile so *incendiary* it had almost set his hair on fire. "I've imagined being with you on more than one occasion."

Back then he'd still been innocent enough to blush.

164

"But—" he began, his thoughts too confused to speak.

"Yes?" she prodded.

They'd been at The White House when she'd told him, in her spacious quarters. In addition to having his nerves jangled by her proposal, he'd also been jangled by *her*.

She'd greeted him wearing a lace negligee that showed him exactly what he'd spent weeks imagining.

"Wouldn't it bother you knowing I was with other women?" he'd finally managed to spit out.

"It's just a service—no different than any other service the people of our class offer, Joss. It just pays better. Please tell me you're not planning to entertain ridiculous, childish emotions like jealousy?"

Well. What could his seventeen-year-old self say to *that*?

If she could conduct their relationship with such sophistication, why couldn't he?

It hadn't been until after he'd accepted her offer and entered the rarified confines of The White House that he'd understood that she wasn't going to be his lover at all; she was going to be his teacher.

"I do love you, Joss, you were one of the few bright spots in my life back then. I'll never forget you protecting me and bringing me food. But the truth is, I prefer women, Joss."

He'd goggled.

She'd laughed. "Come now, you're a man grown, certainly that doesn't surprise you?"

He was too ashamed to tell her that while he'd known about men liking men, the fact that some women liked women, *had* surprised him.

Joss shook his head as he recalled his naïve younger self. It had taken time, but he'd eventually gotten over his boyish infatuation and he and Melissa had become close friends—even after he'd quit working for her.

Still, as close as they were, he couldn't bring himself to tell her about his affair with Alicia. He *knew* she would see past his words to what he was hiding: that he'd fallen deeply, hopelessly in love.

He *did* tell her about Annie on his last visit.

"Don't you know better than to tangle with a young girl, Joss?" She'd looked disgusted.

Joss hadn't pointed out that Annie was not much younger than him. Although in experience, he was centuries older.

"I know, I know. If I could go back—" He'd shrugged. "But there's no use wishing for that. Besides, I'm not sure she'd have taken *no* for an answer." Joss thought of the hateful glares she'd shot his way. "She's a woman scorned, Mel, and I can't help feeling that she's plotting something against me."

That had made her snort, which had kicked off a bout of coughing.

"Serves you right, you shrew," he'd mocked. But Joss had not liked either the look or sound of her coughing. Not that she'd pay any attention to anything he said. But when she'd needed, a few minutes later, to run behind her screen and cast up her accounts he'd been unable to hold his words back any longer.

"You need a doctor, Mel."

"I'll not quack myself, Joss. So save your breath to cool your porridge," she'd warned.

Not that she had stinted any of *her* breath—no she would not be deterred from a path once she'd started down it. "And don't try to change the subject. A girl like Annie has *one* thing in mind, and its nothing more nefarious than marriage."

He'd laughed. "Listen to you with the big words."

She'd pursed her lips, but he could see she was pleased. She'd not gone to school when they'd been young—her mother putting her out to sell fruit or other trifles when she was barely eight, but now that she was well-off, she paid a tutor and could read.

"*Anyhow*," she'd continued. "Just stay away from that girl." Her eyes had gone shrewd then. "Now, why don't you tell me what's really bothering you?"

But Joss had stood firm against her prying.

The last thing he'd wanted to do was admit the mortifying truth: that he'd fallen in love with the woman who employed him.

Chapter Nineteen

As usual, Joss was reading when the knock came.

He glanced at his watch and saw what he already knew: it was well past midnight. He'd given up on her coming and had stopped dressing in the fancy clothing she'd bought for her and waiting.

Instead, he did what a real groom would do and stripped from his work clothing, taken a chilly sponge bath, and slipped on the fancy banyan Belle had sewn him for Christmas and the slippers his sister-in-law Susan had made for him, feeling quite like a king.

He stared unseeingly at the book in his hand. This had to be Annie, who'd left him alone since leaving here three nights ago, crying. He considered pretending to be asleep when there was another knock, sharper this time.

He sighed, stood, went to the door, and yanked it open.

"Joss."

He stared.

"Please. May I come in?"

He stepped to the side and closed the door, turning and leaning against it, watching as she took off her disguise.

"I didn't wake you, I hope?"

Joss just looked at her. Her eyes flickered away from his and stopped on the small table beside his chair. "No, of course I didn't wake you. You were reading?"

"Yes."

"What is it?"

"A novel."

She winced at his sharp tone, but persevered. "Oh? Which one?"

"It's one of the books I had planned to read with Lady Elizabeth. She gave me a copy, even though we won't be discussing it."

"You saw her?" she asked shrilly.

Joss's eyes narrowed. "No. She sent Hiram with it. *He* saw her, my lady."

She flushed and turned away from him, her expression either angry or hurt. Joss *hoped* she was hurt.

He sighed, disgusted by his petty behavior. "Was there something you were looking for, my lady?"

"Please, don't call me that."

Joss raised his eyebrows, but she wasn't looking at him, she was looking at her hands.

"I've come because I no longer need you for—for what I originally hired you for."

Her words were worse than a kick to the gut. But he would be damned if he showed *her* that.

Instead he said, "I'd discerned as much."

The tops of her sharp cheekbones flooded with color at his dismissive tone. "I'm sorry, I should have told you much sooner instead of leaving things . . . hanging."

Joss decided it was actually worse than a kick in the gut. It was the most frustrating, powerless, and belittling sensation he'd ever experienced.

All the power over what they'd had—*if* they'd had anything—was in her hands. He'd always known that intellectually. Now, he knew it viscerally.

"I don't need you *here*, but I still wish to employ you." Her tongue darted out nervously to moisten her lip. "But not to work here," she repeated.

Joss tried to ignore the sinking feeling in his stomach. "Oh?"

He didn't think he'd ever seen her become so flushed before—except when they been in bed together.

"I—" She looked dizzy, as if she might faint.

"Would you like to sit, my lady."

She went to the chair in his tiny sitting area and slumped into it. Joss stood across from her, hands behind his back, and waited, just like the obedient servant he was.

She finally said, "I know where you worked for almost four years."

He shouldn't have been surprised, but he was. He must be one of the stupidest men in Britain.

Joss sighed. "Her Grace of Beckingdon," he said.

Her jaw dropped. "What?"

Joss closed his eyes and covered them with his hand. Oh God.

"You . . . you know the *Duchess of Beckingdon*?"

Joss ignored her question. "Who told you about me, my lady?" He could see she wished to argue, but her jaw tightened and she looked down at her hands, twisting them uselessly in her lap.

"Who," he demanded. He needed to know.

If people were talking—selling secrets at The White House—Melissa would need to know.

She flinched at his harsh tone. "I don't know. I received a message—an anonymous message."

Joss frowned. "Who would do such a thing?"

She refused to meet his eyes. "I don't know."

Joss inhaled deeply, held it, and then exhaled slowly. "Very well, I shall pack my things and be gone tonight."

She leapt to her feet and clutched his sleeve. "No! Don't, please."

Joss jerked his arm away from her, furious. "What do you want from me? An apology? Fine, I am sorry I was a whore years before you met me. Will that suffice, my lady? Or perhaps you want—"

"I don't want an apology."

"Then what the devil *do* you want from me?" It was the first time he'd raised his voice in her presence.

"I can't have you here. But I—I can offer you a different job."

He hadn't thought he could feel any sicker. His mouth curved into a smile and he knew it was not pleasant. "Tell me about this new job."

She opened her mouth and the words tumbled out. "I can pay for a place for you to live—a place where we can meet secretly. I can even find you a position with somebody else, if you like. I-I know lots of people. Or I can simply pay you what I have been and you don't need to work. We don't need to stop seeing each other. It just can't be *here*."

Joss didn't know what was more depressing: that she would make such an offer, or that he would—even for a heartbeat—consider accepting it.

—❤—

Alicia had consumed three glasses of wine with dinner.

At the time, she'd felt confident and fearless. That had all changed the moment she saw him.

She blinked away the moisture that kept gathering in her eyes and forced herself to look up into his face: his rugged, almost homely face, which she treasured more than almost any other.

The truth had hit her the moment she knew she would have to let go of him: she enjoyed his company—both in and out of bed. She loved him. The only person she enjoyed and loved more was Elizabeth.

He rocked back on his heels at her scandalous offer, his lids dropping so low she could hardly see his eyes.

169

The silence grew, along with her misery and mortification. She got to her feet, but then could not move. Her brain encouraged her, strongly, to head for the door. To run. But her body, coursing with memories of their nights together, of their intoxicating, maddening pleasure, refused to obey.

"Don't you have anything to say?" she demanded when it seemed he would not speak.

"I'm wondering what it is, specifically, you wish to pay me for." He fixed her with a stare that chilled her.

"What do you mean?"

One corner of his mouth pulled up. "Do you think everything that is done in a whorehouse is the same?" She flinched at the word whorehouse and his smile grew. "You don't like that word: *whorehouse*." It was not a question. "But yet you want to buy a *whore*."

"Joss, I—"

"If you want to hire me, there will need to be a contract and you will need to be specific, to lay out the terms, *my lady*."

"I will?" It was barely a whisper, but she was past caring. Her legs were so weak she slid back down into her chair.

He nodded slowly, the menace back in his dark eyes the way it had been that first night in her carriage—a sensual menace. "It is a business negotiation—it is how things are done. You tell me what you expect from me and I tell you how much you will have to pay me to get it."

The voice in her head was screaming warnings.

But Alicia ignored it. She licked her dry lips and his gaze dropped to her mouth. "Li-like what?"

He raised his eyes. "You wish me to describe the kinds of *services* women—*ladies*—have employed me to do in the past?"

She wanted to deny it. To yell, *No! No, I don't! I can't even bear to think of you with another woman!* But her head nodded, as if it were fascinated by the amount of pain it could inflict on her heart—her soul.

His smile filled with loathing—for her? For him? For what they'd had?

"You like listening to me speak of such titillating things. The rude, rough words I might use." He cocked his head at her, the sly, cruel expression on his face one that she'd never thought to see. "I wonder if I shouldn't start charging you *now*." He chuckled, and it was a mocking, ugly sound. "Don't worry, I'll throw this part in for free."

Her chest was rising and falling fast. Her face, she knew, would be glowing red; morbid curiosity kept her riveted to her seat.

He fingered his chin thoughtfully. "So many women have come to me with so many needs, where should I start?"

Churning black jealousy threatened to choke her. She'd done this: she'd asked him. She could tell him to stop.

His mouth twisted. "Still, they did tend to fall into certain . . . categories. There were those women who wanted to become my sexual slave—who wanted me to be their *master*." His nostrils flared and his smile grew until she saw teeth. "But I probably don't need to explain much about that to *you*. They did whatever *I* commanded and I used them however I pleased." He closed his eyes, as if at some memory, the look so sensual it gutted her.

As jealous as his admission left her, one shocking detail rose above the rest. "*Other* women have paid you for that?"

He nodded slowly. "Oh yes, many women. Sophisticated, sensual women who knew exactly what they wanted. Women who gave me as much pleasure as I gave them." He hesitated. "But you were different."

Alicia's heart leapt at his admission, as if he'd lifted a five-hundred-pound weight on her chest. "Oh?" she asked, hope blooming inside her.

His harsh features shifted into a gently amused, *patronizing*, smile. "Yes. You were so needy and lost." He paused, his eyes glinting. "Such a charming *novice*, that I've serviced you for free."

Alicia stared, his words echoing inside her over and over.

He grinned. "But I digress—you wanted to know the full range of services I offer. While some ladies want me to master them, some want me to be their . . . slave." His smile grew and it was not a nice smile. He leaned down and put his hands on the arms of her chair. Alicia sat back, but he just kept coming closer.

"That means I will do whatever *you* command me to do. You will own me, body and soul, to use however you please. Perhaps you would like to experience that arrangement for a while?"

She gaped up at him, speechless with hurt and humiliation. And want.

Whatever he saw on her face made him scowl and step back away until he was leaning against the doorway to his pugilism room, his posture insouciant, his expression watchful.

He crossed his arms. "I don't even need to fuck you." She flinched and he smiled. "I can just hold you, stroke you, and murmur how beautiful you are. How much I adore and love you, couldn't live without you. Share the details of my life—listen to your inner most secrets as if I find them *fascinating*. Not much different than what we've been doing, actually." He gave a dismissive shrug.

Each word was like the flick of a whip.

"But it sounds like you have something special in mind for me, my lady. Something exclusive. You want to buy me in my entirety—not just for a few hours a week. You'd like to *own* me, keep me in a house, dress me the way you like, have me ready, waiting, and *hard* to service you whenever you desire. Your private *whore*—just as I've been for you these past weeks."

She recoiled at the barely restrained violence in his eyes, but her body thrilled at what he described: Joss, hers—all hers. An explosion of desire sent hot sparks cascading through her body, a fire settling low in her belly and kindling into a conflagration.

She stared up at him; he was like a wall, a sheer cliff of solid rock. She knew he was angry—only a fool wouldn't see that—but he hadn't left, he was still here. Perhaps this anger would pass. After all, they had shared *something* together.

Surely he wouldn't wish to let it all go.

Surely he needed it just as badly as she did?

"What are you thinking?" She bit her lip as soon as the last word slipped out of her mouth.

He gave a rude bark of laughter and his eyebrows, his most mobile feature by far, shot up. He pulled the sash on his robe and shrugged it off his shoulders, standing naked before her. Erect.

All the blood in her body rushed to her sex. He was so very magnificent, so very—

He gestured to his hips. "That's what I'm thinking. Just like the good whore I am, speaking of such things has made me hard. *You've* made me hard, and ready and eager to please." He wrapped a big meaty fist around the base of his erection and thrust his hips. "I'm thinking about fucking you, my lady. Burying myself inside you, spreading you wide, filling your hot wet cunny, ramming myself to the hilt, until my jewels pound against your ass. Pumping you hard, making you scream, until—"

"Enough!" Alicia lurched to her feet, sickened by the open loathing in his voice, on his face.

She staggered for the door, her head buzzing and pounding and hot; only to be stopped by the sound of his low laughter. She spun around, her mouth open.

He was standing with fisted hands on his narrow, taut hips, his abdomen flexing, the V of taut, ridged muscles even more defined as he laughed. His face was almost unrecognizable, his eyes squished into amused slits by his cheeks, which strained to contain his grin.

Alicia sucked in a breath. "You. . . you . . ."

He pushed back a lock of hair that had fallen over his forehead with a violent thrust of one hand, the motion sending muscles rippling across his torso, his shoulders, his biceps, his—

"Yes, *me*, my lady." He dropped his hand and his smile with it. Fury, and something else, something unidentifiable, burned in his eyes as he strode toward her. Alicia tried to move away, but her feet tripped her up and the chair stopped her egress.

He grabbed her upper arms, his grip like iron manacles He drew her closer and closer, bending low, his gaze unbreakable.

"You want to know what I'm thinking? Do you really even believe that I *can* think? Or feel?" A muscle jumped in his jaw and his pupils narrowed to specks. "You treat me like a whore and then become offended when I speak like one? You think because you pay me a wage that I am willing to sell you every last part of me. As if I'm some sort of toy to be taken out of a box, played with at your leisure and then tossed aside when you tire of me?" The hateful words came out of him like a cauldron that was boiling over.

Her mind reeled at what he was saying. But part of her body throbbed, ached, and burned for him.

He leaned down so their noses were pressing hard against each other. "You dig into my past—*pry* into my life—and then—when you find out what I once did to earn my crust—you banish me from your daughter's presence as though I am a carrier of the plague."

"No!" She winced away at his words. It was the truth, but only part of it. "You don't understand—"

His face twisted until he looked like a stranger. "*Of course* I don't understand," he sneered, his eyes blazed into hers. "How could *I* possibly understand the motivations of an elevated being such as yourself?"

He flung her arms away from him as if she'd burnt him—or as if he could not trust himself to exert control any longer, his chest rising and falling like a massive bellows. "You bloody toffs—you're all the same, every one of you. Treating your servants like possessions, no different than a dog or a carriage or your bloody chamber pot."

He turned his back, leaving Alicia battered, like the victim of a cyclone or avalanche. She could only stare.

The room was so quiet. There was no ticking of a clock or crackling of a fire. Her gaze flickered to the tiny grate and she realized it was cold and dark.

She heard the sound of his cupboard door closing and looked up. He'd pulled on his scarred groom leathers and tossed a worn canvas bag onto his bed. Beside the bag was a small pile of garments and a few books.

"What are you doing?" Her voice sounded reedy, weak, unlike her.

"Leaving." He didn't turn. Instead, he sat on the bed and pulled on a pair of heavy woolen stockings.

Her mind spun, looking for something to say—to defend herself from his accusations. But what *could* she say? His words were true. She *had* pried into his life, into his past. She *had* come here to use him for her needs. She *had* offered to pay him to touch her—to *be* with her.

But she'd not made her offer for any reason he believed: not because she thought him dirty or unworthy or less than her.

She'd made the offer because she didn't want to live without him—wasn't sure she *could* live without him.

Alicia closed her eyes. She'd treated him the same way every man had treated her: like a thing. An object to be used for her pleasure, employing him like a tool to get what she wanted, disregarding his needs, his very humanity.

She opened her eyes at the sound of heavy footsteps. The small pile of garments on the bed was gone, now in his bag. He'd pulled on a roughly woven coat and a brown hat she'd never seen before. He slung his bag over one huge shoulder and was walking toward the door. He was going.

Alicia opened her mouth, but she'd already offered all she had to give. She had nothing else for him. Nothing.

So, she stood by silently, and watched him go.

Chapter Twenty

The thing that bothered Joss the most was the smell.

It had been years since he'd worked in his Da's shop and he'd forgotten lots of things, or put them out of his mind, more likely. But the smell of blood, offal, and death all flooded back to him in an instant.

Still, Joss was grateful for the backbreaking and relentless schedule after too many days and weeks of waiting and wanting.

"To be truthful," Michael had said when Joss showed up with his bag in his hand, "You could not have come home at a better time. Not that I'm glad you were sacked, of course."

It had been easier to tell his family that he'd gotten the sack for talking back to his immediate superior, Mr. Carling.

If they'd have known Carling they would have scoffed at his excuse. Carling was more likely to thrash a disrespectful employee than he was to report such a thing to his employer. But the excuse served well-enough, and all of them except Belle believed it. His sister knew him too well, she knew something was wrong, even though Joss had told her nothing.

"Since Davy Jenkins broke his foot—the clumsy bastard—I've been runnin' about like a duck with two heads." Michael had scratched at his neck, the leather apron he wore every day having chaffed the skin permanently raw. "I like the lad, so I told him I'd hold his job. He says he'll be back in three weeks at most, so I could use your help."

So, here Joss was, back where he'd begun his life.

Of course things were different than they'd been all those years ago. Da was so feeble he no longer got out of bed and it was Belle who kept the house on top of the shop in order rather than their wiry, perpetually angry Nana.

But the hard work, the long hours, and the stench? Those were all the same.

Joss had settled in—too easily in some ways—spending his evenings at home, enjoying the time with his sister, and his father when the old man was aware enough to know where he was, if not who he was.

Belle had always been his favorite sibling. It might have been the fact their Ma left when she was still just a baby and Nana—although she'd looked after Belle's physical needs like food, clothing, and shelter—had had no time for the sensitive girl's loneliness. Nor for her passion for books, a weakness in their grandmother's eyes.

But Joss had understood his sister's sense of loss. His life had changed drastically after their mother left. His Nana said he'd had enough book learning for a lifetime; that at fifteen his father had been working full-time in the shop and so should Joss.

So he'd stopped going to school and had put away the hopes her mother had lodged in his head and in his soul—expectations that he might one day become a teacher—and he'd gone to work.

"Joss?"

Joss looked up from his noontime meal, which he'd not touched, to find his sister smiling down at him. His face naturally creased into an answering smile. "Sorry, Belle, what was that?"

"You'd gone somewhere far away, hadn't you?" Her eyes dropped to the table. "And you've not eaten a thing."

He opened his mouth to promise her that he would, but she waved him down. "I didn't come to scold you. I came to tell you that you've got a visitor—it's Hannah Baker." Her forehead furrowed. "But she calls herself Melissa Griffin now. My, but she looks as fine as a fivepence."

Joss scowled. Melissa—here. Just what he needed.

Belle saw his look and hesitated. "Should I send her away?"

"No, you can show her in."

Belle looked around the humble but spotlessly clean room, her expression doubtful. "In here? Or should I show her into the parlor?"

"She isn't too fine for our kitchen."

Belle nodded uncertainly. She'd been a little girl the last time she'd seen Melissa, no doubt her appearance was an enormous surprise.

She left and soon the door to the kitchen opened. Joss stood.

Mel stopped in the open doorway and cut him a saucy look, one hand on her hip. "You look so pleased to see me, darling."

Joss stared: for all her bravado, she was *gaunt* and hardly looked like herself. He opened his mouth to ask her what was wrong and then glanced over her shoulder, to where Belle hovered.

"Would you like some fresh tea, Joss?"

He looked at Mel and raised his eyebrows. "Would you like some, *Mrs.* Griffin?"

She smirked at his dry tone but gave Belle a kind smile. "No, thank you Miss Gormley."

"I'm fine with my ale," Joss said.

She nodded and quietly closed the door.

Joss pulled out the chair across the table from his. "Good God, Mel, you're skin and bone. It's been what—three weeks since I last saw you? What happened?"

She laughed. "What a silver-tongued devil you've become, Joss. I think you're supposed to tell me how fine I look rather than pointing out how hagged I am."

She was certainly dressed fine; the cut and quality of her garments were as tasteful and expensive as any aristocrat's.

Today she wore a carriage dress of dark ruby wool trimmed with gray. Her hat was high-crowned and bore a cluster of feathers that reminded Joss of a pheasant's tail. The garment must have been new because it fit her rail-thin body like a second skin. She'd lost weight but she was still beautiful. Her green eyes were huge in her heart-shaped face and she looked as fragile as spun glass. But Joss knew she was as tough as hammered steel for all that she appeared so delicate. Although she didn't resemble Alicia in appearance, the two women shared certain characteristics: intelligence, confidence, and humor, for a start. But he thought what they really shared was a history of pain. Whatever it was that Alicia had hidden from him, it was something bad.

"I'm interrupting your meal," she said, laying a blood-red beaded reticule on the table and pulling off matching lambskin gloves.

Joss pushed away fruitless thoughts of Alicia while shoving his plate to the side. He sat back, crossing his arms. "Have you seen a doctor?"

"Not so hasty. I'll tell you everything. In good time."

"How did you find out I was here?"

"Not from you."

He barked a sharp laugh.

"Were you ever going to come and tell me what happened?"

"I've been busy here. Between the shop and my father and—"

She snorted and then reached across and broke a corner off the sandwich on his plate, popping it in her mouth and chewing. "Mmm, this is good."

"I thought you'd *just* had your tea?"

She grinned and took another piece.

"Who told you I was back here?"

She chewed and rolled her eyes in bliss. "Mmmm."

"Mel . . ."

"Oh, hush. You're so theatrical, Joss. You really should be treading the boards. I found out you were here when I sent a message to you at

Lady Selwood's and the messenger returned with the information you'd quit."

Joss felt a prickling of surprise. So, Alicia had not said she'd sacked him. She'd looked so bloody guilty when he'd left that he'd been fairly sure she would not try to wreck his chances for future employment, no matter how cruelly he'd behaved.

"You sent a message? Why? What's happened?"

"I could ask you the same thing," she said, smoothly dodging his question.

He shrugged. "Your messenger was wrong—I was discharged for being insubordinate."

"Surly Joss was insubordinate?" She made an amused clucking sound, not waiting for a response. "That's not difficult to imagine. So, here you are." She made an encompassing gesture with one hand while the other picked away at his sandwich. Joss slid the plate across the table to her and she smiled.

"Here, you look as though you've been starving yourself. Although you sound better than the last time I saw you."

"I was ill, but I'm better now."

He grunted, not wanting her to see how much that information relieved his fears.

Judging by her grin he failed miserably. "It's no use trying to hide it—I can see you still care about me, Joss. Although I certainly wouldn't have known it by the frequency of your visits these past weeks. But if the mountain won't come to Mohammed then . . ."

"What a clever girl you are."

She laughed at his sour tone. The sandwich, which his sister had made to accommodate a man of his dimensions, looked preposterous in her slender hands but she opened her mouth wide and took a bite, chewing with gusto.

"I haven't tasted anything so delicious in ages," she said after Joss slid his mug of ale across the table and she'd washed down a few mouthfuls.

"You employ one of the most expensive French chefs in London," he reminded her, his mouth watering just thinking of the meals he'd had from the kitchen of The White House.

"Yes, but it has been a long, long time since I've had good, honest, rib-sticking English fare."

"You poor darling."

She ignored his taunting. "How long are you going to stay here?"

"My brother's employee should return in two days and he'll no longer need me."

"And what are your plans then?"

He didn't tell her that he didn't have any. Without a reference from Lady Selwood, which he absolutely refused to go beg for, his options when it came to employment—at least as a groom—were slim indeed. He shrugged, not wanting to tell her that he'd already put feelers out to the man who used to set up his fights. The response had been less than enthusiastic.

"Come work for me."

"Mel—"

She raised a hand. "Just listen to me—will you? Please?"

He heaved an exaggerated sigh. She would not stop until she spoke her piece.

She pushed aside the plate and folded her arms on the table, leaning toward him like a woman who meant business.

"I asked your sister how your father was and she said he is quite ill. That the doctor calls on him once, sometimes twice, a week now."

"What of it?"

"I remember what you told me of your plans for you and Belle when your father passed and your elder brother took possession of all this."

Joss cursed himself for sharing anything with this woman. He loved Mel, but she'd been born to manipulate.

It was true he'd made plans with Belle. His little sister was a sweet, intelligent, loving, wonderful woman. But her pockmarked face was the only thing men seemed to see. She'd never had a suitor and odds were she never would.

When Belle no longer took care of their father, there would be nothing left for her in this house. It had been their plan to pool his earnings with the little she'd get from their father and buy a small place where they could live and operate a bookstore. It wasn't a grand dream, but it would be a quiet, pleasant life.

The money he'd saved thus far was not enough to achieve that dream. Not nearly enough. They might be able to afford the lease on a building, but without a reserve of money they would not have a cushion for the lean times.

"Joss?"

He frowned at her. "You know how things ended with us before, Mel. Why are you asking me to do this?"

"You're a man now, Joss—less romantic. You were just a boy then and far too young for what I expected of you. I know that now." She smiled. "You were so ready to be in love. In love with love."

Joss's face heated at her words but he knew she spoke the truth. He wondered what she would say if he told her about Lady Selwood. How much of a grown man would she think him then?

He met his friend's beautiful green eyes. Mel was one of the loveliest women he'd ever seen. For a time, he'd believed she was *the* most beautiful, both inside and out. But there was a hard core of her that remained untouchable, at least to him.

It was that hard core that allowed her to do the work she did. Joss had found being a whore difficult. Beyond difficult: soul destroying.

Yet Melissa had always seemed to be at ease. In fact, there had been times when he believed she took pleasure from the power she wielded over the men who fought to have her.

"There is no easier way for you to make so much money so fast, Joss. And, if what your sister says about your father is true, you will need money sooner rather than later."

"Easy for *you*, Mel." She flinched, but Joss was not finished. "I'm not sure why you make the assumption that being a *whore* is quite so easy for everyone else."

Her face hardened and the expression made her look older, like the woman she was and no longer a girl. "You think this is *easy* for me? I didn't say that—I said it was *easier*, and that is the truth." Her mouth twisted. "How *easy* do you think it was for me to be sold by my own mother? How *easy* do you think it was to become the play thing of a toff three times my age when I was fourteen and passed around among his nob friends, and then discarded when he considered me too old—too used up—at the age of seventeen?"

She snatched up her reticule and gloves and stood. "So when I say I'd rather be in control of who I *fuck* and when and for how much and that I'd rather have a place to call my own, to have a measure of control over my own body, to make decisions for my future then, yes, it is *easier*. I don't know why you were really sacked, Joss, and I don't care. But if you think it is *easier* to earn your crust by living under another person's roof and belonging to them body and soul, far be it from me to argue with you."

She was fast, but Joss was faster. He was right behind her when she reached the door and tried to open it. But his hand was against the smooth wood and it would not budge.

She glared up at him through the feathers on her hat. "Remove your hand."

He cupped her jaw in his free hand. "Shhh, love," he stroked the sharp angle with his thumb, looking past her anger, and seeing a flicker of something else—shame? Pain? Fear?

Her eyes narrowed, and he thought she might hug her anger to her chest; she had a fierce temper and could cut a person out of her life as easily and quickly as a butcher cut the fat from a roast.

"I'm sorry, Mel."

"You great, stupid oaf."

His lips twitched. "Yes, but I am *your* great, stupid oaf."

"Oh, Joss," she sighed and then laid her head against his chest.

"Oh, Mel," he mocked gently. His arms slid around her, his body remembering the shape of hers. He pulled her close, dodged the feathers that threatened to poke up his nostrils, and angled his head to kiss her cheek.

"I need you, Joss. I—I need you to manage for me while I get away." She gulped in a breath. "I sent the message to you hoping you could at least spend some time overseeing Hugo and Laura, but now that you are out of work, I would really love to have you back at the house. To live there. You see, I've been very sick—I almost died."

He closed his eyes. *Ah, God.* "Why didn't you tell me?"

"I—I—" she broke off, but Joss knew what she'd been going to say.

"You would have welcomed it—death." It wasn't a question, but the feathers on her fine hat trembled like a male pheasant on the strut.

"Good God, Melissa! Why?"

"It just seems so pointless—struggling and working and scheming so that I might one day go and live a life of comfort in the country." She gave a watery laugh. "I've never even been to the country—what if I worked for it all this time and I hate it?"

Joss smiled, stroking her fragile shoulders. "You ninny, why don't you go and see for yourself if you like it? Take some time and go to the ocean, or to the moors, anywhere but here. It's so grim and dreary, especially in winter."

"I want to, Joss. And my doctor has said I must do so for at least a few months if I am to ever recover. But I don't see how I can leave. Venetia has sold her remaining interest, which just leaves me with Laura and Hugo. And you know how they are."

Yes, Joss knew about Laura and Hugo, the two most experienced whores at The White House, who hated each other with a passion.

"I need your help, Joss. I just need some help," she murmured into his chest. "You don't even need to take clients, Joss. I—" Her arms tightened until it was hard to breath. "The doctor said I am physically exhausted and the problem in my stomach will only become worse if I don't take time to rest. He said the country air is what I need." She gave a slightly hysterical laugh. "Lord, the country! I couldn't tell him I was more afraid of going to the country than I would be traipsing through St. Giles naked."

He pulled her tighter. "Shhh, don't talk nonsense. Of course, you should go to the country and rest. You will love it—clean fresh air, quiet—"

"Oh, don't! You're just scaring me."

He chuckled, just as she'd meant him to do. "I will help you, Mel." He rubbed her back, the feel of her delicate shoulders making his heart clench. Next to his sister, she was his closest and best friend in the world.

"I will come back to The White House and help."

As soon as he said the words, Joss realized that was exactly where he'd expected to end up all along.

Chapter Twenty-One

Alicia had believed the days after Joss left were the worst in her life—even worse than the hell of living with Edward and David. But unlike the hellish five years as David's plaything, it wasn't the physical part that was soul-destroying. This time it was the mental anguish that tore at her. All the years she'd been married to Edward and subject to his sick demands she'd at least had the hope that she would one day be free and take Lizzy with her.

Now there was no such hope.

David had planned his next move well, almost as if he knew Alicia's schedule.

It was the first time she'd left the house in days—not since that dreadful night with Joss. But she'd needed to go to Connie's.

Her friend had been feeling ill since before New Year's and Alicia had not visited her because it was an influenza, and she did not wish to risk bringing Lizzy.

She'd stayed only an hour, finding Connie weak, tired, and peevish from prolonged bedrest.

"I'm dreadful company, Alicia, but that doesn't mean I don't appreciate you coming. Tell Lizzy I've greatly missed our literary discussions and look forward to resuming them when I'm well enough."

After that, Connie had all but pushed her out the door.

Even before stepping out of her carriage, she'd known something was wrong.

Feehan met her at the front door, his face like a death mask.

"What is it?"

"It's is Lord Selwood, my lady. He, er—"

"My God, man—out with it!"

The old man had jumped and so had the two footmen hovering behind him.

"Lord Selwood came to take Lady Elizabeth home not long after you left, my lady."

Alicia was half-way down the steps before he'd finished speaking. "Fetch the carriage back around!" she'd yelled to whoever was close enough to listen.

Within moments, they were rolling toward Selwood House, Alicia barely able to keep from leaping up on the box and driving the carriage herself.

She could see by Beamish's tighter than usual expression that he'd been warned to expect her.

"I want to see my daughter."

"Lord Selwood will see you in the library, first, my lady."

"I don't *wish* to see Lord Selwood, I want—"

"Alicia, my dear."

She looked up to find David at the top of the stairs.

"David! I'm here to see Lizzy."

He gave her one of his gentle, infuriating smiles. "Please, can we not discuss this like civilized people?"

Alicia knew by his patronizing tone that he would not capitulate. She followed him to the library.

"Please, have a seat."

Alicia remained standing. "What is wrong?"

David turned to Beamish. "Please send—"

"I don't *want* tea, David. I want to see Lizzy."

His smile never faltered, but his brown eyes chilled. "You may go, Beamish." The door shut quietly, the soft click bringing Alicia to her senses.

"I'm sorry, David. That was uncalled for. It's just—"

"You are worried, of course."

Alicia looked up to find him back at his desk, his eyes hooded, his posture alert . . . watchful.

"Yes, thank you. I can see you understand." She folded her hands to keep them from shaking. "B-but why did you come and take her, David?" Her pleading made her sick, but she could not stop. "You promised me if—"

He chuckled and shook his head. "No, no, no. I told you that you might convince me otherwise, Alicia. But I made no promises."

She gaped. He had ruined her life—ruined the little bit of joy she'd just begun to find with Joss and all for—

He gestured to the chair beside her, his jaw hardening. "Now, I said to *sit.*"

She bit her tongue until it bled to keep back the words she wanted to hurl.

He smiled. "There's a good girl. You do tend to get overwrought, my dear." He paused long enough to enjoy watching her struggle to control her fury. "You see, the more I thought about it, the more I realized that I have seriously underestimated your judgement. If not this ... *servant*, there would no doubt be somebody else. If—"

"But I discharged him! I did as you said. I did—"

"Alicia." The word was laced with dark promises.

She tried to get her breathing under control and failed. "You *bastard*," she whispered, unable to stop herself.

His eyes had become so dark he looked like a man on the brink of climax. But his words were like cubes of ice. "I will not tolerate such emotionalism. Nor will I tolerate your disrespectful tone. I am head of this family and in charge of my sister's wellbeing, both bodily and morally. Now, Lady Selwood has returned from the country earlier than expected and that is why I have brought Lizzy home. The best place for her is here, with her brother—with her real family. I am sure we can agree on a schedule of when you may visit. *If* you are willing to be reasonable, that is. But I'm afraid we must postpone such things for a while. The doctor says—"

"Lizzy has seen a doctor?" Her voice was shrill. "She was *fine* when I left a few hours ago."

His lips tightened slightly, the only sign that her interruption displeased him. Even so, he remained smiling. "Yes, I would hardly let my sister sicken and not call a doctor." His voice was a mixture of amusement and reproof. "The doctor said she is suffering from a sudden and virulent influenza which he has seen more than a few times lately."

"That's impossible! She wasn't ill when I left this morning—I don't understand what has—"

He cocked his head. "Are you questioning my good judgement, Alicia?"

"No, of course not," she said quickly. "But if she requires nursing, I could come and—"

He shook his head, his eyes glinting with private glee. "Oh no, I'm afraid not. You see whatever she has caught is quite contagious. I've engaged a nurse for her, a competent woman who is accustomed to dealing with sickness. And Doctor Edmunds will come daily. It has been only a few hours and already the cupping is showing signs of—"

"You're having her bled?" she demanded in a voice at least two octaves higher. "But surely that is not necessary? Have you—"

"My dear Alicia. I have employed one of the best physicians available—a man who has attended the royal family. I daresay he is better qualified than *you* to determine what is best for my sister."

She tried desperately to fix an accommodating and calm expression on her face. "Of course. Of course you are correct, David." Her lips trembled. "May I see her?"

"Oh, not today, I'm afraid. She is sleeping. Rest, that is what the doctor and her nurse say she needs most. And they know best."

"May I come—"

"I think it best if you wait. I will send word when she is feeling up to visitors." He smiled; he was loving this: making her beg, grovel. The last thing he would do is give her what she begged for—not when her suffering was affording him such pleasure.

What could she do? What?

Nothing. That was the answer. It was as if her mind had locked up, like a ship frozen in an arctic sea, so deeply imprisoned in ice it would never break free.

She played her only card. "I am expecting money from the canal scheme within weeks. I could give you a draft against—"

His eyes widened. "Are you trying to *bribe* me to shirk my brotherly duty?"

She stared at his smirking, hateful face and the appalling truth almost choked her.

"I've been such a fool. This was your plan all along."

"You look so surprised," he said gently. "Surely you recall what I said after our last time together?"

Like the fragment of a nightmare, his words from that horrid night came back to her:

"I've enjoyed our time together," he'd said, leisurely buttoning his pantaloons while Alicia studied her rising bruise in the mirror. "You needn't go to servants for a bit of rough, darling—not when I'm always more than willing to accommodate you. In fact, I believe I must insist— for the good of our family reputation—that you conduct any future affairs with more discretion."

She'd not thought then what his words might mean—No, she'd been too consumed with dread at what she had to do.

She looked up from the horror of her memory to find him standing beside her chair, smiling down at her. "That was supposed to be the last time," she said stupidly.

"Oh no, sweetheart, I said nothing of the sort. The truth is, I find nobody else pleases me quite the way you do." He ran the back of his knuckles over her cheekbone—the one he'd struck the last time, his eyelids becoming heavier with the memory of what he'd done to her that evening. "You've spoiled me."

No, getting rid of Joss hadn't been the end of her torment.

It had only been the beginning.

—❤—

Mel made Joss's return to The White House feel like the return of the prodigal son.

The last time he'd worked at the establishment she'd been only second in charge, now she was the controlling partner.

When Joss had visited in the past he'd always gone to her suite of rooms. He'd noticed the changes in quarters over time. Mel's suites became larger and larger, until her current arrangement was not dissimilar to that of Lady Selwood's.

Indeed, Mel's taste was not dissimilar. While she lacked Alicia's flair, she had the same impulse toward clean lines, neutral colors, and a lack of clutter.

His first evening back they met in her study, which was adjacent to her private dining room.

"Are you all settled in?" she asked as she poured him a glass of rich amber liquid.

"Yes. And thank you for the generous accommodations." He took the glass and inhaled, his eyebrows rising. "This smells . . . expensive."

She grinned. "It is."

He raised the glass to his mouth and then hesitated. "You will not join me?"

She made a moue of distaste. "I'm afraid my body does not seem to like spirits any longer." She raised her goblet. "Milk is what the doctor ordered and all I can tolerate these days." She raised her glass. "To friends."

"To the best of friends." The liquid somehow managed to both burn and slide down his throat like silk. His smile turned to a grin. "A man could become accustomed to this."

"A man like you *should* become accustomed to such things."

Joss had heard her opinions before on the subject of what he needed, craved, deserved and he didn't bother arguing with her.

Instead, he brought up the matter of business. "I've closed out my bank account and had this draught made out in your name." He handed her the bank cheque that represented everything he had in the entire world.

187

If she was disappointed by his businesslike tone, she did not show it. Instead she went to her desk and unlocked the top drawer with a key she kept on her chatelaine. "Excellent. And here is the agreement, just as we've discussed." She handed him the slim sheaf of paper and smiled. "You are now one-quarter owner of the finest pleasure house in London."

Joss's face heated at her words. One quarter ownership of a business this lucrative was far more than his money should have purchased. But all his arguments had been in vain. Melissa had employed her not insubstantial will and he had, after too many arguments, capitulated to her generous offer.

Joss took the contract in one hand and raised his glass. "To business *and* friendship."

"To business and friendship." She took a sip. "Thank you, Joss. You know there is nobody else who—"

"Hush, partner—I know. Tell me about my newest investment."

She chuckled and lowered her elegant form into a wingback chair. "You had an opportunity to go over the most recent ledgers?"

"Yes, and a very impressive year it was last year."

"Our best," she said with obvious pride. "Particularly on the women's side of the business, where even with close to a dozen companions I cannot accept all callers."

Mel referred to her female customers as callers, and the men who serviced them, their companions. She said it was important to their female clientele, who didn't care for words like whore or prostitute. Just hearing the word whore made him remember, with some discomfort, that last night with Lady Selwood, and the horrible things he'd said—

He pulled his thoughts back to Melissa. "I'd like to take some time during the coming days to show you the practical side of things. As you know, I employ a man to keep the ledgers and manage much of the financial matters. But I have learned the hard way to keep close watch on him."

Joss nodded. He knew she'd been cheated by a manager several years back. It had not broken her, but it had left the business's finances battered.

"I would like to hand that over to you as quickly as possible."

He lifted his glass. "You trust me?"

"With my life." She was not smiling, and he knew she meant it because he felt the same. "I want you to know that I *do* trust both Laura and Hugo—with the business, if not each other. You needn't be here every minute of the day, Joss. I just need a . . . well, a stabilizing influence—somebody both Laura and Hugo will respect."

Mel's butler—a man every bit as regal as Beamish—entered. "Dinner is ready, madam."

Joss escorted her the short distance into her dining room, seating her at the head of the long table and taking the place to her right.

"I'm having only two courses tonight. I want time to talk," she explained as several servants loaded the table with platters, tureens, and a dozen other items.

Joss gave her a sardonic smile. "Stinting me already?"

She chuckled and poured him a glass of red wine, again abstaining. When the door closed, they served themselves and ate, the first few moments filled with the sounds of two people who enjoyed good food.

After a time, she broke the silence, her eyes sweeping his person. "I approve of your clothing."

"Thank you, I had an excellent recommendation for a tailor." It had been Mel who'd sent him to the man who made his coats and pantaloons, another man for his linens, and a cobbler who'd made him a pair of evening shoes, Hessians, and even top boots, although he had no immediate plans to add a horse to Mel's stable.

"I trust two weeks was long enough to sort out your business at home?"

"Aye, more than enough."

"What is to be the story?"

"I've taken a position with a Mr. Pettigrew, a man of business who keeps a small stable in the city."

"And *is* there a Mr. Pettigrew?"

"Probably. Somewhere."

Mel chuckled. "Your talents are wasted. You should be writing gothic novels."

Joss merely smiled. "What about you, Mel? Have you decided where you will go?"

Her expression turned pensive. "I was thinking somewhere by the sea. I have never spent any time by the water." She cut him a wry smile. "And don't bother to point out how the Thames is water."

"I won't. I agree, a place by the water."

"Have you seen the ocean?"

"It's hard to believe, but no, I haven't."

189

Mel put her elbow on the table and dropped her chin into her hand, staring at him. "Why have we let so much of our lives pass us by without seeing the ocean?"

"We've been busy with the everyday business of staying alive."

"Is that all life is, Joss? Working to stay alive?"

"For people like us, I guess it is. Not that I think we have it bad," he hastened to add, his mind drifting to the countless beggars, prostitutes, and urchins who clogged London's streets and alleys.

"Were you dreading it? Coming back here?"

Was he? Yes—a lot. But he couldn't say that to Mel without hurting her. "No, I wasn't dreading it." He lied with a smile and added, "After all, this is a rather grand opportunity. We both know I purchased a quarter of your business for a lot less—"

"I thought I said that subject was closed, Joss." It was not a question and he could see she didn't wish to discuss the inequitable terms which she'd taken merely to have him come on as part of the establishment. "I want to know how being back here is for you?"

Joss sighed. "To be honest I just feel . . ."

"Numb?" she supplied.

He hesitated.

"We need to be completely honest with each other, Joss."

"Yes, I do feel a bit numb." But then he'd felt numb ever since he'd realized Lady Selwood had been afraid to allow him around her daughter, as if he were a violent criminal or sexual deviant of some sort.

"It's not just coming back here that is eating you, is it?"

"No."

She leaned forward, her brow creased with concern. "What happened, Joss?"

He looked up from his thoughts and shook his head. "Nothing I didn't deserve," he said, taking a deep drink of wine.

Chapter Twenty-Two

"**Y**ou look awful, Alicia, just awful."

Alicia chuckled at her friend's blunt words, but Connie wasn't amused.

"I'm not jesting. Have you seen a doctor?"

"There's nothing wrong with me."

"I beg to differ."

Connie was pacing Alicia's boudoir while Alicia lay on her chaise longue, a half-empty glass beside her.

The younger woman sniffed the air. "And you've been drinking."

Alicia didn't bother to deny it. Why should she? She'd earned her right to drink. Besides, what did it matter? Week after week passed with no clear distinction between the days; a person needed to drink just to bear it.

Connie took a heavy wing chair and dragged it across the floor, not caring that she was scratching the wood and rucking the carpets. She pulled it close to Alicia's chaise and dropped into it, reaching out and grabbing Alicia's hand.

"My God, you are as chilled as a corpse."

I wish I were a corpse.

"Tell me what happened. Please."

Alicia tugged away her hand and reached for her glass. Liquor was the only thing that made anything bearable. She'd never had a taste for it before—not after she'd watched so many people be brought low by their love of the bottle when she was growing up.

But when she'd gone back to Selwood House a second time—the day after David had taken Lizzy—and learned what David had done, she'd come straight home and poured herself a brimming glass of brandy.

"David says Lizzy needed rest and he's put her in an asylum." Alicia tossed back the remains of her glass.

"Good Lord—but why?"

Alicia poured the last of the bottle into her glass.

Connie chewed her lip, clearly at a loss for what to say. "When was this?"

"I don't know—what day is it?"

Connie groaned and grabbed both her hands. "You can't go on this way, Alicia. You can't."

"That is what I'm hoping," Alicia admitted, scanning the room for another bottle.

"We can go speak to David, Alicia. Together. If you stop drinking, we could speak to him in a calm, rational manner—"

Alicia was suddenly furious. "Don't you think I already did that, Connie? Don't you think I have already tried that? Twice I went to Selwood House and, no, I had not been drinking either time. I asked reasonably, I begged, I groveled." Her vision blurred red and rippled with rage at being forced to think about her behavior. "He told me he would *keep* her in a hospital if I insisted on bothering him. He said it was *my* choice. He said he was beginning to doubt that any contact with me was a wise idea—perhaps *I* was the reason she'd become worn down and ill. He asked me these questions: Did I want her to eventually come home? Or did I want her to be in some dreadful hospital for the rest of her life?"

Hot tears rolled down her cheeks, which only made her angrier. "Nothing I could do or say changed his mind, nothing," she muttered.

She couldn't tell her friend what she *had* done, and how it had made no difference to him in the end. No, he was enjoying tormenting her far too much.

Thanks to the clever work of Horace's men of business, she could only get her hands on her quarterly allowance. The rest of it—the bulk of her vast wealth—could not be touched unless she received permission from the trustees. They'd advanced her an enormous sum of money the last time David had demanded it. To get it, she'd needed to lie and tell them it was an investment. She'd not been able to repay the loan; they would not be so amenable again.

"Alicia, why does he do this?" Connie sat back, her expression one of shock. "Why? What is there between you that he must torment you so? He doesn't want to take care of Elizabeth—and I know the countess certainly doesn't. So, why?" She cocked her head, her eyes sharp and piercing. Too piercing.

Alicia pushed to her feet and would have fallen if Connie hadn't taken her arm.

Connie glanced around. "Where is Maude?"

She pushed away from Connie, staggering toward the cluster of bottles on her dressing table. "She's gone."

"Where?"

"I don't know and I don't care. I sent her away." She snatched up a bottle and began to open it, her fingers fumbling and numb, the bottle as elusive as a Chinese puzzle in her useless hands. "Bloody hell!" She flung the bottle across the room. Instead of the satisfying smash she was hoping for—craving—it hit something with a dull *thunk*, rolled, and then broke with a small tinkle of glass.

"Lady Selwood?"

It took a moment for Alicia's eyes to focus, to find the source of the meek voice.

"Ah," she said when she saw the maid hovering just inside her dressing room. "Annie, come here. Open one of these for me."

The girl scurried toward her. "Yes, my lady."

"Alicia, are you—"

Alicia had forgotten her friend was still there. She closed her eyes. "After you open the bottle ring the bell. Lady Constance was just leaving."

She heard a soft gasp behind her and squeezed her eyes shut against the rustle of fabric as her friend stood. "Don't bother, Alicia. I can find my own way out."

Alicia didn't turn around but listened until the door opened and shut, only then opening her eyes, catching the maid watching her with sharp eyes. She dropped her gaze immediately.

"Here you are, my lady. Shall I pour you a glass?"

"Put the bottle down and leave."

The girl instantly complied. "Will you be needing—"

"Get out. I won't want you again tonight."

A lightning bolt of something sly crossed the girl's face before she dropped her chin and dipped a curtsy. "Thank you, my lady."

Alicia waited until she'd gone before locating her glass and filling it. For some reason, she didn't trust the maid and didn't want her around when she reached the point of insensibility. Which is when she started to talk—not that she remembered saying anything, but Maude had told her.

Her eyes watered at the thought of her maid. She wished she'd not sent Maude away. Not that she had, really. The truth was that Maude had left her.

"I'll not sit here and watch you destroy yourself," she'd said after the first week.

"Fine. Go sit somewhere else."

The older woman's jaw had worked as though she were chewing a mouthful of writing serpents. "This isn't you, my lady. It isn't. You are a fighter." The pleading tone in her voice had momentarily caught Alicia's attention and Maude came close enough to take her hand, her gray gaze intense. "You put up with all those sticks in New York, you endured that. . . that—" The expression of revulsion on Maude's face reminded her of everything the other woman knew about David and Edward, and what they'd done to her.

Alicia had snatched away her hand. "Yes, I endured all *that*. And for what Maude? For *what*? So Edward could give control of Lizzy's future to that—" Her mouth had filled with bile and almost choked her. She could not say his name.

"Fight for her, my lady. *Fight*. Just like you always have."

Alicia stared into the eyes of the only person left in her life who'd known Allie Benton. "I'm out of fight and out of ideas. Out. I've done everything I can. Don't you understand," she demanded, her voice hoarse with the need to be understood, for once. Just once. "I have done everything I can short of killing him. Everything."

Maude's jaw dropped. "Please…tell me you aren't—"

Alicia had laughed bitterly. "Good God, what would killing him do? I'd be in jail and she'd be left in someone else's care. Don't you see, Maude. There is nothing I can do. All this," she'd waved her hand around. "And all that money in the bank, and I can do *nothing*. I am a prisoner as surely as if I were in jail."

The silence after that had stung—because she'd known, by the older woman's defeated expression—that she was right.

"Destroying yourself won't help Miss Lizzy, will it?" she'd tried when Alicia turned away.

"No, but it will help me. Now either shut up or get out." And to her surprise, Maude had gone.

Alicia couldn't recall how many days ago that had been.

The girl—Annie—had shown up when she pulled the bell for more bottles and somehow, Alicia couldn't quite recall *how*, she'd become her new maid. Not that Alicia needed one. She was wearing the same clothing she'd worn for days.

She took a drink and grimaced as the liquor burned her throat. No matter how much of it she drank, she never liked it any better. In fact, she hated the taste of it. But she hated remembering even more. Remembering not only what had become of Lizzy, but what she'd done to Joss.

—❤—

Joss decided he would stay with Sundays as his day off just to keep his routine with his family.

Now he had the entire day, but he usually required the first part of it to sleep. Although he wasn't actually servicing callers, he still had to spend a good deal of time mixing with the clientele, on both sides of the building.

Resuming his activities had been difficult at first.

"You've forgotten all that I taught you," Mel said to him several days after he'd come back.

"You're right about that," Joss had admitted.

Women weren't like their counterparts on the other side of the building. They jeopardized everything to come to Mel's and they wanted more than a quick release: they wanted an *experience.*

Unlike their husbands—some of whom were probably in the building at the very same time—they were not the mistresses of their destiny. As wealthy as they were, their options were sorely limited. They could either conduct affairs with their fellow, bored aristocrats or engage a *companion* at The White House.

Joss had resigned himself to what he was doing: helping his friend and also accumulating the funds necessary to take care of his sister.

The way his father had declined—rapidly—Belle would need a place to live far sooner than either of them had expected.

While Joss might be able to arrange to borrow money from Melissa to purchase a house for Belle, it would be years before he could stop working at The White House and join her.

The carriage shuddered to a halt and Joss realized he'd arrived. He opened his door and hopped out.

"Thanks, Harry," he said to the grizzled coachman.

"Aye, see you here tonight, Mr. Gormley." He touched his hat and drove off.

Joss couldn't take one of The White House coaches all the way to his door, so he had it drop him off near a coaching inn that was a ten minute walk from his Da's house.

He enjoyed the walk, even on days like today, when it seemed winter was refusing to release its grip on the city.

He flipped up the collar on his old brown wool coat and shoved his hands into his pockets. The streets were not heavy with foot traffic and he soon fell into a rhythm, his thoughts drifting to where they always went when he wasn't vigilant: to her.

Joss knew it wasn't right—that it was disgusting, even—but he'd used his memories of his time with her so often and so hard they were like a favorite, but worn-out, article of clothing.

He was ashamed at how far he'd sunk since that night—when he'd lambasted her about *her* behavior.

It turned out that she'd been right about him. Once a whore, always a whore—or at least a whoremaster. He already—

"Joss!"

Joss stopped and glanced around. Had somebody—

"Joss, wait!"

He recognized the voice and was tempted to break into a run.

Instead, he sighed and turned. "Hello, Annie."

She grinned up at him, her cheeks like apples, her face framed with a startlingly becoming silk-lined bonnet. "I thought you were ignoring me—I called your name a dozen times and you didn't stop."

"I wouldn't do that," he lied, shamefully recalling all the times he'd ignored her knocking on his door. He glanced around. "Are you by yourself?"

"Yes, I was coming to see you."

Joss bit back a groan. "Oh?"

"I walked all the way from Lady Selwood's."

The name, spoken out loud rather than inside his head, was like a fist around his heart.

"It's cold today, isn't it?" She shivered to demonstrate.

Joss looked down at her, torn. After all, didn't he at least owe her common civility?

Not to mention she can pass along all the little bits of gossip about her.

Joss ignored the ugly little voice and offered his arm. "Why don't you come along and have a cup of tea. You can meet my sister."

Her face lit up like it was Christmas morning and she took his arm with a reverence that should have been flattering but just left him feeling like a heel. He slowed his stride to match hers.

"Where are you working now?" she asked after it became apparent that he wasn't going to start the conversation.

"At a city gent's place," he said, purposely vague.

To his relief, she didn't pry. "Lady Selwood hasn't engaged anyone else to replace you."

His body stiffened and he hoped she hadn't noticed. "Oh? Using Hiram and William for her errands these days?" he asked in a voice that shouldn't have fooled anyone.

Annie's bonnet moved back and forth and she chuckled. "Not hardly."

"What do you mean?"

"I mean she hasn't left the house in weeks."

Joss stopped. "Why? Is she ill?"

Her smile slid away and her full lips pinched down at the corners, the look in her eyes mulish. "What do you care?"

He shrugged, aware that he'd been foolish. "She was an easy mistress to work for, I don't wish her any harm."

Annie's eyes were narrow and suspicious. Joss took her arm and resumed walking.

"So," he asked after a long moment of silence. "What's ailing her?"

"Nothing but a case of bottle fever."

"*What?*"

This time she was the one to stop, pulling away her hand and staring up at him with a dangerous glower.

Joss knew his face would be flaming so he said the first thing he could think of to save the situation. "Surely she wouldn't do such a thing with Lady Elizabeth there."

Mention of the young noblewoman didn't help the situation.

Annie placed her fisted hands on her hips and glared. "Even though she sacked you, you're still sweet on her."

"On whom?" he demanded, another part of his mind stuck on what she'd said: Lady Selwood had said she'd *sacked* him? That wasn't what Feehan had told Melissa when she'd sent a note for Joss.

Before he could ask her to clarify, Annie's voice rolled over his thoughts.

"I don't know which one you're sweet on." She shook her head, hurt and confusion evident on her face. "I don't know—on one of 'em, that's for certain. You get this look whenever they're mentioned."

"What look?" he asked, even though he knew the look she was talking about because Mel had commented on it more than once in the past weeks.

Annie made a noise of frustration. "I didn't come all the way out here to talk about her—or them."

"Why did you come, Annie?"

Her lip trembled at his sharp tone and he felt like an ogre. He sighed and reached for her hand. "Look, Annie, I didn't mean—"

But she wasn't having any of it. "Yes, you *did* mean it. You're just as high and mighty as you ever were. You aren't the only one, *Joss*," she sneered. "There are several other blokes, and they'd give their right arms to be with me."

Joss wanted to ask her why she wasn't with them but doubted that was the way to smooth matters. Instead he said, "I don't doubt that for a minute, Annie. You're a beautiful, smart girl."

She blinked at that, uncertainty mixing with anger. She finally nodded. "That's right. I'm glad to see you realize that. I could've spent today with any of them. But I picked *you*."

"I know. I know you did." He reached for her arm and this time she didn't snatch it away. "Come on. It's cold." She hesitated, but he could see she was wavering. "My sister will be glad to have the company. And so will I," he added.

That did it and she took his arm.

They walked in silence and he realized it was his turn. "That's a very pretty bonnet, Annie. It looks becoming on you."

Her smile turned positively radiant and she gave a little skip as they walked.

Joss felt more than a bit guilty that it took so little to make her happy.

"Lady Selwood gave it to me," she said, not pausing, not looking up. For once, Joss managed to control his body's reaction.

"That's nice," he said, as noncommittal as he could muster. Why the devil was Alicia giving her parlor maid bonnets?

Annie paused and he felt like she was evaluating the situation and considering what she was going to say and whether it was worth the possibility that he might be more interested in the subject matter than her. She must have decided not.

"I'm her maid now."

He was astounded that his step didn't even stutter. And grateful he was too stunned to speak or demand answers, not that she needed encouragement.

"She sacked that sour old crone Miss Finch and raised me up." She hesitated, and sounded significantly less certain when she next spoke. "I only wish she'd have more need of me. But she never goes out and never wears any of her lovely dresses, not even when her friends come to see her. Not that they do any longer, not since she yelled at poor Lady Constance. Fancy that," she said with wonder in her voice, completely unaware of the effect her words were having on him.

Joss cleared his throat. Several times. "Fancy what?"

"Oh, just being able to tell off a duke's daughter the way she did, not that she wasn't deep inside the bottle when she did it. If I thought drinking a load of expensive liquor would help me get brave I'd do it, just to tell off that snotty Maisy Dockins."

For the rest of the brief walk home she talked about her long-running feud with Maisy, one of the other maids who worked for Lady Selwood, leaving Joss free to consider her shocking disclosures and remember things he would've rather forgotten.

Things like Alicia's stricken expression the night he'd yelled at, insulted, and walked out on her.

Chapter Twenty-Three

Alicia was staring at her dead fireplace, remembering another dead fireplace.

She'd woken up on the settee, cold. Why was it so cold? She looked around and frowned, unable to remember. Until her eyes landed on the broken glass that ringed the door to her sitting room. Now she remembered. She grimaced and reached for a bottle. But the table in front of the settee was strewn with glasses, all empty.

She closed her eyes and lowered her head to the back of the sofa, too tired to get up and ring for more. Too worried that nobody would come when she rang.

She'd been quite abusive—and more than a bit dangerous, the broken glass reminded her of that. Memories of the past few days flooded her head. Thankfully a soft scratching on the door interrupted them.

"A message for you, my lady." It was the girl's voice, muffled, from the hall. No doubt she was too afraid to open the door.

"Come in."

The door opened slowly, only a crack at first.

Alicia sighed. "Just bring it to me," she said, somewhere between shame and irritation.

She took the message from the salver. "Where is Feehan?" she asked absently.

When the girl didn't answer she looked up. "Well?"

The girl—Annie, she reminded herself. Since when did she reduce servants to labels like "the girl"? Was what Joss said true—that she didn't believe servants were real, thinking, feeling people. A memory of his face—a face she'd held at bay for days, weeks—swooped down on her like a hawk on a rodent.

"You, er, told Mr. Feehan not to bother you."

Alicia stared at the girl, her attention bringing even more of a blush to her plump healthy cheeks. She was extremely pretty. Pretty and young and wholesome. Just looking at her made Alicia feel tired and old and used up.

Annie was the kind of woman Joss should have—somebody who would love him, appreciate and value him. Give him babies. She shuddered as if struck and swallowed several times before speaking. "You can go," she said, her voice hoarse and raw.

She waited until the door closed before opening the letter, her eye dropping to the signature first: Shelly.

She pushed herself up, blinking away the sleep and grit in her eyes and holding the page closer, her teeth gritted as she forced the letters on the page to remain still.

"My Lady:

I apologize for the delay in responding. My servant forwarded your message regarding the investigation you requested."

Alicia blinked. What investigation? She tried to think back to the past days—weeks?—but could not recall sending Shelly anything.

She turned back to the message.

"I've just completed a project in Brighton and I will be back in London at the end of the week. In the interim, I've taken the liberty of having my associate draw up a list of all sanatoriums, asylums, or hospitals. He's already begun visiting the ones in the vicinity and I will join him upon arriving in London.

Yours respectfully,

William P. Shelly

Alicia lowered the letter to her lap. What the devil? Who could have sent Shelly a letter on her behalf?

There weren't many choices. Connie?

She remembered the last words Connie had yelled at her, just before Alicia had told her servants not to let her in again, or she would sack the lot of them.

"You're killing yourself, Alicia. Committing suicide right in front of me. Do you think I won't do everything I can to stop you?"

Could she be behind this?

Connie knew about Alicia using Shelly for an earlier investigation. They'd discussed it when Connie had needed somebody to look into a matter concerning her new housekeeper—a woman who'd stolen half the family silver during her first six weeks in her new position.

Alicia pushed aside thoughts of Connie's thieving housekeeper and stared down at the letter.

A pale flicker of interest licked at the pain that filled her heart. She might not be able to *be* with Lizzy, but at least Shelly could bring her information. She would not need to sit here, isolated and alone. Good God, why hadn't she thought of this? Why?

Do you care about the whys and wherefores? Or do you care about finding her? It was Aunt Giddy, who'd been conspicuously absent of late.

Alicia's lips trembled into a smile; Shelly would find her if anyone could.

Hope surged in her chest and she tossed the letter onto the nearby console table and stood, alarmed at how wobbly her legs felt.

When she wrapped her robe tighter, she grimaced in distaste: she stank. Revulsion wrapped around her tighter than the filthy clothing and she staggered to the bell pull before lowering herself onto the bench in front of dressing table, the room whirling and swaying around her. When had she last eaten? She could not recall.

Alicia looked in the mirror and winced: the woman who looked back at her was at least ten years older.

Lord only knew how much weight she'd lost, but it all seemed to have come off her face. She was gaunt, her skin paler than normal with an unhealthy, yellow tinge.

She groaned. There was a soft scratch on the door and Annie's low voice, "Yes, my lady?"

Alicia was too ashamed to turn. "Have a bath brought up."

"Yes, my lady." The door clicked shut.

Alicia dropped her head in her hands.

She'd only been weeping and pitying herself for a few moments—or at least she thought it had only been a few—when the door opened again.

"What do you want, Annie?" she demanded, furious to be caught in such a pitiful position.

When nobody answered she looked up to find Maude was standing in the doorway.

"Oh, it's you." She turned back to her mirror, her face tingling and burning, as if she'd developed some kind of rash.

The door closed and her shoulders slumped. She'd left. Alicia had behaved like a—

A loud thump made her yelp and turn.

Maude was still there. The thump had been her bag hitting the floor.

"Yes, it's me." Her hard, gray eyes flickered from Alicia's crown to her feet and then back to her face. "You look terrible."

Alicia couldn't help smiling. "I know."

Maude's mouth quivered, but she was tougher than Alicia. Much tougher. "I heard you'd rung for a bath and wondered if you might be ready to re-join the living."

Alicia hesitated. "I-I got a message and it was from—"

"I know who sent it."

Her eyes flew open. "*You?*"

Maude scowled. "Yes, *me*. Who else did you think would do it?"

Alicia just shook her head. "Why didn't I think of it?"

"You were too far inside the bottle."

She winced at the harsh assessment but knew the other woman was right. Painfully right. So she just said, "Thank you."

"You're welcome."

Alicia colored under Maude's penetrating stare and looked away, unfortunately back at her reflection in the large dressing table mirror. She grimaced and jerked her chin at her image. "Do you think you can do anything about this?"

Maude stumped across the room and came to a stop behind her, her eyes taking in the damage. "Not about the weight. Only time will fix that. But the dark circles, this?" She tweaked a limp strand of greasy hair and nodded. "Aye, I can do something with that."

Alicia's shoulders sagged with relief. And then something occurred to her. "How did you know that I'd rung for a bath so quickly." She frowned. "Just where have you been living?"

Maude's mouth curled into a sly smile. "What do you care?"

"Maude—"

"There was a vacancy above the carriage house. I took it. Had myself a wee holiday." She frowned up at the ceiling, as if deep in thought. "First I've ever had, if I recall right."

Alicia experienced a fierce, and entirely foolish, surge of jealousy at the thought of the other woman staying in *his* room.

God. She hated her own mind. *Hated* it. What good was all the money she possessed if it couldn't buy the things she wanted? Things like Lizzy's freedom and some peace? Or more time with Joss?

Alicia closed her eyes and pushed away the muddle of pain such thoughts brought. She'd destroyed any chance with Joss; he hated her, and had every right to do so.

Instead, she thought of the woman beside her and how she'd introduced a ray of light. She opened her eyes to find Maude studying her, her expression pensive. "I'm glad you came back," Alicia said again.

"I know you are. Now, come along, let's get you cleaned up."

—◈—

"Out with it, now."

Joss looked up. He hadn't even realized Mel had entered his room. He stood, his hand automatically putting the tooled-leather marker in the book and closed it before answering.

"I don't know what you mean."

"I'm to leave this place shortly and I'd like to do so feeling as though you are prepared to take charge of it."

"I am. What makes you think I'm not?"

She placed fisted hands on her hips. "Do you think you are smarter than me?"

Her words startled a laugh out of him. "No. I *know* I'm not smarter than you," he answered honestly.

"Good. So tell me, why have you been looking like a toddler whose best and only toy has been stolen since coming back from your family's place? What happened? Is it your Da? Your sister?" Her green eyes were wide, her forehead pinched with concern.

Joss glanced down at the book in his hand, running his finger over the raised gold lettering on the spine that read, *Antony and Cleopatra*. He was re-reading it, like some broken-hearted, lost fool.

"If we can't tell each other the truth then what do we have, Joss?"

He looked up. Rich yellow candlelight glinted off her smooth, copper chignon, her magnificent green eyes serious. "Please, Joss, you are doing so much for me, everything. Let me help you—if I can, even if it's just lending an ear. I just can't feel good about leaving if you are so *bloody sad*."

Joss set the book aside and gestured to the small settee that directly across from the big fireplace. "Please, Mel. Sit."

She sat and he lowered himself into his chair. "I ran into the girl from Lady Selwood's—the maid named Annie."

"I remember." Mel frowned. "She's the one who was in heat for you?"

Joss cringed at her assessment—which was accurate if brutal. "Aye. That's the one."

"So what happened? Is she still hunting you? Tell her to bugger off."

"It wasn't that, she's not a bad lass, although she is rather persistent. It wasn't seeing her that bothered me—it was what she told me about Lady Selwood."

When Mel didn't answer, he looked up.

Her mouth had flattened into a grim line. "So that's it."

Joss didn't bother pretending. "Yes, that is it."

Mel dropped her head against the back of her chair and rolled it side to side. "Oh, Joss, you *idiot*. You fool. You—you, oh there is no word for you. I should have guessed."

"Why the devil should you have guessed?"

"Oh, all the things you did while you were there—the book discussion club, being included on trips to the theater." He flushed and she sat upright, glaring. "And then there was you being fired for insubordination. You have a temper that takes a year to rouse—I knew something was not right then. Not only that, but I've heard about her. Who hasn't? One of the richest and most beautiful women in England."

Joss didn't like her tone. "Why do you say it like that? As if that is all there is to her? As if—"

She held up a hand. "Are you listening to yourself?" She plowed on, not waiting for an answer. "Oh no, trust me, I don't think you've fallen for a pretty face—and I *certainly* don't believe you've fallen for money, I know you. But I'm sure that a pretty face *and* such marvelous adventures have convinced you that you love her."

Joss shot to his feet and went to stare at the fire, shame and anger and an odd sort of fear roiling inside his gut. "I knew I should have kept my mouth shut. I knew I—"

"Oh, just sit down, you great looby. You should see yourself. No," she said when he began to leave. "Don't leave. I won't mock you. Come here." She patted the settee beside her. When he didn't move, she adopted a pleading, kicked-puppy expression. "Please, Joss, I'm an invalid and you should humor me."

"Oh, bloody hell." He dropped down beside her and she immediately leaned against him, nuzzling his shoulder with her chin until he lifted an arm around her.

"That's better," she murmured into his chest. "Tell Aunty Melissa all about it."

Joss rolled his eyes.

"Come. Tell me, you know it helps to get rid of it. That's exactly what you told me the day I came to beg you in your Da's kitchen."

And so it was.

Joss had encouraged her to talk when she'd not wanted to, he'd known that, but he'd also seen it was burning a hole through her like acid. Was that what Alicia was to him? Acid?

He pulled Mel's small body closer, comforted by the familiar feel of her. "I don't remember you begging," he said into her soft, fragrant hair.

"Hush about that. Tell me about her."

"There's nothing more to tell, you've already guessed the whole pitiful mess. I—well, I became enamored of her."

"*Pfft!* Enamored."

"Fine. I love her."

"And her?"

He pulled away far enough to look at her face. "Are you jesting? What do you mean, *and her*? Of course she doesn't love me."

Mel thrust his arm away, an expression of fury distorting her lovely features. "What do you mean, *of course*? Because she is a countess and you are a groom? Do you think *that* is enough to stop people from falling in love?"

"I think it's enough to keep people from doing anything foolish about it." His words gave her pause. "Good Lord, Mel. You, of anyone, should know how hopeless such emotions are. Is there anything more pitiful or predictable than a whore falling in love with her protector?"

She eyed him scornfully. "So, you think this is all you are to her—a whore?"

Her words hurt, even though he'd said the very same thing himself. "I don't think she wanted to hurt me, but I do think she wanted only to play. And me? Well, I'm not built for such games and have no interest in playing them. It was well enough that the situation came to a head when it did. It is not the kind of life I want for myself." He snorted. "The life of a kept man."

She twisted around in his grasp, staring up at him. "Would that have been so bad? After all, you could have spent more time with her."

"I didn't want her that way."

"Oh, Joss."

He looked down into her sad eyes. "Why do you say it like that?"

"Because you are such a dreamer. Haven't you learned yet that life never gives you what you want? Sometimes you have to take what is offered and shape it to your needs. Sometimes you have to take the best you can find."

Her eyes had gone distant and he knew she wasn't just talking about him.

He wanted to ask her who she was thinking about, but he knew she would never tell him. For all her claim to be open she'd never shared the details of her personal life—at least not the part that dealt with any lovers she might have had. Real lovers, not those who paid her.

"Is it too late?"

Joss blinked at her question. "Too late?"

"Yes, perhaps you can go to her and speak to her—tell her—"

He snorted. "No. It's too late." He recalled her stricken expression—her eyes—from that night.

"No," he said again, more firmly this time. "It is *far* too late."

Chapter Twenty-Four

Alicia held the letter with both hands to keep from shaking:

"*My Lady:*

I have recently learned we have a mutual friend named Joss Gormley."

"Joss." Alicia stared at the page without seeing it. The familiar name was almost enough to cause her physical pain. She lifted up the single page and continued reading.

"*If you are so inclined, I can arrange for you to spend some time with him this Wednesday. All you need to do is arrive at the direction below at 10 o'clock and I will have a carriage waiting for you.*
I apologize in advance if I've been mistaken.
Yours & etc,
Melissa Griffin"

Alicia read the letter through three times, just to make sure she hadn't missed something. That there wasn't more. But there wasn't.

Today was Wednesday.

How had Mrs. Griffin known Alicia wasn't busy tonight?

Not that she wouldn't have cancelled a dinner with the King himself to see Joss again.

This last thought jarred her; she hadn't made up her mind to accept this offer. Had she?

Why not?

She shoved away the thrill of excitement the question generated and reread the letter again, as if she might find more answers.

Who'd told Melissa Griffin about her? There were two people who knew that *she* knew about The White House.

She could rule David out.

And it wouldn't be Joss; he'd looked at her with hatred in his eyes that last night.

Who could it have been?

A memory tickled and teased her, something Joss had said . . .

Alicia sat up straight: the duchess.

Joss had believed the Duchess of Beckingdon had told her.

Alicia swallowed. His words—words she must have purposely pushed to the back of her mind—could only mean one thing: the duchess must have been his lover—or client or whatever they called such women.

"Listen to you, Alicia," she said, startling herself with the sound of her own voice. *Such women.* Who was she to judge a woman for seeking physical pleasure? With Joss. She closed her eyes against the painful image of her lover with another woman and then quickly opened them when pictures flooded her mind.

It had to be the duchess who'd told Melissa Griffin. But why would a woman—one who barely knew her and didn't particularly care for her—do such a thing?

Alicia shook her head. None of this made any sense. But it was the only clue she had.

She pulled the bell, went to her writing desk, and wrote a terse, unsigned note.

She was just sealing it when a servant came—a footman, rather than Annie, much to her relief. The girl had been sullen since Maude's return.

She handed him the sealed missive. "This is for the Duchess of Beckingdon. It is to go *only* to her own hand. Do you understand?"

"Yes, my lady."

"Wait for a response if you find her at home."

"Yes, my lady."

"You may go," she said, turning away from his curious stare. What she was doing was beyond the pale when it came to social etiquette, but Her Grace would either respond, or she wouldn't.

Alicia would have wagered a great deal on the former.

The Duchess of Beckingdon's response was terse in the extreme:

"This afternoon at 5 o'clock. I will be at the Clarendon for one hour."

There was no signature, which was just as well.

Alicia would have preferred somewhere she was less likely to be recognized than the Clarendon, but the duchess had given her no say in the matter.

Her fears were realized the moment she stepped in the door and saw Sir Henry Lloyd, the first lover she'd taken.

Even through her veil, he recognized her, which she supposed was not surprising given that she'd worn a veil to every meeting with him.

"Lady Selwood, what an unexpected pleasure."

"Sir Henry, what a . . . surprise." Except it wasn't. His face was flushed and ruddy and Alicia knew exactly what he was doing here. After all, he'd done it with her on a half-dozen occasions: disappointingly quickly, as a matter of fact.

"Yes, it is a surprise. Lady Lloyd found herself in need of something or other so we trotted into town for a few weeks."

Sir Henry had recently married a rich cit—the daughter of an iron monger—and Alicia knew he'd only married the woman because his finances were at sixes and sevens.

Alicia said a brief prayer that she'd never been so enamored of his handsome face that she'd made the mistake of marrying the man.

A flash of cerulean velvet caught her eye: it was Lady Frampton.

Alicia did not know her well, but she could see the woman was in a hurry to leave. She glanced at Sir Henry and saw him watching the other woman's hasty departure, a smug, satisfied smile on his face.

So, that's how it was. Married less than a year and already dallying. The whole reason she'd broken off their liaison was because of his impending marriage. Alicia refused to wreck a marriage. Especially one that hadn't even begun yet. It seemed Lady Frampton did not have such qualms.

Well, who was she to judge?

"I'm afraid I must dash, Sir Henry," she said when he turned back to her, his eyelids heavy, his full lips moist and repellant. How had she ever found such a self-important ponce attractive?

He bowed over her hand and grinned suggestively. "Have a delightful afternoon."

She felt his sticky eyes on her all the way to the desk. "I am Lady Selwood."

The concierge all but vaulted over his small wooden counter.

"Please this way." He led her away from the large sitting area toward the private parlors, opening the first door.

Alicia hadn't really known what to expect. But the duchess wore her usual, distant smile, and gave a slight nod to acknowledge her.

"Good afternoon, Lady Selwood." She turned to the hovering lackey. "Please have tea sent in."

"Very good, Your Grace." The man departed with alacrity.

Alicia tucked her gloves into her reticule. "Thank you for meeting me so quickly."

"Your message sounded rather urgent. How may I help you?" Clearly the other woman was not interested in idle chit-chat and was eager to get away from Alicia as quickly as possible.

"It's about my former servant, Mr. Jocelyn Gormley."

Red stained the duchess's pale, dignified face like wine on white table linen. The duchess pursed her mouth, resignation and defeat suddenly aging her twenty years. "I thought as much."

An awkward silence followed. Alicia had tried to come up with the correct words a hundred times since making her decision to confront the duchess. What came out was not what she'd scripted in her mind's eye.

"I want to know how you are acquainted."

The door opened and the concierge entered, accompanied by not one, but two, tea tray bearing maids.

By the time the fussing was over, tea distributed, biscuits and cakes declined, Alicia's heart had ceased to palpitate.

The moment the door closed the duchess set down her untouched cup and saucer.

"I would like to dispense with this as quickly as possible. I don't know what he told you, but—"

"He told me nothing."

The duchess's brow wrinkled with obvious perplexity.

"Mr. Gormley told me nothing," she reiterated when the duchess did not speak. "Indeed, he rarely speaks at all, on any subject." She smiled wryly but the other woman did not return the gesture.

"I paid a man to investigate his activities." That much was true, but not in the way it sounded. Still, she could hardly tell the duchess that her stepson was blackmailing her with the information.

"What has he done that you'd do such a thing as have him followed?"

Alicia's face scalded. "He did nothing, Your Grace. As to why? Well, the first time I did it to—"

"You've done it more than once?"

Alicia bit her lip and looked away. She was making a bloody hash of this—and it was unlike her. She took a deep breath and continued. "The first time was because I wished to employ a servant with exceptional discretion." She gave the other woman a pointed look. "A man strong enough to offer protection and also disinclined to chatter."

The duchess chuckled and Alicia's jaw dropped.

The older woman saw her expression and waved her hand in the manner of one waving away smoke and clearing the air.

"I'm laughing because that would certainly be Joss."

Jealousy seared her at the other woman's casual use of his name. A name she'd clutched to her chest like the most precious of all jewels.

"But please, go on, Lady Selwood."

"Yes, well, I had him investigated the first time and The White House came up as a place he frequented." The duchess's eyebrows shot up. "What is it?" Alicia asked.

Color returned to her high, sculpted cheekbones. "Oh, it is nothing. It's just that I'd been told he left some years ago now."

Alicia could imagine too well what lay behind her blush.

"I don't believe he is working there. The man who looked into his activities told me he's acquainted with the woman who operates the, er, house."

The duchess merely nodded, but Alicia would have sworn there was a wistfulness in her sharp gray eyes.

"In the course of his investigation my man recognized you." Alicia lied, her gaze flickered to the other woman's trademark, her distinctive hair. She'd decided to say this instead of mentioning Joss's purely innocent slip.

"And you put that piece of information along with my awkward behavior Christmas dinner?"

It was Alicia's turn to nod. "I did. So it was you I thought of when I received the letter."

"Letter?"

Alicia looked at the other woman's face and immediately knew it had not been the duchess who'd said anything to Mrs. Griffin.

Before she could say anything, the duchess took a deep breath and released it. "I always expected to get caught one day, but I thought it would be a servant betraying me, or perhaps one of the employees from . . . there," she finished lamely, her cheeks again flaring with color and making Alicia understand just how beautiful the woman across from her must have been, and still was. Not only beautiful but obviously *passionate*.

"Please, Your Grace. I don't wish to expose you—I can leave right now if you wish it. I will never say anything to anyone. But—"

The duchess's lips pulled into a wry smile. "But you are curious."

"Yes, I am."

"Do you wish me to frank you?"

Alicia blinked. "I'm sorry—frank me?"

"A turn of phrase. You see, new members are admitted on the word of other members. You need somebody to vouch for you before you are allowed entry. I believe that is true for the other side of the building as well."

No wonder Shelly couldn't buy his way inside.

"But if Joss is working for you perhaps—" the duchess trailed off, her expression embarrassed but also curious.

"No, he no longer works for me."Alicia hastily turned the topic. "What was that you mentioned—franking me?"

"Oh. Yes, well it is the only way to ensure any amount of discretion, and even that is not perfect, of course. But I've managed to escape outside notice for almost ten years."

Ten years! Alicia did the mental math—so that meant she would have been going a few years before Joss and would have been there the entire time he'd worked there.

Lady Beckingdon smiled at whatever she saw on Alicia's face. "Yes, I went to him as long as he was available. I knew him only by his first name and I used an assumed name, of course." She paused. "He is an unusual man," a slight smile tugged at her lips. "In many ways." She gave an elegant shrug. "I found he suited my . . . requirements admirably and I engaged him whenever possible." Her smiled grew, and her eyes sparkled as they looked into Alicia's. "He was in demand and I never saw him as often as I wished. And then," her smiled drained away. "And then one day he was just gone." She stared at Alicia. "It is never enjoyable when a person you have come to rely on—perhaps even like—simply vanishes. But he—" she broke off and shook her head, her expression saying what she couldn't.

Alicia was surprised when compassion mixed with the envy, jealousy, anger, and—not the least—lust that boiled inside her as she looked at this woman who knew so much about the man who'd come to dominate her waking and sleeping hours.

The duchess took a sip of tea but grimaced. "It is cold."

"Shall I ring for another?"

"I'm afraid I can't stay." The look she gave Alicia seemed genuine, almost as if she would have liked to stay. Her next words surprised her.

"I can tell you how you contact Mrs. Griffin, who will then send one of their coaches for you. It is all carefully contrived to protect your reputation." She gave a sad smile. "A shame such Byzantine measures are necessary when our husbands can set up their mistresses and escort them to the theater right before our eyes. But there it is: a woman's lot." Her bitter smile turned almost impish. "But Mrs. Griffin gives us a way to seize something for ourselves—as women, not just ladies. Would you like the information, Lady Selwood? You can use it, or not, it is up to you."

She didn't want to tell the woman that she already had an appointment, but she also didn't want to reject either her offer by appearing above such an arrangement.

So instead she said, "Yes, Your Grace, I would like the information, very   much."

Chapter Twenty-Five

Joss despised himself for his duplicity but could see no other way of finding out how Alicia was doing.

So he'd invited Carling out for a drink, quite shamelessly pumping him for information.

The older man had been open, treating him almost as if they were still workmates. He'd told Joss how Lady Selwood had at last stopped ordering bottles to her room and that her crotchety servant had returned.

"Aye, Miss Finch is a cagey one. It was her who had Feehan deny her drink." Carling had chuckled, his eyes disappearing in mirth. "Lord, you'd have liked to see it, Gormley; Feehan sent running with a flea in his ear."

Joss had laughed, but he hadn't thought it amusing. It had only served to illustrate just how bad things were.

"So, things are back to normal," he'd prodded. "Everyone happy."

"No, not everyone. That Annie," he'd shaken his head, his lips twisted in disgust. "She'd been glad to get Finch's position, which she wouldn't have had if Finch hadn't have refused to bring the countess another bottle. Annie was more than happy to all but pour the poison down the mistress's throat."

"I can't believe she would do that," Joss had felt compelled to murmur.

Carling had eyed him curiously. "Can't you though? I thought you'd done pretty well to avoid her trap—until she came back last half day crowing like a cock about how you'd had her to your family's for dinner; that you two were walking out together."

Joss had flushed at the other man's words and sharp look. He could hardly deny the story without calling Annie a liar—nor confess he'd been using her shamelessly for information, so he'd let it pass.

Carling had taken his silence for something else. "I'll say this, and I might get a pop in the mouth for it—" he'd given Joss a belligerent look that had made Joss laugh and the other man's tension drain away.

"Oh, go on—you'll say what?"

"You ain't courtin'?"

Joss shook his head. "No."

Carling heaved a sigh of relief. "I'm glad. She's a bad piece of goods. Not happy that the mistress is drying herself out. Didn't want to give up her lady's maid position, did she?"

Joss wanted to think the other man was exaggerating but he couldn't forget the glitter of malice in her eyes when she'd spoken of Lady Selwood's condition.

"I'm sure Her Ladyship would be amenable to helping her acquire such a position."

Carling had snorted.

"What?"

"Just stay away from her, lad."

That was Joss's plan. He'd even gone so far as to change his day off, so he could avoid any "accidental meetings".

He couldn't bring himself to *like* Annie, but he couldn't dislike her, either. She wasn't mean spirited, just unhappy with her lot.

Joss would remember that assessment later.

Alicia was headed to The White House in an unmarked, luxurious coach.

He hates you! He hates you! The words spinning around in her head faster than the wheels of the carriage.

The accusation, in one form or another, had not stopped slithering around in her brain since she'd arrived at the boring looking house where she'd changed carriages.

Alicia didn't know what she'd been expecting—hadn't thought of it, really—but it hadn't been what she'd found.

The house on Pultney Steet had looked just like any of the others: quiet gray stone with lights burning in a few of the windows and a footman waiting to hand her from her carriage.

Inside she met a butler as staid as any she'd ever seen, who offered her something to drink. She had just demurred when a door opened and a woman stepped out. An exceptionally *beautiful* woman.

Alicia was about to turn away, her cheeks flaming at encountering another patron when the woman smiled and said. "I am Mrs. Griffin. Good evening, my lady."

Alicia could only stare. *This* was what a madam looked like?

Melissa Griffin was dressed in a dark green silk that was not cut particularly low but fit her shape so intimately it looked to have been stitched onto her body.

Fiery auburn hair and tilted green eyes complemented her pale creamy skin. Not only was she exquisite, but she was dressed with far more taste and fashion than three-quarters of the *ton*.

This woman wasn't only a madam, she was also something else to Joss—a woman whom he'd visited regularly. Was she his lover?

"Will you join me in the sitting room?"

Alicia followed her into a room that was just as simply and elegantly decorated as the small foyer. In fact, it looked like a room Alicia might have decorated herself.

The color pallet was a soothing mix of brown, cream, and beige with a hint of moss green. The furniture was of the type you'd find in a man's study, comfortable rather than decorative.

"Please, sit." Mrs. Griffin gestured to a chair and took the one across from it.

Alicia sat, wondering what the devil was going on.

"You're probably wondering how all this transpired?" Mrs. Griffin had a long upper lip that made her appear kittenish, but her lower lip was all sin. When she smiled, however, her mouth curved into a charming, lopsided grin that was engaging and girlish.

"Yes, I am," Alicia admitted.

"Do you know why you're here?"

Alicia's lips parted.

The other woman laughed, a low, throaty sound rather than the elegant tinkle of bells one would expect.

"I'm not laughing at you, my lady. I'm laughing at my foolish question." The humor drained from her eyes, which became shrewd and assessing as they swept Alicia's person.

She knew she was coloring beneath the other woman's piercing stare. Something about her pitiless eyes reminded Alicia of her husband Horace. The thought was a startling one. What could her ancient homely husband have shared with this exquisite butterfly?

"What I meant to ask was do you know who is responsible for you being here tonight?" Alicia hesitated and again the other woman filled the gap. "Joss is the reason you are here."

Alicia's jaw sagged and she was trying to absorb the other woman's words when she dropped another bombshell.

"Joss did not exaggerate when he described you as the loveliest woman in Britain."

Alicia didn't know what was more shocking: hearing his name out aloud or hearing what he thought of her from the mouth of a beautiful woman. She cleared her throat, jealousy, pleasure, confusion, and at least a dozen other emotions swirling inside her.

"What is this all about, Mrs. Griffin? If Joss wanted to speak to me why didn't he come to me himself?"

"Oh, he wants to speak to you—he just won't admit it." She smiled at Alicia's look of confusion. "You have hurt my friend. Deeply."

Alicia opened her mouth. And then closed it.

Mrs. Griffin nodded. "Thank you for not denying it."

"He told you what happened?"

"He told me no details—Joss is a very private man. He merely told me that you'd discovered where he'd once worked and felt he was no longer an appropriate person to be around your daughter. So he quit."

She felt sick at hearing the words spoken aloud. "That's what he believes. But it isn't true." Mrs. Griffin raised her eyebrows. "Oh, it's true that I no longer had him wait on my daughter. But not for the reasons he believes. My reasons for that decision are not ones I can share."

"I see."

Alicia did not want this sophisticated and obviously intelligent woman to think poorly of her. "I never thought he would do her any harm. He is exceptional. He is unlike any servant I've ever known." A pang of shame followed her words. "I misspoke—he is unlike any *man* I have ever known. He is intelligent, kind, and moral. And I treated him badly—very badly. I knew it at the time. But . . . Well, I thought it was better that way." She gave Mrs. Griffin a pleading look, wanting her to understand. "I expected him to come back—at least to collect the last of his things— but he never did. Nor did he ask for a letter of reference." She couldn't maintain the woman's knowing gaze. "When he didn't, I assumed he either went to work for his father or . . ."

"Or me."

Alicia nodded, unable to speak.

"He *did* go back to his father's. But that business belongs to his older brother now, so he could not stay. He didn't seem optimistic about his chances getting another groom position without a recent letter, so I offered him employment."

Alicia made herself meet the other woman's gaze. "You believe I forced him into this decision."

"Not in the way you think."

Alicia had no idea what that meant.

Before she could answer, the other woman went on. "That you have come here tonight, knowing what you do about his past, tells me you care about him." She paused. "I can have my carriage take you back to your house. Or, I can have you delivered to The White House, to Joss. He does not expect you and I cannot say what reception you will receive." She lifted her shoulders. "The decision is yours."

They stared at each other, with only the sound of the crackling fire, the noises from the street, and the ticking of a clock filling the room.

Isn't this what you wanted? Aunt Giddy's voice was so loud Alicia almost looked around the room for her.

Was it?

Did she really want to be just another of his paying customers? Her stomach clenched at the thought.

She looked up to find Mrs. Griffin waiting, a curiously thoughtful expression on her face. "I don't think I c—" to her shame, her voice broke.

"What is it, my lady?"

Her kindness almost undid Alicia. She squeezed her eyes shut and forced out the words. "I don't think I can be just another of his clients."

The madam gave her a quizzical look. "May I ask you an impertinent question?"

Alicia laughed weakly. "It seems like the perfect time for it."

Melissa Griffin didn't smile. Instead, her green eyes were as hard as jade. "You responded to my letter without hesitation and it is clear you wish to see him. But have you decided what it is you *want* from Joss?"

Alicia could not hold her gaze. She stared down at the richly patterned carpet beneath her feet, the ornate design as complicated as her thoughts—but far more orderly.

What did she want from him?

Alicia knew; but she'd been too afraid to even think the thoughts.

It was time to do so, now.

Shelly was searching for Lizzy and was confident he would find her—sooner rather than later according to his latest message.

When he did, she would take Lizzy and they would go to the Continent. Once Lizzy had time to rest and recuperate from whatever it was David claimed ailed her Alicia would take her on the longer journey to New York.

And she wanted to take Joss with her. If he would come.

And if David sent men after them, well she would deal with that when it happened. Without him bleeding her of every extra dime, she would have ample money to protect Lizzy.

Alicia looked up, weak with relief that she'd *finally* come to a decision.

"I love him."

Some of the hardness went out of Melissa Griffin's eyes and she nodded. "He deserves to be loved." She hesitated, her lips curving into a wry smile. "I will warn you that he has no inkling about any of this—that I am meddling in his affairs." She raised her eyebrows and Alicia nodded. "I know this is not the most straightforward way to do this—"

"But you think this is the only way to get him into a room with me—if he doesn't know who I am?"

Mrs. Griffin nodded. "Yes. But, ultimately, this is your decision—you don't have to do this. You could simply go home and send him a letter."

It was certainly a more mature method. But would Joss even speak to her after the way she'd treated him?

And then there was the fact that her letter writing skills were less than impressive.

No, she wasn't willing to take the risk that he might just ignore her letter.

"I want to do it."

"Very well. I'm going to send you in as I would any client. I've scheduled you for another of our companions—" She smiled at Alicia's startled look. "I'm sorry, I know this seems convoluted, rather than just scheduling you with Joss."

Yes, it did. But she kept her mouth shut.

"If you'll trust me—you'll find I have my reasons. Can you trust me, my lady?"

Alicia hesitated, and then said. "I trust you."

"Good. So, when you arrive you will be greeted by Hugo. However, the way I've arranged it Joss will come to you before you spend more than a few minutes with Hugo. Understand?"

Not at all, but Alicia decided it was better if she didn't know.

She nodded.

"I'm going to give you the orientation I give everyone, just so you understand the lay of the land, so to speak."

"Yes, of course."

"First, you are Mrs. Charlotte Smith. Please use that name whenever you are within the walls of The White House." She paused, "I'm the only one who knows our clients' true identities. I keep that information in a ledger in a vault. Now, the other thing is a mask." Mrs. Griffin leaned over to the chair beside her and picked up a loo mask Alicia had not noticed, as well as a small hat with a rather heavy veil attached. "Wear both at all times."

She held out the mask, giving Alicia a reassuring smile. "Hugo will never know your name or what you look like. In the normal course of events most people remove it at some point during the evening. Naturally, you will not wish Hugo to see your face."

Alicia's hands shook as she took the scrap of black velvet.

Mrs. Griffith noticed. "Please, you must relax. If you decide you don't wish to enter the building, simply tell the driver. He will take you here, or to your house, or anywhere else you desire." She paused and Alicia nodded. "When you arrive, a servant will greet you. Normally, a client will have a specific scenario in mind and they would have provided me with a written description beforehand. To facilitate matters, I have taken the liberty of writing up something and leaving it for Hugo. You won't need it, of course, but I think it is wise if you follow the usual procedures. Do you have any questions?"

Alicia had at least a hundred, but she shook her head.

"So, Mrs. Smith—are you ready?"

Alicia must have said yes because here she was a quarter of an hour later, her carriage rolling to a stop.

She closed her eyes and said a quick prayer that she was doing the right   thing.

Chapter Twenty-Six

Joss was entering the daily paid out receipts into the enormous ledger Melissa kept for that purpose.

As of tonight, he was officially in charge of the entire operation. Melissa had departed earlier in the day for the house she'd leased somewhere not far from Brighton.

She'd taken a handful of employees with her, two of them women who'd wanted a rest from the rigors of whoring and were glad to pose as members of Melissa's household to lend her respectability in the small seaside community she'd chosen.

Joss questioned her decision when it came to hiring whores for respectability, but what did he know about such things?

He'd told her she could stay away longer, but he could see she was already anxious to be leaving for as long as she was.

This was a huge undertaking and the operation of not one, but two separate brothels—the men's side boasting its own hell—required a lot of time and effort and cost a fortune.

There were mountains of expenses: building maintenance, furnishings, food, fine wine, champagne, and liquor, just to name a few.

And then there were the employees themselves.

Joss looked down the ledger to that part of the book that listed employee expenses and shook his head in amazement.

Melissa could have retired five years ago if she didn't pay the wages she did to both whores and servants.

When he'd pointed that out, she'd said, "If I'm going to make money off the backs of other people, I believe they should be amply compensated for it. This assuages some of my guilt. With only a little management, they should all be able to save enough to one day retire."

Joss didn't have the heart to tell her that most of her employees ran through their money like water.

And some of them—Hugo Buckingham's face flickered through Joss's mind—probably *never* wanted to retire because they appeared to love what they did.

Thinking of Hugo annoyed him, just as it always did.

"You are so jealous, Joss," Melissa had teased when Joss had made some scathing comment about the amoral male whore who made more money for The White House—from both male *and* female clients—than any other.

"I'm not jealous," he'd said, only partly lying. "I just don't trust him. He's sly and self-serving and he'd sell us all in a heartbeat if he thought he could make a penny."

Melissa had laughed. "Poor Hugo! What an opinion you have of him."

Joss snorted now as he thought about her defense of the loathsome man. *Was* he jealous? He didn't think so. Although it was true that Hugo was far more popular than Joss had ever been.

Of course, Joss had drawn the line at servicing male clients.

Hugo, Joss believed, would fuck a knothole in a fence if it paid him to do so.

Not only was he amoral, he also had a dangerous sense of humor and it amused him no end that Joss disliked him. He made a concerted effort to discompose Joss in any way he could: parading through the hallways naked and displaying his shockingly huge cock seemed to be his favorite method, but he was always coming up with new ways to annoy him.

For example, just moments earlier the sleek, snake-like, untrustworthy whore had waved around the letter he'd received from the new client who'd booked their diamond suite for the entire evening.

"I almost feel like I should pay *her* for the privilege of this evening," Hugo had told Joss with an evil-sounding laugh when Joss had had the misfortune to run into him outside Melissa's study. "I just spoke to Marcus, who met her carriage, and he said her figure was delicious. As for her face?" He snickered. "Who cares if she looks like the back end of a mule if she keeps her mask on?"

Joss tried to ignore the other man, but Hugo went out of his way to place himself in Joss's path.

Even the way Hugo dressed was irritating and affected: black leather breeches, black linens, a dull black silk waistcoat with onyx buttons, and supple black leather riding boots—although Joss knew for a fact the man had never ridden a horse in his life.

"Listen to this, Gormley," Hugo had said.

Joss could hardly *avoid* listening as Hugo had been standing in front of the office door when Joss returned from his errand—almost as if he'd been *waiting* for him, which he probably had.

Melissa would frown on Joss beating her highest earning whore to a pulp, so he crossed his arms and stared down at Hugo.

"What."

Hugo was not put off by either Joss's tone, dead stare, or bigger body.

"Listen to this," he said.

"I want to give myself body and soul to a demanding master ...."

Hugo had assumed the stance of a Shakespearean actor declaiming a soliloquy as he read the rest of the half-page letter.

Joss wanted to tell him to shut up and to go sod himself, but the more Hugo read; the more interested Joss became.

It was as if this woman—some stranger—had opened his head and looked at his brain: the part that showed his deepest, most private and primitive sexual desires. And then she'd written them all down on paper.

A piece of paper that had the misfortune to end up in the hands of a man who in no way deserved it.

Hugo hooted loudly when he finished reading, startling Joss out of his fugue.

The shorter man had smirked and grabbed his crotch. "Good God! I'm hard enough to break rocks. I'd better get my arse over to the diamond suite before she catches fire." He'd strode off chuckling.

Joss had stood there, rooted to the floor. His groin throbbed like a war drum as he thought about what the woman wanted.

The anonymity of the scene she'd described in her letter meant he could imagine she was any woman.

He could imagine Mrs. Smith was *her*.

Joss closed his eyes briefly, disgusted by his thoughts, by his body's reactions, by his raw lust. Was that really what he'd become?

No, it wasn't.

And so he'd swallowed his desire and turned back to his ledgers.

But here he was, ten minutes later, still fantasizing. He could not get his mind off this woman in the diamond suite. Who the devil was she?

"Just go look up her name or you'll be useless," he told himself, his feet already in motion toward the safe.

As he turned the tumbler, he wondered what the hell he was doing? Finding out her name didn't matter. It still wouldn't be Alicia.

"Oh, what can it hurt," he muttered, opening the heavy door and taking the brown leather ledger from the bottom of the pile.

Melissa was fiendishly organized and kept two lists cross-referenced by their real names and false names. As he flicked to the section where the false names began a small rectangle of paper fluttered to the ground.

Joss picked it up and his jaw dropped: Lady Alicia Selwood.

His fingers worked without any instructions from his brain and turned the card over.

In Melissa's distinctive hand were these words,

"Client has requested anyone but Joss. Has indicated Hugo sounds best suited to her needs."

Alicia could not have said a word even if the man had not already commanded her to silence.

He poured two glasses of something and came toward her.

He was sharp featured and possessed a muscular but sinuous body that put her in mind of a satyr—an erotic, seductive minion of the devil himself.

She told herself it didn't matter.

What mattered is that *she* wore a mask and this man would soon be gone. Or so she hoped.

He handed her the glass, his lips curving in a smile that was without a doubt the most wicked she had ever seen.

"I'd like to see behind that mask," he said in his odd accent, which was rough yet somehow cultured—like a guttersnipe from St. Giles who'd taken elocution lessons from a royal duke.

Alicia swallowed at his words and he chuckled. "Don't worry, I won't make you take it off… yet." He took a deep pull on his drink and bared his teeth while the liquor burned its way down his throat. His teeth were surprisingly white but crooked, and the two canines appeared pointier than usual. His eyes were a dark brown that looked black in the room, which had been lighted so poorly she almost ran into a table on her way in.

He smacked his lips and grinned at her. "Ahh. Have a sip, Mrs. Smith. I insist," he said when she hesitated. His face—which was far too angular and feral too be handsome—became even harder. "I don't like to give orders twice."

Alicia stiffened as his cold command, tempted to tell him what she thought about what he did or didn't like.

But then she realized he was just playing whatever part Mrs. Griffin had written for him, so she raised the glass and took a drink, wondering—worriedly—just what the other woman had written in that letter.

It was fine brandy, but all alcohol tasted like sawdust after she'd realized that she'd almost killed herself drinking.

"Good girl," he praised.

When Joss spoke to her that way, Alicia wanted to drop to her knees.

Hugo made her palm itch to slap him.

"Hold my glass, darling." He gave her his still half-full glass and then reached for the clasp on her cloak. When she startled, he jerked her body toward his.

He might be whipcord lean but he was unbelievably strong.

"I'm removing this, Mrs. Smith. Does that present a problem? You may answer me either *yes, Hugo,* or *no, Hugo.*" He held her close enough to his body that she could feel his heat and smell his skin and hair. He wore some type of cologne that had a citrus-tang to it. He smelled good, but he was not Joss.

And just where the hell *was* Joss ....

"Now, I'm going to take this off."

She swallowed. "Yes, Hugo."

The corner of his mouth pulled up into an evil smile. "Good girl." He unclasped the cloak and then leaned close and pressed his body against hers to remove it from her shoulders. She felt the unmistakable thrust of his arousal against her belly and shuddered.

He chuckled. "You like that, do you? All for you, darling."

Oh God. *Joss, where are you?*

He took the cloak in one hand and sauntered toward a coat rack, draping it over a hook. Alicia felt a bit dizzy and discovered she'd been holding her breath. She released it quietly and inhaled another.

"That is a lovely dress," he said, eyeing her up and down and circling her in a manner calculated to make her even more nervous. "Charmeuse, is it not?"

Alicia swallowed, but before she could answer a hand struck her bottom. She jumped and gave a mortifying yelp.

"When I ask you a question I expect—"

There was a light knock and then the door opened.

"What the bloody hell," Hugo demanded of the cringing lackey in the doorway.

"I'm sorry to disturb you, Mr. Hugo. But I'm afraid you'll need to step out for a moment."

Hugo turned to her, his face unreadable. "I beg your pardon, Mrs. Smith. I shall return directly."

The door closed behind him and Alicia dropped into the nearest chair.

Thank God. She'd begun to wonder if Mrs. Griffin's plan had fallen to pieces. Lord, how would she extricate herself if—

The door opened again and she leapt to her feet.

Alicia would have known him anywhere, even though he was backlit by the lights in the corridor and she couldn't see his face.

Her heart thudded in her chest and she took a step toward him.

He didn't speak when he stepped inside and closed the door. Unlike Hugo, he wore a full-face mask, just like hers.

His evening clothing was that of any gentleman: a black cutaway coat, white linen, and black pantaloons that were so tight they looked as if some lucky servant had merely applied boot blacking to his magnificent thighs and calves.

Alicia opened her mouth to thank him for seeing her, but then he said, "Good evening, Mrs. Smith. Hugo has been unexpectedly called away but I will see to your needs."

His words were crisp and emotionless, not unfriendly, but certainly not warm.

Alicia frowned; did he not recognize her?

She opened her mouth, but he raised a hand.

"You may nod if you wish me to stay or shake your head if you wish me to go. You may not speak unless I give you permission. Once you have made your decision to stay, you will obey me in every way. Nod if you understand."

His words shot through her like a bolt of lightning, ripping down her spine and settling in her sex. She was wet. Immediately. Part of her brain—the tiny part that could still think—wondered why Hugo's orders had not elicited the same response.

"Mrs. Smith." His voice was like the crack of a whip. "Nod yes or shake your head no to be taken home. Do it now."

She began nodding even before he'd finished, the shocking truth mingling with lust inside her aching body: He did not know who she was, but he was obviously more than willing to *service* her; she was nothing but a job to him.

Her body shook with barely suppressed fury. And desire. She wanted to hit him—to yell at him and hurt him—but she also wanted . . . *this.*

How long would it take him to realize who she was?

And just what had Melissa Griffin put in that letter? The way he was behaving ... Alicia shivered.

He turned away from her and opened the door again, exchanging a few words with somebody in the hall. A young woman dressed in a maid uniform entered.

"Sally will take you into the other room and assist you while you change. You will not speak to her. Nod if you understand."

Again her body responded before she gave it permission.

"Good, now go." He turned toward the sideboard that held the two glasses she'd set there.

Sally approached her and gestured to the room beyond. Alicia hesitated only a second but he seemed to sense it—even though his back was to her as he poured himself a drink.

"The next time I have to repeat myself, Mrs. Smith, you will find yourself in the carriage on your way home. You have five minutes to change your clothing."

Alicia burned at his tone, the sort a man—a *rude* man—would use on a disobedient dog.

Resistance and rebellion fought with lust and were easily overpowered.

Her feet—deceitful things that they were—bore her toward the room he'd indicated. It was a dressing room and Alicia saw that clothing—if you could call it that—had already been laid out on the bed. She gaped.

"But—but," she stopped, appalled at how weak she sounded.

The girl didn't comment. Instead she began unbuttoning Alicia's gown.

Time seemed to speed up, every second bringing her closer and closer to wearing . . . *that.*

Go tell him who you are, you fool!

Alicia ignored Aunt Giddy's voice, too stunned by the agonizing truth: Joss didn't care who Mrs. Smith was—he would do this with anyone. God only knew how often he'd done this in the weeks since he'd left her employ.

That unpleasant thought was one more ingredient in the nasty stew that simmered within her. How was it possible that thoughts of him with other women—*many* other women—could revolt and arouse her at the same time? What was *wrong* with her?

Alicia realized that the girl had already removed her gown, petticoat, and stays.

"Please lift your arms, Mrs. Smith."

Alicia complied and Sally lifted her chemise, barely disturbing her hat.

Next, she knelt and untied Alicia's garters and rolled down her stockings before slipping off her evening shoes, leaving her naked but for a hat, veil, and mask.

When Sally brought the garment closer, Alicia stared. It was barely a collection of thin straps holding together sheer black material. Part of her brain—the part not busy being appalled at the thought of wearing the gown—realized it had ties that made it adjustable.

Once the girl had adjusted the last of the panels, she turned Alicia to face the mirror.

She gasped at what she saw.

The garment did *nothing* to cover her! Instead, the transparent material emphasized the shadowy triangle of hair at the apex of her legs. Her nipples—dark and hard—thrusted against the gossamer thin fabric.

It was obscene. Her body was entirely exposed, while her face was a black void where the heavy veil fluttered with each shallow breath.

With no face or head, she resembled a bizarre sort of statue—like the Greek and Roman torsos she'd seen over the years. She was nothing but a . . . body.

"Come, Mrs. Smith." The girl nudged her away from the mirror and gestured to yet another open doorway. This one opened to a bedchamber.

Again, there were only two candles. She was more grateful than ever for the lack of light.

"Wait here and do not move," Sally said, leaving her standing facing an enormous four-poster bed.

There was a fire at the far end of the room but it was far away and the chill was acting predictably, her nipples tightening painfully, her skin pebbling from a combination of cold and wanton excitement. She expected to hear him any minute behind her. Any minute.

But the longer she stood there, the harder it became not to move. Was he never coming? Was this some manner of jest? Could she—

"You were told not to move, Mrs. Smith."

His voice, low and cold and hard, came with a puff of warm air on her right ear and she jumped and yelped.

"Shhh," he whispered, his erection pressing against her buttocks and his broad, powerful torso covering her back.

She felt the phantom touch of his hands on her hips and jolted.

"You are so nervous, Mrs. Smith." He stroked from her hips to her breasts, his hands lingering on the wide strip of fabric that encircled her waist and held her pitiful negligee together. "You look very desirable in this gown—a delicious vessel for my pleasure."

Alicia swallowed convulsively at his crude compliment.

His fingers slid between the slits, his hands warm and rough on her thin, sensitive skin. "Lean forward at the waist and grip the bed."

His voice was a low rumble, the words scraping her nerves like a razor. Her jaw dropped.

She heard him inhale—to dismiss her? To send her away?—and quickly did as he bade her, the position leaving her feeling more exposed and vulnerable than she'd ever felt in her life.

A low chuckle came from behind her. "Very good, Mrs. Smith. I was concerned for a moment that I might have to send you packing." His mocking tone turned her entire body hot with shame and lust.

This time she didn't jump when his hands began to caress her, the movements slow, firm, and possessive as he learned the shape of her too-broad hips.

"You are lush, Mrs. Smith." She felt his body cover hers, his weight pushing her down cruelly, forcing her to struggle to maintain her position. "There is nothing I enjoy more than fucking a lush arse."

Her eyes fluttered shut and her ribcage expanded.

"Ah," he chuckled again, his hand wrapping around her pelvis and pulling away the panel of thin fabric that shrouded her sex. "You like that," he said smugly, his finger pushing between her lips and giving her agonizingly swollen peak the briefest of flicks before penetrating her body.

She gasped at his rough invasion.

"What a beautiful tight, wet cunt you have Mrs. Smith." His finger curled up inside her and she whimpered.

His hand flexed, gripping her mound almost painfully hard. "Not a sound from you. Do you understand me?" he demanded in a harsh voice; the finger buried inside her prodding a mind-numbingly sensitive spot.

He slapped her buttock with the hand that wasn't buried deep inside her. It didn't hurt but it surprised her—and, horrifyingly—excited her.

"You will acknowledge my questions or I will punish you, Mrs. Smith. Do you understand?"

Her body tightened at the word *punish* but she nodded quickly and his hand began to move.

He worked her with all the skill she knew him to possess, a second finger joining the first. When his free hand began to circle her pearl, it took mere moments to bring her to the crest of a climax.

"I want to reward you for your obedience."

She preened at his praise even as she despised her needy weakness.

"I could make you come so easily—make you buck and shudder and convulse as you drench my hand," he whispered, his movements hard and rhythmic. "Or I could just tease you, over and over bringing you to the brink of pleasure and leaving you quivering and wanting."

His words, as much as his skilled hands and fingers, drove her blindly toward orgasm.

"But I'm not going to do either."

He released her abruptly and swatted her bottom *hard*. "Get on the bed, on your hands and knees," he ordered. "Face forward, head up, and remain completely still. You will wait for me in that position as long as I require it. Understood?"

Alicia nodded, embarrassingly clumsy as she crawled onto the bed.

She heard a drawer being opened somewhere as she dropped to her hands, her knees clamped tightly together. It was all she could do not to turn and see what he was doing. Wisely, she refrained.

This time, she wasn't surprised when he made her wait.

She heard the clink of glass on glass and realized he was pouring himself a drink. Rather than fury, it was lust that pounded inside her at his openly degrading treatment.

"Spread your knees."

She gritted her teeth so hard her jaws hurt, but she did as he said.

"Wider—to the width of your shoulders."

Shame and desire became indistinguishable as she spread until only a single insubstantial panel of fabric was all that covered her sex.

"Good." His voice was a low, rough purr. "Now, reach back and lift that fabric out of the way, toss it over your back. I don't want anything to obstruct my view. Once you've done that, drop to your elbows."

Her face burned with mortification and she fumbled to lift the diaphanous panel and shunt it to the side. Her body shook as she assumed the submissive posture he demanded.

He gave a low animalistic groan. "My God, what a beautiful sight. You are beyond exquisite, Mrs. Smith."

His words and the worshipful tone of his voice both thrilled and gutted her. He'd said something similar one evening in their love nest above the stables.

Apparently, he said the same thing to all his customers.

Alicia had to blink away tears. But her sex throbbed for him.

"I could look at you all night long." His voice was still worshipful, but now there was a slight tremor that told her he was not untouched.

She heard the sound of a glass being set down, and then he was behind her again, one big hand resting possessively on her lower back while the other caressed her exposed sex with a light touch that made her bite her lip to keep from whimpering.

He groaned and then pressed something hot and slick against her entrance. "I can't wait any longer, Mrs. Smith." And then his thick, blunt head breached her.

Pain and pleasure mingled as he held her impaled on the impossible hardness of his body, stretching and filling her.

"Mmm." He took her waist in both hands, his fingers almost spanning her, the touch making her feel feminine and desirable.

And then he oh-so-slowly slid out, removing himself delicious inch by delicious inch until only his crown remained.

"So good, isn't it?" he whispered, his hips pulsing lightly.

It was beyond good. It was. . . intoxicating.

She nodded, and he slammed into her.

When she cried out, he didn't chide her.

He pounded her, as relentless as a piece of machinery, pumping her harder with each thrust, until she felt like she would split in two.

But she wanted him deeper, wanted to give him more.

"Yes, just like that." His words made her realize that she was canting her hips and pushing against him.

He laid a big hand in the middle of her back and pushed her lower, the action bringing him deeper.

Alicia began to come apart, her consciousness narrowing to the place where they were joined: she gathered the last of her wits and tightened her inner muscles.

"Ah, God, yes," he shouted.

But then—once again—he stopped.

"Not so fast," he snarled. "Not so goddamned fast."

The harsh sounds of their breathing filled the room and she squirmed against him, desperate for release.

He gave her buttock a stinging slap. "You will not climax, Mrs. Smith. Not until I allow you to do so." He grabbed her hips and pushed so deeply it hurt, making her gasp. Also making her realize she'd failed to answer.

The instant she nodded; he began to move, possessing her with slow, thorough thrusts.

How could she not climax when he was doing *this* to her?

He had never denied her pleasure before—always seeing to her satisfaction first.

Why did her body respond so intensely to deprivation—like a dog groveling to be stroked?

He began to move slower, more rhythmically, but pushing just a fraction deeper each time, his guttural grunts beyond arousing.

"Clench," he ordered.

Without thinking, Alicia obeyed.

"*Yes.* Again. Squeeze me—squeeze me as tightly as you can."

This time, when she tried to obey, nothing happened.

He rammed her hard. "*Clench.*"

Her body responded without her mind ordering it.

"Good. Don't stop."

Each thrust brought her closer, until she was gritting her teeth to hold back her climax, her head aching from the effort of restraining herself.

And still he continued to pound her and pound her and pound her. Until—

He shouted something incomprehensible and then hilted himself, his shaft jerking and thickening as he spent deep inside her.

Gradually, his spasms grew weaker and weaker, until they were mere shudders.

Primed, wanting, and shaking from the effort of restraining herself, Alicia waited for him to see to her pleasure.

And waited.

And waited.

He gave a low grunt of satisfaction, pulled out of her, and then rolled onto his back, his eyes glinting up at her from behind his mask.

"Did I say you could look at me, Mrs. Smith?"

Alicia startled at his cold tone and jerked her head up.

Beside her, he shifted once and then continued to breathe heavily, until finally she couldn't hear him.

Alicia frowned. Was it possible. . . could he have gone to *sleep?*

She whipped around and found him lying on his side, his head propped up on one hand. His eyebrow cocked.

Alicia realized she was still on all fours like some barbaric supplicant and pushed onto her knees, shaking with anger.

His lips twisted into a mean, mocking smile.

"What's the matter, Alicia? Didn't you get your money's worth?"

Chapter Twenty-Seven

Joss couldn't see her face but he could feel the rage rolling off her deliciously sweaty and wanting body.

"You *knew?*"

He snorted and pushed off the bed, watching in amusement as she yanked off her hat and veil and clumsily spun around, still on her knees.

"You really do think I'm an idiot, don't you?" he asked, not waiting for an answer.

Instead, he snatched his half-full glass of cognac off the nightstand, throwing it back in one gulp before tossing angry words over his shoulder, "Do you really think I wouldn't recognize your body? Did you not recognize *mine?*"

A sound of choked fury came from behind him and something hit him in the back of the head.

He turned to find it had been her hat. She was standing beside the bed, her hair sticking out at all angles, her hands fisted on her hips, her impressive bosom rising and falling rapidly.

"What is *wrong* with you?" she demanded.

"I only do what the client asks for." He spun on his heel, heading for the brandy. He ripped the stopper from the decanter and dumped more liquor into his glass, too angry to look at her.

"I don't understand," she said behind him. "Why would you do such a thing?"

"I'm sorry—I suppose those very explicit instructions were for Hugo—anyone but *me*, actually."

"What are you *talking* about."

He swallowed another mouthful and grimaced, suddenly feeling a bit bilious.

Just what bloody game was she playing now? Just who—

She snatched the glass from his unresisting fingers and slammed it down on the table, the contents sloshing over the side.

"What is wrong with you?" she repeated, glaring up at him. "I only wanted to talk."

"Ha! Is *that* what they call it in America?" He strode over to where he'd left his coat draped across the back of one of the chairs and fumbled in his pocket to grab the note. "You mean why did I follow your orders—the orders you wrote out to the very letter?" He thrust the crumpled piece of paper at her and snatched up his glass again before striding back to the chair and lowering himself into it so hard he jammed his tailbone.

"Christ," he muttered, shifting uncomfortably, his eyes sliding to look at her.

She held the letter close to her face, her lips moving slightly, her expression that of a person who'd never seen it before.

The truth hit him like a cold, wet smack in the face: Melissa.

"Goddammit!" he yelled.

She jolted at his yell and looked up. "I didn't write this."

"How did you get in here?" He knew the answer before she said it.

"Mrs.Griffin invited me."

"That meddling, interfering—"

"Joss!" She waved the letter around. "Why would she do this?"

"Because she likes to meddle."

Her face was crimson. "What did you *tell* her about me that would have led her to write such things?"

He snorted. "You mean why is it such an accurate assessment of your desires?"

Her jaw dropped. But Joss knew she couldn't deny it.

Her eyes narrowed to shards of blue ice.

"I told her nothing about what you like in the bedroom, Alicia. Believe me, Melissa needs no help when it comes to such matters—human sexuality is her area of expertise." He thought it would not be prudent to tell her that Melissa had *personal* knowledge of Joss's own sexual proclivities.

Joss wondered if she had any idea how erotic she looked: flushed, angry, and dressed like Salome. He doubted it.

He swallowed the rest of his drink and set down the glass. "I'm guessing she thought such a letter would give us something to talk about. And it has." He hesitated and added, "And I suppose she contacted you because she thought I wished to see you."

"You told her that?"

"No."

She recoiled and he sighed. "I'm sorry, I didn't mean that the way it sounded. Won't you sit?" His eyes couldn't resist another trip up and down her body. "I, er, well, it's difficult to talk when you look—" He waved a hand to encompass her person, which was bloody delicious but not conducive to rational speech.

Joss stood, grabbed the throw rug from the back of his chair, and wrapped it around her shoulders.

"There," he said. "Now, sit."

She sat. "Tell me what you told Mrs. Griffin."

He sighed. Clearly, she was not going to let go of the topic. "I just told her about us. About how things ended." He felt his face heat. "Normally I wouldn't have said *anything* but she kept at me."

"Why would she do that?"

"Because I was miserable." He scowled. "There, I said it."

"You're miserable? Because of me?" Her full lips were curved into a tremulous smile and her eyes were wide.

"Yes, because of you—are you happy to hear that? You certainly look bloody happy."

Rather than appear chastened, her smile grew. "Yes, I *am* happy to hear it. Does that make me a bad person?"

"Probably."

She laughed and his lips twitched.

She stood and came toward him, the blanket slipping from her shoulders. Joss groaned. "Oh god."

She sank to her knees beside his chair, her hands taking his, which he'd been using to cover his erection.

Her smile grew. "Is that for me?"

"No." He grabbed her hands and jerked her up onto his lap, growling when her fleshy bottom settled over his aching groin.

Her arms slid around his neck and she nuzzled him. "I'm probably crushing you," she murmured into his neck.

"Mmm hmm, you are."

Her body shook with laughter. "I've missed you so much, Joss. *So* much. I've been completely miserable without you."

He grunted; he hadn't forgiven her yet—no matter how thrilled he was to be touching her, holding her.

She looked up, her brow wrinkled. "Why did you make that sound?"

"Why did you send me away?" he countered.

Her face lost all its humor and she bit her lip, her expression suddenly closed.

Joss shook his head, his anger flooding back. He stood, lifting her up with him and placing her at arm's length once they were both on their feet.

He turned away but her hand on his arm stopped him.

He whipped around. "What, Alicia? Why are you here? Just for a fuck? I know you might not have written that note, but you're here—in this place. What do you want?"

She stared up at him, her blue eyes wide and hurt. "I just wanted—I need—" her shoulders slumped and he saw diamonds squeeze from the corners of her eyes.

"Oh bloody hell." He grabbed her and yanked her close, holding her like   he   would   never   let   her   go.

Chapter Twenty-Eight

They sat in the small sitting area, both of them wrapped in the luxurious black silk robes they'd slipped into, a generous tea tray between them on a low table.

Alicia had thought he'd make her leave, but instead, he'd pulled the bell and ordered tea.

She looked up from the steaming cup in her hand to find him examining her, waiting.

Something about his very stillness told her that he'd not speak again if she did not say what he needed to hear. But if she told him what she needed? If she told him what she wanted to do? Would he leave everything behind, become a criminal, and come with her?

You have to tell him, Allie.

She put her cup down. "What I'm about to tell you isn't pleasant, Joss. Before I say anything, I want you to promise me something—two things, actually."

"What do you want me to promise?"

"Promise you won't hate me for what I've done."

His eyes closed briefly and he gave a helpless sounding laugh that made her shiver.

"What? Why are you laughing?"

But he just shook his head, an odd, sad smile on his face. "I promise I won't hate you. For any reason."

His words were not as reassuring as she'd hoped. Of course, extracting a promise from somebody before telling them what they were promising was not exactly playing fair.

"What's the second thing?"

"I'll tell you in a moment." Alicia chewed her lip, struggling to gather her thoughts.

It was difficult to look at him—thoughts of what he'd just done to her, and how much she'd loved it, ricocheting around in her head and making rational speech difficult. Especially about *this* subject.

She dropped her gaze to his hands, which rested loosely on the arms of the bottle-green leather armchair. He had the biggest hands she'd ever seen. She loved his hands. She—

"Alicia?"

She sighed. "Very well. My marriage to the late earl was not ideal." She snorted rudely at the horrific understatement. "He needed money. I knew that before we married and I believe the civilized settlements we negotiated prior to our marriage were all he wanted." She cleared her throat, which seemed to have gotten smaller, tighter. "I only learned that he wanted something else after." She looked down at the rich carpet beneath their feet. It was jewel-toned and luxurious, as fine as anything in a lord's house. "He also wanted was a son."

He cocked his head. "But he already has one."

"He didn't want a son for himself."

She could almost hear the machinery churning as he struggled through the various possibilities, discarding them, one after another, until he reached the last one. The most unthinkable one. She knew when the realization dawned on him because he blanched.

"My God."

Now he would know her for what she was. Oddly, what she felt most was relief: there would be no more hiding from him.

"Edward was the consummate gentleman right up to the wedding night. That evening, he called me into the library after dinner. David was there with him. Edward told me I could submit like a good wife, or he could make things very unpleasant for me. He rationalized it—saying he wasn't physically able to bed me, so it was only fair that at least one Selwood could." Her voice had become louder and she swallowed down her rage.

"They were both terrified that David's wife wouldn't produce a son. The poor woman had had miscarriage after miscarriage and the only child to survive was the one girl. If David didn't have a son, everything would pass to a cousin—and they both refused to accept that possibility. So, if David couldn't have a son by his own wife, they'd both agreed that I was the next best thing." Alicia paused her gruesome tale.

Joss said nothing, but his expression spoke volumes.

"He pointed out how handsome his son was, how refined, what excellent bloodlines. In essence, he told me that I should be grateful to be bred by such a fine specimen."

Joss flinched, his hands flexing. "How long did this go on?"

"Until my dear husband shuffled off his mortal coil. And then again when David came back to town this year."

His eyes widened in disbelief.

"Oh, not for a child anymore—lord, but that would be inconvenient to explain, wouldn't it?" Her laughter sounded hollow. "But that didn't mean he couldn't amuse himself with me in other ways. He didn't even want me, er, *sexually* most of the time." She swallowed convulsively and turned away. "You see," she said, not altogether successful at keeping her tone level and normal. "What he really enjoys is inflicting pain. Sometimes, I think he prefers beating me to. . . to . . ."

Joss shot to his feet and came toward her, but she couldn't stop the flow of awful words.

"Somebody found out about us, Joss—about what you and I did in your quarters and told him. He did not appreciate sharing me with a mere servant."

Joss dropped to his haunches beside her chair, taking her hand. "He made you discharge me."

"He said he'd find a way to have you thrown in jail if I didn't. He also said he wouldn't take Lizzy away from me if I showed him that I was respectable and could be trusted." She closed her eyes. "But he took her, anyway, Joss. He took her."

Joss reached out to take her in his arms but she shook her head.

"I won't be able to control myself if you do, Joss."

"Shhh, sweetheart. You don't need to control yourself around me." He enfolded her in his gentle, powerful embrace and she gave up the struggle and just sobbed.

— ❤ —

Joss held her shaking body, struggling to contain his fury as he stroked her hair, murmuring soothing words into the fragrant abundance of it.

She'd been systematically raped by her stepson with the aid and acquiescence of her husband.

Joss simply could not wrap his mind around it. What kind of people did such a thing?

He slid his arm beneath her knees and picked her up, cradling her against his chest as she sobbed and carrying her to the sofa in front of the fire where he sat and held her, letting her cry as long as she needed. Just holding her. Holding her and thinking about Selwood's smug, hateful face and what he was going to do to it.

"Joss?"

Her voice pulled him away from his murderous musings. "Yes, love?"

She gave a watery chuckle and pressed her face into his chest. "Oh, that sounds very nice. Am I your love?"

He hugged her tight. "I'm sorry about tonight, Alicia. I never meant to hurt you or force you to do anything you didn't—" God, he was so mortified by his behavior tonight after what she'd told him that he simply could not find the right words.

"No, Joss." Her sharp tone startled him. "How can you think that what we do together is anything like what David did to me?" She struggled into a seated position, cupping his jaw. "You didn't hurt or force me like he did. I *wanted* you to do all of that—and more." She kissed him, her mouth hot, eager, and salty on his. "I loved it," she whispered hoarsely in his ear. "Does that make me depraved? I—I loved tonight."

Relief and lust washed over him in equal amounts and he said a small, silent prayer of thanks. But then he put her away from him, not finished with this conversation, no matter how much he wanted to take her again.

"I want to know the rest. Please. He made you get rid of me or he'd take away Lady Elizabeth—and then he took her. Do you know where? To the house in the country?"

"No, he's sent her to a place where she can rest and recuperate," her voice broke, and Joss stroked her hair until she could speak again. "I'm so sorry I sent you away, Joss. But I had to try and—"

"Shhh, of course you had to try. I understand." He tilted her chin toward him. "But you can't lie to me again about this kind of thing."

She nodded, her nose and eyes were puffy and red, and yet she was still the most gorgeous woman in the world.

"We will find her, Alicia. There has to be—"

"I have a man looking for her." She gave him a sheepish look. "The same man who looked into your background."

Joss didn't care about that. "Has he found anything?"

"Nothing yet, but he is busily narrowing down the list and has employed two other gentlemen to assist him. He is doing everything he can."

Joss could think of one thing that her investigator probably hadn't tried: beating Selwood until he became more cooperative.

"Joss?" The word came from the vicinity of his right nipple, where she was resting her head.

"Mmm hmm?"

"That promise you made me earlier?"

He had a sinking feeling. "Yes?"

"It's that you won't do anything foolish about David—don't, er, well, *damage* him. It's not that I wouldn't enjoy that," she added hastily. "But he makes a powerful enemy. Besides, Mr. Shelly has things in hand. I'm sure he'll find her soon."

"Hmm."

"So, you'll promise, then?"

Joss felt bad about lying, but not *terribly* bad. "I promise."

She relaxed against him. "That's good. Because I—I care for you a great deal. A *great* deal."

He smiled and kissed the top of her head. "And I you."

"The truth is, I don't want to live without you—it is too miserable, I won't do it."

He held her tight, willing her not to say what he thought she was about to say; willing her not to offer him another arrangement like the one she'd offered before. He was too afraid he would take it.

So he shifted her until his mouth could reach hers, and plunged into her deeply. She made a slight sound and then opened for him, her hands sliding around his neck, her tongue taking up his challenge.

When they were both breathless, he pulled away and she again collapsed against him.

"Joss?"

"Hmmm?"

"I want to talk about this—about us."

"Alicia—"

"Don't say my name that way—as if you already know what I'm going to say—and are going to tell me no."

He held her out so that he could see her face. "Do you think you'll be able to slip away and come here unnoticed to see me? If he knew about what happened in my quarters then he will certainly find out about this."

"That is not what I want at all."

He frowned. "I don't understand?"

"I want to be with you—and not just at night."

Joss stared, not wanting to hope.

Her pale, beautiful face flushed and she looked up at him from beneath her lashes. "Are you going to make me say it?"

"Yes, I'm afraid I am—because I have no idea what you mean."

She closed her eyes, took a deep breath, and then opened them. "Joss, will you marry me?"

—❤—

The second time they made love, Joss made sure she found satisfaction. Several times, in fact.

Afterward, they were lying together, their bodies cooling in the night air. Joss had twisted a long strand of hair around his finger and was admiring the sheen.

"Joss?"

"Mmm hmm."

"You did not answer my question?"

"Oh? What question was that?"

She punched his shoulder.

"Ow!"

Joss released the strand and it unwound from his finger like a living thing. He encircled her delicate wrist with his thumb and forefinger.

"You would be an abusive spouse, it seems." He kissed her knuckles, which were still clenched in a fist, and looked up at her while tracing the seam between her fingers with the pointed tip of his tongue.

She shivered. "Are you trying to drive me mad?"

He kissed her again and released her. "I think you are already mad, Alicia. Have you given any thought to what marriage to me would mean? Are you sure this is not a thought born of the moment—of passion?"

"I think it has been in my mind for a very long time, buried beneath my fear for Lizzy. You don't understand how little I value society. My only friend in London is Lady Constance and she will remain true no matter who I marry or what I do." She placed her hand flat over his heart, her eyes distant and thoughtful. "Besides, when I take Lizzy from David, I shall not be able to return—even if I wanted to." She turned her dark blue gaze on him. "Will you want to be a fugitive—with us? What of your family? Your sister?"

"You are not thinking straight, darling. I am the son of a butcher and you are—"

"The daughter of a whore."

Joss's eyes widened. "What—?"

"Yes, I am a fraud—everything you think you know about me is a lie."

He could only stare.

She shook her head, even though he'd said nothing.

"Oh, it isn't *all* a lie, of course. I was married to Selwood and to Horace Dandridge before him. But what you think you know about me—that I am from Selwood's class? That is a lie. I am from a place that is—"

She sighed and shook her head. "I was born poor. Dirt poor. Alicia isn't even my name. My aunt called me Allie—short for Alice."

Joss tried to tilt her chin up toward him, wanting to see her.

But she stopped him. "No, I want to tell you this but I don't want to see your face. I can't."

Joss frowned but nodded. "Go on."

"We were so very poor. Aunt Giddy took in washing and mending, she worked all the time just to keep us fed with a roof over our heads. She would bring me along when she went to pick up mending. I was too young to be left at home and we had nobody else. I loved my aunt—dearly. But she was always tired, short-tempered, and old before her time. Life at home was miserable and tense. But the places we went?"

She stopped and twisted her head as if to look at him, but instead she stared over his shoulder, into her past. "They were magical. Vast palaces filled with beautiful things. I knew that was what I wanted, Joss. Above all else, I wanted to live surrounded by beauty, comfort, and plenty. I never wanted to fear being thrown out of our meager rooms because we couldn't scratch up the rent. Or to hear my stomach grumble as my body consumed itself because I was so hungry."

Her expression was expectant, as if she wanted him to agree with her. What could he say? He'd never yearned for either creature comforts or luxuries the way she had—but neither had he lived with such grinding poverty. His family had experienced hardship, but nothing like what she was describing. Even so, he nodded.

She rested her chin on the back of her hand and continued. "One of those palaces—the biggest, the grandest—belonged to a man who had no family. Horace Dandridge had been married once before when he was quite a young man. But his wife and daughter had died and he'd never remarried. He was old—older than my aunt—my grandmother's age, if I'd had one. I was only sixteen the first time I saw him, but I already knew he would be the one. I would marry him, and he would save me."

Joss tried not to show the revulsion he felt; who was he to judge her? He who had fucked his way through half the *ton* for money.

"It was not hard to make him notice me," she said, back in the past, her voice almost dreamy.

Joss could only imagine. As a woman nearing forty, she was magnificent; as a girl she would have been just as beautiful, but he imagined her youthful innocence would have been irresistible to some men.

Joss himself preferred a woman with experience, not a girl who would be little more than a child.

"I went with my aunt to pick up the mending—I was carrying it home for her by then, taking on my share of the burden. When she was drinking a cup of coffee with the housekeeper, I took the first step to getting what I wanted. I knew he was home because the housekeeper had mentioned he'd been ill. Both she and my aunt had discussed how sad it was for such a man to be alone."

She paused, but Joss kept up his rhythmic stroking of her back, the tension in her body as tight as a bow.

"I knew which part of the house was the sole purview of the master because I'd planned my move for months. I found my way into the family wing of the giant mansion and Horace was behind the seventh door I opened."

She twisted in his arms, until she was looking up at him, smiling, but there was no humor in it. "He was propped up in the grandest bed I had ever seen. Massive pillars and a canopy that was made from the finest brocade. The bed took a step ladder to mount. There he was, his glasses on his nose, his gray hair askew, the bed piled high with ledgers and papers. I wore the best dress I had," she cut him a brief smile. "I only had three, and that was two more than Aunt Giddy could afford. She'd made them from castoffs. Sometimes she would remove a row of lace or a ribbon, and the owner of the gown would never even notice." Her grin was like that of a young girl who had just filched a sweet.

"The dress I wore was pink with a row of stolen lace at the neck and sleeves." She looked away, her profile every bit as perfect as the rest of her. "Horace looked up and smiled. I will never forget his smile. He was not a handsome man and the years of struggle and hard work were evident in his lined face. But he had the irresistible grin of a rogue. His teeth were crooked, the lids of his astonishing blue eyes drooped with age, and he had a scar at the corner of his mouth that made him look like he was perpetually snarling.

"'*I must have died and gone to heaven,*' he said.

"I'd prepared myself for any variety of responses, but not for that. I had no reply and could only gape. He took pity on me.

"'*Why else would an angel choose to visit such an old lobscouse as me?*'"

"What is a lobscouse?" Joss asked.

"That is exactly what I asked him. It seems lobscouse was some horrid dish from where he'd grown up—in Liverpool."

"Ah."

"Later I learned he'd left England when he was little more than a boy, but he still had an accent that was not from New York."

Joss pushed a stray strand of hair behind her ear and kissed her cheek. "Like yours."

"Oh, no. I sound nothing like the people in my neighborhood. Even before I came to England, I'd begun to affect the accent of the New York elites." Her mouth twisted. "Lord, if you think English aristocrats are clannish high sticklers."

"I can see why he believed you to be an angel."

Her expression became sober. "I was sitting on a chair beside his bed, chatting with him, when the housekeeper found me. Oh, I knew I would be in trouble. Perhaps even Aunt Giddy would lose her work."

She glanced up at Joss. "But Horace began to protect me that very day. *'I'll not have the girl punished,'* he told his housekeeper and my aunt. Even so, I got a dreadful scolding from Aunt Giddy. But then, a few weeks later, we both found ourselves being moved into that great mansion."

Joss tried to hide his disgust, but she could see through him.

"No, he did not make me his mistress. He would not take me to his bed for another seventeen months, until I was almost eighteen, after he'd made me his wife. He was sixty-seven."

A mix of envy and revulsion churned inside him as he thought of a younger Alicia giving her body—her maidenhood—to a man old enough to be her grandfather.

"He was good to me—very good to me—and I grew to love him for himself, not only his money." The words were almost defiant. "He gave me whatever I wanted and crushed anyone who showed me disrespect." Her lips curved into a wicked smile. "The matrons of New York society loathed me. But their husbands—who held the ultimate whip-hands—ensured these women invited me to their functions, allowed me into their clubs, and acknowledged me. But not once did any of them offer to become my friend. It was, quite literally, just Horace and me."

"What about your aunt?"

Her expression softened. "Ah, Aunt Giddy. Well, she was shocked, ashamed, and proud of me in equal measures until the day she died. She wore herself out taking care of me and once Horace took the burden of providing for us from her shoulders she simply faded away. She died the second year of my marriage. She was thirty-eight." A tear trickled down her cheek. "She died when she was younger than I am now."

She stared into Joss's eyes. "I have lived too many years trying to be somebody else—life is fleeting and I don't want to live a lie any longer." She brushed aside a second tear. "I want you. And I want you in my life."

His heart felt like it might explode. She wanted *him*—big, ugly Joss Gormley. Before he could come up with anything to say, she spoke.

"I've been thinking about how David found out about us—I think I know who told him."

"Who?"

"There was a maid—Annie."

The joy in his chest froze. "What about her?"

"Feehan discharged her recently for going through my desk—although she denied it."

"Yes, but how—"

"I saw her one night," she interrupted, her eyes narrowing. "When I came to you. At the time, I thought she must have been visiting somebody else. But it was you, wasn't it, Joss?"

She ran her fingernails down his chest when he didn't answer immediately.

He sucked in a breath when a nail grazed his nipple. "Yes, she came to my room often. I turned her away—all except one time."

Her glare should have singed off his eyebrows.

"Believe me, I have regretted it a thousand times since."

She continued to glare.

"What can I do about it now? It is over and done with."

Her lips had thinned until they were harsh lines. Joss was tempted to tease her about jealousy but did not think she would appreciate it just now.

"When did this happen?"

"Before the two of us were ever together," he assured her.

Her expression remained guarded.

"There hasn't been anyone else since you."

Her eyebrows shot up.

"What? Why are you looking at me that way?"

"But—but you work *here*."

He frowned. "Didn't Melissa tell you what my job is?"

"She told me you'd come back to your old job."

Joss muttered something exceedingly vulgar beneath his breath.

"Jocelyn Gormley! Who taught you to say such things in the presence of a lady?"

"I beg your pardon, my lady." He picked up her hand and kissed the tips of her fingers.

"I'm sure you can beg more prettily than that."

Her words surprised a snort of laughter from him, but he was not finished with the subject of his meddling friend just yet.

"I am merely a part owner and manager while Melissa is away. I no longer take clients, love—only you."

She heaved a huge sigh and rubbed her body against his in a most pleasing fashion. "I am *so* relieved, Joss. You have no idea what was going through my head."

"Oh, I can imagine," he said. "It would serve Melissa right if I packed my bags and went down to whatever little village she has sequestered herself in and—"

Alicia's hand slid down his chest, beneath his robe, and over the thin skin of his tight abdomen. "Shhh, you're blustering."

Joss's hips jerked at her touch. "I don't think that's what it's called, sweetheart."

She gave a wicked chuckle. "Besides, if you get in a carriage and go hunt her down you will need to leave me here alone." She stroked his cock from root to tip.

Joss made a gurgling sound and barely forced out the words, "Good point."

She dragged her thumb across his glans. "Yes, isn't it?"

No rational conversation was had for quite some time.

Chapter Twenty-Nine

Joss was entering the receipts from *two* days, rather than one, since he'd not done the work he was supposed to do last night.

He was also thinking of everything he and Alicia had said: the plans that had been spoken of, but not yet formalized, the problems that faced both of them.

It was. . . daunting.

But it was also thrilling. She loved him. Alicia loved *him*.

"Why do you have that stupid look on your face? Or is that just the way your face is?"

Hugo's grating voice jarred Joss out of his very pleasant reverie and he put down his quill before he gave in to temptation and stabbed the other man with it.

"Don't you ever knock?"

Hugo smirked—which *was* the way *his* face looked most of the time. "There's an old bird out front to see you."

Joss sighed.

Hugo's eyes went wide. "What? Why are you giving me that, *God, Hugo! You are too horrid to be borne* look?"

"Because you *are* too horrid to be bloody borne, Hugo. Did you get a name?" he asked before the other man could respond.

"No. She didn't want to give one, did she?"

Joss stood, removing the ink cuff from his left arm. Something suddenly occurred to him. "What the devil are you doing answering the door?" That was the last thing this business could bear: Hugo as its goodwill ambassador.

"Herman is down with a cold and Gerald ran off to do something for, hmm ..." He took his chin between his forefinger and thumb and gazed theatrically ceilingward. "Now who would have sent Gerald off at this time of day?"

Joss snatched his coat from the hook and grunted as Hugo helped him struggle into it. "Yes, yes. *I* am the one who sent Gerald off."

Hugo adjusted the collar of Joss's coat, plucking a piece of fuzz from one shoulder, and then scrutinized Joss's cravat, his hands lifting.

"Touch it and I'll break your fingers."

Rather than look insulted, Hugo's eyes widened theatrically. "Oooh, careful with that treacly talk, big lad. You know how much I love the rough trade, *Jocelyn*." He turned on his heel, chuckling as he sauntered away, swinging his arse from side to side. "Shall I show her into the receiving room?"

"Yes, Hugo, that seems a better idea than showing her into the kitchen or broom closet."

Hugo just laughed.

Joss stared at his ruined cravat in the mirror, momentarily annoyed he'd not let the other man tweak it. Instead, he did what he could to neaten his appearance and then took the door that led from the study— or the *office,* as Melissa called it—through a middling sized dining room that sometimes was used for private parties—into the receiving room.

And also right into the middle of a rather heated conversation.

"—and before that would ever happen you'd find your prick twisted into a knot you'd never be able to untie," an American voice Joss recognized said.

Hugo threw back his head and roared with perhaps the first genuine laughter Joss had ever heard.

"Miss Finch?" Joss said, unable to keep the disbelief out of his voice.

The older woman turned to him, her poke bonnet obscuring her face from any angle except straight on.

She stood up from the wing chair where Hugo had seated her, and upon the back of which the other man was now leaning, his curious, sharp eyes flickering from Joss to Miss Finch and back again.

"Mr. Gormley." Her eyes rolled over him with the crushing weight of a mail coach. "Look at you, fine as a fivepence."

Hugo gave another delighted laugh. "I *like* her."

Joss looked up from the tiny woman. "Thank you, Mr. Buckingham, you may go."

"Actually," Hugo said his eyes flitting between them, "I'd rather stay, if you don't mind. If Miss Finch here is to be a new member, I'd like to be the first to offer my services."

"Hugo."

"Hmmm?" His dark eyes shifted from Miss Finch, who'd been staring up at him with an expression that should have turned him into a pillar of stone.

"You may go, Hugo."

Hugo heaved a dramatic sigh. "Very well. I shall have tea sent up." He strolled toward the door, taking his time and making sure Miss Finch had ample opportunity to see all his wares. The door closed and the woman turned to him, shaking her head.

"It's true, then—this is an expensive molly house—complete with man whores. Who'd have thought such a thing?"

Joss was astounded to feel his face heating. "Please, won't you sit?"

She pursed her lips and lowered her tiny form into the chair she'd just vacated, her hands closed protectively over the reticule she clutched in her lap. That was how Joss knew she was not quite as comfortable as she might appear.

"I apologize if Hugo said anything to upset you."

She barked a dismissive laugh. "I thought you knew me better than that, Mr. Gormley."

Joss just smiled.

"I suppose you're wondering why I'm here?"

Among other things—like how she'd found out about the place to begin with. Had Alicia told her?

"I found the letter Mrs. Griffin wrote to her ladyship."

Joss's eyebrows shot up.

"You needn't give me such a snirpy look. I knew she was up to something—and I had a feeling you were part of it." Her hands flexed restlessly on the bag in her lap. "She's been a wreck since you left." She cut him a sharp look. "I trust that is all sorted out now?"

Joss opened his mouth, but then closed it. It was hardly his place to tell Alicia's servant what they'd decided in between their lovemaking sessions.

"Oh, don't feel like you're betraying a confidence. I could tell how it was when she came early this morning. She is, at long, long last, happy."

Joss could not keep the smile from his mouth.

"And I know she is confident her man Shelly will find Lady Elizabeth. I daresay the two of you have made plans. I already know she means to take Miss Lizzy away from that disgusting monster." She stopped, her chest rising and falling so violently that she had to take a moment to compose herself. "But I know something her ladyship doesn't know—I know why Miss Lizzy might not have enough time to wait for Shelly to find her. I think you need to know the truth." She inhaled and held it, and then gave Joss a look he'd never seen on her face: one of fury, revulsion, and despair.

Joss's happiness drained away. "Why are you telling me this? Why aren't you telling her?"

"If I tell her, she will kill him."

Joss slumped back in his chair. "Good God, what is it?"

"I fear you might do likewise when I tell you."

They locked eyes, a sick feeling welling inside him.

"You must give me your word that you will not kill Selwood in the course of helping Miss Lizzy. You must. If you do not, I'm afraid you are condemning that poor girl to a nightmarish future."

The door opened and one of the maids entered carrying a tray.

"Thank you, Mary. You can just put it down; Miss Finch will serve."

The door closed behind the maid and Joss shoved both the table and tea-tray out of the way, and then leaned forward and rested his forearms on his thighs.

"I will not kill Selwood. Now, tell me all of it. Do not hold anything back."

Chapter Thirty

Alicia was in her study looking at the newest report from New York on her canal investment.

She had a man who saw to her general business—she read far too slowly to be able to deal with it all herself—but the canal scheme was a pet project of hers.

Right now it looked like all stumbling blocks had been removed and the project would move ahead. Not on schedule, but no more than eight months late.

A sharp knock on the door made her look up from the spidery handwriting of her business associate in New York City. Maude entered before she could speak.

"Please come in," Alicia said dryly.

Maude ignored the unsubtle dig. "This just came for you."

She glanced down at the handwriting and did not recognize it. When she broke the seal her eyes dropped to the bottom: Joss.

"Darling,"

Alicia read the word at least four times—and for once it was not because she couldn't understand it.

"I'm terribly sorry, but I'm afraid I have to put off our meeting tonight. I have a family crisis I must attend to. I'm not sure how long it will take, so don't expect me tomorrow night, either. Don't fret, Alicia, it is only a short delay. Know that I love you and will be thinking of you every moment we are not together.
Your devoted love,
Joss"

"Well?"

Alicia looked up in surprise. She'd forgotten Maude was still there.

"Why do you have that foolish grin on your face?" She dropped her jaw and goggled with a star-struck look.

Alicia laughed; there was nothing quite like a conversation with Maude to bring a person back to earth. Abruptly.

"I shan't be meeting him tonight—and maybe even tomorrow."

Maude grunted. "It's all for the best."

Alicia had to bite her lower lip to keep her mouth shut. She'd almost immediately regretted telling the older woman her plans—but then Maude would need to understand what was going on if she were to move swiftly when word came from Mr. Shelly that he'd found Elizabeth.

"Is everything ready if we should need to leave in a hurry? Have you gone through my dressing room and packed my trunk?"

Maude smirked at such an obvious dismissal. "I have. Would you like to inspect the contents?"

Alicia turned back to the desk, which was covered in papers she still needed to read. "No, I would like you to leave me alone."

"You will be dining in tonight?"

"Yes. In fact, tell cook that I'll just have something up here. I daresay I shall be here late into the night."

"That sounds an excellent idea."

The door shut behind her before Alicia could ask her what was so bloody excellent about it.

❤

Joss hated leaving The White House in Hugo's hands, but after speaking to Maude that afternoon he'd known he had little choice. He needed to see Selwood *now*—if not yesterday.

He'd warned Maude to be ready to leave on a moment's notice. He'd also sent her with a message for Alicia, begging off seeing her tonight and tomorrow. He'd hated to lie to her, but telling her what he was going to do would only cause her pain and worry.

Joss walked up the steps to the front door of Selwood House just after dark. He wasn't surprised when Beamish informed him that the earl and countess were not at home to visitors this evening.

Undaunted, Joss had given the old butler a message for Lord Selwood and had gone around back to wait by the servant entrance.

Lord Selwood kept him waiting until ten-thirty before he sent his messenger.

Joss saw Annie before she saw him. She poked her head out the servants' door and squinted into the dark alley that ran back to the mews.

Joss stepped out of the shadows and Annie started.

"Well," she said, after giving him the once over, "Look at you."

He could have said the same thing. Annie looked as if she'd aged five years in the few weeks since he'd last seen her.

"How do you like working here, Annie?"

She snorted. "Well enough, not that I had any choice."

"I heard you were caught stealing—you're lucky you aren't in jail."

She propped her fists on her hips and glared up at him. "And who might you have heard that from? That old cat who wanted her job back, I'll wager." She gave him a scathing look, her sharp eyes cataloguing his clothing. "And you—back working for her, are you?"

"Did Lord Selwood send you to fetch me?"

"I certainly wouldn't come looking for you otherwise."

"Then perhaps you should take me to him, Annie," he reminded her gently.

She turned on her heel and Joss followed. It was late and the kitchen was empty but for a pair of young scullery maids sleeping in front of the massive stone hearth.

Annie turned to Joss as she led him up the servant stairs.

"You know that old witch got me dismissed without even a recommendation."

"You ended up here quickly enough. Don't try and say you weren't taking money from Selwood to spy, Annie."

"Oh, Mr. High-and-Mighty—like you've never done anything wrong." Her eyes narrowed to slits. "You're a *whore*."

If she thought the accusation would hurt him, she was even more naïve than he'd believed.

"That is true, Annie."

She deflated before his eyes. "I'm sorry for sayin' that, Joss, I am." She launched herself at him, almost setting them both on fire when she forgot she was still holding a candlestick.

Joss took it from her tightly clenched fingers and set it on the step above before taking her in his arms.

She cried so hard he worried somebody would hear her. But nobody came and Joss let her weep until only small sniffles were left.

He gave her back a last stroke and then set her at arms' length.

"Oh, don't, I must look a fright."

Surprisingly, she didn't. Annie was that rare woman whose looks were enhanced by tears.

"You know this house is not a good place for you."

The look she gave him told him plenty.

"Has he tampered with you, Annie?"

She shrugged, her eyes hopeless. "Oh, what does it matter? He's not the first—although I think I'll tell him it's his baby I'm carrying."

"Oh, Annie."

JOSS AND THE COUNTESS

"You needn't worry," she snapped, "we both know it's not yours." She spun around, striding ahead of him.

She opened a door and gestured him into a library. The Earl of Selwood was sitting behind his massive desk.

"Thank you, Annie." The earl didn't stand, but watched Joss with a wide grin, his eyes glittering with amusement. "You may leave us."

Joss felt, rather than saw, Annie hesitate beside him.

"That will be all, Annie." This time the earl was not smiling and the door immediately clicked shut.

Selwood lounged back in his chair. "What a surprise to see you, Gormley." His brow wrinkled. "Were you here to apply for the groom position?"

Joss ignored the feint. "I think you know why I'm here, Selwood."

"That would be *my lord* to the likes of you." All traces of humor were gone.

Joss merely looked at him.

"It would seem your association with my *dear* step mamma has given you an inflated notion of yourself."

"I know what you've done to your sister." Joss could see the other man was far too interested in playing a game of cat and mouse and the last thing he wanted to do was give the earl what he wanted: the pleasure of tormenting him.

Selwood's eyebrows shot up and he steepled his fingers, resting his elbows on the arms of his chair. He cocked his head. "Oh, and what is that, pray?"

"Do you really want me to say the words out loud?"

Selwood gave an insouciant shrug. "I have no idea what you are talking about."

Joss made no attempt to hide the loathing he felt. "She's your *sister*. How could you rape anyone, not to mention a crippled young girl in your care? Your own flesh and blood? Your—"

Selwood waved a negligent hand but his facial muscles had gone taut. "Oh please, save your drama for those who would believe such lies."

"Release her into the care of her stepmother and I will not expose you for the monster you are."

The earl laughed. "Do you really think anyone would take *your* word over mine?"

"I think enough people would pay attention that your credit in society would suffer." He hesitated, and then decided to set the hook deeper. "And Alicia has told me how much your reputation matters to you. *She,* on the other hand, has no interest in politics or the *ton*. She also possesses enough money that she doesn't need to care. She tells me that you are not nearly so downy. In fact—"

Selwood lunged to his feet and gripped the edges of his desk. "You *dare* to threaten your betters."

Joss snorted, "If you are my better, then I am grateful to occupy the position I do."

For a moment, Joss thought the earl might come for him. But his expression shifted in a heartbeat, going from condescending to amused.

"Oh, and what position is that? Between Alicia's thighs?" He gave an ugly laugh. "Trust me, lad, I've occupied that position—and a good number of others—far more often than you can imagine."

Joss had warned himself he would have to deal with this and more.

"The difference between you and me, Selwood—well, at least one of the differences—is that I don't force myself on women. Now, tell me where your sister is being held or I'll have to employ a bit of persuasion."

Selwood laughed, but Joss saw a flicker of worry in his eyes.

He *should* worry because Joss could inflict a lot of damage before anyone could answer the earl's summons.

"It wouldn't do any good if I *did* tell you. You'd need a battering ram to get to her without my approval."

"You just leave that to me, *my lord*. Now, I'll have the name."

"Just what do you and that American slut—"

Joss hadn't even realized what he was doing until his fist connected with Selwood's jaw. It all happened in slow motion: the sound of teeth clicking, the grinding *thud* of bone striking bone, and Selwood's body slamming into a table full of decanters behind him.

The sound of crystal shattering was deafening.

Joss leaned down and picked Selwood up by the throat, shoving him against the wall, and not caring when Selwood's shoulder went through the portrait of some long dead ancestor.

He held the earl with one hand, pinning him by the neck. "Where?"

"Sod. Off."

Joss backhanded him so hard he worried he might have knocked him out. But, no, his eyelids fluttered open.

"Next time you shan't get the back of my hand," Joss warned. He squeezed Selwood's throat, horrified by how rewarding the sensation was.

The earl wheezed out a word but Joss couldn't understand. He leaned closer. "Come again?"

"Bethlem."

Joss reeled back as if struck. "You bloody, fucking animal—your own sister, in *that* place."

Selwood cracked a gruesome smile, blood covering his teeth and dripping from the corner of his mouth. "You'll never get her out."

Joss struck him once in the solar plexus, driving him to his knees. "That is for Alicia," Joss snarled. "And this," he drew back his foot and released all his pent-up rage. "*This* is for your sister." His boot caught Selwood square in the chest and knocked him back a good three feet.

Behind him the door flew open and Joss heard the trampling of several sets of feet.

"My lord?" Beamish dropped into a crouch beside his master. "Are you hurt?"

Selwood was motionless, a thin trickle of blood running from the corner of his mouth.

The butler sucked in a horrified breath. "I—I think you've killed him."

"I doubt we shall all be so lucky."

Selwood made a gasping, coughing sound and Joss turned on his heel and strode toward the door, where two men stood, one in the livery of a footman, the other wearing the rougher clothing of a groom.

"Escort Mr. Gormley off the property," Beamish called out behind him.

Neither man looked willing to lay hands on him, but they certainly stayed close enough, and seemed intent on frog-marching him all the way out to the street—through the guest entrance this time.

He ignored the footman and turned to the groom. "Thank you. I can find my way from here."

The man crossed his arms. "We'll just watch and see you do."

Joss headed across the square.

"And don't come back, if you know what's good for you," the footman called after him.

Joss just laughed.

—❤—

Joss met Alicia's investigator in a dirty inn on Lambeth Road that some enterprising wag had named *The Laughing Lunatic*.

He could spot Mr. Shelly easily by Miss Finch's colorful description: a dried-up stick of a man no bigger than a minute.

While he hadn't met Shelly, the other man had certainly seen Joss before.

"Ah, well met, Mr. Gormley."

"Mr. Shelly."

The smaller man flushed at Joss's significant look. "Er, I've taken the liberty of securing a table in the corner. To qualify for such a premium—and private—location I've had to order us meals."

Joss glanced around the place, which looked as though it had last been cleaned during the reign of Henry VIII.

They'd barely lowered their arses onto the rickety chairs when a slatternly serving wench set down two heavy trenchers with a thump.

"Two kidney pies, mash, and peas." She stared at Shelly with disdain before turning her greedy eyes to Joss, her smile thawing. "And what can I get you to drink, Goliath?"

Joss gave her a slight smile—as if he hadn't already heard it a thousand times. "A pint of your house brew." It had been one of his father's few maxims that the only safe drinks to order in most tap houses were those brewed on site. Not that Joss had any intention of eating *or* drinking anything in this place.

The wench sauntered off, her hips swaying in a manner that certainly caught Mr. Shelly's attention.

Joss cleared his throat.

"Ah, yes." Shelly leaned across the table, although nobody at any of the nearby tables appeared to be listening or interested.

"After I received your note earlier, I immediately got in touch with one of the wardens on the incurable wing. He owes me a favor for getting him out of a tight spot. He said there are several rooms on the third floor of the west wing, which is the women's side. Most of the cells are located off the main galleries, but there are two at each end that are self-contained. He says it is commonly known that some of the physicians take, er, special patients. Also, the patients in these rooms are not available for viewing."

"Good God—they still allow that?"

"It is difficult to stamp out, especially at night when only the floor wardens remain. It is a way of earning extra money that they are reluctant to give up."

"So, you're saying that paying them is the best way to gain entry?"

Shelly nodded. "Do you think Selwood will send extra men? Could he be moving her tonight?"

Joss pushed aside the congealing pie before propping his elbows on the table. He thought about the condition he'd left Selwood in a few hours earlier. He'd looked barely able to lift a finger, but it was better not to take chances.

"Let's assume he might and plan for every eventuality. If we can get past whoever it is that watches the front entry, how do we get into those rooms?"

"He said they usually keep the keys on their person—that we'd need to get our hands on one of the warden's keys for that particular floor. He was going to wander over there tomorrow night and then we might—"

"We don't have time for that; we need to go tonight."

Shelly had started shaking his head before he'd even finished. "I don't think that is wise, Mr. Gormley. We have no idea what kind of situation we'd be stepping into. If Lord Selwood is committed to keeping his sister restrained—and actions like this would indicate that he is—perhaps he might even engage Runners or contact a constable."

Joss smiled. "Yes, I daresay you are correct. But we'll have something far   better,   Mr.   Shelly."

Chapter Thirty-One

Alicia had only just fallen into a light doze when somebody knocked on the door.

A candle flickered at the end of her bed. "My lady?"

She sat bolt upright, blinking against the light. "Is it time, Maude?"

"Yes, I just received word from Mr. Shelly. We are to wait at the Swan with Two Necks for Lizzy. It will be sometime four-thirty or five."

"But—" Alicia glanced over at the clock. "It is already four."

"Then we should make haste."

The servants loaded up her trunk while Alicia dressed in her warmest traveling clothes.

Maude had suggested bringing a similar valise for Lizzy, just in case she had to leave wherever she'd been kept without any possessions.

While Alicia struggled into her clothes, she thought about Joss. Oh, how she wished he'd been able to come to her tonight!

Her face heated at her selfish thought; it sounded as though he had his own family problems to manage. Alicia prayed that nothing terrible had happened.

She wouldn't be able to say goodbye, but at least she could leave him a message to let him know that Mr. Shelly had found Lizzy much faster than he'd hoped.

Alicia wished with all her heart that he could come with them to France tonight, but he'd warned her that he was tied to London for at least the next month..

"I'm sorry," he'd said, gently stroking her jaw. "But I can't leave Melissa in the lurch." His thin lips had quirked into a wry smile. "No matter how much I would like to give her a piece of my mind about her tricks."

"Oh, hush, Joss." She'd kissed the end of his crooked nose. "Her tricks brought us together."

"Yes, and not without affording her a fair amount of entertainment in the process."

While they might have disagreed on his friend's methods, Alicia had agreed with him when it came to keeping his word to Mrs. Griffin.

"I'm hoping Shelly will find her soon, even though that will mean we must be parted," she'd said.

"But not forever." He'd kissed her breathless. "And we can make the most of tonight while we have it."

And they had, oh, they had.

But now she needed to write him a letter—even though she wasn't quite sure what she could tell him other than she loved him and was leaving.

Alicia had just finished struggling through her very brief missive and was sealing it when Maude appeared.

"My lady, the carriage is ready." Maude was holding her heavy fur cloak. "I thought I'd bring this—in case she is cold."

On their way to the carriage Alicia stopped to talk to the young footman, who looked wide awake for all that it was so early in the morning.

"See that this is delivered to Mr. Joss Gormley first thing in the morning."

The boy's eyebrows rose slightly, but he took the letter and was quick to nod. "Yes, my lady."

Once they were in the carriage Alicia was assailed by a sudden qualm as she saw the house—most likely for the last time.

She grabbed the smaller woman's hands and squeezed them tight. "Is this the right thing to do—taking her away? It is, isn't it?"

Maude's face was exceptionally grim and she squeezed Alicia's hands until the bones hurt. "This is the only thing you can do, my lady."

—❤—

Joss looked at the two women across from him and repeated what he'd just said. "Are you certain you wish to do this? There is danger involved, I can't say how much—but it might be significant.

Ella and Julia were fairly new to The White House and hadn't been around the last time Joss worked for Mel. He'd chosen them for two reasons: they were both fit and could run if necessary, and they'd both come to Mel from a place so vile they had a deep-seated hatred of men who abused women.

"You say this arsehole put his *sister* in Bethlem?" Ella repeated.

"Yes."

"And you just need us to lure the men keeping her away?" Julia asked.

263

"Yes. I think if you go in and ask to see the lunatics and offer to pay them—I'll give you money to wave around."

Ella laughed. "If we can't wave around something of our own to make them follow, then we've lost our touch."

"Yes, well, I don't want you getting trapped by them. There is also the danger more men may have arrived. If so, we may have to come up with some other approach."

"We're game, boss," Julia, an exquisite blond with doll-like blue eyes said, hiking up her skirt and pulling a wicked looking blade from a holster on her calf.

"Good God. Do you wear that all the time?"

"I'm never without it." The cold look in her eyes told him all he needed to know. Joss had realized a long time ago that most of the whores who came to work for Mel had arrived there via the hard route. Joss, with his happy childhood and relatively close-knit family, was the rare exception.

"Well," Ella said, getting to her feet, a huge grin on her full-lipped, sensual features, "I'm ready."

That was an hour and a half ago. They'd arrived at the spot where he'd agreed to meet Shelly—the overrun gardens to the north of the old building

The older man was speaking to somebody who could only be the warden he'd mentioned. Joss and the two women approached and the warden stopped talking, his eyes shifty and nervous.

Shelly turned to him. "He wants £4 to let the four of us in."

Joss eyed the warden. "That is extortion. What do you usually charge for entry?"

To his credit, the man's pockmarked face flushed a dull red. "If I do this, I'll have to make myself scarce for a few days.."

"Has Lord Selwood sent more men tonight?"

"No, just the same two as always and the woman who watches the girl."

Joss nodded and reached into his purse, which he'd filled with money from Melissa's safe before leaving.

Before the warden could close his fingers around it, Joss grabbed his wrist and yanked him until their chests were touching.

"You are not by any chance leading us into a trap?"

"God no." His eyes were wide with terror. "I'm not. I swear."

"Repeat the plan as Mr. Shelly told it to you."

"I will let in the women first and tell the floor warden they want to see the lunatics. While they distract him, I'll admit you two. Once you have the key you can release the girl and I'll lock up the nurse."

"And the two men with her," Joss added.

The man swallowed. "Aye, 'course. And the two men. And you'll take the girl and nobody will be the wiser until they come to check on her tomorrow in the late afternoon."

Joss cocked his head. "Until who comes?"

"Why, the Earl of Selwood and his lady wife, sir."

It was closer to five-thirty when Shelly arrived in a rented carriage. Alicia had walked a rut in the floor of the private parlor by the time the innkeeper showed the small man into the room.

"You have her?" she demanded.

"Yes, my lady. She is even now being transferred into your carriage."

"Transferred? By whom?"

The door opened behind Shelly and Joss entered.

"Joss!" Alicia made a choked sound before launching herself at him.

"Shhh, my love," he murmured, his chest rumbling beneath her ear. "You must make haste." He held her away and leaned down to kiss her tears of relief from the corners of her eyes.

"What are you doing here?" she asked in between sniffles.

"Miss Finch will explain it all to you. But come, darling, you need to be on your way, it's already later than I'd like."

Alicia's traveling coach waited in the courtyard with a team of six, the postilions already mounted.

Joss opened the door and handed in Maude before turning to her.

"She is sleeping," he gestured to the forward facing seat, where Lizzy was sitting upright, her body listing to the side. "You will need to keep hold of her, she must have been given some manner of sleeping draught and is impossible to rouse."

Alicia's heart drummed in her ears. "Is she all right?"

"I believe she may have fought her captors and they decided it was easier to drug her. Physically she appears sound." He glanced into the coach and nodded at Maude. "Miss Finch will tell you everything on the way and Mr. Shelly will fill in anything she does not know. He will assist you when you reach Dover." He leaned down and gave her a hard, swift kiss.

When he pulled away she realized everyone around them must have been shocked by his actions and were now studiously looking in the other direction.

"Now, you must go."

Before she knew it, she was seated beside Lizzy's still form, Mr. Shelly on the bench across from her with Maude.

Joss flipped the steps up and gave her a last lingering look before saying, "I wish you safe travels." And then he shut the door.

◄ ♥ ►

Joss considered going directly to Selwood's house and confronting the man's wife this time—demanding an answer. But he told himself to let the matter go. Nothing could be done about it and Lady Elizabeth and Alicia would be better served if he did not stir the hornet's nest he'd already kicked over. No doubt he would already have his hands full when they discovered Lizzy was gone.

He summoned a hack and directed it to take him to The White House, settling back into the cold gloom of the interior before allowing his mind to retrace the path of the past few hours.

He and Shelly had discussed what they'd learned about Lord and Lady Selwood on their drive to the Swan with Two Necks and had decided the information was best held in reserve. They could always use the truth if they the earl and countess tried to go after either Joss or Alicia and Lizzy.

Joss's heart ached when he thought of Alicia's anguish when Maude told her the truth.

And then there was whatever nightmare story Lizzy would have to tell. And it *would* be a nightmare because the scene in Bethlem hospital, even the private room she'd been confined to, was something Joss would never forget.

The building was newish, but the construction methods had been so shoddy it was difficult to believe it wasn't the old Moorfields hospital.

All three floors had galleries that ran down the center with cells off to the sides. Some of the inmates roamed at will, some were chained bodily to metal bars from which they could not have moved more than a few inches.

The warden who'd guarded the wing Lizzy was in had been dead drunk when they found him, making the task of lifting the keys that much easier.

The two men Selwood paid to watch the door had all but run to Ella and Julia when they'd strutted down the gallery. It had been only the work of a moment for Joss to subdue one of the men into

266

unconsciousness while Ella held the other at the point of her wicked blade.

Lizzy's room had been small and clean enough, but the air had been frigid and reeked of stale spirits. The source of the stench was the nurse, who snored heavily in the room's only chair. The half-empty bottle of laudanum attested to the source of Lizzy's unnaturally deep sleep. All in all, it took less than two hours to get in, get Lizzy, and return her to the waiting carriage.

The hack stopped and Joss leapt out without bothering with the step. He paid the driver and let himself in with his own key. The front door was locked to the public at four a.m. each day and unlocked again at six p.m.

Somebody had thoughtfully left a candlestick for him and he yawned hugely as he made his way all the way to the quarters he kept in the private portion of the house. Nobody was stirring, not even the charwomen, when he reached his room.

He'd not slept for two nights running—yesterday evening with Alicia being *far* more enjoyable than tonight.

His body had begun to shut down from lack of sleep and even his whirring brain had begun to grow sluggish after almost forty-eight hours without sleep. He'd only managed to toe off his boots and remove his coat and cravat before crawling beneath the covers of his cold bed. He was asleep before his head hit the pillow....

❤

BANG! BANG! BANG!

Joss jerked upright and stared from the door to the clock; he'd been asleep no more than twenty minutes.

"This had better be important," he yelled hoarsely.

The door opened and Hugo stood in the opening. For once, he wasn't smiling.

Joss swung his feet to the floor. "Well?" he said when Hugo didn't speak.

"There are two constables here for you, Joss."

Well, that was fast. He nodded wearily and stood, going to his bureau and removing a fresh neckcloth. He tossed it on the bed and poured some cold water into his wash basin. "Tell them I will be down shortly.

"Er, you already know why they're here?" Hugo sounded tense and unlike himself.

JOSS AND THE COUNTESS

Joss plunged his face into the freezing water, scrubbed briefly with his hands, and then grabbed the towel and dried himself before answering. "They're here about the girl? About Bethlem hospital?"

Hugo's brow wrinkled. "What? No," he said before Joss could answer. "They're here about Lord Selwood."

Ah, so that was it. The man would have him throw in jail for assault. Well, it had been worth it.

Joss picked up his neckcloth and tied the world's worst knot, surprised when Hugo did not take the opportunity to comment.

Still, he'd be damned if he wasted time on his cravat if he was going to Newgate for beating a lord. He snatched up his coat, which he'd carelessly thrown over the back of a chair—that alone enough to attest to how exhausted he was.

"I'm afraid I engaged in an altercation with Lord Selwood last night and I daresay he will take his pound of flesh." He turned to Hugo, who'd helped him shrug into it. "You're going to be in charge for a while, Hugo, until I can contact a solicitor and see what can be done about getting me out. I'd rather not disturb Melissa with this if it can be helped. You'll need to tell Laura and the two of you can manage together." He gave the whipcord lean man a hard look. "Just save your machinations for when I return, if you don't mind."

Hugo shook his head, his mouth open. "Joss, I don't think you understand—Lord Selwood, he—he isn't the one who sent the constables. Lord Selwood is dead. And they are saying that you are the one who killed him."

Chapter Thirty-Two

Many things could be procured within the cold, thick, and unforgiving walls of Newgate, but all of it required money. Lots of money.

While Joss had *some* money, he did not feel like wasting it on more comfortable accommodations. So that is how he came to be crowded into a cell with perhaps two dozen others.

Joss had nothing to fear physically—he was the biggest man their by half—but the filth and stench were almost worse than the loss of liberty.

Time passed slowly and it was agony without a book.

On the second or third day—it was difficult to gauge the passage of time—a jailer pulled him out and escorted him to a tiny cell which he would have all to himself, although the trade to private quarters also included the addition of shackles.

He'd spoken to nobody save the jailers and the two constables, who'd kept him up another eight hours after his arrest.

They'd told him the evidence against him—damning—and they'd also disclosed the cause of death: a poker to the back of the head.

Joss had declined both the opportunity to confess or to request legal representation. He was hoping Hugo would carry out the last orders he'd given him. Although. . . knowing Hugo's unsavory sense of humor it was possible *nobody* knew of Joss's incarceration. Although he could not imagine that would be true for long. Such a juicy story—the violent murder of a well-respected peer by his stepmother's ex servant—was likely to be in every paper.

Joss was lying on his dirty straw pallet, trying not to think of what was making him itch so badly, and watching two rats fight over his uneaten meal when the hatch on the door opened.

"You've a visitor. You'll have fifteen minutes and no more." The hatch slammed shut, keys rattled, and the door opened.

Joss scrambled into a sitting position, trying to avoid moving overly much as the shackles on his wrists and ankles had begun to chafe.

He grinned. "Belle, what are you doing here?"

His sister's white face collapsed and she rushed toward him, but he shook his head and held out one hand, wincing as the heavy metal bracelet tugged against his skin.

"Stay back. I am absolutely *covered* in something that bites." He grimaced. "I'm guessing fleas or something worse. And I smell revolting."

She stopped where she was, throwing her hands over her mouth and laughing through her tears.

"Oh, Joss, how like you to worry about such a thing at a time like this."

The door clanged shut and they both startled.

"Pull that stool a bit closer, Belle."

She'd brought a large tapestry bag with her. "I've been trying to get in since I heard, but they wouldn't let me see you. I've brought you some things."

"Who told you I was here?"

Her flush told him who before her words did. "A gentleman who works with you? Er, a Mr. Buckingham?"

Ah, so Hugo had done what he'd asked. At least part of it. She took out a package wrapped in paper, a towel, and a stoppered jug.

"I imagine it is all over the papers?"

She frowned, digging in the bottom of her bag until she found what she wanted—a small book.

"It has been dreadful. Lord Selwood's murder is on the front page of everything and they've mentioned your name as the only suspect."

She took out a wax-cloth wrapped package and then put her bag aside and came toward him.

"It is a sandwich, Joss—tongue, your favorite."

"Thank you, Belle." He took the package and made himself open it, even though he had no appetite.

"I tried to come to you immediately but they wouldn't let me," she said again, glancing around nervously.

Joss chewed and swallowed and she startled as if he'd said something.

"Oh, what a ninny I am—here is this, a little bit of ale."

He took the jug, happier for the beer than the food. He'd not had anything to drink almost since entering. He'd broken down and taken a dipper of the brackish water they brought, but he had a terror of contracting some jail-house malady.

"Mr. Buckingham came to me only hours after you'd been taken."

Joss silently apologized for maligning Hugo's character.

"He told me you wished to wait for a man—a Mr. Shelly."

"Yes, that is correct."

"Mr. Shelly, it seems, was delayed and he only just arrived back this morning."

"He's been gone four days? Is anything wrong? Did something happen to Lady—"

He only realized he'd raised his voice when she glanced nervously toward the door. As if on cue, the hatch opened.

"Oi! Keep it down in there."

Joss slid back down to his pallet.

Belle leaned toward him. "Nothing happened to Lady Alicia, Joss." Belle smiled. "She is the loveliest woman I have ever seen."

"Alicia came to see you?" he asked stupidly.

"Yes, she arrived with Mr. Shelly."

Joss closed his eyes and his head dropped back against the stone wall with a dull *thunk*. Why had she come back? If they hadn't found out about Lizzy's disappearance, which seemed bloody unlikely, they would eventually. And when they did, they'd have a second suspect.

"She wanted to come see you," Belle's words made him open his eyes. "But Mr. Shelly said that would not be wise at this juncture."

"Thank God one of them is showing some sense."

"Oh, Joss, you cannot mean such a thing! She is so kind and clever and—and she says she loves you very much." Her eyes were so wide with disbelief he laughed.

"That's not very flattering to me, Belle."

Her cheeks reddened. "I didn't—"

"Hush, sweetheart. I know you didn't." He chewed his lip, trying to think of a way to tell her that Alicia needed to leave. Now. Or better yet, yesterday.

"You'll never guess what she said to me, Joss."

That was probably true. "What's that, darling?"

"She said I could come and live with you both in France."

Joss stared—no, he wouldn't have guessed that. Although he wasn't sure why. Alicia was loving and caring and had always been fascinated by his family.

"I told her I didn't think my husband would like that."

Joss's jaw dropped and she gave a low chuckle.

"That's not very flattering to me, Joss," she said, her words a mocking echo of his.

"Who, Belle?"

Even in the dim light of the cell he could see her cheeks color. "You remember the new doctor who came to see Father?"

Joss did remember him; he was far younger than their old doctor and a handsome young man. "Doctor MacLellan?" he said.

She looked pleased. "Ian MacLellan." Belle swallowed hard. "He said he loves me, Joss. And," she dashed a tear from one cheek with the back of her hand. "He says he never even noticed the marks."

Joss grinned. "Of course, he didn't notice them, you looby." He hesitated, wondering how to couch his next concern.

"I was worried that having our last name in the paper might cause problems for him," she said, as if reading his mind. "But he said notoriety is always good for business."

Joss gave a weary chuckle. "He sounds like an excellent man."

"Oh dear, how could I be so selfish to be wasting our time with that when you're suffering in here?" Before Joss could tell her just how much her information relieved his mind she went on, "I almost forgot." Belle opened her reticule and took out a folded piece of heavy cream stationary he knew well. "Lady Alicia said to give this to you. That it would explain everything."

Joss took the single piece of paper and stared at it. Only one page? To explain everything?

He shook his head and then cracked the seal.

—◆❤◆—

Alicia waited until the girl crossed the square and turned onto Bruton Street before rapping on the panel.

It slid open immediately. "Aye?" the grizzled driver asked.

"That's the girl there, the one just ahead."

Alicia put back her veil and tapped on the window as they came up alongside her. Annie Philips glanced at the carriage and then stopped, gaping.

Alicia opened the door. "I'd like a moment of your time."

The girl had beautiful eyes which were as round as guineas. "I—"

"Get in."

She flushed a dark red but climbed into the carriage and shut the door.

"Where were you going?"

Her pretty face was sullen. "Nowhere in particular, my lady. It is my half-day and I was just going to walk and look."

Alicia tapped on the roof. "Take us around the Park," she told the driver. When the panel shut, she looked at the girl. "I think you know why I am here?"

"Is this about Joss?"

Hearing his name on the young girl's lips was like coal to the inferno of jealousy raging inside her. She'd never suspected she was jealous and she certainly was not enjoying the experience.

"I won't beat about the bush, Annie. Tell me what happened the other night after he left?"

The girl chewed her lower lip before saying, "Mr. Beamish had the footmen move Lord Selwood to the settee in his library and then summoned Lady Selwood to ask her what they should do. His lordship was unconscious and Mr. Beamish was that nervous that he would do the wrong thing."

Alicia recognized the smug satisfaction on the girl's face because she felt it herself at the news. "He's interfered with you, hasn't he—Lord Selwood." It was not a question, but the girl nodded.

"Was it against your will?"

Annie opened her mouth, but then hesitated.

"You can speak openly, in fact I wish you would."

"He told me I could be head parlor maid if I let him—" she stopped and then shrugged.

"Did he hurt you?"

Her dark eyes flickered to Alicia and she saw surprise in them. "Yes, my lady. And then I—" She stopped, uncertain.

"Go on."

"And then I found out he'd promised the same to all the girls. I went to him—"

Alicia winced and the girl nodded. "Yes, he was not happy."

"Are you with child?"

Annie's face reddened and she swallowed. "Yes."

"Is it his?"

"No, it's . . . somebody else's."

"How far along?"

"Two months, my lady."

Alicia didn't want to ask, but she had to. "Who is the father?"

"Don't worry, it wasn't Joss."

She wanted to weep with relief, but now was not the time. "Who, Annie?"

"I'd rather not say, my lady. He—well, he said he wouldn't marry me. That he didn't believe it was his. He said everyone knew I was a s-slut."

Her eyes were glassy and Alicia shook her head, anger warming her chest. "Every woman has to tolerate those accusations, Annie. All of us. Don't ever let what some man says diminish you." Not that she'd ever taken her own advice.

The girl sniffed and wiped her eyes.

"You know Joss did not kill Lord Selwood, don't you?"

Annie hesitated, and then nodded.

"You weren't just going to look at shop windows today, were you?"

"No."

"How much money did she give you to hide?"

"I wouldn't have done it, my lady. I wouldn't have—"

"How much?"

"One hundred pounds." She saw Alicia's look of disbelief and her eyes sparked with anger. "I know it's nothing to you, but it's the difference between starving on the street to me. And—and I never would have allowed Joss to hang for it." She could not hold Alicia's eyes. "I just needed to have a little something for when the baby comes."

Alicia tapped on the roof.

"Take us to Mivart's," she said when the vent opened.

Annie cocked her head. "Where are you taking me?"

"It is a hotel. You will be able to rest and tell me what you saw. And then you will wait for me there, while I go and speak to Lady Selwood."

—❤—

Beamish's face was redder than she'd ever seen it.

"Tell her I am not leaving until she sees me, Beamish. And tell her it is in her best interest to do so sooner rather than later. Every minute I have to wait is a minute angrier I will become. Her ladyship does not want to make me angry."

Ten minutes later Lady Rebecca Selwood came into the smaller sitting room—the one that was tiny but had only one door and was in the corner, so had only two sides on which eavesdroppers could listen.

"Alicia, I am sorry you had to wait. I should have told Beamish that my orders did not apply to family." Rebecca's eyes were suitably red-rimmed, as any devoted widow's would be.

Alicia had no interested in small talk. "I know it was you, Rebecca."

"Me? I'm sorry I don't—"

"I know you killed David."

"Are you mad?" Rebecca whispered, her usually placid face a mask of terror as she glanced at the doors.

"I will not permit Joss Gormley to suffer for your sins. And I have a witness."

The other woman made a noise of pure fury. "That girl! I knew I should have—"

"What? You should have killed her too?" Alicia could see by the other woman's flush that was exactly what she meant. "And what about Lizzy—would you have killed her, too? Or just left her locked up in that dreadful place?"

"She wouldn't have been in that place if she had simply shut up and done what David told her to do."

Alicia had not expected *this*. She stared at the other woman with open, seething loathing. "You—you *monster*. It was your idea."

Rebecca tossed her head, the gesture oddly girlish on her middle-aged face. "What good was she doing anyone? This would have been a way for her to help all of us."

Alicia was simply too sickened to speak.

Her silence infuriated the other woman. "What about me? Do you think I've enjoyed being pregnant almost constantly for twenty years? Do you? And nothing but disappointment after disappointment. And then the last time left me—" she stopped and bit her lip.

"You are not pregnant at all, are you? You were only pretending until Lizzy had the baby. And then, if it was a boy, you would have claimed it as your own. And if she didn't have a boy? What then? Would you have just kept using her as David's *broodmare*?"

Rebecca surged to her feet, shaking with her rage. "Don't use that tone with me—you who were his *whore* for years. If you'd done what you were supposed to do your precious Lizzy would have been spared."

"You're mad. You're absolutely bloody mad. Do you think your husband's—and his father's—mania to preserve their precious bloodline was worth rape? Worth *incest*? I could almost feel sorry for you if not for the fact you have done this to Lizzy and would now watch an innocent man hang for murder."

Rebecca raised her hands. "Please, don't be so hasty. Let me explain. I wasn't—I wouldn't," she lowered herself onto the settee beside Alicia.

Alicia shot to her feet. "Get away from me! You are a *vile, vile* abomination of a human being. You make me physically ill."

Tears rolled down the other woman's cheeks.

Her weeping just angered Alicia more. "Why did you do it?" She didn't have to explain what she meant.

"I had to kill him." Rebecca's shoulders shook. "I should have done it years ago."

Alicia couldn't have agreed more.

"He said—after that man beat him—that he would have to let Elizabeth go or there would be trouble. He said he would just have to find another way. And—and I knew then what he'd planned. I could see it in his eyes." She dropped her head and sobbed.

"So, you did not want what had happened to Lizzy to happen to your own daughter."

"You don't understand what he was like. You don't know…You just don't know…." She kept whispering, staring at her clenched hands, her tears rolling down her cheeks.

Alicia pulled on her gloves and walked toward the door, afraid of what she would do if she stayed.

Rebecca's head whipped up at the sound of Alicia's steps. "Where are you going?"

"Where do you think I am going? To the authorities."

"No!" She lurched off the settee and came after her. "You can't—you can't."

Alicia fumbled with the door handle, the slick leather of her gloves unable to gain purchase. Rebecca—who was heavier, if not taller than her—grabbed her by the shoulders and slammed her against the wall.

"You can't! You can't tell anyone, ever! I will have to make sure you don't tell—I'll—" her wild gaze settled on the marble bust beside the door and she reached for it. Alicia took the opportunity to kick her as hard as she could in the leg.

Agonizing pain shot from her toe up her leg but Rebecca released her and Alicia lurched toward the door. Not until she reached the foyer did she understand the other woman had not followed her. Beamish, who must have been waiting off the main hall came rushing toward her.

"Is aught amiss, my lady?"

Alicia caught a glance at herself in the glass. She hadn't realized she'd lost her hat and her hair had come down on one side. She also had scratches on her neck.

"Lady Selwood is not well," she told the white-faced butler in a shaky voice. "You must send somebody up with her—perhaps even two people, a maid and your biggest groom. She should not be left alone. She has already killed one person and just tried to kill me."

Beamish was clearly aghast. "But-but—"

"I am going to the authorities, Beamish. But shall have to watch her. They will come here sooner rather than later, and when they—"

The crack of a pistol cut off the rest of what she was going to say.

"Oh my God," Alicia ran toward the stairs, other servants emerging from rooms. She was heading toward the sitting room she'd just left when a scream came from the library.

A maid came running out, still screaming, not stopping when she saw Alicia.

Both doors to the library were open and there was Rebecca. She was slumped in David's chair and had obviously found David's gun.

Epilogue

Five Months Later
A Chateau Outside Paris

Alicia watched Lizzy and the baby from the terrace.
She'd had one of the ground floor rooms in the chateau converted into chambers for the girl and her child; that way Lizzy could roll her chair out into the sunshine whenever she wished.

She heard a light step behind her before two hands landed on her shoulders. Joss kissed her temple and she leaned back against the solid familiarity of him.

"How is she today?" he asked, his voice a low rumble against her back.

"A little better every day. I think Natalie has given her a reason to live."

Alicia had been concerned Lizzy would hate her child because of who the father was, but instead she'd clung to Natalie since the first time she'd seen her.

Joss turned her to face him. "And how are *you* today, my lady?"

Alicia slid her arms around his neck and smiled up into his harsh-featured face: a face that was more beloved to her than any other except Lizzy's.

"I'm better now that you are here. Did you see you have a letter from Mrs. Griffin?"

His eyes glinted with amusement. "Yes, I'm almost afraid to open it."

She chuckled. "Coward."

Joss had ended up staying behind in London for two months.

The first month was to complete his promise to Melissa Griffin.

He'd been concerned his notoriety would be bad for Melissa's business. Instead, both men and women had flocked in greater numbers, drawn by the scandal.

His father had passed away quietly in the middle of his time at The White House, so Joss had stayed another month to help with the burial, various family matters, and attend Belle and Ian's tiny wedding ceremony. Belle had decided it was better to offend propriety and marry Ian than to be a burden on her brother Michael and his wife for a year of mourning.

Alicia knew that Belle's seemingly happy marriage was a great weight off Joss's mind. They were looking forward to a visit from the newlyweds, sometime in the fall, hopefully around the time of the christening.

Alicia disengaged herself from his embrace and picked up another letter. "This also came—for both of us."

He glanced at Lady Constance's direction on the envelope and looked at Alicia. "Ah, news about Annie? What does it say?"

"Annie has had her child, a son. She is happy working for Lady Constance and has already met a very kind—and handsome—footman on the duke's staff who has taken a shine to her."

Joss chuckled. "I can only imagine."

She smacked him with the letter. "You will restrict your imaginings to your wife, Mr. Gormley."

"Temper, temper," he teased, catching her so quickly that his hands were a blur. He pulled her close. "Too much excitement is bad for our daughter," he whispered into her temple, and then began to trail kisses down her jaw.

Alicia pressed her body against his, her heart pumping faster at what she felt. "You already seem rather excited."

"Excitement is *good* for your husband," he murmured.

Alicia laughed and gave herself up to his caresses. "How can you be so certain it will be a girl? Don't you want a son? I thought every man did."

He nibbled her ear. "Why would I want a big ugly blighter like me?"

"Maybe I would," she said, groaning when he thumbed one hardened nipple through her gown.

"You've already got a big ugly blighter," he reminded her.

She chuckled, melting against him. The fact that she was pregnant for the first time at almost forty was a miracle she gave thanks for every day.

He slid a massive arm beneath her knees and swept her up in the way that always left her breathless.

"Joss," she said laughingly. "What are you doing?"

"It's a secret." He stopped in front of the door. "Open the door, darling."

She complied and he didn't bother closing it before striding down the wide corridor toward the stairs.

Alicia had leased the beautiful, serene chateau for two years. She'd spoken to Lizzy and Joss and they'd all agreed that time away from scandal and England would give them all a chance to heal. But neither of them wanted to live here permanently.

As for Alicia, she didn't care where she lived as long as she had Joss and her daughter with her. In her experience, it was the people you loved, and not the country, that made a place feel like home.

The scandal over David's death and Rebecca's suicide was still mentioned in the papers from England, even months later. The news of Joss and Alicia's marriage had quickly crossed The Channel and caused the matter to resurface.

Likely there would always be scandal associated with their names—both because of Joss's initial arrest for murder but more for his role as the enterprising groom who'd somehow managed to marry the American Ice Countess.

Fortunately, Lizzy's part in the drama remained a secret. Although her daughter might never be able to walk, she'd become leagues healthier in the months she'd been away from David.

It would take years for her to put the worst of her nightmarish past behind her, and she would never be able to forget completely.

Alicia wanted to stay as close to Lizzy as the young woman would allow, and Joss agreed. The two got along better than ever now that they were free to become friends. They still had their reading salon every week and Alicia occasionally joined in.

She'd finally shared the truth about her problems reading and writing with Lizzy and Joss and she no longer felt so ashamed. They both loved her no matter how quickly she could read, and that, somehow, made the process of completing a book considerably less daunting.

"Where are we going?" she asked as he began to take the stairs, two at a time.

"For such a clever woman you ask some rather silly questions," he said, not even winded as he reached the second-floor landing and began the ascent to the third.

"But it's the middle of the day," she protested laughingly.

"I *know*," he said, swooping down to kiss her hard as he reached the landing. "I've already let the first half of the day go to waste."

She relaxed in her husband's arms with a sigh. "You're correct—you've been horribly lax," she chided. "I shall give you one last opportunity to make it up to me."

"Ahh, well I suppose duty calls," he said with an exaggerated, martyrish tone as he came to the bedchamber they shared.

This time Alicia opened the door without being asked.

■■

About the Author

SM LaViolette has been a criminal prosecutor, college history teacher, B&B operator, dock worker, ice cream manufacturer, reader for the blind, motel maid, and bounty hunter.
Okay, so the part about being a bounty hunter is a lie.
SM does, however, know how to hypnotize a Dungeness crab, sew her own Regency Era clothing, knit a frog hat, juggle, rebuild a 1959 American Rambler, and gain control of Asia (and hold on to it) in the game of RISK.

S.M. also writes under the name Minerva Spencer

Read more about SM at: www.MinervaSpencer.com